I0645267

MAD, PLAID AND DANGEROUS TO MARRY

BOOK IV OF THE HIGHLAND BRIDES

ELIZABETH ESSEX

to Tracy Brogan,
brilliant author, steadfast friend and
superlative road trip companion
for teaching me that all the small moments
could add up to something much bigger,

and

to Celeste Bradley,
another brilliant author and steadfast friend,
who was kind enough to suggest the change from the Byronicly-inspired
original title to the far more delightful
Mad, Plaid & Dangerous to Marry.

Author's Note

December, 2018

My Dear Readers,

I am very pleased to bring you this second edition of this story with a new title, new cover and selective edits to the text, originally published in April of 2018 as "Mad, Bad & Dangerous to Marry." But never fear—behind these changes it is the same story of loyalty, devotion and and unwavering belief in true love. I hope you will love Greer and Ewan as much as I do. So I will wish you, as always, Happy Reading!

Cheers, EEx

PROLOGUE

Edinburgh, Scotland
September, 1792

EWAN CAMERON, Duke of Crieff's joy was a rare and exhilarating thing, like the hot tot of strong Scots whisky he tossed back to celebrate his good news. The letter in his hand settled it—he was going to be the happiest man on earth.

He was going to be married.

In two days' time, the woman who had been chosen to be his bride would arrive at Castle Crieff, and they would at last become man and wife.

He was ready—in fact, he had never wanted anything more.

Let other men gnash their teeth and complain of the parson's mousetrap—he would step gladly into the Eden of having the woman he had admired, adored, and grown to love over the course of ten seemingly short years of correspondence, at last by his side.

All was in readiness. The final settlements were signed and sealed. The hall and drawing rooms of Castle Crieff glowed with polish. The chambers he had refurbished for his intended bride were everything refined and serene.

It only remained for him to finally meet her.

Lady Greer Douglas
Dalshee House
Perthshire

1 April, 1782

Dear Lady Greer,

I thank you for the honor you do me in consenting to be betrothed to me. I look forward to the day in the future when we shall eventually be married. It is a great relief to know my future, and the future of Crieff, is secure. I hope you will like me.

Your servant, Lord Ewan Cameron

Lord Ewan Cameron
Castle Crieff
Perthshire

14 May, 1782

Dear Lord Cameron,

I thank you most kindly for your letter of congratulations. Mama (who helps me write this) tells me it is I who am honored by your kind condescension, and that I should pledge that I will use the years between now and our marriage to make myself into a help-meet worthy of both you and Crieff, though I had rather just ride my pony up the moor. But I do hope I shall like you, too. That would be nice. As nice as if you liked me, too, though Mama says that it is my place to make myself pleasing to you. I suppose I might do so, if I knew what you thought pleasing. But all that seems terribly complicated ~ let's just like each other, shall we?

Your devoted friend, Lady Greer Douglas

CHAPTER 1

Castle Crieff, Scottish Highlands
September, 1792

IT WAS ALWAYS GOING to be a delicate, tricky thing, to marry a man one had never met before one's wedding day. But until the moment Lady Greer Douglas was seated in the carriage, on her way to her bridegroom, she had not suffered a single twinge of worry—for all that she had never met her bridegroom in person, she and the Duke of Crieff knew each other well.

Well enough to marry, sight unseen.

True, she did have a miniature of the duke, tucked safe in her pocket, like a map to show the way in a foreign city. But the painting was from some eight years ago—he would have changed since then. He would have grown into a man.

Yet despite not knowing his face, she knew his character. She knew him by the hundreds of letters they had exchanged since the day they had become betrothed, some ten years ago. Letters he had faithfully—and hopefully, joyfully—written to the last, setting the date for their wedding.

That last letter—the one telling her he was ready to marry, if she were also—along with the first he had ever written her, were folded deep in the pockets beneath the petticoats under her silk wedding-day gown, tucked away for safekeeping with the miniature—sacred talismans she could touch for strength and reassurance.

And she needed that reassurance now, as the carriage at last began the long descent from the moor down toward the village of Crieff. This would be her home now and forever-more, this side of the mountains, this village, these people. She would be responsible for them and to them.

Just as it should be. The bright morning sun slanted through the trees and dappled the carriage windows and making the sunlight dance across the seat cushions, as if nature herself were as simultaneously excited and delighted as she.

Greer let down the window sash so the late summer wind could blow the uncharacteristic nervous excitement from her mind. It was natural to be both excited and nervous— after all, it was her wedding day.

That nonsensical thought put a smile curving across her lips just as the coach began to shudder to a sudden stop.

"Whoa there!" The coachman, Fergus Fenner, was sawing at the reins to bring the team of four horses to a jangling standstill.

"Fenner?" Greer exchanged a puzzled look with her parents, the Earl and Countess of Shee, before she called, "What is the delay?"

"There be a mon in th' road, mileddy."

"A man? What do you mean?" Greer craned her neck out the window. "What does he want?"

"Jesus God," the coachman swore. "I think 'ee mebbe dead."

Dead? Greer was already out the door and onto the dirt of the road.

"Greer! Wait for your father—" Mama called after Greer. "Oh, for goodness— Mind your skirts!"

Greer dutifully grabbed up an armful of the embroidered cream silk taffeta, but what were clarty skirts to the life of a man, whoever he was? He was sprawled face-down in the mud and damp of the road, the back of his head a blackened, bloody welter of dried blood and dirt.

The sight knocked her to her knees. "Oh, sweet Lord."

"Be he dead, mileddy?" The coachman was still fighting to keep his nervous team under full control.

"I can't tell."

"Stand back, my dear," Papa instructed.

But, of course, she did not—Greer had never been the sort of person who could stand by when she might be actually doing something useful. "I think his chest is moving." She carefully put her hand to the fellow's grimy, outstretched wrist, feeling tentatively for some pulse of life.

His skin was cool and damp to the touch, and his clothes were torn and ragged and soaked, as if he'd been caught out in the rain. But the weather had been unseasonably sunny for days—Greer had thought the fine, early autumn weather a good omen for her future.

And yet, here the man was, white with cold—or perhaps from blood loss. She moved her hand to touch his neck, and he groaned away from even that slight pressure.

But alive, then, God help him. "He lives."

"Get a rug!" Papa ordered the groom.

"Get two!" Greer added. "One to cover and warm him, and the other to get beneath him to carry him—where?"

"The coach." Papa, bless his steady heart, didn't hesitate.

"We'll take charge of him to the village. Come help me," he called to the groom.

Greer touched her hand to the injured man's chest. "Can you hear me?" she asked the insensate fellow. "We're going to help you."

A low sound crawled from his mouth.

"He's trying to say something!" Greer bent her head low to the man's battered lips.

He made the barest breath of sound. "Crieff."

"Aye, of course. We'll take you to Crieff straightaway," she assured him, though she had no idea if the man meant the village or the castle. But really, it did not matter—time was of the essence.

"Robbie," she called to the groom, "fetch my medical case from the boot of the coach, if you please. Quickly now, before we move him." She had perfected the case, adding and subtracting medicines and supplies through the past year of travel on the continent. She had intended to bring such preparedness to Crieff, so that in the future, she might convince her bridegroom that he could travel in comfort and health. "We'll staunch the bleeding and bind his head up before we put him in the coach, and take him on to the village."

The village was closer than Castle Crieff, and a doctor was more like to be found there.

"Yes, let us get him there immediately," Mama agreed from the carriage. "I bid you consider, Greer, darling, that good men are seldom set upon for no reason, while bad men are invariably set upon for very good ones. And Crieff may not approve of your bringing a nearly dead vagrant with you to your wedding."

Surely the Duke of Crieff would approve. But Mama did not know Ewan as intimately as Greer did—she was sure her bridegroom would not mind if she finessed the niceties. "I am confident His Grace would be gratified by my swift application of both charity and bandages to bring one of his injured retainers to him, instead of letting the fellow die by the side of the road."

"Quite," Papa agreed. "Let us proceed."

Greer gingerly wrapped the man's head in linen bandage strips before she took the blankets from Robbie. But the injured fellow was far too large for her to shift on her own. "Robbie, I need you there." She directed the young groom opposite. "Can you lift him so?"

"Can I be of assistance, mistress?"

Greer turned to see a wizened, tweed-clad man setting his brake and alighting from a sturdy working cart in the direct, no-nonsense way of a working man who knows his profession and his own worth. He introduced himself with a simple tug on his tam. "Billy Dewar, mistress. Moorkeeper tae His Grace o' Crieff."

"Oh, yes!" Relief was like a heartening cup of tea. She knew the older man's name the same way everything she knew about Crieff—from Ewan's letters. He had described the moorkeeper with much admiration. "Thank you, please, Dewar. If you could just help me shift this rather big man onto the rug? He's badly injured."

"Aye, mistress." But when the elfin moorkeeper came close enough to get a good look at the injured man, Dewar let out a low Scots Gaelic curse and dropped to his knees on the road. "Jesus God, lad."

"Do you know him?" Curiosity warred with relief—it would be a great help if Dewar knew where the injured man ought best to be taken for help.

Dewar shot her a surprisingly sharp glance. "Do ye no' recognize 'im, then?"

"No," she admitted, puzzled by his question. "I can't think he's from Dalshee"—she cited her father's estate, located on the eastern divide of the moor—"or one of us"—she indicated her father, the coachman, and the other servants—"would likely recognize him, blood and all. But we're so much closer to Crieff here. And he said something that sounded distinctly like 'Crieff.'"

"Oh, aye?" Dewar was all skeptical reluctance. "I reckon he'll be a local lad—he does ha'a look that's perhaps familiar. Though it be hard tae tell frae sure, mistress."

"Aye," Greer agreed. "He is rather badly cut up. Even his hands. But do you have an idea of where we should take him? The direction of the doctor in the village, or the apothecary?"

"Ah, weel, tha' might do." The odd fellow shifted his cap, but then nodded, as if he had arrived at his final decision. "But best if you leave 'im tae me, mistress, and be on yer way."

"Oh, I had not thought of that." Greer knew it was the emotion of the moment that made her loath to put the injured man into the hands of this ancient stranger, however much it would ease their way to Castle Crieff. But Ewan had often written of his reliance upon Dewar, and his absolute confidence in the moorkeeper—surely she would be well-advised to do the same? "You will make sure the poor fellow is seen by a skilled, experienced medical man?"

"Indeed." Her father agreed, drawing out his purse and handing a golden guinea coin to Dewar. "For his care," Papa instructed. "Or for arrangements, should they need to be made. A Christian burial, in the village churchyard, certainly, not a pauper's grave. You may apply to my man at Dalshee, if such funds prove insufficient." The earl stood. "Robbie, fetch Dewar's cart up here, would you? We'll load the lad into that instead of the coach, and inform His Grace of Crieff's household of the arrangement when we arrive at the Castle."

Dewar seemed to suddenly awaken to the identity of his new acquaintances—he belatedly tugged his cap. "Yer pardon, Milord Shee. On yer way tae Crieff, are ye? Then ye'll have gotten the news?"

"That His Grace is to marry today? Most assuredly." Her papa was all burnished pride. "I bring him his bride, my dear daughter, this very morning."

A sort of stunned stillness came over Dewar's craggy face, as if he had not yet understood that the young woman before him was to be his new mistress at Crieff. Which was strange —Greer would have thought the entire village would have been making ready to drink a punch in toast to the health of their new duchess. But perhaps in Ewan's travels back and forth to Edinburgh to make things all right and tight with the lawyers, he had not yet given the word that the long-standing betrothal was at last to conclude with their marriage.

But whatever it was she saw in Dewar's expression was quickly masked when the moorkeeper turned to the business of hoisting the injured fellow's long frame into the back of his sturdy cart.

Greer seized hold of the injured man's cold hand as it fell slack from the blanket, as if she might somehow give him some small bit of comfort and warmth. "Mind there's a fearful gash on the back of his head," she cautioned. "I fear his skull might be broken."

"Aye, mistress," answered Dewar, just as the lad in his care let out a terrible groan.

"Gently there," Greer cried, abandoning any attempt at detachment to bundle her voluminous lace-trimmed linen *fichu* under his head to cushion it.

"Not the Brussels lace," Mama muttered from her viewpoint in the window of the carriage, but she was too used to her daughter's brash chivalry—for Greer was forever giving the shawls off her shoulder and the shoes from her feet to unshod beggars—to put any real heat into her objection.

And Dewar was already straddling the fellow to position his fractured head on the square yard of delicately embroidered fabric, while perhaps also purposefully shielding Greer from getting too close a look at the fellow's grimy, bloodied face, as if the moorkeeper feared the sight would be too much for her.

But Greer had never taken to being shielded, however much men had a dreadful, and frankly infuriating, tendency to withhold both experience and information from women. Even her papa, who knew better than most men, had upon occasion forgotten his pledge to treat her as an enlightened, thinking woman who could make her own choices and decisions.

So she stepped around the side of the cart to get a better look at the fellow. It seemed important to *see* him, to fix him in her mind, perhaps so she might help Ewan and Dewar identify him.

Grime and blood spattered the man's bruised and swollen face. Merciful heavens, but he'd been beaten so badly, his own mother would be hard put to recognize him—at least one of his eyes was purpled and completely swollen shut, and his pallor beneath the blood and bruising was a fearfully pasty white. "He's had an awful time of it, hasn't he?"

"Aye, mistress. Had a terrible millin,' 'ee has. I don't 'ave too much hope." Dewar took off his own tweed coat and laid it over the fellow's shoulders. "I'll see tae him either way."

"Thank you." How terrible, the moment she should be starting a new life, this young man—though it was hard to tell his age under the welter of blood—might be losing his. It was a sobering, somber thought. "You'll keep His Grace apprised of his condition?"

Dewar spared her another sharp glance, no doubt wondering why a woman of her standing should be so concerned for an injured villager. "Aye, mistress."

"Thank you, Dewar." Greer could not keep her smile from spreading despite the terrible circumstance. "I'm very happy to become your new mistress—I've looked forward to marrying His Grace of Crieff for a very long time."

Dewar shook his head and nodded, and then, of all things, patted her hand as if he were her father and not an odd, wizened old moorkeeper. "Ye trust 'im tae me, mistress," Dewar swore. "I ken what's needed."

Greer tried to feel relief and satisfaction that the incident was well-concluded—here was nothing more she could do. "I thank you for your kindness to him."

"Aye. I'll see tae him as if 'ee were mine own." Dewar climbed atop his cart, ready to be off.

"Right, then." Greer ought to have been happy—happy they had done the right thing, a good deed for a stranger in grave need. But she couldn't seem to cast off the ridiculous feeling that she ought to do more. That this man needed *her* help, not Dewar's.

But she had other responsibilities this morning. So she stepped back. "Godspeed to you both, Mr. Dewar."

The moorkeeper raised his hand in silent farewell, before slapping his reins and trundling away.

Greer swallowed her misgivings, shook out her clarty, bloodied skirts and climbed aboard her own carriage. She tried to settle back her seat, but as the Douglas carriage wheeled forward to take her to her wedding, she could just make out Dewar's last words. "Jesus God, lad. What in the hell have they done tae ye?"

Lord Ewan Cameron
Castle Crieff
Perthshire

1 April, 1784

Dear Lord Cameron,

I am ten and four this year, and as an acknowledgment to my advanced age, my mama has at last given me permission to correspond with you—hoping that you shall not mind being corresponded with. But I think as our futures are to be entwined, I should rather tell you my news than anyone else. Pray, if you are amenable, please write, so I may tell you all.

For instance, I have now a new pony of my own to ride, bought special for my use. He is the prettiest chestnut of 13 hands ~ quite the tallest I have ever ridden. I feel like I can see the whole of the world from his back.

Papa has promised me that once I am well used to riding him, I will be allowed to take him up the long miles to Glas Maol, which Papa says is where Crieff and Dalshee lands meet, which makes it my favorite place in the world. Should you like to meet me there some day so we might know each other?

I await your reply.

Your friend, Lady Greer Douglas

Lady Greer Douglas
Dalshee House
Perthshire

6 May, 1784

Dear Lady Greer,

My grandfather has given me permission to answer that I think it a fine thing for you to write me. And I congratulate you on your pony. What have you named him? I myself have a fine riding horse of 17 hands, bred here at Crieff. Cat Sìth is his name, on account of his black coat and white star on his chest like a mountain panther. I should think it a fine thing to take him up the long mountain pass to Glas Maol to meet you, but as Grandfather is taking me with him to Edinburgh on estate business, I fear we shall have to postpone the expedition until later in the summer. So we shall have to make haste slowly—as my grandfather is always cautioning me—in our friendship. I hope this day finds you well.

Your servant, Lord Ewan Cameron

CHAPTER 2

T**HE PAIN** reached down into the darkness and dragged him up into the punishing light. Everything was an agony. Every thought. Every breath.

But he *was* breathing. He was alive somehow, though he felt none too sure that the condition would last—the Devil and all his minions were pounding at his brain with pick axes, piercing his skull with such fierce deliberation that death seemed a viable alternative.

But still, he breathed.

He screwed his eyes tighter against the bright agony of the light, but the movement brought a roiling in his gut and a hot bitterness to his throat. It was pain to move, and pain to lie still, panting like an injured animal.

That's what he was reduced to—nothing but animal instinct to escape.

An overloud voice made the ache in his head intensify as if it were being crushed in a grinding vise. "Are ye still wi' us, lad?" A cramped hand gripped his shoulder, bringing a host of lessor pains shouting in his ears like a sergeant major. "Yer no good tae me dead."

He gritted his teeth, tasting the metallic tang of blood on his tongue. "Not dead yet," he attempted, but the words were nothing but a moaning gibberish.

"That's it, lad," the voice encouraged, nonetheless. "Stay wi' me now."

It was everything he could do to obey, because if this was what being alive felt like, he wasn't sure he didn't want to be dead.

"Devil take it," the voice ground on, "but someone wanted ye kilt. Yer hair and skull is sae blacked with blood, I dunno what—" The gruff voice was choked with fear.

That made two of them.

He slitted one eye open to see an auld fellow wearing a weather-beaten face leaning over him, inspecting him like a gralloched deer on a game larder hook.

"No one beats a mon so badly unless they want him dead," the man grumbled as he poked painfully at his split and cracked lips. "Weel, even with that thrashin', ye've still got yer teeth, ye lucky bastert."

He felt anything but lucky with the pain cleaving him in two.

"Let's gee a drop o' water in tae ye. Though I reckon it'll go a treat easier if there's a wee dram o' whisky in it."

Tepid peat and spirit-infused water dribbled into his mouth, and he had to concentrate to swallow it down. The effort left him gasping with pain, but holding his thick, split lips open like a nestling bird. "More."

"Easy, lad. One swallow at a time." The auld man held the cup to his lips, as patient as Job. "Hell mend ye, but yer that lucky tae be alive."

Lucky. At this moment, luck seemed a lot to ask for. But ask, he did. "Crieff?"

"Aye, lad. I've got ye home—I've got ye tae Crieff."

Inchoate relief made drawing his next breath easier than

the last, though the pain was still like a granite boulder on his chest. "Don't want…die," he panted. "Want—" He could not remember what he wanted, or exactly what he had been doing before—before the pain.

One fragment of thought, a memory as thin and insubstantial as a cobweb brushed across his bashed-up, splitting brain—an image, as bright as a penny in his palm. "Penny."

"Wheest, lad. No need for money." The craggy voice rasped in solace. "Yer home."

Home. The thought conjured the same word to the front of his brain—Crieff. But what it meant was an empty void— the darkness of his mind yielded no answer.

There was only loss. And fury.

And pain.

Lady Greer Douglas
Dalshee House
Perthshire

1 July, 1784

Dear Lady Greer,

I thank you for your last. I have returned with Grandfather from Edinburgh, but it has been decided that I am like a great hunk of Highland granite and need polishing—I needs must be sent to France for schooling. I own, I do not like the idea of going so far away from home—my idea of what is perfect would be to stay always at Crieff, for here is all my happiness. There will not be hills and moors and guns and dogs and horses of my own in France. Nor, I greatly regret, any trips to Glas Maol. I hope that you will forgive me not keeping our appointment there, but I will pledge to do so upon my next return.

Your servant, Ewan Cameron

Lord Ewan Cameron
Castle Crieff
Perthshire

12 August, 1784

Dear Lord Cameron,

How disappointed I am that we cannot meet. But you must go to the Continent! How I should so dearly love to travel, but I have never been farther from home than Inverness, which is certainly not Paris! But now that you must go ~ even if it is only to school ~ you must write me of your travels, and cure me of my itch to be gone away. All the wonders that you see ~ the buildings and forests, the people and their costumes, the food and the drink and music and dance ~ all must be reported!

As to polishing, if you who are so learned ~ Papa says you have had a tutor these many years ~ need polishing, I despair that I will be hopelessly gauche! In an effort to prevent that, Mama ~ who says that I am everything rash and brash and hoydenish ~ has made me pledge to apply myself to my studies ~ which are in reality only accomplishments and not learned study ~ with renewed attention, especially my application of the French language, so we may converse easily upon your return. Therefore I will bid you not goodbye, but au revoir,

From your chère amie, Lady Greer

P.S. Mama bids me ask you to excuse my evidently scatterbrained sentences. Your pardon.

CHAPTER 3

REER'S STRANGE SENSE OF LOSS—the unquiet feeling
that she had somehow mismanaged things and
made the wrong decision to let the moorkeeper
take the injured man away—lasted only until the coach
passed through the tall stone gates to the estate and up the
tree-lined drive to Castle Crieff. Her giddy excitement
returned in earnest as the carriage rolled to a jangling stop,
and the grey gravel crunched under the groom's running
feet.

This was the moment she had been waiting for—the start
of the life she had been wanting, preparing and planning for
ten years to lead. But now that the moment was here, her
stays felt suddenly too tight—her stomach rolled and dipped
as if she were still at sea, crossing the Channel to hasten
home to Ewan.

She had never expected to feel hesitant—she who had
always known what she wanted, and always thought she had
the courage of her own convictions. But her palms had gone
hot and clammy inside her kid gloves.

Her sudden nerves must have shown—from the backward facing seat, Papa beamed at her, all pride and support. "You look beautiful."

"You *are* beautiful." Beside Greer, Mama gave her words an entirely different, but no less heartfelt, meaning.

"Thank you, both." Greer knew she was no conventional beauty—she was too ordinary, too sharp-jawed and flame-haired to be considered bonnie anywhere but Scotland—but she knew she was loved. Which gave one a different sort of beauty—a beauty that came from confidence in one's merits instead of solely one's looks.

So if her knees were knocking together, it must be from excitement, not apprehension. Because any moment now, her friend Ewan Cameron, His Grace, the Duke of Crieff, was going to throw open the doors to Castle Crieff and greet her with the smile she had been waiting ten years to receive.

She herself was already smiling in near giddiness, so happy to meet the man she loved that her cheeks began to hurt.

And yet, he and his smile did not come—the door remained closed.

"Curious." Papa stepped down from the coach and took a fraction of a moment to show his disapproval of this illogical lapse in protocol by straightening his sleeves. "Robbie," he instructed the groom, "pray ply the bell and inform the household that His Grace's betrothed has arrived."

Greer certainly felt as if she had arrived—in more ways than merely standing on the doorstep of her soon-to-be home. After years and years of preparation—of travel and study and accomplishment—she had arrived at this day ready for her future.

Greer took another moment or two to admire the beau-tiful grey and white crenellations of Crieff's immense stone keep, its harmonious imbalance and pleasuring asymmetry. Ewan had described it so perfectly, with his characteristic easy understatement, she felt as if she were coming home, instead of coming to a place she had never been.

And to a man she had never actually seen.

The miniature in her pocket was of a fair-haired youth, still largely unformed by the world. Not that looks mattered so very much—her own were nothing special. She had heard herself described as a handsome young woman—handsome being what people said when they couldn't say beautiful—but hoped Ewan would love her for her enthusiastic disposition and sharp mind, rather than the rather ordinary arrangement of her face. She hoped their marriage would be as equals, much like her own parent's happy, affectionate union.

From inside the carriage, Mama reached for Greer's hand, and gave it a reassuring squeeze.

"It's quite all right, Mama." Greer smoothed her skirts, made herself everything calm and unruffled, like a swan gliding along the top of the water, while beneath all was determined, paddling work. She couldn't have them thinking she was a heedless heathen with no sense of occasion. Today she would be on her best, most lady-like manners. She would do her Mama proud. "I am sure it will all be right as rain."

"Good lass." Mama patted her silk and lace clad arm. "No need to fret or fash."

And yet there was a need for…something.

Because still, no one came.

Greer had expected that a signal would have set up from the gatehouse and her betrothed would have been out on the forecourt waiting to greet her—she would have been, if their situations had been reversed. For goodness sake, they had been betrothed for ten long years—surely some sense of occasion was warranted?

"Come, my dear." Papa reached for her hand to alight,

because the massive double door finally opened to disgorge a man in black wearing the badge of the house steward.

Greer began as she meant to go on—confidently. "You must be MacIntosh. His Grace has told me so much about you, I feel as if I know you already."

The steward was just as Ewan had described him—thin, angular and proud, with a stoic demeanor. "Aye, mileddy." He bowed deeply at the waist. "We were no' expectin' ye. But I welcome ye to Castle Crieff."

A rush of heat suffused her skin. Gracious, what a cock-up that would be if there were not to be a wedding. Greer took a deep breath to keep her mortification from spreading —she had no desire to look like an overripe strawberry to her bridegroom.

"Thank you." Greer moved toward the door on her own, as Papa was handing out Mama. "But I wrote to His Grace from Dalshee, that he might expect us this day. Did he not receive my missive?"

"I cannot say, mileddy." The grave-faced steward conducted her through a lofty entrance hall bristling with displays of arms of Camerons past. "If you'd like to wait here, mileddy?" He indicated a smallish bench against the wall, before he bowed deeply to her father and mother, as well. "Milord Shee. Mileddy Shee."

But an entrychamber was not where a new duchess ought to be received. "What is wrong?"

Mama made a calm motion for Greer to cease and desist, and Papa warned, "Now Greer, don't borrow trouble where none—"

But Greer could not stop the overwhelming sense that something was deeply, indelibly wrong. "Where is His Grace?" she demanded.

MacIntosh looked almost anguished—he pleated his lips between his teeth before he spoke. "It pains me, mileddy—"

"I am here."

Greer turned toward the voice in glad expectation of every happiness, only to feel her warm smile freeze to her face as if it were covered in a rime of cold frost.

The man before her could not be her Ewan.

Nothing about the handsome, but severe man in the black silk suit—which, by the way, needed tailoring to fit properly —was familiar. His hair was nearly white, not wheaten blond, as Ewan's was in the miniature. True, hair color might dull with age or change with fashion, but Ewan's eyes—the bright green of Crieff's forest—would not have suffered a sea change to this man's blue. The man before her was tall, to be sure, but not so tall and ungainly that he might frighten wee children, as Ewan's had once joked he was.

And furthermore, no spark of welcome, no soft flare of recognition lighted his blue eyes. Everything was stiffness and unease. Everything was wrong.

"I'm afraid you have the better of me." The man before her was as correctly polite and formal as if they were strangers. As if she did not already know the private longings of his heart, and he hers.

Papa drew himself up. "I am Lord Charles Douglas, Earl of Shee. My lady wife, Lady Flora Douglas, Countess of Shee. And this is our daughter, Lady Greer Douglas."

Greer dropped into a deep curtsey because she had been raised to be everything polished and polite despite her brash nature, and because several other people, Crieff's—and very soon her own—retainers had come out into the entry hall to gape at her in her clarty, blood-stained skirts. She would not falter. "I am Greer."

The dark-suited man drew in a sharp breath, as if to steady himself, and then he smiled awkwardly. "I see now. The betrothed."

"Yes." Why was he acting so strangely? What was wrong with him?

An unwelcome, entirely disloyal thought jumped into her head—what if all his letters they had written to one another, all the sentiments she had cherished and practically memorized for the past ten years, were a lie? What if they were not two souls in perfect harmony? What if he had made it all up —the dry good humor and understanding and camaraderie?

What if he really didn't *like* her?

She could see a clenching along his jawline, a twinge at the corner of his red-rimmed eyes. And the patent discomfort in the thinned line of his mouth, which he opened and shut twice before he could find the words to speak. "I am Malcolm Cameron."

"Oh, I see." For that short moment, Greer felt the sweetest relief—Ewan had not lied to her. This was all some terribly awkward misunderstanding. "Where is His Grace?"

This Malcolm Cameron spoke again. "It falls to me to tell you that I am now His Grace of Crieff." He looked away, as if he did not want to meet her eyes, or Mama or Papa's. As if he were trying to distance himself from whatever impossible thing he was continuing to say. "I am very sorry to have to tell you that my cousin, Ewan Cameron, is dead."

Lady Greer Douglas
Dalshee House
Perthshire, Scotland

8 October, 1784

Dear Lady Greer,

I have come to the appalling conclusion that I am not a man for travel. How I long to make haste far more slowly than the current speed of our swaying carriage. While my companions have found delight in every part of our journey, I must admit that every step away from Crieff feels a punishment. My companions—I gang on with three other sons of Scotland—Alasdair Colquhoun of Strath-cairn, Archie Carrington of Aiken, and Rory Cathcart of Edin-burgh—the Four Cees, we've taken to calling ourselves—tease me unmercifully, so I am forced to admit that I am an un-manfully poor sailor—I was wretchedly ill for the Channel crossing, which was prolonged due to contrary winds. The length of the journey only added to my agony, but did not cause it, as I was ill from the moment we were put on board.

You will be disappointed in me, for such poor sentiments I am sure, but thoughts of you, safe and solid in Dalshee, have been my solace. How I long to be walking the high, unmoving hills with you and not sailing the unhappy seas with Alasdair, Archie and Rory. But needs must, and I needs must become a gentleman of culture and learning worthy of both Crieff and you, so on I press.

From Calais we traversed narrow, dusty roads to Paris, and are now fairly comfortably ensconced in our new home—the hôtel, or private mansion, of a friend of my grandfather (who also stayed here when he took his education) on the Rue Malebranche, which—

the Malebranche—we are told laughingly, are demons depicted in Danté's Inferno. Clearly there is so much we do not know, but must, if we are to survive, learn.

I trust that your days are spent more pleasantly—oh, please tell me they are.

Yr. svt. E. Cameron

Lord Ewan Cameron
7 Rue Malebranche
Faubourg St. Michel
Paris, France

12 November, 1784

Dear Lord Cameron,

Poor Ewan. I am sorry for your distress. I have decided that while you send me all the news of your travels ~ which I long to make ~ I shall send you all the news of your longed-for hills of home. This morning, I made the very long ride atop my pony Dunnie ~ I hope you like that name, for he is a brown, mischievous imp ~ all the way up the solid, unmoving mass of Glas Maol for you. The wind was wild and wet, and everything inhospitable, but still I kept on with the Ghillie Jock Keith laying ahead, feeling that I would be disappointing you if I turned back. And so I was rewarded, for as we crested the top, the clouds lifted and the sun seemed to shine straight down upon us. And from there I could see for a hundred miles, all the way across the glen and the high moorland loch to Crieff land.

I held the sight of the green, green braeside ~ green is quite my favorite color now, you know ~ to my heart, so you might know it is cherished in your absence.

Please know me to be,

Your friend always, Greer Douglas

CHAPTER 4

*H*E WAS JOLTED back to painful reality by a rough hand to his shoulder. "Are ye still wi' me, lad?"

It was day, though the light was fading, and he was still alive.

And he was damn thirsty—God, but he was hot.

He roused himself to speak, but the voice that came from his mouth was nothing but a whispered croak that was more moan than words—a parched frog at the edge of a dried-up pond.

"Aye, lad. Ye've the right o' it." The familiar, craggy face of the man he had come to think of as his savior swam into focus above him. "But yer safe here. I'll see tae ye."

As he'd no idea where in hell *here* might be, or how the devil he had come there, he simply made a frustrated sound of assent—this wizened auld man had kept him alive, and therefore must know what he was about.

"Ye come an' go a fair bit," the fellow observed. "How's the pain?"

"Pure louping," he tried to say. But the words came out of his mouth garbled and nearly unintelligible to his own ears.

But the other man seemed to understand the gist of it. "Get a bit o' this in tae ye." The auld fellow dipped a spoon in a steaming cup and dribbled some onto his lips. "Willow bark in broth. For the pain."

He sucked the liquid in. Hell mend him, but it was braw—warm and salty and damn near life-giving. He wanted to speak, but all he could seem to do was make a sound of inarticulate thanks.

The savior fellow's large hand came to rest briefly on his shoulder. "Ye'll do. They may have thought they boxed and buried ye. But we ken better don't we? It'll take a vast deal more than that tae kill Crieff, eh?"

The word caught in his brain and ricocheted around like a bullet.

He wet his lips so he might speak. "Crieff?"

"Aye." His craggy savior stopped and peered at him, hard and probing. "Yer Crieff." And then the auld fellow's eyes widened. "Devil set us all on fire. Do ye no ken *who* ye are?"

Who was he? It ought to have sprung to his lips, his name. It ought to have been there, obvious and waiting on the tip of his tongue. But here was nothing. Nothing when he opened his mouth to speak. Nothing when he tried to turn his mind inward and search his thoughts. Nothing beyond the beginning of the pain.

His skin began to crawl with something colder than the chill—fear, like an icicle dripping onto his chest.

The old fellow tried another question. "Lad, do ye ken who I am?"

"Brought me here." The words sounded as if they had been gnashed between his teeth.

"Aye, lad. I did bring ye here. Damn, but I fear yer brain's been sadly disordered—ye took quite a blow." The auld fellow gave him a wry twist of a smile. "Though a lad with a thinner skull might not have survived."

"I will." He gritted the words out. He would survive. Damn him if he wouldn't. "Your name."

"Dewar. I'm yer man." Dewar gripped his hand hard. "Never doubt it. I'll see you healed up if it's the last thing I do."

He wanted to joke that he hoped it wouldn't be the last thing either of them did, but the words whirled across his brain like storm clouds, roiling in the ether above. Only one word was important enough to stick in his brain and come quickly off his gnarled tongue. "Crieff."

But he would learn the other words. He would learn and remember them all. Damned if he wouldn't. "More."

At his request, Dewar spooned some more broth into his mouth. "Aye, best get as much in tae ye as we can afore the doctor gets 'ere. I'll have tae cut yer ruint claes off so he can have a look at ye. It'll no' be a comfortable thing being bound up, I reckon."

Comfort was a moveable thing. Comfort would be learning to drink without having to have liquid spooned into his mouth like a wee bairn. Comfort would be finding a way through the darkness of his brain to locate his memories in whatever dusty, forgotten corner they were hidden, and reclaiming them as his own. As Crieff.

Whoever, or whatever that was.

But that was what he would do—he would find his bloody way back if he had to fight every inch of the way. He would survive.

He lost track of time until a second grim-faced man appeared above him—the doctor Dewar had warned him about. "Ye've made a good start."

"Aye." In another moment a warm cloth began to bathe his face and neck and arms and hands. Every inch of him was exposed, but the warm wetness turned cool in the air—a blessing against the uncomfortably tight heat burning under his skin.

"Who is he?" The new fellow was younger than Dewar, but just as terse and serious.

"One o' my lads," Dewar's gruff, familiar voice answered. "Nobody special."

Nobody special. The words—and the accompanying sense of loss—hit him deep, carving him out.

He was nobody.

And yet—he was somebody enough that someone had tried to kill him.

The thought gave little comfort.

"Who in this village would beat a mon so badly his own brother'd be dashed tae recognize him?" the doctor asked. "Heavy boots, I reckon, from the look o' these bruises—a kicking vicious enough tae break three, probably four ribs, as well as his nose. Though who knows? From the look of his hands, he might'a given 'em as good as he got."

"Not much of a fighter, our lad, though he were built fae it. Too kind, 'e is. Wouldn't think tae use 'is fives 'til it were too late."

He felt another portion of relief sag through him, quieting the shallow desperation shoaling his breath. Whoever he was, special or not, this man Dewar knew him, even if he no longer knew himself.

"I can't feel as there's any bones broken in his skull, tho' his scalp's mashed tae a bloody mess." He felt the doctor's fingers sifting through his hair, cutting away. "There's silt and grasses in his hair. Where'd ye say ye found 'im?"

"I didn't," was Dewar's terse reply before he relented. "E were found on the road by 'er young ladyship Douglas of Dalshee."

Dalshee. This word, too, echoed around in his head like the shout from a distant moor top, growing fainter with every repetition, until it was blotted out completely by the obliterating agony of being turned over.

"What d'ye think?"

He couldn't think. He couldn't fathom anything much but the hard plank of the table beneath his cheek. He couldn't remember what had happened before. How he had been in the road or came to this place. It was maddening.

"He'll be some time healing."

"But he'll heal." Dewar's words were a declaration—a statement of intent.

"Too soon tae tell," the doctor cautioned.

He mustered every last ounce of his strength and where-withal. "I will."

He would will it so. He tried to recall that fragment of an image, that memory as thin and insubstantial as a cobweb—a bridge, and woman, as bright as a penny in his palm.

But there was nothing more. Nothing but the mad agony in his head. And the single word that kept repeating itself over and over in his brain—Crieff.

Lady Greer Douglas
Dalshee House
Perthshire, Scotland

20 December, 1784

Dear Lady G,

Thanking you for your last. I will own that Paris is not as bad as I had feared, but mostly because my studies keep me too busy to sulk, and my companions are too jolly to admit any low spirits from me. With them, I find it easier and easier to bear the separation from home.

To celebrate the Yuletide season, Rory has arranged for us all to sit for portraits, each to be sent home as a gift to our families. He has charmed the favorite of the Queen—a woman artiste of some renown—to be our portraitist. After a few awkward sessions, I begin to enjoy the quiet of the posing for Mme. Vigée-LeBrun, who is both captivating and clever, and whom I think you should like very much. But we will see when the portrait is finished how captivating and clever she has been.

But in the meantime, Madame bids me gift you with this—

Wishing you the joy of the season,

Your servant, E. Cameron

Lord Ewan Cameron
7 Rue Malebranche
Faubourg St. Michel
Paris

28 January, 1785

Dear Lord Cameron,

I hope you passed the Christmas season in the same comfort and joy you have given to me with the gift of the miniature copy of your portrait. It is now my most treasured possession, though now I must worry about all the captivating and clever women you must be meeting. And so I feel obliged to warn you that in your absence ~ and perhaps in wanting to be more perfectly united with you in clever, scholarly pursuits ~ I have grown bookish. Mama is constantly telling me to put away my book or I shall ruin my eyes, but Papa has thrown open his library in sympathy.

What a world there are inside books! Mama says I must tell you so you may inform me if you object to a bookish wife, but I fear, my lord, that the damage is already done, and my mind is already quite improved, and I do not want going back. Still, I will await your opinion on the matter (though I have already quite made up my mind!).

Your devoted friend, Lady Greer D.

CHAPTER 5

"$\mathcal{I}$T CANNOT BE."

It couldn't be true. Ewan couldn't be dead. She had his letter. It had all been arranged.

He couldn't possibly be dead.

She would have known, would have felt the loss, surely, if something had happened to him. She was closer to Ewan that to any other person under creation. She had waited so many years to be ready, to be worthy of him—he could not now be snatched away at the last.

She would demand that this impostor tell her the truth.

But Malcolm Cameron's silence—his awful growing silence—cut as hollow as a blade. He looked at the ground—anywhere but at her—before he finally steeled himself to meet her eyes. "I'm afraid it's true."

The reality hit her like a scythe, cutting her down even as she tried to deny it. "Nay. Please. Please!"

Someone rushed toward her—Mama in a swirl of soft silk arching out her arms.

But Greer barely felt the embrace. She was supposed to be in *his* arms—the man she loved. Loved, liked, respected and cherished. The man she had looked forward to marrying. The man who was supposed to finally be her own.

Her throat tightened, hot tears burned behind her eyes, she couldn't draw breath.

Papa came to her other side, propping her up. "Pray fetch some brandy or sherry, before she takes a faint."

"Nay." Greer had never in her life taken anything so weak as a faint. She had crossed oceans and scaled mountains without needing to pause for breath. She had always stood on her own two feet.

But today was different—horribly so.

The way was cleared, with Mama on one side, and Papa on the other—their firm embrace keeping her from shaking like a leaf—they maneuvered her from the empty reception room into a private drawing room, where there was an upholstered settee upon which they sat. Some well-meaning person pressed a sherry into her shaking hand, and Greer drank, dutifully gulping down the potent fortified wine, though nothing could ease the cold ache in her throat.

How could this have happened to her Ewan—he who was so careful and methodical in his habits? Where had he been that such a thing *could* have happened?

"If I may ask, how did he die?" her papa was quietly inquiring.

Malcolm Cameron's eyes shied away again, as if the topic were too painful. "An unfortunate accident, is all we can surmise. He disappeared, we are told, after a night of heavy drinking, as was his wont."

Disappeared? As was his wont? The sheer wrongness of such a statement hit her like a bracing skelp across her face.

Nothing could be farther from the impression of the man she had come to know over ten years of correspondence. The very notion was an insult to his memory, an assault against all she had held dear. She refused to listen to such tripe.

Her canny Papa, bless him, gave voice to the questions she could not ask. "Where did this occur?"

Lord Malcolm Cameron—for she couldn't yet make herself think of him as Crieff—hesitated, but finally answered. "He was last seen in Edinburgh."

Ewan's letter had told her he had business in the capital. He also had friends there. Friends, like Alasdair Colquhoun, the Marquess of Cairn, or Archie Carrington, who ought to have been with Ewan, and kept him from 'disappearing.' Oh, why had they not?

Why was nothing, nothing, nothing, as it ought to be?

There were so many questions—Greer picked the most pressing one. "When?" She had had a letter from him only two days ago. His next to last letter had found her in Holland ten days before. Ten days spent in travel, crossing the Channel and hieing up the Great Northern Road as fast as a post chaise could take them.

"Forgive me, but I was under the impression the lady did not even know my cousin." Malcolm Cameron shot a chary look at the steward, MacIntosh, as if seeking information and confirmation.

"They had not formally met," Papa replied. "Though the betrothal was of long-standing. However—"

"Greer and His Grace wrote often," her mama explained. "They must have written hundreds of letters."

Four hundred and twenty-six letters, to be exact—Greer had counted. She *did* know Ewan. Through their correspondence, they had shared their thoughts and feelings in a way that some married couples who lived in the same house might never have done.

But Malcolm Cameron was frowning at them, as if he

could comprehend neither the reasonable explanation, nor her unreasonable emotional state.

Greer would not apologize for her feelings—they were honest and right. "His Grace and I were betrothed for ten years, my lord." She still could not bring herself to call this man—Ewan's cousin, it seemed, though she had never heard of him—by Ewan's title. "We had every expectation of a long and happy life together. His death"—even saying the word brought a searing pain to her chest and heat to her eyes—"has come as a very great shock."

For the first time in her life, Greer felt fragile, as if the next blow might shatter what was left of her composure into a hundred broken pieces.

"Then I am doubly sorry to be the bearer of such bad news." And he did look sorry. He looked as devastated as she —there were dark circles of grief under his red-rimmed eyes.

Greer tried to set her own shock aside—such news must have been as hard for him as it was for her. It was not his fault that no one had known to send word to Dalshee.

She tried to be logical, but there over the drawing room mantelpiece was a portrait of Ewan. The young lad in the portrait stood with his parents in the park with Castle Crieff in the background, his vivid green eyes and quiet smile a younger version of the youth who gazed at her from her miniature.

She wanted to see to Ewan, himself. For the first, and final time. "I should like to see him now. To pay my respects."

To see him at last, and to say her private goodbyes with the tender care and affection she had harbored within her for these long years.

But her request was met with a terrible silence while Malcolm Cameron stared at her, aghast. "I beg your pardon, but that is not possible." Malcolm Cameron looked away to another soberly clad man who stood to the side—a secretary or some such functionary—as if he needed to confirm the answer. "The body has not yet been recovered."

Wild, unsubstantiated hope kindled like a flame in her chest, burning away all logic. "But, then how do you know—" Her mind raced to the possibilities—perhaps they were wrong. Perhaps it was all just a miserable misunderstanding, and Ewan was alive. "Disappeared, you said? Then he might yet survive! There was a man on the road—"

"Greer." That was her father's voice, as full of grave caution as her Mama's hushed whisper.

"You go too far. Pray do not let your imagination run away with you in so serious a matter."

But Greer was already on her feet, full of the volatile combination of hot, burning indignation and hope, advancing toward Malcolm Cameron as if being closer could force him see the possibility more clearly. "If he has not been recovered, how come you to wear his ring?" She knew the heavy, black onyx seal—as she knew *all* things of Crieff— from Ewan's description and recounting of the day the ring had come to him on his grandfather's death. And yet here it was on Malcolm Cameron's hand, even when Ewan's body had not yet been recovered?

Cameron's left hand shifted to touch the ring on his right, as if slightly astonished to discover he was really wearing it. "I wish to God I wasn't. But the ring was sent to me. As proof. When the authorities sent word." Malcolm Cameron seemed to gather himself together before he faced her. "I didn't like to say in front of ladies, but his body *has* been found—dead. Quite dead. Though it has not yet been brought home to Crieff, as it ought."

"Oh." The hot ember of hope in her chest was stamped out. "Oh, I see."

"We expect his body to be delivered directly." Cameron looked to his secretary again before turning to her papa. "My

Lord Shee, I would ask that you and your countess and daughter stay for the service and burial, though it may be some days, as arrangements are still being made." Cameron nodded to his secretary in confirmation.

"Yes, of course," Papa demurred at the same time that Greer objected.

"But I cannot stay here." Not in this house that would never be her home. "Not now."

"Greer, dearest." Mama rose. "We have an obligation, to say nothing of our Christian duty, to stay and pay our respects. It is the very least we can do."

"I understand that you have suffered a loss, my lady," His Grace, Malcolm Cameron, said. "But—"

"Nay." It was more than a loss—her grief was a gaping hole in her very being, her soul. Her loss was a well that could never be filled.

"Yes," her mother countered without raising her voice. "We have all suffered a grievous loss and endured a terrible shock. Your Grace, I offer you and the House of Crieff my sincere condolences."

"Perhaps we all need some short time to recover ourselves." Malcolm Cameron was clearly working hard to mask his sorrow behind an admirable show of responsible civility. "But when that time is over, I should like to think things can…" He paused, and glanced at Greer, before he finished. "And should, I think, remain the same."

"What do you mean?" Papa was as bewildered as she. "What things should remain the same, Your Grace?"

His Grace of Crieff did not answer her papa but instead crossed to Greer's side to take up her hand and gaze into her eyes as if he were swearing an oath. "I stand ready to honor Crieff's commitment to you. I stand ready to honor the marriage settlements and make you still Crieff's bride. In fact, I am sure my cousin would have wanted it that way."

Lady Greer Douglas
Dalshee House
Perthshire, Scotland

11 April, 1785

Dear Lady G,

In answer to your last—I hope you will enjoy the enclosed.

Yours, E.C.

Lord Ewan Cameron
7 Rue Malebranche
Faubourg St. Michel
Paris

17 July, 1785

My dearest Lord Cameron,

I am in receipt of your last, and the enormous parcel of <u>BOOKS!</u> you have so very kindly sent to me! I am all agog, and frankly near overwhelmed at your generosity. Would that I had something of equal value to give you. Alas, I have only my friendship and loyalty to offer in return. Perhaps when I am grown older, and you are at last home, I shall think of something better with which to thank you.

In the interim, I remain,

Your most devoted friend, GD

CHAPTER 6

$\mathcal{E}$VEN MAMA GASPED.

Greer shook free of Malcolm Cameron's hand. "Nay." Every feeling forbade it.

She sought out the miniature tucked away in her pocket, as if the beloved talisman could ward off such an ill-considered prospect. Though she could no longer hold back the tears scalding her eyes, she found enough pride and indignation to stiffen her legs along with her spine. "That is impossible."

She could not imagine that Ewan would never have wanted any such thing—the rapport between them was unique and special and not to be fobbed off on whomever came next in the succession.

"While your offer is no doubt well-intentioned, Your Grace, the timing of such an offer is highly inappropriate." Papa's tone was cooler than was strictly civil.

"Forgive me." Malcolm Cameron was instantly contrite, and, judging by the flush creeping across his high cheekbones, suitably abashed. "I spoke too soon. Such things belong to the future, not now. Let me see that you are shown to your rooms, so you might recover."

"Nay," Greer insisted. "I cannot stay. I cannot."

"Greer." Her mother's voice held another warning. "Let your Papa handle this."

Wait for your father. Stand back. Don't put yourself forward. Watch your tongue.

She couldn't. She cared nothing for manners or civility or precedence at that moment. She couldn't possibly— "I want..."

She wanted privacy to curl up in the comfort of her mother's lap and cry herself to sleep. She wanted the solace of her dogs and her home. She wanted the last half-hour to never have happened.

The crushing reality of it all was like to suffocate her. "I need air."

She needed to be alone, outside, where everything was green and alive and she could feel close to Ewan—out on the land he loved more than anything else in the world. "You will excuse me, please—"

Greer picked up her ruined hems and ran out the way she had come in—through the oaken door MacIntosh rushed to hold for her, and across the now-empty forecourt.

She chose the direction of her flight instinctively—even if she had never before walked the paths from Castle Crieff, her heart could still navigate its way toward the craggy outcropping of rocks known as Glas Maol.

She took the first path that showed itself at the edge of the tall, sheltering cathedral of the fir trees, letting the wild reverence of the wind whipping through the branches silence the screeching sorrow in her soul, driven by something pressing, some weight that needed to be carried high into the open vastness of the heather-covered hills. But exertion and grief stole the air from her lungs, and she had to stop before the last of the trees gave way to open moorland to catch her gasping breath.

She dropped her skirts—it did not matter now if the hems of her beautiful wedding gown were dirtied or even ruined. She would never wear them again—the gown would forever remind her of this ruined day, this relentless, burning sorrow.

A noise in the underbrush startled Greer into realizing that she was not alone—a clarty little dog appeared to have been creeping along behind her in tentative accompaniment. The poor animal looked as bedraggled as she felt.

"Here, lad," she called the mud-speckled spaniel near. "Oh, you poor thing," she crooned as the taffy-colored dog melted into a grateful puddle of animal pleasure at her feet. "How long have you been out here on your own?" Greer ran her hands over the dog's ribs to try and reckon how many days he might have gone without food or care.

Her answer was a sweet, wiggling kiss, but behind the spaniel's long silky ears she discovered a leather collar, with a wee, dingy name plaque.

Her fingers stilled even as her heart kicked over within her chest. "I am a Gent," Greer read the brass plaque sewn onto the leather. The fresh tears that dampened her cheeks were immediately dispatched by the demonstrative little animal, whom Greer clutched to her chest. "Oh, poor, sweet Gent."

For she knew this dear dog in the same manner that she knew all the things of Crieff—and because she had given the wee spaniel his name at Ewan's behest. She should have thought to ask after Ewan's pet dog, who looked much the worse for wear—his coat hung slack on his spare frame and his feathery legs were fringed in mud.

"But you'll be fine now that you've found your way to me, Gent—I'll see to you in your master's stead." She ruffled the sweet animal's soft-furred head. "I'll take you home to Dalshee where you can be with my own dogs. We'll be a quadrumvirate of our own."

Gent could never take the place of Ewan, but the wee dog would be a lovely, lasting connection to him and the special rapport and friendship they had forged over the years.

Greer's tears finally gave way to a smile—for who could not smile under the adoring gaze of such an animal, who, after his gyrations of ecstasy were exercised, followed her back toward Castle Crieff, rising grey and tall out of the surrounding green.

The place she had thought to call home. The place she had been prepared to *turn into* her home. The place where she had prepared to become…herself—the wife and partner, the duchess she was always meant to be.

But no more. The smell of ashes—of all her burnt hopes and dreams—filled her head. But no, it was only a whiff of wood smoke, borne to her on the wind from a snug cottage some ways down the woodland path, which looked, from the pony cart still hitched in front of the cottage, to be the moorkeeper's.

A keener glance told her the cart was not Dewar's, but was a doctor's gig, with all the chests for medicines and the like built-in—perhaps come to attend to the lad.

The impulse to turn that way, to involve herself, was nearly impossible to resist.

"Come, Gent." Greer picked up her skirts and hastened for the cottage, determined to set at least some part of her troubled mind at ease.

"Lady Greer."

Greer was forced to turn—Malcolm Cameron stood at the edge of the gravel forecourt as if he were waiting for her.

She stifled the mad impulse to run away from him. "Your Grace."

Cameron raised his hand in companionable greeting, as if they were two friends on a Edinburgh parkway and not at the edge of a wild wood on his dead cousin's estate. "I thought it best to make sure no harm might come to you out here, alone."

As if this citified man might help her, who had practically grown up on the moorside.

She spread her hands. "As you see."

"Yes, I do see." He gave her that tight, uncomfortable smile. "That dress is very becoming. It suits your coloring."

While it was generally a rather nice thing to be flattered and fed compliments, her head was too full of loss—of the fact that this was to be her wedding dress, and that it was soiled with blood and dirt, which strangely Cameron did not remark upon—to be properly receptive to his pretty blandishments. She was most decidedly not in the mood. "I am sure you mean to be kind, though I apologize for my appearance. I was on my way to the moorkeeper's." But to forestall him from accompanying her, she gestured to the clouds beginning to pile up from the west. "I fear it's coming on to rain rather hard shortly."

"Is it?" Cameron frowned up at the sky. "You'll know better than I, of course—I'm no countryman to be scrying the weather." He backed up a pace or two, but held as firm as he could in the face of the uneasy threat of a highland storm. "It is so difficult here at Crieff, and without a wife to help me through the difficulties, and in understanding all the arcane traditions." He drew in a pained breath. "But until such happy day, perhaps you might see your way to...offering me some neighborly assistance."

His appeal softened some small part of her impatience. She was the heiress of Dalshee in her own right, and had been raised to be a duchess, educated in all the disciplines needed to manage vast estates—agriculture, animal husbandry, forestry, geology, geography. She liked to think she had been as well prepared as any Old Etonian or St. Andrew's Magistrand.

But the unfortunate truth was that she could not be a duchess without a duke.

So it behooved her to be polite to this duke, no matter her feelings. "I thank you for the compliment you do me, Your Grace, but if it as a matter of tradition, I should advise you to turn to MacIntosh, or Mrs. Peddie—the housekeeper," she clarified at his blank look, "—who know better how things are to be done here at Crieff."

"Clearly you are far more conversant with the staff here at Crieff, than I," he admitted. "Actually, I wanted to seek your counsel on the more private and delicate matter of the service and burial for my cousin."

"Oh." The heavy press of grief fell upon her like a shroud —she hated to even contemplate such a thing. But who would know Ewan better than she? Certainly not this cousin she had never heard of. "You might plant a rose," she began and immediately wished she had not.

Ewan had likely never told anyone else that he himself had planted rose bushes—one for each of his parents, as well as for his grandfather—so that the shoots could grow entwined in the hillside plot where generations of Crieff ancestors had been buried.

But *she* ought to be the one to plant such memorial—a climbing rose, naturally, as Ewan had often remarked upon his towering height.

"Yes, of course." Cameron was all graceful concession. "Thank you for that suggestion. I am honored by your insight and shall see that it done."

"Well then." She attempted a smile for politeness's sake, but knew it was likely more of a grimace. But it was the best she might do under the present circumstances.

"I'm sorry. I won't detain you any longer." Cameron stepped back with his hand across his chest in apology. "Forgive me. There is no good way to bear or receive such bad news."

"No," Greer agreed. "I fear not." She tried feel for him, for his situation was undoubtedly as painful as hers—they had both lost someone very dear to them. "How did you find out"—she forced herself to use the correct address—"Your Grace?"

He seemed relieved to be able to talk about what must have been a trying circumstance. "In…in Edinburgh. I called for Ewan there, at Cameron House, only to find he had gone out and not come back." He shook his head at the sad wonder of it. "He never did come home."

Greer willed the tears to stay dammed behind her eyes, even as she answered. "It is very hard."

"Yes. Out with his friends, those disreputable fellows—" He did not finish whatever he had been about to say. But it was no less than she herself had thought about any friends that would not take care of one of their number.

Malcolm Cameron sighed and looked about him, and back at the Castle. "And now Crieff must be my home. It is all so strange and…difficult."

It was difficult for all of them. "Time, they say, heals all wounds," she ventured, though she disliked such platitudes—if time was to heal her wounds, it would be because she had taken every step to help it along, distracting herself from the loss with good works and better thoughts. "I am sure that you will feel more at home as you become accustomed to your new responsibilities." Ewan's responsibilities—the responsibilities he would have shared with her. Responsibilities she would have taken on with her eyes closed and one arm held behind her back.

But it was not Malcolm Cameron's fault that he had not

been raised and educated to be a duke—he seemed to feel the lack of training acutely. "Thank you," he said with a stiff nod. "You are very kind, and under difficult circumstances."

She acknowledged the compliment with a simple nod. "I suppose we are under the same difficult circumstances. We neither of us could have planned this."

"No," he concurred. "But we can make the best of it, as he would wish. I admired him, greatly, you know."

Such welcome sentiments helped plaster up the cracks in her wounded heart. "As did I."

This time, his quiet smile was genuine. "We are united in our grief."

Greer could not help but be moved. "Thank you. Your cousin was a great friend to me. I was quite attached to him and will miss him deeply."

This surprised him a little—his dark eyebrows lofted like black grouse wings for the barest fraction of a moment before his face regained its pale, solemn visage. "I had not imagined such a friendship possible," he remarked.

"Friendship between a man and a woman? Or a friendship with one's betrothed?"

"Both, I suppose. Either."

"I don't think either your late cousin or I could have imagined marrying someone who was not a friend. When we became betrothed, we set out to become the best of friends—confidants even. As a result, I trusted him implicitly." Greer regarded him evenly, willing him to really understand. "My own parents are an example of just such a match—mutual affection and respect govern their conduct, and as a result, all is harmony and peace."

"Harmony and peace." He said the words with the same touch of disbelief as he had 'friendship' —as if they were even more improbable.

"It is possible," she assured him. "It is more than possible —it is necessary."

He smiled a little, and then bowed, still clearly not believing. "May I escort you back in?"

Greer strove for more polite patience. "I thank you, no. I mean to visit—"

But before she could relate the tale of the man in the road, she caught sight of the moorkeeper, Dewar, turning his pony from the path, as if he didn't want to disturb them.

But here was her chance for better news. "Dewar," she hailed him as she hurried down the path.

"Mileddy." The moorkeeper reined the pony to a halt before he tugged his cap to Malcolm Cameron. "Yer Grace."

"I wanted to inquire after the injured man," Greer said. "How does he get on?"

"What man?" Cameron asked from behind.

"Local lad, Yer Grace," Dewar explained with an offhand nod in the direction of the hills. "Accident up the moor."

There was something sharp and uncomfortable about Dewar's tone that sent Greer's attention prickling under her skin—they had found the injured man on the road to the village, not on the moorside.

But perhaps Dewar was a just a prickly, private sort, as Highlanders often were—long hours alone on the moor rarely made a man a brilliant conversationalist.

She would help him along. "Were you able to fetch a doctor for the lad?" She used Dewar's word, though it seemed strange to call so large and obviously grown a fellow a lad.

"Aye, mileddy." Dewar nodded, and then touched his cap and adjusted the reins to move along, as if their conversation were at an end.

Greer put a hand to the pony's bridle to stop him, but the

movement brought the wee dog out from behind her skirts and to the attention of the moorkeeper.

"Ah! There 'e is." The old fellow's relief and delight were evident in the crinkled corners of his eyes. "Been lookin' for him for days. Did ye find him, mistress?"

"Gent was loose up on the moor." She did not try to censor the chiding tone of her voice. "I should like to keep him—if I may, Your Grace."

Dewar looked none too happy at the suggestion. "Valuable stud dog, that, well trained."

Cameron ignored Dewar's comment, and smiled at Greer. "Then I shall make him a gift to you."

"Thank you, Your Grace." She took the dog in her arms and turned her attention back to the moorkeeper. "But the injured fellow—is he doing somewhat better, I hope? I thought I saw the doctor's gig at your cottage?"

"Eh, weel…" The moorkeeper pulled a wry, unhappy face.

It was like fishing for salmon in the Shee, talking to Dewar—she had to keep trying until she found the right bait. "Is it a matter of the fee? I'll bear the cost if there is something more that might be done."

"Nay. There is naught more can be done, mileddy." Dewar took his hat off, and then looked her in the eye. "He's passed."

"Passed?" A chill blew across her skin like an ill wind. "Oh, no."

The grief she had momentarily held at bay was like a hole hidden in the path—pain wrung its twisted way through her. "I had so hoped."

"No, mistress." Dewar softened his voice, but his tone was emphatic. "He's passed on, the lad has. Died."

"Oh, I am so sorry." She felt hollowed out—empty of every hope. So much loss.

Malcolm Cameron appeared at her elbow for support. "Did you know this lad?"

"No. But..." Greer found herself giving much the same answer as she had earlier to his question about Ewan. And with just as much sorrowful confusion. "We just..." She took a deep breath and tried again. "We found him in the roadway, my parents and I, and tried to do our best for him before Dewar came along, and took charge of him."

"A local fellow?" Malcolm Cameron shifted his gaze sharply to the moorkeeper. "From Crieff? Ought I to know who he was? And what happened?"

"A ghillie, Yer Grace." Dewar addressed his laird with solemn courtesy. "Hunting accident. It's wilderness up these glens. Dangerous wild lands. One misstep..." Dewar let the ominous warning die away unspoken.

Wild, yes, but dangerous? Greer supposed it must be so to people who had not lived there all their lives—to strangers like Cameron. Still, a ghillie was a guide who ought to have had significant hill-craft, and a superior understanding of the mountains, moorsides and glens.

And they hadn't found him up the moor—he had been on the road near the village.

It didn't quite make sense.

But this loss struck a blow far harder than it should for a stranger she had merely chanced upon. "So sad," she found herself saying to fill the yawning gulf of pain inside. "So much death." A sigh wrung itself out of her aching lungs. "Life is so very fragile, is it not?

"Indeed, that it is." Malcolm Cameron reached out, to touch her hand as if in support and understanding. "Come, led me lead you back where you belong."

Lady Greer Douglas
Dalshee House
Perthshire, Scotland

18 October, 1785

Dear Lady G,

Paris begins to grow on me—like a moss on the back of Scottish granite. The city is fascinating and beautiful in a way that I had not imagined a city could be—spacious and grand and civilized in a way that neither London, nor certainly Edinburgh are. And every day, with every sight, I think my Lady Greer would delight in Paris even more than I. You ought to come—perhaps the earl and countess would delight in the journey as well, although I know your father, the Earl of Shee is devoted to his lands, which may keep him from thinking of so many months away. But perhaps in the spring —after the planting is done would be a perfect time for you to visit, for I find myself anxious to see you. Pray tell him I advise it. I will await your response.

Yours, EC

Lord Ewan Cameron
7 Rue Malebranche
Faubourg St. Michel
Paris

14 January, 1786

Dear Lord E,

Papa says that sixteen is still too young for a grand tour of my own, and must make do with yours for now, and content myself with reading of such places. It is of course his 'for now' which gives me hope that one day in the future I will be allowed see the boulevards of Paris and attend the opera there. And with you, whom I am anxious to see as well! How I long to travel and see such spectacles! Such passion and drama!

I have only been to Edinburgh at Christmas, where there were only concerts, but I purchased some music of young Herr Mozart that I like very much. Have you been to the opera yet? Pray go as soon as you are able, so you may tell me all about it when you come home.

Oh, when shall you come back to Crieff? It is strange to be so apart from one another. I feel as though I miss you when you are so far away. But I am being nonsensical ~ as Mama often tells me I am. And yet I find myself quite in love with you, all the same, and I long for just one kiss from your lips. Pray don't tell a single soul I said so, or I shall never be allowed to meet you before we are married. Until then, I remain,

Your Greer

CHAPTER 7

"**D**EVIL BREAK DOWN THE DOOR, lad." The auld man's voice, low and laced with urgency, roused him from a fitful sleep. "As soon as the sun sets, we've tae hide ye away."

He was too exhausted by pain to feel much more than mild alarm. Wrapped in bandages and a thick wool tartan, he had to keep his eyes closed to stave off the pounding in his brain that made it hard to speak.

But Dewar was already at his side, hauling him up. "We've got tae get ye out o' here, lad, and hide where no one can find ye. Can ye stand on yer own?"

A grunt sufficed to say not bloody likely.

"We'll manage," Dewar assured him. "Trust me—ye can't stay."

He had no choice but to trust the auld fellow—there was simply no one else. "Where?" The word seemed at least intelligible, or perhaps he was just getting used to the harsh, wounded way he sounded.

"Up the moor, I reckon," Dewar gestured with his gnarled thumb. "There's an auld bothy up the last glen, on t'far side o' Crieff land, close by Glas Maol. The glen's a good twelve miles out, and empty, so ye'll be safe enough there 'til we can get ye braw enough to sort th' business out."

Glas Maol—another place name that bounded around in his mad brain, clamoring in the emptiness, along with Crieff and Dalshee.

Dewar had no time for his scattered remembrances. "Get some o' this in tae ye." Dewar shoved a cup with that brilliant bitter mixture of willow bark tea and whisky into his cramped and bruised hands.

He managed a few good gulps while Dewar scrounged around the bed chamber to find clothing. What little dignity remained to him goaded him through the slow, painful process of being dressed in a rough linen shirt, a leather jerkin and a pair of thick wool breeches—when Dewar fished his long legs into the breeks, his bare legs and feet stuck out like empty winter branches.

"Weel, they didn't beat the height out o' ye," Dewar joked. "I'll have tae see what might be done tae cage ye some larger claes, but for now—up ye git." The wiry auld coot inserted himself under his shoulder and levered him up. "That's it, lad. Easy now."

A wave of pain swamped him, but Dewar held fast, and together they shuffled in slow progress to the low-sided wooden cart with the stoic highland pony in harness.

"Steady, lad, steady. Back yer way in, lad, and then push back so's yer legs are stretched out."

He did as instructed, coming to rest on a pallet of hay lining the narrow well of the cart. And they were off, trundling away from the cottage into the falling dusk. He was too exhausted to mark the way, but there was clear, clean sky above him with the smell of pine forest filling his senses, and the whisper of the wind through the trees filling the emptiness in his head and ears. Offering him what simple solace it could.

Under his back, the wagon creaked and rattled across rutted tracks, tossing him to and fro on the pallet Dewar had made to try and shield him from the roughness of the journey. But there was no softening the ride, no blunting the pain—despite the laced tea, the ache was omnipresent, burrowing into the hollows of his bones, leaving him alternately scalding hot and mercilessly cold. This was why he had always hated travel—this debilitating queasiness.

Travel?

But that thought dissolved into the night as the pain swamped him again. While the long hours of the journey wore on, he kept himself tethered to the world by cataloguing the more insistent aches and pangs within him—the back of his head, and those broken ribs the doctor had mentioned.

Damned if he hadn't had the complete stuffing kicked out of him with those wicked boots the man with the blade had worn.

There it was, a picture in his sad, mad brain—a pair of down-at-heel hessian boots flecked with mud. And a dirk. Grating against the pavement like an announcement of intent.

An intent to kill him. "Murder."

Dewar hauled the pony to a hasty stop. "What say ye, lad?"

The word was like the taste of blood from his mouth—he spat it out. "Murder."

"Devil spare ye." Dewar nodded in understanding. "But they failed, aye? Didn't count on ye bein' as hard an' strong an' stubborn as these hills."

"Aye." It was good to hear he was hard and stubborn—he

would need such otherwise dubious qualities to see him through.

The realization helped him breathe easier, despite his broken ribs, and the tapestry of sounds from the moor gave him comfort. The wind picked up, swirling through the fir trees and over the heather, bringing a waft of something sweet and fragrant. He inhaled again, breathing in the ease, wrapping it around him like a blanket.

Dewar drew the cart to a noisy halt, the jangle of harness tack sharp and over-loud in the sweeping quiet. "We're here, lad."

He gritted his teeth against the pain as Dewar helped haul him upright. Waves of nausea battered at him like a storm. But somehow he moved. Or *they* moved, Dewar propping him up to shuffle a few steps, and then a few more, until they arrived at the darkened doorway of the bothy.

"Yer pure done in, lad. Let's gie ye doon." Dewar levered him toward the slab of rock that made a bench in front of the stone bothy.

"God almightily," he cursed. "I'm weak as watered whisky."

"Ha!" Dewar mouth twisted into a wry smile. "Weel, that's twa things in yer favor—ye know what good whisky is, and ye've no' lost yer sense o' humor."

"Managed to lose near all else," he muttered.

Dewar shrugged. "We've yet tae see how much. But I reckon it'll just take time tae suss it all oot." He arranged a thick straw pallet before the heath, before he lit a low burning peat fire. "This'll give ye light and some sma' comfort. But best to bank it durin' th' day," the man instructed, "lest anyone smell the smoke and come nosin' round. Tho no one should be up on this side o' th' moor this time o' year."

"Aye, I ken." He might be mad but he wasn't stupid.

"Good, lad." Dewar eyed him critically. "Ye've done the hard part and can rest."

Rest—it was all he could do to breathe.

"I'll be back every day," Dewar went on. "Or as near to it as can be managed. I've left ye a stout broth in yon pot. Just keep it simmering. An' stay close—hide yourself away in here should anyone come. But no one will—there's nothing round for miles and miles. You'll be safe enough 'ere." The fellow moved toward the low door and paused. "Will ye mind, do ye think, bein' alone for a spell?"

"Nay." He could work to build up his broken body in peace and safety, and practice mangling his words without anyone hearing.

"Right then." The fellow turned back from the door. "Ye do ken where y'are, lad?"

"Aye." No matter that he was most of the way up a moorside, he felt at home. "Crieff."

"Aye, lad. And *ye* are Crieff." Dewar grasped his hand again in one last heartfelt grip. "Remember that if nothin' else, as we puzzle this out. And when we do, by God, we're going tae make the bastards that done this tae ye—tae Crieff —pay."

Lady Greer Douglas
Dalshee House
Perthshire, Scotland

11 March, 1786

Dear Lady Greer,

At your suggestion my companions and I have taken ourselves to the opera house to hear—and see—a performance of Iphigenia in Tauris by the famous Herr Gluck. We felt passably pleased with the performance, though we are told by ears more discerning that ours that the opera is a wild success—the French esteem it highly. I do think that you, with your love of drama, would enjoy seeing the Greek mythologies played out in musical spectacle. I liked it better thinking of your enjoyment. Perhaps I shall go to the opera again for you, and find something by your young Herr Mozart.

Which means, of course, that you shall have to make another pilgrimage to the top of Glas Maol. For which favor I send you an imaginary kiss.

I hope it shall suffice until a real one is available.

Yours, EC

Lord Ewan Cameron
7 Rue Malebranche
Faubourg St. Michel
Paris

26 June, 1786

Dearest Lord E,

I will certainly give you your wish to visit Glas Maol. In fact, I do it now—I have brought pen and paper in a satchel, and after the long climb, am finally sitting in what I have come to think of as our spot, atop the outcropping of bounders looking from the top of the hill across the loch toward Crieff. The soft breeze is blowing sweet heather dust up from the south, and I can hear the capercaillies nattering at each other from the woodland below.

You are quite right to think of this spot as heaven on this earth, and I will keep it ready for your return. Or at least until news of another opera! But I accept with vast pleasure your imaginary kiss and send you back one of my own. More than one, if I'm honest, for you shall have all my kisses, always.

Until we meet to kiss in person, I remain,

Your devoted friend, GD

CHAPTER 8

GREER LET MALCOLM CAMERON return her to the castle, where the steward and housekeeper stood ready to escort the Douglas family to their rooms.

"If you'll follow me, mileddy?" Mrs. Peddie offered.

"Please," Mama concurred.

As little as Greer liked staying, she dutifully followed her parents up the grand staircase, but at the top of the stair, the steward led Mama and Papa up another story, while the housekeeper directed her to the Cameron family wing. "This way, Mileddy Greer."

"Oh, no, ma'am." Greer objected. "I should much prefer not to be away from my family." She needed their quiet, unfailing support now, more than ever.

"Forgive me, mileddy, but His Grace, Laird Malcolm, ordered it so." The housekeeper stepped close and lowered her voice to speak confidentially. "But I thought as the room was done up fae ye on His Grace's—that is, His Late Grace, Laird Ewan's—particular direction, ye might at least want tae see it. Had it done special fae ye, he did, with plasterers and painters here fae nigh on a two-month. I thought as ye'd a right tae see what was meant tae be yer room as duchess. But if ye'd prefer tae keep elsewhere once ye've seen it, I can arrange that verra easily, mileddy."

Done special for her. Scalding heat pooled behind Greer's eyes, and the ache in her chest rose to her throat. "Aye. Of course." Greer took a shaky breath to draw herself together. "Thank you. Please, I should like to see the chamber."

Mrs. Peddie led the way down a narrow stone corridor to the far end of the wing, whereupon she opened a double door to a tall chamber that was a complete contrast to the dark, narrow medieval corridors—the room was light and airy, its walls painted in the freshest, softest blue, with exquisite white plasterwork and beautiful watered silk draperies, which dissolved before her eyes as the tears she had thought she would be able to keep at bay fell unchecked.

All this, Ewan had done for her. He *knew* her—knew what she would love and had surrounded her in it.

"I'm so sorry." She fumbled for a handkerchief but could not free hers from her pocket before Mrs. Peddie whisked one from her sleeve and pressed it into Greer's hand. "Thank you, Mrs. Peddie. I'm not usually such a watering pot. It's just that it's so beautiful."

"Aye, 'tis bonnie, mileddy. I will make arrangements fae ye tae be moved closer tae the earl and countess, but I thought ye would like tae see this room. Brought that fabric back all the way frae Paris, he said he did, afore the Revolution."

So Ewan had kept some secrets—in the midst of so many different gifts over the years, he had kept his particular evidence of his thoughtfulness a surprise.

"Oh, it is so very lovely." She ran her hand reverently along the fall of the delicate silk draperies. "It must have cost him a fortune."

"Nothing was too good fae ye, he said. Bought it the moment he saw it, he said, thinking of ye."

Just as she had been thinking of him, every day, all these years. Their connection had been true. And real. So very real.

The heat in her eyes and throat were abominable. She could not stop the hiccup of emotion that escaped her chest.

What a difference a day made—this morning she had set off with every expectation of being married, but come nightfall she felt like a widow. Except that she wasn't—she wasn't even betrothed anymore. She was only dreadfully, dreadfully bereaved.

"I miss him so." Greer fumbled to dash away the dampness in the corner of her eyes.

"Oh, mistress, so do I." Mrs. Peddie, too, dabbed at her eyes with her lace apron. "Without our laird, we're all tae sixes and sevens. Oh, I am sorry," the poor woman flustered. "I oughtn't have said anythin.' Forgive me, mileddy."

"Please." Greer put her arm around the tiny woman's shoulders, and guided her to the chaise in front of the window. "I am so sorry for your loss. For all of Crieff's loss." She had been thinking of Ewan as hers alone, but he had been theirs—Crieff's—for far longer.

"Bless ye. Thank ye, mileddy."

"Lord Cameron—the duke"—Greer knew she must reconcile herself to calling him His Grace, if only to his face—"must feel it quite acutely, too, to lose his cousin so suddenly."

"Oh, aye. I s'pose," Mrs. Peddie agreed, but said nothing more of the new duke's finer feelings. "A'course, we don't know him weel, His New Grace. Ne'er visited mor'n three or four times in his life, in all the time I've been at Crieff. His father, that is His New Grace's father was the old duke's second son—that is, our Laird Ewan's uncle. I do remember them coming when his lordship, the old duke's heir—that is tae say our Laird Ewan's father—passed away. His lordship were eight, and Mr. Malcolm no mor'n eight or nine."

"So they weren't close?"

"Not as I could say, mileddy, but there was no reason I should know." Mrs. Peddie stood and smoothed down her skirts. "Though they do say His Grace, our late Laird Ewan, received the mon—Lord Malcolm—at Cameron House in Edinburgh frae time tae time, Lord Malcolm had no been a guest here fae many a year."

No wonder Malcolm Cameron was such a fish out of the loch in the highland countryside.

"Thank you, Mrs. Peddie. I appreciate your candor." Greer rose and shook out her own skirts. "Will you let me know when His Late Grace's body—his coffin—arrives, please? I should like to visit privately, if I may. To say my own private goodbyes."

Mrs. Peddie's face crumpled into tears. "Oh, 'tis double sad tae think we've lost both His Grace, our Laird Ewan, and ye at the same time, mileddy."

It was as if the spigot Greer was trying her best to keep shut had suddenly broken—tears, hot and stinging, singed her eyes and made their wet way down her face. The ache in her chest threatened to grow into great gulping sobs. She had to turn away to pull herself under control and wipe her cheeks.

"I'm that sorry, mileddy." The housekeeper tried to console her. "I didn't mean tae upset ye so."

"It's quite all right, Mrs. Peddie. You only said what I was thinking and feeling myself. I, too, had looked forward to making Crieff my home, and being your mistress. Very much." She wiped her cheeks with the back of her hand. "Very much so."

"Sae were we, mileddy. It's been a long time since Castle

Crieff has had a mistress tae see that things are as they ought. I've done my best fae us, but—"

"But there are only so many hours in a day," Greer finished for her.

"Aye, mileddy," the housekeeper sighed. "And now with staff let go—" She shook her head. "The castle is that big, I can't always see everythin's done as I like. And with retrenching, we've not even been able tae order crepe and put up proper mourning."

"No?" Greer had been too preoccupied with her own sorrow to note the lack of mourning furnishings upon arrival. "Retrenching?"

"His Grace, Mr. Malcolm, when he come two days ago, told us he had gone through the books and was making changes, cutting excesses, he said—let half the staff gang off that day. Went through the house like a chill wind it did, room by room, 'til MacIntosh could gather us all up in the servant's hall tae gie us the terrible bad news." The house-keeper sniffed into her apron. "Some of those girls ha' been wi' me since they were wee lassies. And how they're all tae find work in the village, I don't ken. I can't like it, mileddy. Can't like it a'tall."

"No. I daresay not even His Grace himself likes it. It must be very difficult for him to be in such a position." Though Greer had trouble imagining the pressure—or the misman-agement—that would force him to let so many go. She would speak to her mother immediately to see if there was some-thing they might do to employ at least some of the people at Dalshee.

"I'm sure I don't know, mileddy." Mrs. Peddie tied to draw herself together, as if she knew it was her duty to defend Crieff—whomever the embodiment of Crieff might be— from any suggestion of shoddiness. "I do beg yer pardon, mileddy, but as ye were tae be our mistress, and as they say....

Weel, it's all so devilish confounding. We ne'er had a moment o' worry about things under Laird Ewan. And they said His Grace, Laird Ewan, were out carousing in Edinburgh, and ne'er came back. But that don't sound like our laird tae me."

The relief of finding an ally was nearly as sharp as Greer's original alarm. "Nor to me, Mrs. Peddie," she agreed. She had never thought there had been anything hazy or carousing about the man with whom she had corresponded for ten years. Nothing slipshod or unclear. *Make haste slowly*, he had always said. Everything she had read spoke of a thoughtful, methodical man—her thoughtful, methodical, lovely man. With whom she would now never make haste slowly.

The tight heat in her throat was abominable.

"Here, mileddy, get some of this in tae ye." The housekeeper poured her a dish of tea.

Only it wasn't tea, but some sort of unholy concoction of Scotch whisky and honey that burned its way to her belly. "Gracious."

"Aye," Mrs. Peddie agreed. "But it'll help you rest. Poor lass—you're going tae need it."

Rest she did—going to bed and sleeping until the grey light of dawn sent her to the bell.

Mrs. Peddie, herself, attended Greer. "I've brought your morning chocolate, mileddy, just as Laird Ewan said ye liked, God rest him," she set the tray on the bed before she moved to Greer's trunk. "Is there something particular ye'll want for the service, mileddy?"

Grief turned the chocolate to ash in her mouth. "Then they've recovered him?" Greer got out of bed immediately to begin dressing. "I still want to see him, if I may, to make my private goodbyes before the service." Without anyone else there, even her parents. Goodbye and hello all at the same time.

It was awful.

But what could not be avoided had to be addressed with as much courage and poise as she could muster. "The grey silk redingote, then, with the black velvet trim." She had purchased the ensemble in Belgium to impress Ewan with her worldly fashions.

So much for worldly—all she wanted now was the comfort of home.

"Aye, mileddy." The housekeeper set out the redingote along with the requisite under clothing. "Though I can't like this havey-cavey burial before a single prayer has e'en been said o'er the poor mon's body," Mrs. Peddie sniffed.

"What?" Alarm crept under Greer's grief and settled cold in her chest. "But surely the service will be said this morning, Mrs. Peddie, and the burial after, so there's no fear of that."

"Weel, mileddy." Mrs. Peddie managed to look both uncomfortable to be giving Greer such news and outraged on her own behalf. "Ye asked tae see the coffin, but it's impossible—it's no' in the keep. But there's a fresh mound o' earth in the family plot up the braeside." Mrs. Peddie's indignation spilled over her professional reticence. "I don't know 'oo else it'd be, but our Laird Ewan. And they've not let us have the coffin out in state in the great hall, nor put out so much as a vase of mourning flowers, the way they ought."

Something hotter and more biting than alarm began to burn its way through Greer's chest—indignation and outrage that Ewan was not being honored as he was owed. "And who is 'they' exactly, Mrs. Peddie? Who made such a decision?"

"I had it frae Mr. MacIntosh, mileddy. Don't know as 'oo told 'im, but I suspect it were that Mr. Gow, as is His New Grace's secretary. Erasing all trace of him, our Laird Ewan— e'en the portrait that he had made fae ye in Paris, our Laird said, and hung there"—she gestured to an empty space along the wall—"fae ye, they've taken away."

It must have been the full-sized portrait by the famous

favorite of the queen that matched the miniature in her pocket. He had posed for it, for her. He had hung it here, for her. But it seemed that the opportunity to see Ewan, at last, had been taken from her.

The unexpected loss was so sharp and piercing Greer felt her eyes go hot and itchy again, but not only with sorrow—anger, hot and bitter, surged into her blood.

The new Duke of Crieff's reasons must be his own, but she did not have to like them. And she refused to understand them—he had robbed her of her fitting goodbye.Malcolm Cameron's thoughtlessness or mismanagement—it did not matter which—had hurt her in every way imaginable.

But what was she to do about it? As much as she might like to give Malcolm Cameron a sharp piece of her mind, she had to do what was best for Crieff, not suit her own selfish needs—Lord forbid she should cause Mrs. Peddie, or anyone else on the staff, any more grief.

And so she banked her ire. "I'm sure it will all be fine in the end, Mrs. Peddie. Our prayers will not go amiss, no matter the order in which they are said."

"I suppose sae, mileddy," the housekeeper sniffed. "I hope sae."

"I *know* so, Mrs. Peddie. Because we will make it so," she assured the woman. "I thank you for both your frankness and your kindness, Mrs. Peddie. You've given me much to think about."

And much to do—finding the truth beneath the freshly buried lies.

Lady Greer Douglas
Dalshee House
Perthshire, Scotland

11 August, 1786

Dear Greer,

We have gone out to see some of the sights in the countryside, most notably the Palace of Versailles, and its inspiration, Vaux-le-Vicomte. Nowhere else on earth are Descartes's words more happily illustrated: "Science should make us the masters and possessors of nature." Though, I will admit that I rebelled when first reading the great scientist and natural philosopher—being Scots, I can't agree that man is the sole possessor or complete master over nature. I think instead that there is too much worth and beauty in the wildness of the Earth, and that nature may exist in perfection without man's interference. I daresay Descartes might have felt so, too, if <u>he</u> had ever seen the view from Glas Maol.

How I should like to be there now—or actually tomorrow, on the Glorious 12th, when I might be with my grandfather on the moor, hunting up grouse. Alasdair agrees with me, for there is nothing like the beginning of the grouse season to make us miss the Highlands and moorsides of our homeland. And the beauty and wildness that live so companionably side by side there.

I also daresay that, despite my Scots fondness for wildness, I am becoming more and more educated as a gentleman. My eye begins to discern differently, my ears begin to refine. I have even begun to appreciate art. Under Rory's superior eye, I have made my first purchase as a collector. We all have—even Archie, who prefers to concentrate his appreciation on books.

But what I should like more than anything in the midst of all this manicured countryside is a word—a glimpse—of the beautiful wildness of home. Might I ask that of you?

Yours, EC

CHAPTER 9

GREER THOUGHT IT BEST to prepare her parents.

"His Grace has allowed the most unimaginably horrid thing," she warned when they joined her in her sitting room before going down to the chapel. "I'm afraid they've buried Ewan already."

Mama put a hand to her throat, but kept her comment to a civil, "How irregular. Are you sure you didn't misunderstand?"

"I have not misunderstood—I had it from Mrs. Peddie herself. And I can see with my own eyes that the grave is closed." She gestured out the window to the fresh heap of soil atop the grave on the otherwise green braeside.

"Hellfire," was her Papa's thankfully less measured response. "That's...blasphemous."

"Indeed, Papa." His indignant anger somehow made it easier to control her own. "And now the whole of Crieff, as well as us, is denied their proper goodbyes. Poor Mrs. Peddie was beside herself with the impropriety of it all. Though I feel as if I ought to have done...something to prevent it."

"What could you have done?" Mama asked. "You are not

mistress here. It is not your duty to assist or correct His Grace. There is no shortage of people at Crieff to whom he might have turned for guidance, I'm sure—the steward, for instance—if he has no sense of his own to guide him."

"But as Ewan's betrothed, do you think I ought to have helped? I might have easily prevented this miscarriage of ..." What was it—lack of knowledge? Or lack of respect?

"Common decency and common sense ought to have prevented it. And the priest, surely, ought to have given some direction or advice." Mama controlled her censure into a sigh. "But what's done is done—I don't suppose they can un-bury him."

"No." Greer unclenched her hands from her skirts and took a deep breath to counter the ache in her chest. What could not be avoided, must be faced with all available equa-nimity—though her reserves were already considerably depleted as it stood. "Best get on with it."

They did so, making their mournful way across the grounds from the Castle to the ancient kirk of St. Bride, set apart on the grounds where the old village of Crieff had once stood before some industrious Cameron ancestor had moved the whole of the village—less the kirk—to its present loca-tion two miles down the glen.

"My Lady Greer." Malcolm Cameron greeted her at the door to the kirk with both obvious pleasure and apparent relief. "I am glad you have come to condole with me." He bowed over her hand with more warmth than mere correct-ness would otherwise dictate, before turning to her parents. "And my Lord and Lady Shee, my thanks."

Mama pursed her lips to keep herself from saying anything unkind, but Papa gave a pointed look at the plot up the brae and said, "Highly irregular, young man. Badly done, Your Grace."

Greer, too, chose not to be charmed by Malcolm

Cameron—she had come for Ewan's sake, not his. And though she might have blamed herself for the lapse of protocol—if such a glaring fault as burying Ewan's body before the service could even be called a *lapse*—she was not in any mood to forgive Malcolm Cameron's oversight of common decency for allowing the mistake in the first place.

Yet Cameron was oblivious of her disapproval, smiling at her in that contented manner as if he had no thought of having done anything wrong. When she refused to return his smile, he patted his hands against his sides, as if he were searching himself for small talk, and hoped to find a few handy words stashed in his pockets. "You look well."

This, of course, was a monstrous falsehood. She had a mirror, and knew she looked like nothing less than a stewed beet—the tears and sadness that came with realizing the full extent of her loss had left reddened rims and dark circles below her eyes.

Yet, if she could not be anything more than polite, she must still be civil—her sense of what was due the occasion demanded it. "Your Grace, I hope it will give us all some small measure of peace to lay my beloved betrothed to rest."

He nodded in solemn agreement. "Yes, quite." And then offered his arm. "Shall we go in?"

"Where are the rest of the mourners?" There was only Cameron himself, Greer and her parents, and the priest. Where were Ewan's friends? Where were the staff and retainers, and the villagers who owed their livelihoods to Crieff? And where were the landowners from other neighboring estates? In his letters, Ewan had written that both the kirk and the lane that led toward the village had been crowded with mourners when the old duke, Ewan's grandfather, had passed away. "Has no one else come to pay their respects?"

"I did not like to invite anyone who was not family." His

answer was firm and pat—almost as if it were prepared in advance. "Knowing my cousin's reputation, I had not thought there would *be* anyone else."

"His *reputation?*" Greer struggled to keep her voice down, but she could not keep either her astonishment or anger from her tone. Nor did she want to—first Cameron was doing it too brown with his compliments, and now he was doing it too black with his disparagement.

The new duke straightened his shoulders and looked away, though two spots of color showed themselves high on his cheekbones. "Unlike my late cousin, I prefer to be a private man, Lady Greer. I cannot change the past, so I prefer to bury it quietly with my cousin. This is a family matter, and it were best for Crieff and the future for this to be a private service to put such a man to quiet, private rest." He bowed correctly but stiffly and gestured into the kirk. "If you would."

She was burning with a fury that made it impossible to see straight, let alone put one foot in front of the other. She refused to entertain this version of Ewan his cousin put forth. She *knew* Ewan. She knew that four hundred and twenty-six letters over the course of ten years could not be lies. She knew that Malcolm Cameron could not know Ewan better than she herself did.

That Ewan was a "private man" *had* been her surest belief. He had been quiet, and modest, but more particularly, she had been sure that he had been esteemed as a man acutely aware of his public responsibilities and the honor that he owed Crieff. How could such a man have a *reputation?* How could he not be admired or esteemed?

This recasting Ewan as a profligate was not just disrespectful—not just a case of not knowing how to manage things correctly. It was something more. Something more personal and vindictive—an attack on his very character.

Ewan may have no longer been able to defend himself, but she certainly would. "No matter your personal feelings, sir, your cousin deserved better from you. Crieff deserved better. When you diminish Crieff, you diminish yourself."

That sharp piece of her mind delivered, Greer turned her back, but continued to punish him by waiting very correctly for her parents to precede her—she was not above showing Malcolm Cameron how things ought to be done by example. But once she had given way to the heated impulse of the moment, Greer was sorry she had done so—Ewan's funeral was not the place for a show of childish pettiness.

It was all so…infuriating and demoralizing and wrong.

And achingly sad—anger was no antidote to the fist of grief that grabbed hold of her at the sight of the bare altar. A plain altar cloth covered the ancient stone table, making the lack of the coffin, which ought to have been present and covered by the ancient family standard—that even now flew high atop the castle—all the more glaringly absent.

The service itself did nothing to alleviate that sadness—the rite was regrettably short and lacking a eulogy, or any actual mention of Ewan and the remarkable person he had been.

It was all so grievously wrong—surely the rector of St. Bride's had known Ewan well enough to make some kind of personal remark upon his character, or praise his work on behalf of Crieff's people? Why did they not, at the very least, say how much he had loved Crieff? How thankful he had been for Crieff's people, who had buoyed and steadied him through his grandfather's death, and eased his first days as duke?

Instead, the rector only read the lesson from Revelations, and the blessing, "Look, we beseech thee, with compassion upon those who are now in sorrow and affliction; comfort them, O Lord, with thy gracious consolations; make them to know that all things work together for good to them that love thee."

Her sorrow and affliction were physical weights that threatened to crush the last of her hope. Ewan seemed already gone and forgotten—erased, even. Indeed, that his body had already been consigned to the plot up the brae was confirmation of that fact.

The heap of raw earth looked obscene, a scar upon the hillside, a glaring anomaly against the soft green and gray of the hills. It was an affront to all her feelings—the climbing rose she had ordered sent from Dalshee's glass house had not even been planted.

She wanted something more—some sign of reverence and respect, some reminder that even if Ewan might have been flawed or made mistakes, her betrothed *had* been part of this life. He had been part of *her* life. He had been deeply loved and had at least tried to be worthy of Crieff.

She needed some reassurance that his life, and her love, had not been wasted.

But there was none.

With every moment, every solemnly intoned piety, the end came nearer, and Ewan slipped farther and farther away. Ashes to ashes and dust to dust.

Greer had to shut her eyes against the hot rush of hopeless tears as she whispered her private goodbyes. "Fate gave the word, the arrow sped, and pierc'd my darling's heart; And with him all the joys are fled, life can to me impart.'" She swallowed over the tight pain. Oh, how Ewan had loved Burns' poetry. "I love it, too," she told him. "I loved you, too, truly. I will miss you always."

The tears of sorrow she had fought to control could not be checked. But Greer did not care—let them see. Let them see her loss. Let them understand that Ewan would never be forgotten.

Not by her. Not ever.

While the new laird could not forget soon enough, it seemed—Malcolm Cameron had already turned away from the grave to make his swift way back to the castle.

Like a man fleeing the scene of a crime.

Some of the tightness in her chest eased. She had not been wrong to trust Ewan with her love, but from this day forward, she would not trust Malcolm Cameron.

No matter how he charmed or flattered, he would find no welcome from her. No matter that he was a duke, with a veritable kingdom on offer, she was not the sort of woman whose admiration could be bought. Nor the kind of person who would stand by silently while he spouted outright lies.

The words "out carousing with friends" leapt back into her mind—"those disreputable fellows," Cameron had named the *quadrumvirate*—as Ewan's letters called them—of Alasdair, Marquess of Cairn, the Honorable Archie Carrington, and Rory Cathcart. Where were they, who had accompanied Ewan through every other journey in his life? Why were they not at Crieff to mourn his passing?

Unless they had been pointedly not invited.

Well, Malcolm Cameron was not the only one who might write—Greer had questions that needed answers.

And while she was riled up and taking people to task, she was not yet done speaking to Malcolm Cameron. She followed him back to the castle. "We will be off as soon as the carriage is made ready, Your Grace." And as soon as they had changed into more practical traveling clothes. It had been one thing to make the journey to Crieff in her elaborate silk wedding gown skirts, as she had wanted to make something of a first impression, but now she had no such excuse, only the comfort of the familiar.

"Certainly. You'll of course take some refreshment before you make the journey back to Dalshee?" He smiled as if he were hosting a tea party and not a funeral. "Unless I can prevail upon you to enjoy Crieff's hospitality and spend some longer time with us?"

Greer wanted no convincing—she wanted the solace of the familiar and was heartsore enough from the cheerless day to say so. "There is nothing more to keep us here, Your Grace. Now that Ewan has been laid to rest, I want the comfort of home."

Home. It felt strange to say the word standing in the place that she believed would be her home forevermore. Greer could not keep herself from casting one more glance around the comfortable room, much as she had done upstairs in the chamber Ewan had furnished for her. Of seeking one last time the serene beauty of the portrait of Ewan and his parents painted with the parkland and Castle Crieff in the background.

But where the family group had hung above the mantelpiece, there was now an empty space. Greer's temper, already made thin and volatile by the events of the day, flared at this latest erasure.

"But while we are speaking of comfort, if it is not too much trouble to locate, Your Grace, I should like the portrait of the late duke you had removed from the duchess's chamber. As the portrait in question was intended as a gift to me and is clearly no longer wanted, I should like to take it with me."

Malcolm Cameron's reaction was all open chagrin—those hot spots of color rose across his cheeks. "Removed? Ah, yes. We are in the process of going through the rooms, moving things about, finding things more to my taste to decorate the public rooms."

"Indeed. I am sure there is more than enough to suit your tastes in Crieff's magnificent collection, that you won't miss one portrait."

He shook his head in sad denial. "A collection acquired, I'm afraid, by much debt."

This time, heat rose in her cheeks—every fiber of her being tensed in rejection of his assertion. "Debt?" She raised her voice so her father, who had been more privy to Crieff's ledgers over the years in making the marriage settlements, and would know even better than she what was the truth, might pay heed.

For her own part, Ewan's letters had never spoken of such a thing—indeed his every word and action had been indicative of fiscal prudence. *Make haste slowly.*

"Yes," Cameron insisted. "I suppose I ought not say so publicly, but I should like to think you are—or will be—my friend. I can safely confess to you"—he lowered his voice to impart his confidence—"that I find Crieff in a terrible state of finance."

Greer risked a glance at Papa, whose forehead was creased with a terrible frown, but who thankfully held his peace, though he continued to listen. "How distressing," she offered. "But if that is so, then perhaps it would be more appropriate for me to offer to buy the portrait in question."

His Grace's brows rose at the suggestion, before he pleated his lips in contemplation. "I'm not sure I should like that. How strange it would be to think of the young woman sighing over a portrait of one's ri—one's relation, like an old widow, not a beautiful, young, unmarried lady."

For the strangest moment, she had thought he had been about to say "rival." Was that how Cameron had seen his cousin, as a romantic rival? How ridiculous.

She rephrased her request in a way that might not ruffle his proprietary, masculine feathers. "I should only like to have a gift that was promised me—a remembrance of a friendship that afforded me great pleasure over the years, Your Grace."

"Will you not call me Malcolm? After all, we are to become friends, are we not?"

There was enough warmth in his expression to tell her that His New Grace of Crieff indeed intended to persist in courting her—whether she wanted him to, or not.

"I don't see how, Your Grace." On such a day, she did not want to be flattered—nor would she flatter. "We aspire to different things in this life, Your Grace." He wanted Crieff made over in his own image. And she—she still wanted Ewan.

More than ever.

Lord Ewan Cameron
7 Rue Malebranche
Faubourg St. Michel
Paris, France

8 October, 1786

Dear Ewan,

My apologies for the lapse in writing ~ I have been kept busy as a bee in a summer hedgerow by my new governess. Her name is Miss Fiona Hally and she is the most frighteningly intellectual woman I have ever met. Naturally, I adore her because with her help I feel like I might almost catch up to you and your continental education. Of course, I shall never be as worldly, for I cannot travel as you have. Still, Dear Hally is not one for simply sitting in the school room ~ our discourses on natural philosophy take place on horseback as easily in a library. Our lessons on the new systems of agriculture are accompanied by careful observation of the fields and flocks of Dalshee.

And to that end, I have a new horse, as I have sadly outgrown my poor sweet pony, Dunnie. Dunnie will still pull the governess cart, but Papa has gifted me with a startling bonnie white mare, come all the way from Leith ~ where I am sure you know there are horse races. I kept your Cat Sìth in mind while naming her ~ what do you think of Nicnevin, the Queen of the Fairies? I must admit I am quite in love with her. She has the roundest, most beautiful eyes, and is quite the pluckiest mare that ever lived, taking me up and down the braeside with nary a nicker.

I hope your travels out in the wide world ~ Ah, Paris! ~ fare as well as ours. But as you have asked me for more of home, I enclose a gift

~ which I am happy to say necessitated a trip to Inverness with Dear Hally. I hope you enjoy the book of Poems, Chiefly in the Scottish Dialect by Mr. Robert Burns, a poet of Kilmarnock. I hope they give you as many hours of pleasure in Paris, thinking of your homeland, as they do me, still situated in the midst of Perthshire. And I hope it will also give you pleasure to imagine me reciting said poems at the top of my lungs to the wind atop Glas Maol. I fancy if you listen hard enough, the north wind will blow them your way, with a kiss from me. I remain,

Your poetry-reciting friend, Greer

CHAPTER 10

S HE WANTED EWAN so badly it was a physical ache
that had to be exercised out of her soul. "I want to
ride home. Over the moor," she told her parents. She would
not even have to change—the practical warm woolen redingote and quilted petticoats of her traveling costume would
suffice for riding her stalwart mare, Nicnevin, who had been
brought to Crieff along with all of her personal possessions.
"I need air."

She needed the wind to blow the cobwebs of doubt and
confusion from her mind.

"If a groom can be spared..." her mother hedged.

"Nay." Greer wanted solitude nearly as much as she
wanted speed—a groom would only slow her down. "Mama,
please."

"Let her go," her papa counseled. "She'll be safe as the
Bank of Scotland on that mare. The ride will do her good."

"Aye." It might do her good, and it certainly wouldn't do
her any harm. "I'll take the dog, Gent. He'll protect me as
well."

"If you must," her mother sighed. "Keep an eye out for the weather."

"Of course."

Greer took her time making her way up the unfamiliar paths, climbing slowly but steadily upward. The knotted reach of the roots across the path made steps to guide her mare onward toward their special, secret place, though it really could not be much of a secret—half of Crieff and all of Dalshee must know that she liked to head for Glas Maol.

The Green Hill was the high outcropping that marked the dividing line between the vast reaches of Crieff and Dalshee seemed the only place where she could could mourn Ewan properly, as he would have wanted. There was something reassuring about the wild ancient hills—something about their vastness that made her feel small and lucky and glad to be alive all at the same time.

Privileged, that's what she was, to live in a place with such raw, natural beauty. She had missed that sense of enduring force when she had gone away, touring the Continent. Just like Ewan had.

She had not been to the magical place of her youth, in quite some time—she had wanted her first trip back after her year of travel to be with Ewan.

After four hours of steady climbing, she and Nicnevin reached the top, and paused to take in the glorious view. The whole of the day stretched before her like the heather covering the braeside—as far as she could see.

Forever—the whole of her future. Alone.

But perhaps she could still make the life she wanted, even if she were alone. Could find purpose and joy in managing Dalshee, and being its mistress without a husband. She might not have her father's title—or Ewan's—but she would still *be* Dalshee in a way that she never could have been Crieff.

She turned back for one last look at Ewan's land, and saw

a thin plume of wood smoke wafting its way skyward from an old shepherd's bothy.

Strange. There were no flocks in the glen—they should have been moved to lower pastures by this time of the year.

She retrieved her spyglass from her saddlebag, and focused it more closely on the bothy, only to find a man—a tall man with a bandage circling his head—at the end of her glass.

Greer's heart kicked hard against her chest in instant recognition—the man injured in the road. Surely it was he.

But Dewar had said that man had died. So who was this?

A surge of irrational hope filled her blood like hot whisky. Her brash, rebellious heart had already raced to its own mad conclusion without consulting her mind. But once there, the idea could not be called back.

He could be Ewan.

No. That was impossible—the raw earth of the Cameron family plot stood as proof. She was trying to soothe her grief with unreasonable hope. More likely, and more logical, was that he was the injured man from the road.

He had to be. A ghillie, Dewar had called him, and there he was, in homespun shirtsleeves, leaning against a stone wall beside the bothy. He was tall—at least as tall as the fellow from the road—but leaner, almost too-thin. The wind blew his linen shirt taut against his arms and shoulders, exposing a lean, wiry frame. But more telling, his head was wrapped in a linen bandage, and beneath it, his scraggly hair was cropped unevenly, as if he'd gone after it with a pair of hedge shears. Exactly as one might do to rid oneself of the ferocious mat of blood and mud.

The scraggly beard, too, might be the result of the fact that he would have neither the opportunity nor the need to shave in the primitive setting of the bothy.

Yet the moorkeeper Dewar had said that the lad from the road was dead.

Why? Why would he have told her something that was clearly not true?

Greer's curiosity would have her marching across the glen to find out, but prudence warned her not to approach a strange man alone on the moor—if Dewar had put the fellow here, he might have his reasons.

She steadied the glass against a boulder to watch the man work. He moved slowly, piling the heavy stones in place with careful deliberation—or as if the action pained him. Indeed, he propped his forearm on the wall for a moment to survey his handiwork, before he stretched his back from the laborious heavy work, unfolding himself like a windblown weed opening to the air. He turned his face upward to the autumn sun, closed his eyes and drew in a long, aching breath, as if he knew what it was like to feel suffocated within his own chest.

Greer's wounded heart lifted in some strange but sure recognition—this feeling she knew. She, too, felt near suffocated by her grief.

The surety that this fellow was the injured lad from the road also eased some of that ache—no matter that he was a stranger, she was inordinately glad to see him. Glad he was well, or at least better. So very, very glad he was not dead.

Still, he looked the worse for wear—his face was discolored with splotches of bruising, with dark, livid black eyes that spread across the bridge of his broken nose. He looked a brute.

A new, more prudent thought intruded—her mama's warning that good men were seldom beaten for no reason. Greer should return to Dalshee immediately and tell her father and his moorkeeper what she had seen—injured or not, this fellow might be a squatter upon the land, taking advantage of the bothy to hide.

But then why was he working so laboriously to improve the wall? And it surely could not be a good thing for a man so badly injured to be so alone. He looked tired. And cold. And hungry.

But she ought to be sure. She ought to what her father would urge her to do—make a better, more reasoned judgment. She would stay safe—she had the dog and she had her fowling piece strapped to her saddle, and she would stay on Dalshee land, on her side of the wide burn. And honestly, he looked as gentle and lost as a lamb left behind on the moorside—all alone.

And because she had felt so alone, she could not bear for him to feel that way.

Greer picked her way carefully down the slope, moving stealthily from cover to cover, stopping every now and again to re-train her glass on him—at one point he disappeared into the bothy, and at another he walked stiffly to the edge of the burn, where he slowly knelt on his hands and knees to cup water into his mouth.

And then like a deer sensing danger, he looked up. And saw her.

Her breath bottled up so hard in her chest, she could feel her blood pulsing at the hollow of her throat. Her hands went cold and slick where she gripped the spyglass—it was such an unnerving feeling to be spied upon. And quite worse to be caught spying upon him.

He raised his hand in slow, tentative greeting, as if he were as unsure of her as she was of him, with his too-big linen shirt flapping like a loose sail in the wind.

He looked harmless—vulnerable even, and the pity that welled within her was more than she could bear. "Hallo," she called.

"Hallo." His cautious return was carried across the burn by the wind.

At her side, the wee dog Gent, who had so obediently clung to her skirts, pricked up his ears and put his nose to the wind to sniff suspiciously, as if he might divine some arcane truth of the man from his smell.

Greer waited for the wee dog's instinctive animal assessment—her papa had often said that he never trusted a man who didn't like dogs, but he always trusted a dog who didn't like a man. And Gent had definitely made up his mind—the wee dog burst from her side and tore down the hillside.

There was nothing she could do but call after him, "Gent, nay!" She let out three sharp whistles to call the disobedient animal back. "Come! Come away from there."

But the dog ignored her, bounding down the glen and splashing across the cold burn, barking madly as he ran, tearing straight for the tall injured man as if he might do him grievous harm.

The thought was not to be borne. "Gent!" Greer had no choice but to grab up her skirts and run after him.

Lady Greer Douglas
Dalshee House
Perthshire, Scotland

11 December, 1786

My Dear Greer,

My apology for not writing sooner, but in an attempt to further our education and enlightenment, we have taken ourselves to tour Italy to round out our taste and erudition. Our first sojourn finds us in Florence, a city where the Renaissance is alive at every turn. Art and sculpture and architecture come together in such a harmonious way as to be entirely seamless—one cannot imagine the great cathedral without its immense, astonishingly powerful baldachin over the altar, or the Baptistry of San Giovanni—St. John the Baptist to us—without the impressively beautiful bronze doors called the Gates of Paradise.

But all the sights—so much adornment and finery everywhere we look, makes me long for the simpler pleasures and familiar sights of home. Of the medieval imbalance of Crieff, with its pleasing lack of artifice or ornamentation. Of you, with your pleasing lack of artifice. I cannot express how much your honest enthusiasm and forthright opinions mean to me. It gives me much relief to know that you are, and will be, as true a friend and helpmeet to me as my boon companions. In fact, you <u>are</u> my companion—you accompany my thoughts as surely as Alasdair, Archie and Rory accompany my person. And now I have your marvelous book, as well.

Therefore, it is with profound, heartfelt thanks for the Scots poems —which are superb, and which I cherish both for your thoughtfulness and their merit—that I send you this particularly lovely gem *of a picture. It is called a <u>landscape</u>, and it is by the artist who invented this way of looking at the world of the ancients. I hope you will like it, for it made me think, for some unaccountable reason, of you.*

I remain steadfastly yours, EC

THE MOMENT HE SAW HER, Dewar's caution flooded his brain.

Hide yourself away should anyone come.

But he was too far away from the bothy to hide. And she had already seen him.

And she was only a lass.

Lass—the word slid seamlessly into his mind like a friend announcing himself at home. How he knew it, he didn't know. Elusive, that's what the words were, darting in and out of his brain. Sometimes they were there, and sometimes gone, like strangers who disembarked from a carriage and walked away, never to return.

But this stranger was here. Standing like a wee figurehead on the opposite side of the burn, with her autumn-bright hair streaming in the wind like a standard flying atop a castle.

A lass. A lass with a dog.

A *spaniel*. Another word he knew without thinking.

This particular spaniel dog was hurtling down the braeside, barking like mad as it charged across the burn, splashing and streaking toward him as if its wee life depended upon it. But when the wee beastie reached him, the animal simply hurled its wet, soft and silky self into his arms, and began to lick the very skin off his face with such plaintive whines of intent and entreaty that there was nothing to do but accept the press of adoration.

He fell to his knees to try and contain the gyrating jumble of joy, jumping and turning and curling into his legs as if the animal could not get enough of the rough, joyous contact.

"Gent!" The lass's voice was high and clear like a lark. "Gent, come!"

Aye. *Gent*—the dog plastering itself loyally to his side as if it were loath to let him from its sight.

She stood on the other side of the burn, this bonnie, ginger-haired lass, who steadied her wary stance and lifted her chin before she spoke. "I'm so very sorry if the dog or I startled you. Gent's usually better-behaved."

"Nay," he managed. "Gent." After her clear voice, his sounded harsh and raspy. Rusted from recent abuse.

But she made no mention. She frowned at the animal pressing itself into his leg. "Gracious, but he seems to like you very much, though I apologize if we've intruded upon you. I saw you from over on Glas Maol." She gestured toward the mountaintop that loomed over the glen like a raptor.

"Aye. Glas Maol." These words came out of his mouth more easily—both his tongue and his brain had become more familiar with the name. Because he'd practiced it— along with the other words he was desperately trying to keep in his head—day after day, alone, talking to the wind to make himself remember. "The green mountain."

"Aye, just so." Her mouth softened into a small smile. "I'm glad to see you're better—that you're up and about." She took a step closer to the edge of the burn. "I'd been so very worried."

"You know me?" The thought gripped him tighter than the binding around his head and ribs.

"Well, aye," she qualified. "Do you not remember me? The carriage? We helped Dewar, the moorkeeper, and put you into his care. I assume he knows you're here?"

The stark image of bloodied lace against the polished wood of a cart, along with the sickening feeling of jolting over a rutted road leapt into his head, but things were all tangled up in the fog that crept across his brain, concealing and revealing in unpredictable turn.

Aye, of course, he wanted his mouth to say. *Aye, I would definitely remember someone as bonnie and lovely as you,* even if it were a lie. Even if he could not recall her place in the events that brought him here. Because there was something about her—something, if not familiar, then stirring. Something in her kind smile that made him want to know more of her, despite Dewar's warning.

But the words remained trapped inside his own head. Because in that moment, he was keenly aware of being less than he wanted to be—though he could not know what he had been, only what he was now.

Yet, he felt diminished. Especially before this creature, this *lass*, with her soft voice and small, hopeful smile.

"Hit my head." But that was not right either—some*one* had hit him on the head. Someone had tried to kill him.

"Aye, so I see." She picked her way across the rocks in the burn. "I'm so glad to see you're better." And then she stepped forward through the rough grass, and held her hand out to him. "I'm Greer Douglas. I've come from Dalshee."

Dalshee—the land on the other side of the burn. "Aye, yon moor." And then for no reason, his brain prompted him to say in a voice as creaky as a rusted farm cart, "Crieff."

"Aye, this side of the burn is indeed Crieff." Her warm smile was like a balm. "I can't tell you how glad I am to find you better. Or at least on the mend."

She came close enough that he could see the warm kindness in her clear eyes and smell the divine soft scent of blossoms. Better than the dog, who smelled wet and earthy, although the creature still twined about his legs was lovely. But the lass was lovelier.

"Are you all alone here?" she asked. "I had hoped Dewar would be able to return you to your family. Do they know you're here?"

Too many questions at once. "Nay. I—" His mad, damaged brain struggled to keep up.

"You have no family?" she finished for him. "Oh, I see." But she looked around at the stone bothy as if she did not see at all.

"Nay. I have—" Hell and blast. The damn truth was he had *nothing* that he could remember beyond auld Dewar. He had only the bloody blankness in his brain and the unreliable strength of his slowly recovering body.

"You *do* have family?" she assayed. "Is that what you were trying to say?"

He had no idea what he was trying to say. He only knew that he was trying to say something. That some part of his darkened brain still knew that this is what one did—one carried on a conversation by speaking when one was spoken to.

"Friends," he said. But he sounded deranged to his own ears, as if the words got all mangled on the way out of this throat. It was ugly and frustrating and hard, bloody damn hard. Because how he knew he had friends, when there was no evidence of such beyond auld Dewar, he could not say.

His head began to ache.

"It's quite all right," she said, laying her gloved hand on his forearm in a gesture he understood to be kind.

And because she was soft and kind, he could not seem to stop himself from grasping the comfort she offered. From taking her hand and pressing the warmth and softness of her palm into his like a brand, heating him through to his bones.

She stilled, like the deer in the glens when they hear something, looking up at him with the same sort of wide-eyed, wary intensity.

Don't go, he wanted to say. Please stay. Stay and let me thank you. For your kindness. For your warmth and beauty.

He wanted to reassure her that he was not as mad and strange as he must sound and look, living out in the wilderness like a hermit in a hut. But he could not. Because he feared the words would come out in some mangled, twisted moan that would startle her into flight like a deer at the sound of a gunshot.

He closed his eyes for a long moment, trying to sort out the feelings in his head, trying to make his brain force the words from his tongue. But the damned hills shifted under his feet, and the vertiginous swirl of the wind pushed him sideways.

"Oh, gracious." She caught him up by his forearms, trying to take his weight upon her own. "Easy there. Let's set you down on that bench."

"Nay." But he knew she was right, and that he needed to park his arse on the flat slab of stone next to the bothy, where he sat to recover himself in the afternoon sun, resting like a great serpent on a warm rock, exhausted until his blood heated again.

But she was the sun, warming him to his core, easing the aching fists of pain gripping his chest. The heavenly scent of her filled his head—soft and bright with the scent of flower and citrus. Soft. Soft in eye and tongue and manner.

So he let her lead him to the bench. "My thanks." His bony arse hit the stone with a jolt, and he leaned his head back against the wall to make the damned inconvenient whirling sensation stop. When it finally did, he opened his eyes to find her still there, not staring at him, but looking around with her hands on her hips and her bright, intelligent eyes narrowed at the corners, as if she were taking some sort of stock.

"Well. Clearly you oughtn't be left alone—I can't imagine why Dewar did so." She smiled even as she frowned—quite happy taking charge. "But now we're here to help. Gent seems quite taken with you." She looked at the wee dog, who still pressed his furry muzzle into his palm. "I think he likes you very much. He's lost his master, you see, and he's been feeling a bit...lost." Her smile turned bittersweet. "Like you."

Lost. "Aye." He was lost inside his own mind, as mad as a March hare in a hedgerow.

"Have you been seen by a doctor? Has anyone been up here to see you?"

"Aye. I reckon—" He stopped and shook his head as if he might clear it, but the action created another wave of threatening blackness that hovered at the edge of his vision. "I'm fine."

"Yes, I can see that," she disagreed with a wry sort of kindness. "Do you mind if I take a look at your injury to your head? I've some experience with medicine." She pointed toward the back of his head, which stung and itched off and on. But as the stinging and itching was a hundred times better than the incessant ache which had accompanied him up the moor, he would not complain.

He bowed his head—frankly it was easiest to hold his temples in his hands—while she came to stand with one knee upon the bench, close by his shoulder. Close enough so he could smell the bright scent that wafted off her—summer sunshine and something as sweet and simple as new mown hay. So close that he felt the soft breeze of her breathing on the skin of his neck.

It was heaven, even if he was in this forgetful hell.

"Do you mind if I take the binding off to have a look? The Swiss and French advise leaving a healing wound open to the air." She unwound the bandage without waiting for his answer. "The flesh looks healthy, though I should think you'll have a magnificent scar."

"Aye." A scar was a small price to pay for being alive.

"But at this stage, I think it best to bind it back up." She did so, but when she was done, she stepped away, and it was as if every last ember in the fireplace had gone out, so complete was the loss of warmth.

"Not much in the way of creature comforts, is it?" She was poking her head through the open door of the bothy. "Still, it looks well-built and in good tick—snug enough to keep a lashing wind and rain out. And you've several good thick wool plaids."

His face grew strangely hot at the thought of her looking at his narrow cot.

If she noticed, she made no mention. "What have you for food?"

"Dewar," was all he managed.

"He's the one who left you that pot?" She disappeared inside, only come back holding the hot handle of the blackened pot with his only other shirt. "Why, it's almost empty. No wonder you're in such a state. Why on earth he left you up here, when the keeper's cottage is far better suited to the purpose of nursing a gravely injured man back to health than a remote, drafty bothy, I'll never understand," she tsked. "And how is a man to recover from such an injury without the proper nourishment? I'll have Mrs. Malloch make up a hamper full of fruits and cheese and bread to have on hand. Wee nourishing bits to eat besides a stew cooked to treacle for days."

"But—" She regarded him gravely. "I'm sorry, but can you eat such things? I'm sorry to pry, but your teeth?" She gestured to her own, and then to his mouth, as if she thought him as diminished and mad as he felt. "Were any of your teeth loosened in the…accident?"

"No accident." This he knew. He didn't know how he had been unseated from his horse, tipped off the road and fallen down the gorse-ridden braeside into the burn—but he knew he had been beaten to within a hair's breadth of his life.

"Do you mean—" She immediately laid her hand on his arm. "What happened?"

And there it was—the roaring sound of the burn filling his head with the sick sensation of falling.

He grasped at it, but it was like holding a cobweb—so unsubstantial his mind retreated to the damned blankness.

He shook his head. Mad and injured he might be, but he was still enough of a man to bridle at admitting his diminishment. Instead, though he was as sore as a bear, he smiled to show her what Dewar had claimed—that he still had his teeth.

"Oh, gracious." Her checks pinked as she mirrored his smile. "Yes, I see. But the bruises are rather splendid—your nose looks quite broken."

"Aye." He felt the achy bump across the bridge of his nose. "And ribs."

"Is that all? You poor thing." She raised her hand to his face slowly, as if she still thought him a dumb animal and wanted to show him she intended no harm, and slid her hand along the rough, bristly contour of his jaw. She went gently, as the left side of his face and jawbone were indeed still sore with bruises he could not see but felt acutely.

But when she turned her hand to carefully trace the knot on the crest of his nose with her slender index finger, the pad of her thumb inadvertently rested against his lower lip.

For a moment he felt like a dumb, brute animal, to have her look at him with the same curious detachment she might have displayed checking a horse's teeth at a fair. But he was no dumb animal. Though he was as cock-brained as they came, some part of his mad mind still prompted him to open his lips just wide enough to rasp his teeth along the flesh of her thumb.

She drew back her hand as if stung—her face flushed a bright pink the hot color of the sunset over the hill.

His own body roared to unruly, if vigorous life—the feeling was damn near electrifying.

She turned away, distancing and busying herself with the making of plans. "I'll get a salve and some foods to help you heal," she said. "To nourish and help you get stronger. Oh— here!" She pulled something from somewhere in the thick folds of her wool gown. "A good Perthshire Drummond pear, ripe and soft. Let me cut it for you."

She magiced a wicked wee dirk out of her bodice, and before he understood what he was doing, he flinched away.

It slid into his mind's eye so clearly—that image of the dirk in the boot coming toward his head—and so vividly, he could almost feel the sick impact of the hard kick against the base of his skull.

But as soon as it came, it was gone.

"Are you all to rights?" She hunched down upon her heels to peer at him.

"Aye." He took a deep breath and accepted the piece she held out. The flavor of the ripe fruit exploded in his mouth, racing up his jaw, almost painfully good. He made a sound that was half groan, half slavering.

She would think him more than merely mad—she would think him an animal.

It was almost more than he could bear.

"Please." He heaved the word out of his mouth like a heavy boulder rolled in front of a cave. "Stay." He didn't want her to leave. He wanted her to stay and feed him sweet ripe fruit always.

She drew back a bit, even as she smiled kindly. "I wish I could. Though I think the dog will stay." She bit her lip between her teeth, trying to decide, before she asked him. "Would you like that?"

"Aye." The wee dog would be more than welcome, though a poor substitute for her. "Come back?"

"Aye." She briefly touched his knee in gentle consolation. "I'll come back as soon as I may—to check on you and Gent, both."

"Thank you," he managed. "You're"—he worked to enunciate the words carefully— "kind. Sweet." His brutish brain miraculously found him another. "Thou bonnie gem." The words found the way out of his mouth, though he did not really know what he meant.

A flush painted her face, lighting her like the rarest jewel. "Robert Burns—my favorite." The moment hung between them while she decided what else to say. "I had a…a friend who liked Burns especially," she said carefully. "I sent him the poems when he was away and homesick for Crieff." She tipped her head to one side to carefully consider him. "I'm sorry, I don't think I asked, but what is your name?"

All the pleasure that he had felt was swallowed whole by the mortification of being so mad—so diminished—that he did not know his own name.

He could not tell her that. And so he reached out to touch

her hand. To tell her with his body what his lost and twisted words could not—that he needed her.

She answered with a small sunrise of a smile, so pink and kind and bittersweet it made her something more than bonnie—it made her beautiful. "Never mind. It doesn't matter."

But it did matter. He was sure that nothing in the short, painful extent of his memory would ever matter more.

Lord Ewan Cameron
Palazzo Lanfredini
Florence, Italy

1 February, 1787

Dearest Ewan,

I would value any gift that you should give me ~ and how you spoil me ~ first books and now this! Sunrise! The painting is in itself exquisite, but, oh, that it made you think of me is beyond thoughtful. Mama is concerned for the impropriety of the nude bathers depicted in the clear, green water of the river, but I think they are beautiful in their wild, natural beauty, and find the picture quite, quite lovely. I adore it both for itself, and for you, <u>yourself</u>, and ~ dare I say it? ~ for your thinking of me when you looked at those frolicking bathers.

I am becoming quite beholden to you for a vast deal of my education—in less frolicking matters, your mention of Descartes sent me to my father's shelves, and a long, determined read of the Discourse on Method. My French is of course not so good as yours must now be, but I found by the end of my reading that I rather favor your treatise ~ that man, or woman for that matter, should not be the sole possessor, nor the complete master over nature. Indeed, I believe it to be quite impossible. No matter what man's improvements or changes, no matter the quantity of the stone or paving, nature will find a way ~ along the garden wall, where the gardener has carefully trained the apple trees into precise espaliers, seeds will find a way to take root, even somewhere so inhospitable to their growth as the steep vertical wall. And any walk through an old abandoned castle or monastery will show us that nature ~ wind, rain, earth and growth ~ will eventually subsume the building stones, and that a river shall find its course no matter the dams that force it into deep pools.

But enough of philosophy. Today I will look at my new painting by Monsieur Claude and be so very, very happy. I will hope fervently that this letter finds you the same.

Your Greer

GREER SPRANG UP from the depths of sleep in an instant, her heart pounding like her mare's hooves on her chest. Awoken from a vivid dream of him.

Of Ewan.

It was not the first time she had dreamt of Ewan—her girlish fantasies of her betrothed had taken many different forms over the years—but this was the first in which she had seen his face.

But instead of the Ewan she knew from her miniature, the face in her dream had been the bruised and beaten man on the moor.

Yet, in the dream she *knew* the injured man was Ewan— she knew it by the feeling of perfect harmony between them. She knew it by the kindness in his eyes. They had been together in Paris, Ewan and she, walking in a sunny, light-filled garden, arm in arm. She had turned to him, and known he was her husband because of the feeling of abiding rightness and sweetness that had filled her being. And they had kissed, his lips pressing to hers and opening her mouth, filling her with the feel of his tongue tangling intimately with hers. She had pressed herself to his body, strong and warm, clasping her hands around his wide shoulders. And she had felt wonderful and full to her brim and blissfully, blindingly happy.

But now she was awake.

And logic and reason and the damned dirty burial plot on the hillside at Crieff told her Ewan was gone. Nothing would change the past, and nothing could fix the future.

Except, perhaps, helping the injured man who was very much alive, and who had made such an indelible impression upon her.

What had she been thinking to touch him so?

She was thinking he was gentle and lost, though his mind was clearly not entirely right. But whether this was from his injury or some inherent madness, her learning was not sufficient to tell.

Still, *he* must be a man of some learning—that telling snippet of poetry could not otherwise have found its way out of a mind so disordered and a body so badly beaten it was a miracle he was not dead.

He was like Lazarus, risen—

Nay. It was impossible.

She knew it was dangerous to even entertain the notion that Ewan might not be dead. Knew she was making something extraordinary out of an ordinary man to fill the well of loneliness that Ewan's death had opened within her. Knew she ought not give in to such a rash notion.

Yet, the moment she felt his hand upon hers—felt the roughened texture of the fingertips with which he had quite literally clung to life—she had felt a strange connection. A surety that even if he could not seem to speak or think perfectly, his simple touch told her more about him in that one moment than another man might have revealed in five minutes of rational conversation—that he was good and kind.

And grateful for the contact, starved for affection and company as much as he was fairly starved for food—his clothes, such as they were, hung from his lanky frame like drapery from the rod of his bony shoulders.

So company he would get—though it was an emotional wrench to leave sweet Gent. Yet, the wee animal was clearly smitten, clinging to the fellow's side as if he knew him of old. As if he really were...

Ewan.

Nay. Greer forced herself to stop from continuing along that particularly dangerous path of thought. She would find out more before she leapt to any untenable conclusions. She would concentrate on what she already knew, and that was that her new friend's need for simple companionship was, at present, clearly greater than hers—she had her own dogs, as well as Mama and Papa to turn to always, while her new friend had no one.

Nay. He had her now—she would be his advocate and his friend.

Indeed, if the dog trusted him—and dogs were notoriously reliable judges of character—so would she. And here was a purpose that would push her up and out of her grief—here was a chance to do all the good she could, by all the means she had at her disposal, to this person she had found in need.

If there were another reason, a secret wish of her foolish, unyielding heart, she would keep that to herself—a talisman to ward off the ache of acceptance.

She would return to the bothy with foodstuffs as soon as possible. A well-cured ham—something he would not need to cook, but only cut and feed himself for nourishment. Apples from the harvest, and other fruits from Dalshee's well-maintained glasshouse, as well as a thick, hearty stew to stick to his ribs.

She would take action. Greer threw back the covers and immediately stepped upon the scattered stack of letters she had read late into the night, which were now strewn across the counterpane and onto the floor. There, on the rug next to the bed, was his last letter, crushed and smudged by the clutch of her hand.

Yes. Let us be wed in two days' time—nothing could make me happier.

Nothing could make her happy now.

Loss was like stepping in a hole she had not marked, twisting her heart instead of her ankle—hobbling her just the same. Greer's eyes went hot and itchy but she had already cried until there were no tears left to wet the pillow.

And those letters which recounted his travels across the years reminded her that there were others who loved Ewan at least as much as she had. Others who had known him just as long. Others who might have been with him that fateful night in Edinburgh.

She wrapped a warm plaid around her shoulders, and went immediately to her writing desk, whereupon she wrote long, candid letters to Ewan's friends, asking all the imprudent questions, though she knew she might not like the answers.

So be it. Until that unhappy time, she would act, and do all the good she could for the fellow at the bothy.

She dressed in one of her rugged wool redingotes, and headed straight for the kitchens. But how ought she to explain such a request to the housekeeper? And to Mama and Papa? There was something curious—almost disquieting— about the fact that Dewar had told her the lad had died, when the clear truth was that he was recovering.

Perhaps Dewar was simply one of those old-fashioned,

pig-headed sorts of old men who disdained any help from a female? He wouldn't be the first man in Scotland—or the last —to depreciate her 'managing' tendencies.

But she wouldn't apologize for her character—Ewan had never seemed to mind her speaking either her heart or her mind to him in their letters. And she had been raised and trained as the heiress of Dalshee to make decisions—about staff and the estate alike—and to hone her experience into instinct that rarely let her down.

Her instinct was now to tread lightly until she could learn more.

"Oh, mileddy." Dalshee's housekeeper, Mrs. Malloch looked up from arranging a laden breakfast tray when Greer burst into the kitchen. "Yer lady mother was just askin' for ye at breakfast. They've a letter from His Grace of Crieff."

"Thank you, Mrs. Malloch. I will go directly, but in the meantime, I should like a hamper packed for a very hearty picnic, if you please."

"Enough fae two, mileddy?" The housekeeper's sharp eyes were bright with question.

"Aye, if you please," Greer answered. "With a ham and good deal of fruit, if we can spare it, please." That would do nicely to keep her friend in good kip for several days, she hoped.

"I'll have it reddy fae ye and His Grace in no time, mileddy."

"Oh, nay. I meant a *charity* basket not a picnic for—" Greer felt her cheeks flame with equal parts embarrassment and indignation—that Mrs. Malloch should think her already courting Malcolm Cameron so soon after Ewan had died, was mortifying.

And yet, she swallowed the protest poised on the tip of her tongue—perhaps it were better to keep her friend in the bothy's presence a secret until she could divine more about him.

"Thank you," she said instead, though she could do nothing about the riddy heat in her cheeks. "I'll send for it presently."

"There you are, my dear. Do come and break your fast, Greer, darling." Mama's gentle but insistent voice advised. "You're looking rather too peaked. The nourishment will do you good."

"Indeed," she agreed. Though she had not spent more than a moment in front of the looking glass, she knew her eyes were still red-rimmed and itchy with tears. The arduous climb back to the glen at Glas Maol would do her good, but a hearty breakfast was needed first.

"Still nothing—no notice in the Edinburgh papers," Papa groused. "I'll have to speak to His Grace about how things are to be done." Her Papa looked up from his newspaper to smile at her as she retrieved a plate full of kippers and eggs. "Ah, Greer. Good to see you up and about this morning, my dear." He passed her a letter across the breakfast table. "See what you can make of this."

"From Malcolm Cameron? What does he want?"

"To sell me a piece of Crieff farmland."

"Arable land? I thought all such land was entailed upon the estate?" Greer had read—and understood—all the fine points of her marriage settlements.

"When you read his offer, you will see that he says the field he seeks to sell is outside of the entail—though I have my doubts—and is not accruing necessary profit."

Greer applied herself to reading the letter, making note with her finger where she stopped. "This land he's talking about is on the south end of the upland loch near Glas Maol? Where it is protected from the wind, but still he claims is making no profit?"

"So he says." Papa's tone was everything skeptical. "The last I recall, William Cameron—His Grace's grandfather—had always sowed those four hectares with high quality barley that had always been slated for use in Crieff's distillery."

"Has the crop been cut?" Greer asked. "But what would Crieff use for their distillery if they have no barley? This figure he names is too steep, even with a crop. And he certainly can't think to sell it fallow for that price?"

Her father shook his head. "I can't imagine what he is thinking."

Greer weighed the possibilities. "He did say that the management of the estate was a bit beyond him—that he had not been raised or educated with any expectation, or understanding, of estate matters. That he found his new responsibilities strange and difficult."

"He will find it stranger and more difficult still if he does not come to grasps with crops or budgeting. Still, the land would be a good investment for Dalshee." Papa reasoned.

"Why don't I ride up to the loch to take a look at the hectares in question? That way, you shall have an answer about the crop by dinner without the need to write and wait for His Grace's reply." And she would have the perfect excuse to spend the day in the glen.

"Excellent, my dear," Papa answered. "I am glad to see you taking Ewan's death so well. Very practical. We are not made for grief, you and I. We must act and be happy."

Even if she did not exactly agree with him, Greer answered obediently, "Aye, Papa."

"Aye," he rejoined as he patted her hand. "Life does go on. And you are a young woman with responsibilities here at Dalshee, even if you will no longer have any at Crieff."

If she did have any responsibility at Crieff, she would keep it to herself. Do good by stealth, she reasoned, was what the Bible and her parents had always taught. And although she had never been stealthy, or kept a secret from her parents before, she would now. For some reason she could not yet articulate, but understood to be true, her friend in the glen needed her protection.

From whom, she was not yet sure—possibly from Dewar, who had said the poor fellow was dead, and had all but abandoned him to his fate in the high moor. But until she knew for sure what and who had brought the gentle giant to such a pass, she would keep silent.

"I'll go directly."

But Greer was waiting outside the kitchens for Dunnie's saddle baskets to be packed with the foods Mrs. Mallach mercifully provided without further comment, when her Papa found her.

"What's all this?"

The compulsion to lie, to say it was nothing more than a charity basket, lay hot on Greer's tongue. But while an omission was one thing, a blatant lie was entirely another, and Greer had too much respect for her father—and for herself— to point herself down that tangled road. "It's for the young man from the road—you remember, the injured lad from Crieff that the moorkeeper Dewar was seeing to?"

"Aye? Is there some difficulty?"

"It's very strange. He's abandoned the lad"—so much easier to speak of her friend to her father as if the injured man were just a lad—"to that old stone bothy just up the glen from the upland loch under Glas Maol."

Her father knew the remote spot. "Alone?"

"Aye. So I'm taking him food." Greer hesitated for only a moment before she confessed all. "And there's something about him, Papa—something fine that puts me in mind of Ewan."

"Greer." Her father's tone was discouraging.

"Really, Papa," Greer pressed. "There is something noble and fine in him, despite his rough speech and appearance. Something that speaks of a strength of character, despite the ordeal he has suffered—or perhaps because of it."

"My darling girl." Papa's tone was more than discouraging —it was adamant. "I know how attached you were to Ewan— I was as well. He was a singular individual, a wonderful young man, and your marriage to him would have given me great delight. But it is not to be. You must put away this flight of fancy. You must."

"Papa, I'm not being fanciful, truly."

"Greer, as difficult as it may be, you really ought to put your mind to your future. You must turn your attention to other prospects, other suitors." He touched her chin in a gesture of parental fondness. "I'm not getting any younger, my dearest, and neither are you. His Grace, Malcolm Cameron, seems everything sincere in his offer for you, even if he needs educating in the ways of managing an estate."

"Papa." Her voice held its own desperate warning—it was *too soon.*

"Why not?" he asked. "You would be just the wife for him —for you have exactly the knowledge he lacks."

"Papa, I am not a school teacher." She couldn't exactly say what it was about Malcolm that put her off, but she was like a cat with her fur rubbed the wrong way, all tail-swishing annoyance. Mama always said she was too quick to judge, too hard on everyone, including herself. She held everyone to the same impossible standard to which she held herself— to be like Ewan.

"Promise me you will consider, if not him, then someone else."

Greer knew she would not be given leave to go until she agreed. She did so on a sigh. "I promise." And she always kept her promises.

Papa kissed her forehead. "I know it is hard, my dearest. I can see that. But what cannot be avoided must be faced with—"

"Aye, equanimity," she finished.

"You are young and will recover. You must. Your future, and the future of Dalshee, must rely upon that."

"Aye, Papa." Greer knew he was right, but she did not want to think of the future—she only wanted to think about now. And her friend in the glen, who already haunted her dreams.

Was it wrong to want or uncharitable to use her injured friend as an escape from her cares?

Was it her grief—the crushing disappointment of having all her hopes for the future overturned—that made her want to cast both Ewan and the injured man as paragons of virtue? Although she had never thought Ewan was perfect—he had flaws enough, as did she, that he had never tried to conceal from her—he had been perfect for her.

Or so she had thought.

The image from her dream was baffling. No wonder she wanted the concrete action of charging up the moor as if she were riding to the rescue—it was something she was sure was right.

Lady Greer Douglas
Dalshee House
Perthshire, Scotland

24 May, 1787

My dear Greer,

I hope this letter finds you well, as I have not had a letter from you in some time, which occasions some worry. We have travelled onward, or should I say southward, to the ancient city of Rome. While Florence was a city of the Renaissance, this is a city of the Ancients.

They say when in Rome, one must do as the Romans do, and therefore we four world travelers are wearing our shoes to scraps of the thinnest leather in walking all about the ruins and touring all the grand churches filled from terrazzo floors to painted ceilings with the most marvelous works of art, sculpture and architecture. You would wonder at it all. Often I think to myself—Greer <u>must</u> see this. So I rush to put pen to paper and tell you all.

I also put my pen to paper to thank you again for the superb book of poetry. Mr. Burns has become a steadfast friend, to whom I turn whenever I need a dose of home. The cadence of the words, and the images they evoke, cure my homesick heart more surely than almost anything—except a letter from you.

I enclose a rather heated, passionately Italian kiss for you in the hopes that you will write me back for more.

Your devoted friend, EC

Lord Ewan Cameron
Piazza di Spagna 74
Roma, Italia

28 July, 1787

Dear Ewan,

Rome! Oh, how I long to see it. Both Dear Hally and I are in agreement with you that I must indeed travel ~ if not to Rome, then at the very least to London, if I am to be a fit helpmeet and companionable wife to you. We have thus both applied separately to Papa, who unfortunately, still holds firm in his belief that I am too young. I am resolved to be everything calm and mature until I might convince him. Though I must say your passionate Italian kisses leave me nearly too giddy with delight for anything approaching calm.

Pray do send more ~ as many as you ever can, so I may remain,

Your devoted Greer

CHAPTER 13

AFTER THE LONG CLIMB, Greer found her new friend dozing in the late afternoon sun on the bench, his long legs stretched out in front of him, his shaggy head tipped back, resting against the stone wall of the bothy. His eyes were closed, but his still-bruised face was turned up to catch the warmth of the early autumn sun.

He ought to have been the very picture of rest and recovery. He ought to have looked calm and serene in the easy arms of sleep. But there was something tense, something watchful about him, even in repose.

"Hallo?" She called to wake him. "I've brought you food, just as I promised."

He woke with a start, jolting to uncomfortable, probably painful, consciousness, while the silent dog came quickly forward to greet her with gyrations of delight.

"Good lad, wee Gent." Greer dismounted, and let the sweet wee dog jump into her arms. It felt good to hold the demonstrative little animal again, and to see that she had done the right thing in trusting this man with Ewan's beloved pet. "Has he been keeping you good company?"

"Aye." He pushed to his feet as his face lit with recognition and pleasure. "You came back."

"Aye. Just as I said I would. I always keep my word." It was the granite bedrock upon which she had been taught to build her character, as solid and true as the Highland hills.

"Thank you, —" He paused, searching, his hands clenching momentarily into tense fists. "Sorry. I've forgotten your name."

"Not at all. I'm Greer," she told him. "And not to worry if you still can't place yours," she said with a cheerful briskness she did not exactly feel. "We'll think of something else to call you."

He closed his eyes, and clenched his fists again, as if he were trying to physically grasp something. "It's lost." He shook his head. "Some words are fixed." He closed his eyes to recite them. "Crieff, Dalshee, Dewar, Gent. And now Greer." His smile was rueful, though she could glimpse what it cost him. "Others have simply…wandered away."

"Well." For his sake, Greer forced a confidence she did not feel into her smile. "Hopefully the condition is only temporary. So we must help you recover. I've brought all sorts of good things for you—fruit and fresh bread, and a ham from Dalshee's larder." She let Gent down and set to unloading the densely packed, linen-wrapped parcels Mrs. Malloch had diligently prepared. "We'll have you back to fighting weight in no time."

"Fighting weight?" His brow furrowed in wariness, and he looked down at his still-clenched fists in dawning horror. "Do I fight?"

"Oh, nay—tis only an expression." Though he certainly did have the look of a losing prizefighter—all bruised hands and face and broken nose. And he was an uncommonly tall, with a fighter's long reach.

Gracious but they seemed to grow them big in these glens

—Ewan had often remarked upon his towering height. This lad looked to be something well over six feet.

Nay. As tempting as it was to mark the similarities, she would guard against such rash, illogical impulses "I meant you will recover your weight and strength," she clarified. "The food will help that."

"Oh, aye. I ken." He frowned again, and closed his eyes, as if thinking pained him. "Fighting weight," he repeated before he opened his eyes. "Fourteen stone."

"Oh?" Fourteen stone was the weight of a well-muscled, fit man. "Were you fourteen stone once? Before your accident?" She didn't know what else to call it, though he had said the circumstance of his injury was no accident.

"Aye. I think so." He winced up one eye, as if he were not quite sure of his answer. Then he scrubbed his hand into his shaggy, uneven hair, as if he could physically chafe the memory out of his head. "It's lost in my cracked brain."

"Oh, no." How devastating must it be not to know—to have one's very identity stripped away. Perhaps he really was a prizefighter—they were said to go mad from the blows. But he seemed too gentle, too thoughtful, even with his present deficiencies, for such a brutal sport. Too much like Ewan, who made haste slowly.

Nay. "Do you remember how it happened? How your head got cracked?"

"Nay." Even with that simple word, she could hear the frustration, and even loneliness, in his voice. "I only remember…" He spread his hands in a gesture that took in the bothy and the hills and the whole of the glen. "…Crieff."

"Yes. You're a local lad," she supplied—as if such scant information would encourage him.

He didn't seem encouraged—he seemed resigned. He shrugged. "Aye. A crack-brained local lad."

"Well, then." Greer turned her mind to practical solutions

—if she could not recover his memory, she could at least help him recover his strength. "Then when you are feeling stronger—when you've gotten the whole of that ham tucked away—we shall have to venture down to the village, to see if anyone there can remember you."

"The village?"

"The village of Crieff," she clarified. "It lies about ten or eleven miles south." She pointed across the loch. "In that direction."

"South," he repeated, as if he were firming that word, or idea, or concept in his head. And then he turned. "East." He pointed, and then changed his stance. "North." He faced each new direction. "And west."

"Yes—the cardinal directions." How astonishing to watch him recover information that she took for granted—an understanding that was all but bred into her bones. "Is it coming back?"

He stood still for a moment, as if that might help his memory, and then he shrugged. "Compass rose. What is that?"

"That is what we call the formal depiction of those four cardinal directions. Sometimes it looks more like a four-pointed star, or the rays of a sun."

"Aye, I ken. The picture came to mind," he explained. "Then the words. Sometimes they're together. Sometimes not."

It was the longest speech she had yet heard him make. "Then that is progress. With time, and encouragement, more will come back," she said with more confidence than she felt. "It is just a matter of time."

"Aye." He nodded, though he didn't sound convinced. "T'was what Dewar said."

"Then it is sure to be true." Though if Dewar knew this lad—and surely he could identify him by now—why did he not simply tell him who he was? Why did he bring him all the way up to this remote bothy to heal on his own?

It made no sense.

Unless… Unless Dewar had good reason to keep him away from the rest of Crieff, and the rest of society. Unless Dewar also knew why the fellow had been beaten to within an inch of his life. Mama's warning that good men were seldom set upon for no reason, while bad men were invariably set upon for very good ones, re-echoed in Greer's ear.

As much as she wanted his injured young man to be Ewan, the bald truth was he could indeed be anyone, from a prizefighter to even a murderer. Even if he did seem as gentle as a lamb, he was a stranger, set apart from his people quite on purpose, it would seem. And she was alone with this disheveled, "crack-brained" stranger a good eight miles of windswept, empty moorland from home.

She ought to have been more cautious. She ought to have been less *fanciful*, drat it. "I can't stay, I'm afeared. Just wanted to make sure you had food." She busied herself unloading the rest of the carefully packed goods—the apples, and jars of berries, and stout loaves of bread, along with the ham and a roasted chicken. "I should eat the chicken first, were I you—the ham will keep longer as it's been cured and spiced. And there's a crock of butter, and some jam, for your bread, along with some hard cheese."

She lined the foodstuffs up on the stone bench—it would be foolish to put herself in the close confines of the bothy with him. "Will Dewar be back to see you soon, do you think?"

"Hope so. Though he's not so sweet as you."

She smiled despite her best intentions not to be charmed by him, or fooled into misjudging him as a harmless, gentle giant—even below "fighting weight," he was easily twice her size. "Good. Then I'll bid you good day. And good luck."

She swung herself into the saddle, intending to leave straightaway, without any fuss, but he had followed her to the mare, and took up Dunnie's lead to hand to her.

"I thank you." He stepped back and laid his hand across his heart in an entirely genuine gesture of thanks. "For the food. And Gent. For being so kind. I'm grateful." And then he bowed as elegantly as a French courtier.

Manners maketh the man, her mama had always said. But for once in her life, Greer didn't know what to make of the man before her.

"I'll come back," she vowed before she could school herself to prudence. "It might be some days, but I'll come again, I promise." And because she had spoken too solemnly, she smiled, and tried for humor. "So I can see if you're well enough to give me back my dog."

He smiled then, a smile that curved up one side of his mouth with such rueful charm, that it simply slayed her. "And now, I'm not sure if I ever want to get that well."

Lady Greer Douglas
Dalshee House
Perthshire, Scotland

2 March, 1788

Dear Lady G,

I write in the hope that this finds you well, in good health and spirits. I read your last with a heart not as full of longing as I might have thought, for I—and my Scots companions in study—have been declared nearly polished after this trip to the Low Countries, and ready to be sent back to Scotland by the end of Easter Term. Already the air smells sweeter! For once, I am ready to make haste more quickly!

However, I must warn you that my trustees, who, along with my grandfather, have all the say in such things, declare that I needs must be sent to St. Andrews—for I would not countenance either Oxford, Cambridge, nor even Edinburgh, which are all too far from home—for university learning. There, I hope to study something more to the point in managing Crieff, and advising you in stewarding Dalshee, in agronomy and agricultural management. Yet, theory is no substitute for experience, and I wish with all my heart that I were coming home to stay.

And perhaps, with your permission, to kiss you in person.

Your devoted friend, E

Lord Ewan Cameron
Rapenburg 94
Leiden, Netherlands

20 April, 1788

Dear Ewan,

How exciting for you to study at university! I am once again all jealousy for your coming time in St. Andrews ~ I can see you already with your long academic gowns flapping at your heels as you run down ancient porticoes and across green quadrangles. Just the words make me dizzy with delight.

But lest you think I am too dizzy for deep thought, Dear Hally and I are making a course of study to learn all that I can of current best practices of the three-field rotation of crops, to which I am also adding a thorough study of chemistry, so as to properly understand the makeup of the soil at Crieff. Also, what is the underpinning geology of Crieff? We here are on granite, so I supposed you were too, but I should hate to get it wrong if you were on limestone, or heaven forfend, chalk. Please enlighten me, soonest.

Hoping you passed the feast of Easter in all comfort, so you might come home to Perthshire as soon as may be. And do please bring your kisses with you!

I am waiting in happy anticipation of being,

Yours, G

CHAPTER 14

N SOONER HAD the lass, "Greer"—he said her name again out loud, to savor the tart, lemony taste of it in his mouth—disappeared over the crest of the ridge, than another voice hailed him.

"I see ye dint listen. Ye've had a visitor."

"Aye." He turned away from the last sight of the lass to greet Dewar, who appeared as if out of thin air. "I have." Even he could hear the defensive defiance in his voice. "She gave me the dog. And brought food."

He set himself to endure Dewar's lecture, but it didn't come.

"She did, did she?" Dewar whistled so the dog would come forward, wagging his feathery tail. "Damned if she didn't."

"Gent, he is. To keep me company, the lass—Greer—said." Though he hadn't felt alone until she came, with her smiles and her dog and her loveliness.

"Weel, aye. But she's no lass, lad—she's a leddy." The old fellow spoke as if the difference were important. "Leddy

Greer of Dalshee." Dewar looked at him quizzically for a long moment, as if testing the limits of his memory.

"Aye, Greer," he assured the auld fellow. "I remember."

"Do ye? Do ye remember she's the one as found ye? Or do ye remember anythin' of 'er frae afore?"

There was nothing from before the beating that stole his mind from him. Nothing but a penny in his palm. Bright and shining. Like the lass's hair—

But nothing else. "Nay."

"Just as well, I suppose." Dewar rummaged around the parcels still arrayed on the stone seat. "Coffee and tea, as well. No expense spared. What'd she say?"

"That she found me on the road." He was pleased to pull the memory so quickly from the jumble of his brain. "That she came from Dalshee."

"True enough. Reckon ye might no' have lived had she not got tae ye there. Her skirts were black with yer blood."

Dewar's words painted an ugly picture—but not a picture he could remember. He put a hand to his head, almost as if to reassure himself it was still there, and in—relatively speaking —one piece.

"How did she find ye?"

"Here? She was there." He pointed to the ridge across the glen. "On Glas Maol." He was even more relieved to have this place name to hand—it gave him more and more hope that she was right, and that all he needed was some time to recover his senses. "I like her." It was like manna from heaven, her gifts. And her presence. Mayhap, it was the talking to her that helped loosen the stiff rigor of his mind. "She was bonnie."

"Oh, aye?" Dewar didn't sound convinced. "All young lasses are bonnie. What'd she want?" The moorkeeper sat on the stone bench and tore off a hunk of bread.

"To give me food. To help me recover to fighting weight."

"Ha!" Dewar tossed his head back in amusement. "Said that, did she? She's got gumption, that lass, I'll gie her that. Damned if ye don't look a bit like a prizefighter, so pummeled were ye. But I reckon yer talkin' better. And yer upright, on yer own two feet."

"Aye." He had fought hard to do so, pushing himself to his limits. "Mended a bit of the wall, there."

"Oh, aye?" Dewar swiveled to take a look at his handiwork. "Looks solid enough."

He took a deep, relieved breath—Dewar's approval was important to him. As important as the lass's company.

Dewar reached into the game bag slung over his shoulder. "Weel, I brought ye bannocks and barley pudding, though it'll be nothing tae what she's brung ye."

"I'll get back to fourteen stone, Greer said."

"The Leddy Greer said that, did she?" Dewar asked, though his tone was tart. Disapproving. "Ye'll want tae be careful with lasses and leddies alike, lad. Careful o' that one especially. No tellin' what she might say, or 'oo she might tell up the castle."

"What castle?" he asked, but an image of a huge grey stone edifice arose in his mind's eye.

"Castle Crieff." Dewar hooked his thumb toward the west. "D'ye remember?"

"Some. Maybe. I was remembering more things when she was here." Something about her—her swift confidence— seemed to loosen his mind, and his tongue as well.

"What things?"

"I remembered a compass." Another image arose beside the glassy yellow and black rays of the compass rose—a large colorful orb spinning. "A globe." A globe in a comfortable wood-paneled room—a library, full of red and green and blue leather spines. "Books. Reading."

He closed his eyes to probe the shifting sands of his

memory, to will the scene in his mind to reveal more telling details. But just as quickly as they came, they vanished.

His head began to throb. "Hell of a thing not to know. Not to know myself." To have his memories come in dodges and feints, teasing him with these glimpses of what once was. "Do you know who I am?"

Dewar took a long time before answering. "Aye."

His heart throttled in his chest at the revelation—here at last was an answer, a way out of the darkness. But Dewar would not strike the match. Instead the silence lengthened between them. "Will you not tell me?"

"Nay." Dewar wouldn't meet his eye. "Because it's no' safe fae ye."

"To know who I am?" It was as if he were being assaulted all over again—the feeling of helplessness and rage roiled in his gut. "How could that be?" He had to saw in a breath before he could force his aching brain onward. "It's all I think of—my name. All I try to remember."

Dewar was unmoved. "Ye've tae gie it time, lad."

He felt trapped by time—penned in by knowing nothing of his past. And his head was pounding. "Why?"

"Because it's dangerous," the auld fellow insisted. "Ye'd be in over yer head."

A sudden image filled his mind—the black void of cold water closing in over his head. Drowning.

A new, more terrible, more painful thought intruded— what if he had deserved this painful beating, this awful reckoning? "What else are you keeping from me? What did I do that was so bad you won't tell me?"

"Easy now." Dewar put out his hand. "It's no like that, lad. It's the ones that done this tae ye—until ye remember enough tae ken who *they* are, they're the ones ye have tae fear. They're the ones that're dangerous. They were bloody willing tae murder ye, afore—I don't reckon they'll hesitate tae try again. And if ye tangle with them afore ye're ready, lad, afore ye're healed, they'll be the devil himself tae pay."

"So I'm to sit here?" He felt choked with helplessness. "And just *hope* whoe'er did this to me won't find me?"

"Aye." Dewer shook his head. "I don't like it neither, but I don't ken anyplace safer. No one—save that bloody persistent lass—has ventured anywhere near here in ages. You need tae sit right and tight, and let it come back natural like. Tis dangerous fae you tae gang out in the world, not knowing."

"It's stranger yet, to think you do know, but you're not willing to tell me."

"Lad, it's fae yer own good. And what if I did tell ye? Like as not, it'd make no difference."

"Then what difference does my not knowing make?"

"Lad—"

"I'm no lad." His pain and frustration boiled over his better sense. "Look at me—I'm a man grown. I must have responsibilities I've left behind. There must be people— friends or family—waiting and counting on me. Looking for me." They haunted him, these imaginary people, whirling around in his head in the dark of the long lonely night, like ghosts whose faces he couldn't see.

Driving him mad.

If he was a fighter, he needed to fight. And to fight, he needed knowledge. He needed to know.

But Dewar saw it differently. "And there are people out there who want tae hurt ye—look what they've done tae ye thus far!" The auld codger was adamant. "Why would ye expose yerself tae them afore yer healed through and through?"

"Because I must know who I am in order to heal through and through. I can't just sit here wishing and wanting and waiting." He was like to grow madder still from the long empty days and longer, emptier nights. "What if it never comes unbidden?" He gave voice to his darkest fear. "What if I never remember? Am I to hide in a damp bothy for the rest of my days?"

Dewar let out a mournful sigh, and touched his shoulder, as if in support. But his words offered no consolation. "I don't ken yet, lad. I'm sorry, but I just don't bloody know."

Lady Greer Douglas
Dalshee House
Perthshire, Scotland

5 September, 1788

Dear Lady G,

Enclosed with my highest and kindest regards,

EC

Lord Ewan Cameron
St. Salvador's College
St. Andrew's, Fife

20 October, 1788

Dear Ewan,

More books! Such treasures you send to me! I had no idea how interesting and fascinating the study of geology and soils could be. You have more than my thanks ~ you have my delight! And certainly my encouragement to send along whatever else you may lay hands on to improve me for Crieff.

Send as many as you like ~ as many as you can carry! (Although one hopes some future parcel might contain nothing but kisses!)

Mama obliges me to tell you that she does not allow me to spend all my day with my nose in books, and asks me to tell you of my other accomplishments ~ that I can wield an embroidery needle to tolerable (but only just!) result.

But I will tell you I think all my accomplishments nothing alongside my ability to climb to the top of Glas Maol. (And I hope you will smile to read that, for that is my goal.)

Your devoted, G

Lady Greer Douglas
Dalshee House
Perthshire, Scotland

22 November, 1788

Dear G,

I cannot keep from smiling. Pray do not tell your lady mother, the countess, that I depreciate all your learning and accomplishments in favor of your climbing abilities—she will think me foolishly sentimental. But I confess it makes my heart calm and glad to think of you up there in the wind looking over from Dalshee toward Crieff. Shall you go up today? The weather is clear here on the coast, and perhaps if you go to the top and stand on tiptoe, and I climb to the top of the highest tower in St. Andrews, we might see each other across the miles.

Your devoted servant, EC

CHAPTER 15

THE LASS CAME over the lip of the ridge like the sunrise—sweeping the glen with light and warmth. Not that he had been watching for her, but the peregrine falcons high on the cliff tops had nothing on him for sharpness of eye.

He had been up with the dawn, keeping busy with chores —putting the tiny bothy to rights, gathering, splitting and stacking wood for the fire, setting another portion of the ancient tumbledown stone walls to rights, and when the sun was warm enough, washing himself in the cool of the burn.

But mostly watching for her. For Greer.

It had been two days since she had promised to return. Two long days, and two longer nights without her glad presence to relieve the lonely drag of time.

But return she did, riding her slender white mount while leading the dun-colored highland pony laden with wicker baskets. Just as she had promised.

"Hallo!" She reined to a halt and slid easily from the saddle before he could move to help her. "Good morning, Gent," she greeted the dog before she turned to him. "Good morning…" She tipped her head to one side as she contemplated what to call him. "…friend."

Her welcoming smile and confident cheer were like a tonic—he immediately felt better. Stronger, calmer. "Good morn, Greer."

"You look better," she observed. "Your eyes are clear. Why, they're green."

"Are they?" He had no idea—the reflection on the surface of the burn was no pier glass.

And there it was—the image of a mirror. Oval and ornate and standing in the middle of a chamber reflecting his own form back to him. The mirage arose in his mind like a ghost, gone before he could see anything more substantial. Yet he was glad for even that insubstantial glance—the images came infrequently when he was alone, but something about her presence seemed to make them come with greater ease. And clarity.

"What color were my eyes before?" The words and sentences were coming easier—or at least he seemed to be remembering them more easily after days of practicing speaking into the silence of the glen—making it more of a pleasure and less of an effort to converse with her, who was everything of confident grace and ease.

"Blood red." She shook her head as if she didn't like to remember it. "And swollen closed the first time I saw you. It was terrible to see."

While she was everything bonnie and wonderful to see —*mirabile visu*. Her eyes were a clear grey blue and her freckles a lovely warm brown—the rich color of expensive sherry.

But how in the hell did he know what expensive sherry was? And *mirabile visu*—that was Latin. He closed his eyes to try and conjure up some image, some other word, some clue to this knowledge.

But she misinterpreted his frown as pain. "Is the ache in your head quite bad?"

"Nay." He opened his eyes to see both her concern and her kindness writ across her face. "I'm not so pure done in as before. I feel much better."

She let out warm sigh of relief. "That's good. And encouraging. And I mean to encourage you further." She went to the pony's wicker saddle baskets. "I've brought more food, as well as some clothes that might suit you better than what I imagine must be Dewar's ill-fitting cast offs, as those breeks are Crieff's plaid—you must be a good foot taller than the keeper. But we've several lads at home who are closer to your height, so I've brought you some shirts and breeks so you'll have a change of clothing to—Wait! What are you doing?"

Trying to shuck off his soiled shirt—he had bathed his body, not his clothes.

"Nay. Stop." She waved her hands at him in distress.

Damnation. He had forgotten more than just the words—he had forgotten how to behave.

But when he tried to reverse the action to cover his nakedness, she stopped him again. "Nay—I meant your ribs. I forgot you were all bound up. Here, let me help." She moved to ease the shirt from his elbows.

It was rather nice to have her so near. Better than nice. So much better, it gave him ideas. "Ought to take the binding off, I suppose. I'm not so sore anymore, and I reckon I could breathe easier without it."

Her hands stilled. "How long did the doctor say your ribs ought to stay wrapped?"

He didn't remember much of what the doctor had said, apart from the fact that he'd been kicked by heavy boots. So how did he know his ribs ought to be healed? How did he know Latin and sherry?

He searched the dusty attic of his brain, but nothing came out into the light.

It was so bloody damn frustrating.

Yet his frustration disappeared the moment her cool fingers grazed against the skin of his shoulder. "I suppose the practical thing to do is to give it a try," she murmured, "and see how you feel without the binding. We can always do it back up."

What he felt was the subtle press of her clever fingers untying the knot in the bandage. And the cool drag across his sensitized skin as he slowly turned so she could unravel the cotton swath. And the disorienting ecstasy of being so near to her.

But it was somehow she who became dizzy—she stumbled and faltered. "Gracious me."

He put a hand to her elbow to steady her. She was so close—close enough for him to see the bright flush across her cheeks and feel the sweet warmth of her body next to his. "Are you all to rights, lass?"

"Oh, aye," she said, but she sounded like he had the first few days he tried to walk more than a few steps—as winded as if he had tried to run all the way up to Glas Maol. But she was herself again in no time. "There." She shook out the bandage and stepped away. "Can you manage the rest without my help?"

"I hope not."

"Oh." She looked confused. She did not understand that he was teasing—flirting, actually.

Flirting. It was what one did with a lovely lass. And yet he knew—knew in his bones—that he had never flirted in earnest in his life. Never felt this strange, damn near disorienting physical attraction to a lass before.

"Then let me help." She was easing the clean linen shirt carefully over his head, standing on tiptoe before him so her cool, articulate fingers could guide the fabric over his shoulders and across his ribs. "There." She stood back. "Better?"

He was infinitely better for her nearness, but he could not say the same for her—her face was flushed with color and her bright, clear eyes were shining with something he could not place. "Aye. Much, much better."

"Oh, good. Well, then, I'd best see to—" She turned away and busied herself with the wicker saddle baskets for a good long time while he took himself behind the door of the bothy to finish changing into the clean breeks.

He returned to present himself for her inspection. "Will I do, lass?"

"Aye." The flush in her pretty checks had subsided, but her lips curved into a charming, bright smile. "Indeed, you don't look like you're about to split the seams of those breeks anymore."

He stretched and crossed his arms in front of his torso, testing the fit. "Aye. I thank you, Greer."

His relief at bringing her name so readily to hand was as physical as removing the binding on his broken ribs—he could breathe again. He had kept her name on the tip of his tongue for days, whispering it like an incantation to ward off the loneliness. Keeping him sane.

"Greer." He tried it out on his tongue again, like a savory lemon tart.

Another thing his brain revealed even as it concealed—he had no idea how he knew what a lemon tart was, or how it tasted. But he knew he liked it.

"Aye" Her sweetly pleased smile was worth every effort. "Any progress on remembering your name? Has Dewar not been back to offer you any help?"

He opened his mouth to reply when Dewar's adamant cautions came roaring back. *"Careful o' that one especially. No*

tellin' what she might say up the castle," Dewar had warned.
"They're the ones that are dangerous. The ones ye have to fear."

But surely this sweet, kind creature who kept her word
was not to be feared? "I'm recovering," he said instead. "Day
by day. Bit by bit." It was all he hoped, prayed for, even,
staring at the black ceiling of the bothy through the long
lonely nights.

"It will come back," she assured him. "Given time, and
patience. Though I do feel strange not knowing what to call
you."

"What is your favorite name?"

"Ewan," she responded immediately, without the slightest
hesitation. As if she knew her own mind so well, this trivial
fact was close to hand.

Ewan. The name sat on his tongue like a hot coal, and his
skin felt strange and tight, as if his scalp were being pricked
by pins and needles. Yet his balky brain could give no reason
for him to feel that way, or why it might matter. Only that
it did.

So he paid attention. "Might you call me Ewan?"

Everything sunny and animated within her stilled so
swiftly he was sure he had made some great mistake—some
mad misstep that would drive her from him.

"I—" she began, and then broke off as she struggled with
some unknown emotion, looking at him with such minute,
particular attention, as if she might find the answer writ
large across his face. "Mayhap," she finally assented quietly.
"Would you like that?"

"Aye. If it would please you."

She nodded slowly. "I believe it might. Thank you. For
asking."

"You are most welcome." If what he had felt before was
relief, what he felt now was pure exhilaration. "That's grand."

He tried it out again to let some of the heat—the importance —out of it. "Ewan."

"You don't mind?" she asked.

"Nay." Why would he object to anything she suggested? Everything she had done or helped him do was welcome. "It's an improvement on 'lad.'"

"Oh, aye." She gave him one of her slow, bright smiles. "You're not a lad, you're a man grown. And a gentleman by your manners and speech."

The pleasing idea that he was a gentleman was at war with his present circumstances—he lived in a bothy on a moor, not in a fine house, and he wore cast-off clothes. "Dewar said I was a local lad—nobody special."

"Did he? He's said a lot of things that aren't necessarily true." Her tone was as tart as her name. "Even if you are local, you don't talk like Dewar, or the villagers. I think you've been educated."

Had he? If so, his cracked muddle of a brain held only the remnant—fragments of Latin and sherry and medicine.

But what else had Dewar said—about who he was or what he owed Crieff?

Now that he needed the information, his brain remained stubbornly closed to him. The harder he tried to remember, the more the words and ideas swirled together until they were knotted in a tight, impenetrable coil.

As if she sensed his growing agitation, she turned the conversation to practical matters. "I've brought you fruit— oranges as well as grapes from the glasshouse." She began to fetch one of the wicker baskets from the pony.

"Let me." He might not know who he was, but he was no longer so weak or confused that he was useless. "I've repaired the stile, and near finished the wall."

She glanced toward the great pile of rock that he had sorted from the tumbledown stile. "You've made great progress. Dewar and the head shepherd will thank you next spring," she observed, "when they'll have no worries about ewes slipping upland onto the moor to lamb. Poor daft creatures."

She must think him a poor daft creature as well—a madman with a cracked, slipshod brain, and no clean clothes. He felt like a madman, talking to no one but the wind for days at a time. Until she came. "I'm not mad."

"No. You're not," she said with a determined sort of kindness that seemed particular to her. "Though you do *look* a bit mad, with your purple and yellow bruises, and your hair all at sixes and sevens."

"Is it?" He ran an embarrassed hand into the uneven mop, still damp from his hasty dip in the burn. "I reckon the doctor sheared it when he bound up my head."

"Yes, I supposed that was what happened. But…" She paused and frowned as if debating what to say. "I brought some sewing scissors, in the hamper." She hesitated again. "I could trim it up for you. If you like."

If he liked.

The words tumbled slowly into his head, landing with weight. He would like so many things it seemed impossible to pick only one—his memory, his health, his very life. But having his hair cut so he did not look like a madman would do.

Especially if she were the one doing it.

"Aye." And because his broken body fairly hummed with heat at the very thought.

"Perhaps the chair…" And she was off before he could help her, hauling the stout oak chair through the doorway and into the sun with a practical, competent briskness. "Why don't you sit there?"

It seemed impossible that he could comply—his muscles bunched with the need to take off running down the glen. To exercise the sudden spate of restless energy that tumbled through him like water racing over rocks.

But he sat. Backwards on the simple slatted chair so he might have something to hold onto. Facing away down the glen, so he could concentrate on the loch. Or the curlews. Or on anything that wasn't the feel of her standing close behind him, grazing her torso lightly against his back. So close, he could feel the heat of her body across his back and shoulders.

He closed his eyes to savor the contact and hold it close. Close enough to last him through the long, endlessly lonely nights.

"I'll just tidy it up," she murmured. "Make it an even length." And then her hands were in his hair, combing it through her fingers, gently pulling the strands to and fro as she settled on her approach. "It's damp."

He swallowed. "I wash," he explained. "In the burn."

Behind him, he felt a frisson, as if she had shivered.

"It's no' that cold," he assured her.

"Gracious, it's positively arctic. You're a local lad, all right." He could almost feel her smile. "*No' that cold,*" she repeated with a little hum of a laugh.

It vibrated through him, that little sound of pleasure, and set up buzzing through his blood. He heard the wicked snick of the scissors and felt the cold line of steel against his nape as she began snipping. But it was her hands he felt most—the slender, articulate fingers, sliding through his hair and cradling his near-broken skull.

"It's almost a shame to cut it." She let the strands sift through her fingers. "It must have been lovely."

Must have been. For a moment, he felt that awful sense of diminishment, but her touch made him feel something stronger—alive and vulnerable and exposed and at a loss in a way that he couldn't articulate. But mostly alive—his blood was singing through his veins.

She stayed for the most part behind him, only venturing around the side of the chair as far as his ears. But finally, after what seemed an age of tugging and snipping, there was nothing left but for her to come around the front where he could see her. And because there was a God, his eyes were level with the lovely curve of her bosom.

And then she stepped nearer, between his outspread knees.

It was everything he could do to sit docile and unmoving with his palms flat against his thighs—not to let his hands stray to her waist. Not to trace the sinuous curve of her bodice and follow it up and around. Not to touch.

He closed his eyes and tried to simply be, to inhale the soft, bright scent of her. To luxuriate in the pleasure of her presence. It was an eternity, and only a moment before she stepped back.

"There." She lingered, letting her fingers play with his hair as she surveyed her handiwork. "Well." She drew in a sweet sigh of a breath. "Well, if you aren't a handsome fellow, Ewan." She said the name quietly—reverently almost.He felt his chest expand as if he were inhaling every last breath of air in the whole of the glen.

She thought him handsome.

He could die happy. Except he had no thought of dying— only of living and living for this lass. For her company, and smiles, and her good opinion.

And then, as if sensing she had been too solemn, added, "Broken nose and all."

He felt his face split into a smile. "Thank you, Greer." The words came without effort, without torturous thought.

"You're quite welcome, Ewan." She brushed some hair off his shoulder. "Is there anything else you can think of that I can get for you, or help you with?"

He could think of a million things, and also just one. But

he remembered himself enough not to say it. "Have you got a razor?" he asked instead.

This time it was a sensation—the cool slide of a sharp blade drawn down his cheek—and the idea of being clean, rather than an image, that filled his mind.

"Oh, I hadn't thought of that," she confessed. She almost touched the bewhiskered line of his jaw. Almost. "I don't think I could be trusted with a razor."

"I would trust you with anything," he responded. "I would trust you with my life—for I already have."

Her surprised smile grew still. "Aye, I suppose you did. And I'm very glad to have been of assistance. Very glad." She brushed a stray clipping off his sleeve. "Anything else I can do?"

"Come again," he reached for her hand. "Please. As often as you can. As often as you'd like."

She didn't try to pull away. "I'd like that."

The rush of emotions—the relief and giddy hope colliding inside him—took the last of his words. But though he could not seem to think enough to speak, he could feel, and so he raised her soft, capable, caring hands to his lips, and brushed a kiss across her knuckles. Like a gentleman.

This time, there was a voice in his head to match the image of a tall white-haired man. *Like a gentleman, lad.* A deep voice, low and stern and loving.

Grandfather.

He had a grandfather. A family. Somewhere. Perhaps even looking for him. Perhaps looking for him now. "I have a family." He was so elated he wanted to kiss her—to pull her flush against his chest and cover her soft mouth with his and—

"Oh." She took a tentative step backwards, out of his reach. "How lovely. Who?"

"I don't know who. Not yet." But it was lovely. And she

was lovelier. And his life *was* getting better by the day. For the first time, he felt himself truly relax. Because he could truly believe that he really *was* going to recover. "But I will remember. I promise you that."

And no matter who he was, he was determined to be a man who kept his promises.

Lord Ewan Cameron
St. Salvador's College
St. Andrew's, Fife

6 March, 1789

Dear E,

It has done nothing but rain, rain, and rain for four whole days—such buckets of water from the sky, the dogs and I have been confined to the house. The dogs are about to go mad, and I, even madder! It is so dreich, Mama fears the influenza. I have curled myself up in a dry corner of the library where I have taken to re-reading your letters and putting pins in the globe to mark your journeys across the world. Papa promises that once the weather has cleared and the roads are dry we will make a visit to Edinburgh! Papa has business to attend to, and Mama should like a chance at the drapers' warehouses. I am pinning all my hopes on a new pair of half-boots as I have worn my old pair out beyond the repair of the village cobbler with all my walks up to Glas Moal in search of a glimpse of you far to the east.

I know you yourself have been to Auld Reeky, as Papa calls it. Is there anything you most recommend I do? I promise to make a good accounting of myself and not act the country bumpkin, although I fear I am sadly lacking in airs and graces. But how else is one to attain them, than by going to the city and finding that out?

I remain, your devoted, G

Lady Greer Douglas
Dalshee House
Perthshire, Scotland

1 April, 1789

Dearest G,

It is my decided opinion that the only air you need is mountain air, and the only grace required is what you clearly already have in abundance. The only reason you should travel is to enjoy yourself and see the things that are not available at Dalshee. The world is a large and interesting place, but the important things—honor, friends, family—already abide with you in Dalshee. Travel if you must, but never forget that home is the most important place there is. And whatever you do, don't believe a word of anything an Edinburgh buck might say to you—they are all blether and havering. And pray don't accept any kisses other than the ones I send you here. I pledge to send you more, while I remain,

Your steadfast servant, EC

GREER RETURNED to the glen the next morning as early as the long ride—and necessary subterfuges to leave Dalshee undetected—would allow. She wanted to forego the inevitable lecture on the dereliction of her duties at Dalshee should her Papa find out she was still visiting her friend in the glen.

And touching him. And letting him touch her. And calling him Ewan.

It had seemed harmless—even helpful—at the time, to let him have the name. It had seemed fitting, and apt. Because her stubborn heart could no longer resist the notion that he could be Ewan.

She knew it was wrong, and even dangerous to let her feelings and imagination and grief run riot over her better self. To let herself construct such a fantasy of her betrothed out of whole tweed cloth.

But he might be. Maybe. It *was* possible.

And even if he weren't *her* Ewan, it was such a pleasure to be with him—a pleasure to do something concrete to help someone who asked nothing of her in return.

Nothing but her company. And her kisses.

She could still feel the warm press of his lips against her hand, shocking and soothing all at the same time. She could still see the sheer, unadulterated happiness that shone from his eyes like a beacon when he looked at her.

If the eyes were the window to the soul, Greer felt as if she could see something within his—something beyond the confusion and frustration and determination to return to his former self—something hopeful and warm and inviting that despite his apparent madness, spoke to her of trust and honor. Something that moved her to quietly saddle her mare and sneak away from Dalshee with no one the wiser just as dawn was lighting the eastern sky.

This morning she took a different path following the run of the burn down into the glen. The clear morning sun shone down on the ribbon of water that led like a green and silver path to—

Ewan.

Greer instantly halted. He stood waist deep in the deep pool that formed just below the rise, half-naked—his big, bare body glistening in the morning sun.

She knew it was he from his close-cropped hair, like a bright otter pelt. But everything else that filled her sight was astonishing and intriguing—the tapered line of his flanks, painted with streaks of dull, yellowing purple of his bruised ribs. The sleek muscles of his shoulders, flexing and bunching as he sluiced water through his hair. The smooth contour of his chest shimmering as the glistening droplets of water ran down his bare skin.

He was not so big and muscle-bound as the farrier or the teamsters working the plows on Dalshee's home farm, but he had gained flesh in the past days. Enough that his body was beautiful, though sleekly fashioned—honed down to the essential elements, as if there were nothing extraneous, nothing but the honest, essential man himself.

Nothing overwhelming. Nothing, surely, to frighten.

So why had her mouth gone dry? Why was her heart clamoring like a kirk bell within her chest? Why did her skin suddenly feel tight and strange, as if she had taken a chill? And why was she staring at his chest as if she had never seen one of the farm lads leave off their shirt before?

Was this why she wanted so badly for him to be Ewan— so she might feel alive and aflame instead of half-buried in grief? Was her interest in this man that selfish and shallow?

And still she did not move. Did not stop staring.

Instead she watched with breathless interest as he dove forward into the water, leaving her an absolutely spectacular view of his bare round buttocks as they slipped under the water after him.

Oh. Gracious. Lord.

He was naked.

Entirely, gloriously naked.

There were his clothes on the bank, draped across the heather, warming in the sun. As if she needed to see them to confirm that he was not wearing them—to understand that his body was as unclothed and finely made as the marble statues of the ancient gods and pagan heroes she had seen in Rome and Florence and Turin.

But those statues had not moved, had not had warmly tinted nipples or a golden trail of fine hair running down the flat of their taut abdomens. Those statues had not been so gloriously alive.

Before she could come to a prudent or even rational decision as to what was best to do—retreat up the hillside, or simply stay where she was and hope he did not see her—he rose from the waist-deep water, and made for the bank in all his naked glory, pausing on the mossy verge to sluice water from his skin and shake the droplets from his hair.

And then he turned. And saw her.

For the longest moment neither of them moved. Or so much as blinked.

Everything within her was aflame with heat and confusion and hopeless arousal.

And then the wee dog, Gent, barked and bounded for her, and Ewan calmly turned and reached for his clothing, while her legs and her courage gave way—she simply dissolved into a puddle at Nicnevin's feet, hiding amongst the gorse and heather.

Oh, the ignominy of being caught ogling his body like a chambermaid.

Oh, the absolute, enlightening glory.

"Greer." His voice rolled up the brae from somewhere nearer by.

There was nothing to do but brazen it out. She stood. "Oh, hallo!" she called back, putting her hand to her hat, as if perhaps it had fallen into her eyes and she hadn't seen anything at all—anything more than *everything*.

He had recovered his breeks, but his chest was still just as gorgeously naked and bare and intriguing as it had been in the water. He took no notice his dishabille, but stood a few feet off with his shirt in hand, waiting patiently for her to venture near enough to speak. "Good morn, Greer."

There was something about the way he said her name that made it an endearment. Something that made her feel... different—different from the expectations and responsibilities that went with being Lady Greer, and the Earl of Shee's daughter, or the once-future Duchess of Crieff. As if she were just a lass meeting a lad on a moorside.

It was a willful, almost defiant, daydream, that she was simply his dear friend.

"Are you hot from your ride? Your face has gone red," he observed when she ventured nearer. "You could have a go at the pool, but I'll warn you, it's damn cold."

"No. I thank you." She tied to cover her embarrassment with a smile. "I'm only— The wind was just—" She was too unaccustomed to lying to have an excuse readily to hand. "I brought you something." She retrieved the well-worn book of poetry from her saddle bag with more triumph that was strictly warranted. "I thought I might read to you, and see, if…well, if you liked it." She took a breath and brought her wayward thoughts under firm control. "Or perhaps if it helped remind you of anything. It's poetry."

He looked at her as if he could not fathom her intent. "What would poetry remind me of?"

"I don't know," she admitted. But she had not forgotten the line from Burns that he had recited—*thou bonnie gem.* Surely it meant that he was educated—it only remained to discover how well. How much more alike Ewan he might be. "But I like the poems, so I thought you might, too."

"If you like," he agreed. "But don't be disappointed if I can make no sense of it."

He took Nicnevin's lead and walked the horse beside her on the path, totally unconscious of his naked torso, stark and pale in the blaze of morning sun.

And then he did the most unusual thing—he took her hand. As if it were the most natural thing in the world. As if he had no idea his touch made her skin hot and tingly. Or made her heart tumble head over heels within her chest. Or made awareness of her own breathless body slide deep into every bone and sinew.

He just scooped her hand up in his left, palm to warm, strong palm, while he led the horse with his right. His long, callused fingers meshed with hers, his knuckles snugging comfortably between hers. Easy and natural.

And after the delicious shock of the moment subsided, it *was* the most natural thing in the world. It felt comfortable and right. Secure. Her hand fit within his larger one just so. His thumb brushed over hers, back and forth, in unconscious reassurance. Warm and casual and intimate all at the same time.

Heavenly.

This was what she had always dreamed being with a man —with her husband—would be. What being with Ewan would be.

The feeling of ease—of *rightness*—urged her on.

She offered him the book. "I brought you an old favorite of mine." And Ewan's. "It is a volume of poetry by Robert Burns."

"Burns?" He said the poet's name the way he said all things he was trying to remember—trying it out like a taste on his tongue. "The name brings nothing to mind."

"He's Scots, Robert Burns is, from Ayrshire. He farmed in Dumfriesshire and wrote his poetry about farming and the countryside for the most part—it's not at all high blown fineness, poetry. And you seemed to know some of his verses before, that first day I met you here."

"Did I?" He shook his head as if it might loosen a recollection. "I don't recall."

But he tethered the horse and subsided onto the stone bench beside her with a smile that told her he was willing to gang along with her flight of fancy if it pleased her. "Gie it laldy, lass."

She opened the slim volume, and firmed her grip, lest her excitement be revealed by shaking pages. "To a Mountain Daisy: On turning one down with the plough," she read. "Wee, modest, crimson-tipped flow'r, Thou's met me in an evil hour; For I maun crush amang the stoure. Thy slender stem: To spare thee now is past my pow'r—"

"Thou bonnie gem," he finished on a note of wonder.

An eerie tingling seeped under her skin—hope, trying to catch hold within her. "Aye!" Greer tried to keep her excitement in check, but her heart was starting and stopping and clamoring inside her chest like mad. She had to swallow to find her voice. "You remember it. That was the line you recited before, that first day. That's why I brought the poems, in the hopes they would help you remember who you are. And who you were."

"Aye," he answered. "But I've no idea, no recollection of how I know the words. They just came." He rubbed his hand through his cropped hair as if he could shake loose more such thoughts from his disorganized brain. He snugged up closer, resting his chin on her shoulder to look at the open page of the book. "Read it again."

"Thou bonnie gem." Greer put her finger upon the next line, so he might follow along as she read. "Alas! it's no thy neibor sweet, The bonie lark, companion meet, Bending thee 'mang the dewy weet—"

"Wi' spreck'd breast," he read. "When upward-springing, blythe, to greet The purpling east." He closed his eyes to recite the next line. "Cauld blew the bitter-biting north, Upon thy early, humble birth; Yet cheerfully thou glinted forth, Amid the storm, Scarce rear'd above the parent-earth, Thy tender form."

"Just so," she whispered. Joy, pride, gratitude and hope—ridiculous, inappropriate hope—made a hot brew behind her eyes.

Indeed, he looked as astonished as she felt—he was staring at her as if he'd never really seen her before. "Thy tender form," he repeated, his breath warm against her cheek.

His gaze dropped to her lips.

Her breath, her whole body felt tight with anticipation—

with wanting. Wanting to give in to the sweetness of the moment. Wanting to know, after all these years of imagining, what it would be like to be kissed. Wanting with all her heart and mind and body for him to be Ewan.

If she kissed him, she might find out.

She would know him somehow, would she not? She gave in to the dangerous impulse, leaning toward him. Toward his lips, where she settled as light and careful and sure as Burns' lark upon a flower.

He kissed her back, moving his lips slightly, in an unhurried, easy buss. Letting her explore slowly, as if there were no rush. As if she could stop whenever she pleased. As if she could make haste slowly.

He closed his eyes and tipped his head so she could taste his lips from a different angle. So she could get closer still.

He cupped her cheek to draw her mouth back to his. "There, in thy scanty mantle clad," he murmured against her lips. "Thy snawie-bosom sun-ward spread, Thou lifts thy unassuming head, In humble guise."

He was wooing her with poetry—seducing her with the same words she had hoped would awaken him. But it was she who was awakened to the exquisite feel of his lips upon hers. Enchanted by the power of his hands spanning her back to hold her to that lean, braw chest.

She wrapped her own arms around his neck, feeling the heat of his naked skin, hot and alive against the flesh of her palm, pressing herself to his lips, his chest, his being.

There were no words to describe the pleasure, no thought for what came next— nothing between them but want and curiosity and delight, flowing through her veins like French champagne, all bubbling, effervescent pleasure.

It was like a dream, the elation, the suspension of every other concern. It was every daydream she had ever had of kissing her Ewan under the wide blue sky. But she wanted it to be more than just a daydream. More than just a kiss.

Everything within her, every ounce of her breath and every hope of her soul, needed him to be Ewan, who loved Burns. And who loved her.

But the chance was so slim it was as thin as gossamer.

And she, Lady Greer Douglas, heiress of Dalshee, with all the education and erudition and responsibility that went with an estate so great, ought not take chances. Ought not be kissing a man who didn't even know his own name.

To do so was neither smart, nor responsible. It was foolish.

Foolish to allow herself to forget who she was under the guise of helping him to remember. Foolish to set herself up for heartbreak.

"Perhaps it were best if we stuck to the poetry," she suggested, though her voice sounded as thin as a whisper.

"Nay," he whispered back, his breath brushing across her ear, and along the sensitive side of her neck. "I'd rather stick to the kissing." His clever lips found the edge of her ear before he kissed his way back to her lips.

And oh, it was so much nicer to be kissed and kiss, kiss, kiss him back than to think about remembering and responsibilities. So much nicer to simply feel.

And feel such delight.

Greer closed her eyes and shut her mind to everything but him—his strength and his passion. His tender insistence. His need for her, and her need for him.

His lips were rough beneath hers, chapped by wind and weather, but careful, taking only so much and no more. Oh, but she wanted more. More of the feel of him smooth and warm beneath her palms. More of the taste of him wild and heady as Highland whisky. More of the fresh scent of wind and wood smoke that seemed as much a part of him as his green eyes and wheaten hair.

She gave in to the sweet rush of sensation and pushed her hands into his cropped hair, doing now what she had kept herself from doing the day before—letting her own wants take the lead, glorying in the feel of his hair beneath her palms.

She held his big, beautiful, fragile skull and kissed him again and gain. She opened her mouth to him, sliding her tongue against his, filling her senses with the heady taste and feel of him, the warm press of his chest against hers.

Behind the confines of her stays and chemise, her breasts went tight with need.

She wrapped her arms around him, pressing herself against the smooth warmth of him, trying to assuage the aching need that held her tight.

His clever, capable hands spanned the small of her back, urging her close, and closer still, until there was nothing between them but the last vestiges of her modesty.

His hands thrust into her hair, tipping off her hat, scattering pins that slid silently into the carpet of heather. His fingers speared through the ginger strands, fisting up the lengths to tug her head back to deepen the kiss until they were both gasping for air and grasping for composure.

Because she wanted nothing more than to forget who she was, and be nothing more than a lass, sunward spread upon a carpet of moss on a hillside of heather. Kissing and being kissed. Loving and being loved.

But she didn't love him—she couldn't. She didn't even know who he was, and neither did he.

Yet that was the beauty of his kiss—he wooed her for herself, and nothing more.

"Greer lass." He said her name as if it were an incantation —a prayer from his lips to God, the breath against her cheek a plea for divine assistance. "I feel as if I'm going to go mad. Mad for you. Mad to love you."

"I know." She must be mad as well, to think such thoughts. To want what she wanted. To forget herself so completely to do so. "We ought to stop."

"I don't want to."

Neither did she, but the honest fact of the matter was that if they didn't stop, they wouldn't. They would do more than kiss. Much, much more.

The thought was enough to bring her back to the solid earth of the glen beneath her feet—she made herself move away. "I think it's safe to say that you liked the poetry."

He laughed. "I did at that, lass. I'd like to read it every day, if that's the result." His smile curved up one side of his mouth and carved a dimple deep into his cheek.

She couldn't help but reach for him. Couldn't help but delve her thumb into the impression, and then along bristly line of his jaw, and then the taut curve of his lower lip.

"Aye, lass." He pulled her to him, kissing her again and again. "I ken how you feel."

She felt happy and stupid and determined. "I feel I ought to get you more books, if this is the result."

"As many as you like, lass. As many as you can carry."

Her heart leap like a highland dancer at his words—for surely they were her words that she had written to Ewan?

But his face showed no recognition, so she said, "I will do so. In fact, there is a bookshop and subscription library in the village of Crieff." If he was Ewan, he surely would have gone to Blanchard's shop. "We should go there. You're remembering more—perhaps it's time to see if anyone remembers you?"

Everything that had been relaxed and happy in him stilled into wariness. "Dewar said I ought to stay put, and simply give it time."

"Oh, did he? I suppose." It was prudent enough advice, she supposed. But she felt sure they were so close to some revelation. She wanted to be know, to be sure, to end the dreadful, hopeful suspense. To know for once and all. "It's only that I've to go there myself—to the village," she coaxed. "And I thought perhaps you might want to journey there with me. It might help you remember."

He was so quiet and wary—as still and alert as a stag in a mountain glen—that she was instantly sorry she had asked. "Nay, never mind. I was wrong to suggest it."

"Nay." He shook his head, and took a deep breath, as if he had come to a decision. "If I'm a fighter, then it's past time to fight my way back. Lay on, lass, and lead me the way."

Lord Ewan Cameron
St. Salvador's College
St. Andrew's, Fife

2 November, 1789

Dearest Ewan,

How I envy you your sex and your freedom! You may have to do the bidding of your tutors in matters academic, but you may live your life, and spend your time otherwise as you please, with no one to tell you how you must gang on in the world. Or the drawing room!

And yes, I am out of charity with my Mama, who carps and harps upon my hoydenish behavior. Today she rebuked me in front of company for having mud on my hems when we took refreshment at Lady P's on an afternoon visit. And yet if I had held my skirts up free of the mud and slush, she would have upbraided me for indelicacy. I cannot win, and so I have given up trying. I have decided to please only myself, and no one else ~ except you when we are married, for you are logical and will never upbraid me for things which cannot be helped, will you? I hope not, for that would ruin a great many of my plans for our domestic happiness. But if I err, I pledge myself to make it up to you with kisses.

Now, enough of my spleen. Tell me all of your life in St. Andrews. When I ask my papa about the place, he only laughs and talks about the golf games there, with no knowledge of your academic life. What are you studying this term? What must I read to keep pace with you? Please give me direction, or I shall go mad with the illogic of my hems.

Yours, Greer

THE MOMENT he capitulated like a lovelorn swain, she rewarded him by throwing her arms about his neck.

"You won't regret it. I promise. I'll make sure that you won't." She was all happy anticipation. "Nicnevin should be able to carry us both if we keep to a fairly sedate walk."

As he hadn't done much more than a sedate walk himself, this seemed like a more than sensible idea. "Excellent."

He watched with something more particular than admiration as she untethered her mare, took up the reins and mounted her sidesaddle without waiting or asking for him to leg her up. Competence—that's what she was, all able, graceful competence, completely at home on the animal.

"Nicnevin—Queen of the Fairies. She's a grand horse."

"Aye. That's another thing remembered." Greer's smile gleamed down at him. "And she is grand, isn't she, though she's nothing so magnificent or celebrated as Cat Sìth."

"Cat Sìth?" The name set off that familiar feeling of awareness, but no particular remembrance. "The mountain panther that was said to prowl the Highlands?"

"Aye. You've remembered the folklore, anyway," she answered, watching him closely, as if she expected the name to mean something more to him. But when it didn't, she simply urged the well-bred mare next to the stone bench, so he could slide onto the animal's back without over-testing his strength or risking his dignity.

Still, he hesitated to throw his leg over the mare's back—what if he did not know how to ride? What if he had never ridden a horse a day in his life?

"Ewan?" She offered her hand. "Ready? Or are you remembering something else?"

"Nay." But he supposed he was ready as he would ever be to leave the only place he knew as home and go out into the world to face his past. And his future.

He bade Gent to stay, took his misgivings in hand, accepted the arm she offered him. He made the made the most of the situation by wrapping his arms tight around her trim waist, and snugging himself up to her back, close and comfortable. Because it was a long way to the ground, and the unpredictable vertiginous feeling he could keep at bay with his two feet on the ground was bound to swell up any moment.

Best to hold on tight. And inhale the soft scent of her hair. And enjoy the physical intimacy the long ride would afford him. "Gie it laldy" he said, more for his own benefit that hers. Let her think him amorous rather than afeared.

And frankly he *was* amorous and growing more so with every sway of the horse that brought her sweetly rounded bottom in contact with his groin.

And she wasn't indifferent—she slowly relaxed back against his chest as they went along, even as she was her usual, curious, confident self. "Why did Dewar tell you not to leave the glen, do you think?"

His misgivings returned as he searched for how much of

an answer to settle upon. "He said I needed to remember more about myself before I should venture out."

"I should think the venturing out might help you remember."

Her supposition was so reasonable that he began to feel foolish for having allowed Dewar's fears to dominate him. "It already has helped," he assured her.

"Just so." She smiled at him over her shoulder. Her confidence gave him courage, and her kindness gave him hope, although her warmth gave him something altogether earthier —his attraction to her was a physical thing that made the blood leave his brain and depart for climes further south.

He relaxed into the rhythm of the animal swaying beneath them and began to enjoy the day and the beauty of the canopy of trees arching above.

The image of another tree-lined lane through a forest, with a grey stone bridge seen ahead over his horse's ears, slid into his mind's eye. He could see himself riding, alone, atop his own mount with his feet in the stirrups and his hands on the reins.

The memory was as liberating as she had promised. He reached for the reins. "May I?"

"Of course," Greer answered, sliding her fingers back to give him control. "Her mouth is very soft," she instructed, referring to the mare. "Quiet hands on the reins."

A soft mouth. A firm but gentle touch.

He understood without thinking—his hands knew what to do without any interference from his brain. And it felt... good. He felt in control—in control of the animal, and of his own fate—for the first time in a long time.

"Hold tight." With his heels and his legs, he urged the mare into an easy, controlled canter along a flat in the path.

His lass immediately wove her hands into the horse's mane, and leaned forward, giving him room to do the same.

As the mare was bearing their weight easily, he wrapped a strong arm around Greer's waist, and urged the animal into a gallop.

They streaked down the path like thunder, the animal's easy turn of speed eating up the distance. Excitement pounded through his veins with every step, every smooth gait forward.

He let out a great hoot of delight at the thrill of it all—at the speed and control. At the joy of remembering. At the sublime feel of his lass in his arms.

It all felt so right. Greer was right, too—venturing out was good for him. And it was fun. He used to have fun all the time—with Alasdair.

The image of a laughing, red-haired man with a wicked, slow smile swam out of his memory. His friend, Alasdair.

God, how he missed him.

He kissed Greer's neck, and drew the mare back to a walk before the path narrowed and became steeper.

"Gracious," Greer said. "I don't think Nicnevin has ever led such a charge." She gave her beloved animal a reassuring pat on the neck. "Well done, old thing."

The phrase rang in his head like the kirk bell echoing in the distance ahead. *Well done, old man,* in a low, droll man's voice—a man who wasn't Dewar or the doctor, but Alasdair.

Concentrate, Ewan, concentrate, old man. He could almost hear Alasdair exhorting him.

But that couldn't be right—Ewan was just the name she had gifted him. It couldn't be his real name.

He was disconcerted enough to give over the reins to Greer, who halted the mare at the gate marking the boundary of Crieff land. "There it is—Crieff village."

The wee village was situated on the banks of a wide river that wound down the seam of the glen. After the silence and vast openness of the moor, the town was a revelation. The buildings were pressed one against the other like stones in a wall, with a dirt street snaking through the middle. He could see people—a seeming swarm of them—moving about like bees darting from one wildflower to the next. He could hear a cacophony of sounds—dogs and people and rolling drays, hammering and shouts and laughter.

And with the sights and sounds came memories—a farrier, sweat-soaked and sooty from his forge, laughing into his beard. A merchant's wife smiling and beckoning him into her shop. A well at a crossroads, busy with horses being watered and women filling buckets for their washing. He could see himself, riding down the middle of that street. Meeting a man in black robes—a priest. "The kirk is on the left." Tucked up against the hillside.

"Aye," she answered. "Over there." She pointed to a square stone bell tower rising through the trees to the southeast. "Saint Columba's. You remember."

"Some." He was still hesitant—the memory that swam into his brain didn't jibe with the fairly large kirk below. His remembrance was of a smaller interior, with a blazing swath of color—a stained glass window at the altar end. And another, different room with a long table, with men seated about—a magistrates' council.

Too many images to catalogue at once or make sense.

His arm tightened about Greer's waist.

She understood without being told. "Perhaps we should go by the kirk first?"

"Aye," he finally agreed, though his body was so tense his hands had knotted into fists against her skirts. A Christian kirk couldn't be dangerous. A vicar wouldn't kick a man in the head and leave him to die.

"Ewan?" She put her hand over his in reassurance. "It will all come right. I promise. We can stop or turn back whenever you want. You have but to say the word."

He wanted to thank her. To assure her that he was fine. That his palms were not growing slick, and blood was not pounding in his ears as if he were about to take one of Archie's dares.

His breath stopped up in his chest. Archie, another of his greatest friends. Alasdair and Archie, and…someone else.

He closed his eyes to concentrate, to take a deep breath into his lungs, but his nose filled with the distracting aroma of baking bread. "The baker is on the corner."

"Aye." Her enthusiasm was more carefully muted—respectful of his wariness. "You have been here before." She smiled at him in that encouragingly kind manner that made him want to do anything rather than disappoint her.

And if he did not find the courage to face his past now, when would he? Though every fiber of his body was tense with unease, he nodded her on. "Aye. Let's gang on with it."

Greer urged the mare through the gate and down the slight incline to where the fields gave way to muddy street. She chose the way past the back of an inn yard, which opened to the lane.

"Oh, sir!" A young ostler leading two horses had stepped out into the lane in front of them. "Good to see ye. I feared the worst, sir when the horse come back riderless—"

"You know me?" Ewan spoke with more heat than he intended, for the ostler drew instantly back.

"Nay, sir. I wouldn't presume—just concerned, was all. Yer pardon, sir." The ostler knuckled his forehead and drew back to let them pass.

Sir, the ostler called him, though he was dressed as simply as the ostler was, in a linen shirt, leather jerkin, and sturdy breeks.

"It's quite all right." Greer dismounted and hastened to reassure the lad. "We're only seeking information. Do you recognize my friend?"

"Aye. I thought so."

Ewan tensed, ready to absorb the blow, filled with a sudden dread that he was about find out something he didn't want to know—something he didn't want *her* to know about him.

"Or thought I recognized 'im, was all, mileddy," the ostler hedged. "Didn't mean tae interfere."

"Not at all," Lady Greer assured him, all cheerful confidence. "You work at this inn?"

"Nay, mileddy. At the Inn at Bridge of Shee."

There it was in his mind's eye—the narrow stone bridge, arching over the dark river flowing below. He could almost feel the icy cold slide of the water across his skin.

"Heading back there now, mileddy," the lad was saying. "Fetching carriage horses back."

"Oh, aye, of course," Greer encouraged. "We've often stopped at your inn—it lies at the crossroads that leads in one direction west toward Crieff, and in the other north toward Dalshee," she explained to Ewan before turning back to the ostler. "But you saw my friend there, perhaps?"

"Weel," the lad hedged. "Thought as 'ee had come through there on a grand mount heading south, some while back. Might not remember him so much as the horse—warm-blood, big-chested stallion, black with a white star on his chest." The ostler's enthusiasm was professional—all for the horse. "Grand looker of an animal."

He could instantly conjure an image of such a beast—tall, seventeen hands, a hundred odd stone. A magnificent animal with the sweetest, easiest disposition, like a fairy creature. Black with a white blaze across its chest like the legendary black cat that prowled the Scottish Highlands.

Cat Sìth—the name cracked across his mind like a gunshot in the glen.

"Thought 'is lordship," the young fellow went on, "were

his rider, though I can't be sure." The lad gave him a quick once-over, taking in his simple wool breeks and leather jerkin—working man's attire. "But the horse come back tae the inn yard riderless, few days later. Landlord bid us keep 'im while 'ee sent for 'is lordship. Valuable animal, that. Well trained, easy disposition."

They had to all move aside as a carriage rumbled out of the inn yard and past them up the lane.

"His lordship?" Greer's voice was higher, and sharper, impatient at the delay. "*This* man was riding that memorable, particular horse?"

"Aye, thought so." The ostler nodded again, shifting his glance between them. "Remember a big mon, well set up, riding that powerful big horse. Generous, 'ee were—tipped me a vail. Dismounted and asked me tae water the beast. Those were his words—'Water the wee beastie, there's a good lad.' The innkeeper, 'ee come out tae greet him. 'Milord,' 'ee said, and bid him take his ease. But 'ee asked only that land-lord fetch him out an ale to drink to his health, as 'ee were sore anxious to get tae Edinburgh. Smiling 'ee was. Said as 'ee were getting married. Tossed me a sovereign when I wished him happy."

"Oh, aye?" Her voice rose on a rush of breath. "Married?"

Ewan was as stunned as if he had had the wind knocked out of him—breathing became suddenly impossible. He searched his brain frantically for some image—a face, a name—to form in his mind at such a revelation.

But nothing came—his brain stayed stubbornly blank.

How could he not remember such a thing? There might be a woman out there, somewhere, worrying and wondering what had happened to him. Yet he had no recollection of her.

It was hell not to know, not to understand who and what he was.

It bothered Greer, too—she was practically shaking with some tense emotion. "You're sure?"

"Aye," the ostler ducked his head respectfully. "Ye don't forget a mon generous wi' money and a horse like that, mileddy."

"No, you don't," Greer agreed, though she looked more and more in the grips of some strong emotion—her color was high and she was gripping her skirts to stop her hands from shaking.

Ewan forced himself to take part, to try and make sense of it—to find some other fact to spur a memory. "When did this black horse come back riderless, exactly?"

The ostler scratched his head. "Must be nigh a month now, sir."

"That was when we found you on the road." Greer turned back to him, her eyes round with revelation.

"Aye." He took her hand to keep her from trembling. "I could have fallen." Perhaps he had been unseated from his mount and fallen into a ditch after all, instead of being beaten to within an inch of his life.

And yet he could not make himself believe it. "What happened to the horse?"

"Kept him some while, sir, afore someone came fae the beastie."

His wee beastie. His Cat Sìth.

His blood began to pound in his ears again—the image of those bloody boots, sheathing a dirk that was just out of reach, slid back into his brain like a blade. Dewar's warning rang like a peal in his head—*There are people out there who want to hurt ye.* "Who came?"

"Don't rightly ken," the lad answered. "I was across the yard, helping the farrier that afternoon."

Bitter disappointment that the horse was gone, and relief that the animal—his magnificent animal—was cared for, made a sour brine in his belly. "Was the horse marked in any way? Was there any blood?" Head wounds were notoriously bloody—Dewar had said that Lady Greer's skirts had been dirtied with his life's blood.

"Nay, sir. But lathered 'ee were—spooked like. And the rein broken like 'ee'd stepped on it loose."

"Nothing in the saddle bags?"

"Don't reckon there were any, sir. But now I do think on it, when t'horse come back, there weren't no saddle." The lad shook his head, as if unsure of his recollection.

That made two of them. "How far is this Inn at the Bridge of Shee?" he asked, though he felt a prat for not knowing how to get to a place he was supposed to have been.

The ostler frowned at him—clearly doubting if he were the man he remembered.

"Thirty and six miles, sir. On t'other side of the moor, at the top o' the strath."

Too far to go now, riding double on Greer's mare. Too far to go alone, not knowing the way, not knowing what dangers might be lurking. And not just for him. If he enlisted the Greer's help—and he knew no one else he might ask—he might be leading her into danger.

There are people out there who want to hurt ye.

"Thank you," Greer was saying to the ostler as she fished a coin out of her pocket. "You've been most helpful. I'm sorry I can't be so generous as to give you a sovereign, but we thank you for your help."

"Welcome at that, mileddy." The lad took the coin with a polite knuckle to his brow. "Happy tae help ye, sir."

"Thank you," Ewan added, though he had more questions than answers.

When the ostler was safely down the lane, out of ear shot, Greer gripped his arm. "Oh, Ewan," Her face shone with pleasure. "Do you not see?"

"Aye. We'll have to go there, to this inn—at least I will."

"Nay. Does none of it make awful sense? Does none of what he said make you remember?"

"Aye, some." But she was fairly shaking herself apart at the seams with whatever it was *she* had made of the information. "What is it?"

She lowered her voice to a trembling whisper. "I think I know who you are."

"Who?" The weight of possibility squeezed his chest like a binding.

She took his hand and pulled him back down the lane the way they had come, away from any prying eyes or ears. And still she whispered. "I think you're Ewan Cameron, Duke of Crieff."

Dewar's words rang in his head—*Yer Crieff.* But the Duke of Crieff? Surely he would have remembered that? Surely he would have some residual understanding of what a duke did, or what he had to know, or who depended upon him?

It was impossible. "Nay."

Greer set herself to convince him. "You're titled—'his lordship' the ostler called you. And the horse you were riding? I know that horse—Cat Sì—"

"Cat Sìth. Aye." Perhaps there was something to what she was saying—a man would have to have some wealth to afford such a magnificent beast. But still, there was a fair distance between having enough money for a horse and being a duke.

"And if the horse came riderless to the Inn at the Bridge of Shee, then you were on your way home, from Edinburgh, most likely, for your wedding."

"I'm not married." The words came unbidden, before he could think them out.

"Oh, aye." But she was taken aback by his vehemence— she clutched the mare's rein tight, as if to keep herself from falling. "But...can you not remember?"

He could not. But he shook his head as if he could will the truth into his brain. "A man would remember something like that. Someone so important." And a man certainly didn't like to admit such a gaping hole in his memory to the lass he had been kissing—and dreaming of doing more than just kissing. Dreaming of *being with*.

"You don't—" She took another careful, almost pained breath. "You really don't remember, do you?"

"Nay." His voice sounded bitter—hell, he was bitter. He was trapped in a damned limbo by the holes in his memory, stuck between future and past with no sure way forward except back. "I should have listened to Dewar. I should have stayed put and waited for it all to come back."

She looked at him with a sort of dawning horror, as if she could not believe him.

And he felt all her horror, all the damn *diminishment*. He felt inadequate to the moment. And to her. "I don't think I can be who you want me to be."

"Dear Lord, Ewan." Her voice caught as if each word was a punishment to her—tears began to fall unchecked across her cheeks. "If I'm right, you have no bloody choice."

Lady Greer Douglas
Dalshee House
Perthshire, Scotland

6 February, 1790

Dear Lady Greer,

The chief focus of my studies at the moment is in the rather less classical science of Agronomy, specifically the propagation and use of Cocksfoot, or Orchard Grass, for grazing, and Lucerne as feed in enclosed fields at Crieff. Such seeds have been seen to good use at Holkham in Norfolk, and I think will do very well for Crieff. I am attempting to convince my grandfather to make a gradual change to Cocksfoot, using own seed, so the layout of investment is not so great, and seeing how the grass takes in our pastures before proceeding. Pray, what grasses have you got at Dalshee? Do ask your father for me, as I should be curious to know, and most obliged by your answer.

Your EC

Lord Ewan Cameron
St. Salvador's College
St. Andrew's, Fife

18 March, 1790

Dear Ewan,

Gracious, so formal. So disinterested. Well then.

I am gratified to learn that your studies go well in St. Andrews and are so very much concerned with Crieff. Very well.

As to the Cocksfoot ~ Papa and I are are <u>both</u> members of the Dishley Society, and receive the latest information of the Society on all manner of husbandry and agricultural improvements. We have made some success, Papa and I, with the Cocksfoot, although my concern has long been for the peaty make up of a great deal of Dalshee's bottom land pasturage, where the Swiss variant of seed fares better.

We have, however, been significantly more successful with breeding long-wooled style, hearty sheep of our own, better adapted to forage on the upland heather than other, more celebrated southern breeds, whom we find too fine for our moorland living. Pray do keep us informed of your progress in the theoretical study of these matters. We are happy to compare our <u>results</u> with the latest theories.

But I, for one, liked your letters better when they were full of passionate kisses and not bloody Cocksfoot.

Regards, G

*E*VERYTHING GREER had prayed for—every whispered bargain with God, every plea in the dark of the night—had been answered.

Ewan was truly alive.

And yet somehow, everything was still wrong.

He shared none of her joy at the revelation, and none of her recognition—he did not know her. He did not even know himself enough to believe her.

Disappointment, guilt and sorrow converged into a pain that squeezed the blood from her heart. And not three hours ago she had blithely assured him everything would be fine. How wrong she had been.

It was Dewar who had the right of it—she should not have brought Ewan out of the glen. She should have left him safe and sound in the bothy. If the ostler—who was not even from Crieff—had recognized Ewan, so too would others. Rumor spread like stink—insidiously—and word would inevitably get back to his murderers, no matter if they were here in the Highlands or in Edinburgh.

"We need to get you to a safer haven." She would correct

her mistake by taking him home to Dalshee, where he could take his time and recover in peace without the possibility of discovery, and where she could shield him from anyone who might wish him harm.

"Aye." He nodded grimly. "I can't like the feel of this place." He looked impatiently down the lane where a sharp-eyed woman leaned over her gate, eyeing them openly. "Come, let me toss you up."

She let him give her a leg up into the saddle. "I'll take you home with me, to Dalshee," she suggested. Greer was sure her parents would not object—in fact, she was sure they would do everything in their considerable power to help him. To help *them*. "We'll keep you safe there."

She knew in an instant that she had said the wrong thing —his face closed off, as if a cloud had passed in front of him, and his hand raked through his cropped hair in a gesture of agitated frustration. "I'm not some lad in need of a lass's protection. Or Dewar's. I told him, I'm perfectly safe on my own. I'm a man grown, and I can make my own way. I'll not take you into danger with me." And off he strode, toward the treeline.

Leaving her behind.

"Ewan, please," she called after him. "Please. Now is not the time to argue." Not when half the village might be looking and listening to them—the woman down the lane had attracted friends and was now pointing their way.

Greer turned the mare for the forest path, but by the time she got through the gate, Ewan was nowhere in sight. "Ewan? Please. This is too important—there is more I need to tell you."

He made no answer. He had already abandoned her. Again.

Greer hauled in a deep breath to try and draw the sting from the blistering hurt. It was everything she could do not to burst into tears in the middle of the lane, so abominable was the hot ache in her throat. Because the cold, awful, worst fact of the matter was that the friend she had made really was the man she loved, but he did not remember her at all.

A man would remember something like that. Someone so important.

She had always thought she was as important to him as he was to her. But evidently not.

The thought was enough to make her chest ache so badly it made it hard to breathe. But breathe she must. And help him, she must, even if he were not yet ready to help himself. Because her memory and knowledge were intact, and she knew things he didn't.

She knew Ewan was alive, so the burial of body in the graveyard—if there had been a body and not just an empty coffin—had been an elaborate ruse. She knew that Ewan must have been attacked nearer to the Inn at the Bridge of Shee Water and not in Edinburgh, because the horse could not have come riderless all the way from Edinburgh.

What she didn't know was why Dewar had told her Ewan was dead? Except that he had said so in front of Malcolm Cameron—might he have said something different if she had been alone?

Gracious, but there were enough questions to go around, for she still had not had any letters from Ewan's 'disreputable friends' in Edinburgh.

It was enough to make her as mad as a march hare—madder, even. Because when they had robbed Ewan of his memory, they had also robbed her of her future.

But it was a future she would not give up without a fight. "Ewan!" she called. "Please! Come to Dalshee."

But he did not answer back. Clearly, he did not want to be found.

With that particularly discouraging thought, she turned

for home, taking the more direct southerly route across the moorland, in the hopes Ewan might follow her to Dalshee on his own.

But without him snugged up tight and warm and strong against her back, the long afternoon shadows lengthened into chill. Still, she was glad of the solitude, and glad of the necessity to direct the horse over the uneven ground so she wouldn't have to think, wouldn't have to ponder out all the questions swimming in her head like bream fry in a moor-side burn.

"My lady!"

A hot ember of hope had Greer twisting in her saddle, only to snuff itself out at the unwelcome sight of Malcolm Cameron hailing her from some distance behind.

He was riding a magnificent, tall black horse with a white star on his chest—Ewan's Cat Sìth—though she noted the stallion had been fitted with a hard, curbed bit. She might have told Cameron such a bridle seemed an over-zealous choice for such a well-trained animal, but His Grace was not alone—behind him was the military-looking man who had quietly advised him that very first day at Crieff, and behind *him*, on his stout highland pony, was the moorkeeper, Dewar, looking as inscrutable as an old mage.

"Your Grace." Greer had no choice but to greet them.

Cameron returned the politeness. "My lady, what are you doing this far south on Crieff land?"

"I made a trip to Crieff village, Your Grace." She gave way to a protective lie. "The bookseller there promised me a copy of…a novel"—she chose the type of story least likely to raise his interest—"A romance."

"Never tell me you ride alone." His tone was incredulous.

"Oh, aye." She had been the recipient of similar questions all her life. "Always have, always will."

"I beg you would curb such impulse," Malcolm Cameron

said. "For I've had an alarming report that a dangerous man was seen in the village and disappeared back into these hills. Have you seen anyone?"

Greer at first worked to keep her alarm from her face—they must be speaking of Ewan, and if they had seen him, they had seen her with him—but decided that alarm was just the emotion the situation called for. "I saw and spoke to several people in the village, but no one who might be thought dangerous." She cast a careful glance at Dewar. "Do you seek this dangerous man now? All three of you?"

For it struck her as strange that Cameron would attend to such a report himself—Dewar could probably track a man as easily as he could track a stag—without anyone's help. But Dewar, she could only hope, had no interest in tracking this particular man, if she could somehow communicate to him just whom she had been with—

"Best for the villagers to see that I am a man who tends to my duties no matter how trivial they are," Cameron answered.

"Indeed," was all she could think to say to that particular piece of havering. Cameron seemed the kind of man who rarely attended to what he considered trivialities—his handling of his cousin's funeral was proof enough of that.

"Who did you talk to from the town?" This question was asked by the man behind Malcolm Cameron—his servant or secretary.

And while Greer had no pretentious to snobbery, or acting high in the instep, there was something in his tone, something impolite, or perhaps only dismissive, that stiffened her spine. She raised an eyebrow along with her ire. "And you are?"

He belatedly doffed his old-fashioned tricorn hat. "Mr. Gow, my lady."

His accent was English—perhaps that accounted for her instinctive distaste.

"Forgive me," Malcolm Cameron gestured to the man. "Lady Greer, this is my secretary, Gow."

"Thank you. Mr. Gow." She acknowledged the introduction with a little bow. "I did come from the village, as I said, and chatted with a number of people"—two was a number, certainly—"as I said, but have not seen a soul on my journey this way."

"You are fortunate." Malcolm Cameron gave vent to his concern. "You may not realize how vulnerable you are as a woman alone."

It was not the first time Greer had heard such sentiments —they were too common to merit anything above notice. But that this man—who knew nothing of the Highlands, or of her life—thought he needed to tell her—about her vulnerabilities in the world, was laughable. That he felt he needed warn her, who had traveled to and from the Continent and felt its perils, was annoying. And that he thought her so insipid or uneducated or uninformed as to be unaware of dangers she assessed every day, was condescending in the extreme. "I most often bring my dogs to ensure my safety, and—"

"Dogs are no match for a man with a gun."

She disliked his lecturing tone and wanted to scoff at him for thinking her so foolish, or unprepared that she did not have her own gun—indeed her fowling piece, which she had been about to point out to him, was in plain sight, attached as always to her mare's saddle—but she began to think it best not to antagonize a man so set on being right. "Come, Your Grace, I doubt anyone would want to shoot me."

"Accidents happen all the time, my lady." His tone was all grave concern and instruction. "We are in pursuit of a miscreant roaming these glens—this madman seen in the village who haunts these hills. It's wilderness up there, as Dewar here has said, ripe for malefactors. Raised as you have been—sheltered and alone—you cannot know what men are like."

She knew exactly what men were like—more often condescending than not, as well as patronizing. "Your Grace, I have been neither sheltered nor alone. I have lived and traveled in the world and on the Continent, amongst a variety of peoples. I have also ridden in these hills all my life. I doubt there is a person, or a stag, or even a tree within a hundred miles that I do not know on sight or by reputation."

"Yes, of course you do," he assured her, changing his tone to soothe, as if she were a whinging wean and not a woman full grown. "Nevertheless, I'll accompany you home. If I may."

His tone told her he wasn't asking for her permission, but demanding it as his due.

Greer postponed giving him a sharp piece of her mind—it was undoubtedly cleverer and more prudent to draw him off with her. If he followed her to Dalshee, he couldn't track Ewan.

She gave in with as much good grace as she could muster. "If you insist."

"I do." He put his hand over his heart in that gesture that was meant to convey a heartfelt oath-taking. "I feel I *must* accompany you home. If something were to happen, I could never forgive myself, nor face your father again."

Her pride, she supposed, would not let her acquiesce without having her say. "I am quite safe, Your Grace. Dalshee lands are very nearby, and I know my way by heart, as does my mare." And she was armed—with a wicked dirk in her boot, as well as her gun.

"But there is no telling where this blackguard is, or where he will strike next."

"Strike?" It seemed a rather incendiary word for an injured man who had been living quietly in a bothy. "Has he struck already?"

"Not exactly," Cameron hedged. "But he is a trespasser, my lady, a lawbreaker by definition. Who knows what mischief the miscreant has caused, or what stock he must have stolen to keep himself alive?"

That he had kept himself alive on Dalshee ham and hothouse oranges freely given, did not seem opportune to confess. "Our stockmen have reported no losses," she said instead. "But our flocks and herds have been prudently moved closer to the home farm at this time of year." Which he ought to know as Crieff's laird.

Talk of agricultural husbandry held no interest for Cameron. "Gow, you go with the moorkeeper. Report back." He was already turning his mount onto her path. "After you, my lady."

Greer gave the mare her head along the familiar, well maintained paths, urging Nicnevin to just enough speed to bedevil Cameron, until he at last manhandled his poor, double-bitted mount alongside her.

"I am glad of a chance to speak to you alone." He angled Cat Sìth closer to Nicnevin's flanks. "The last time I saw you at the funeral it didn't seem…appropriate."

"Please, Your Grace." Every feeling rebelled against the thought of any repetition of a proposal. She must put paid to any romantic ideas—even though marriage alliances were sought for many other reasons than love, she could not countenance one without both affection and respect. And especially not one without trust. "I appreciate the—"

"Please." He stopped her by angling Cat Sìth across the mare's path. "I am not an eloquent or romantic man, Lady Greer. I am out of my depth and know it. But my wishes have not changed since you first came to Crieff. I admire all I know of you, and I should still very much like the opportunity to fulfill the promise Crieff made to you. To make you the Duchess of Crieff, if that is what you still desire."

It was impossible. Impossible to accept his proposal. Impossible not to be tempted by her own ambition to be a duchess. No matter if she was to inherit her father's entire estate, which was not entailed away to the male line, she could never inherit his title. If she married Malcolm Cameron she would be Duchess of Crieff and have all the things—the duties and responsibilities, and above all the rights and recognition—she had always imagined.

The only problem was what she *desired*, was something entirely different from ambition—she desired Ewan. Or at least the version of Ewan she had constructed from his letters, not the man who did not remember anything about her.

Greer strove to keep her fresh grief, and the frustration it engendered, from her voice. "It is too soon, Your Grace."

"Is it? But I could not miss this opportunity to express my feelings to you most ardently."

She shook her head. "Your Grace, we do not know each other well enough for ardency. You don't know me."

"Do I not?" He shook his head, as if she must be mistaken. "I know my own wishes, my own heart. I may be new to the countryside, but I am a man of the world, my lady. I have lived in London. And I know a remarkably beautiful woman when I see one."

Greer dismissed his blandishments as easily as he had her concerns. She knew beauty was entirely in the eye and ambitions of the beholder—character was the thing for women as well as men. If there were anything remarkable about her, it was her dowry. And her own ambition.

"All I ask is that you consider my proposal," he concluded, before he added, "but while you do so, I also wanted to advise you, that I have uncovered something…irregular going on at Crieff."

As decidedly irregular things were to her certain knowledge going on at Crieff, Greer said nothing beyond a non-committed, "Oh?"

"Unseemly things," he went on.

More unseemly than inheriting a title when the previous incumbent was not yet dead? Gracious, but there was too much to choose from.

"You will have noted I am sure, the dreadful irregularity of the funeral—how the casket was inadvertently buried before the service."

"Gracious," was all she chose to say while she tried to decide how much of her own knowledge—that the man who was supposed to have been buried in that casket was at that very moment alive and roaming about the moor—to share.

"It has preyed upon my mind as to why that happened," Cameron went on. "Why the men were instructed to do so, and by whom?"

"Was it not yourself?" Who else had so little regard for tradition or understanding of protocol? Who else had the authority? It certainly hadn't been the rector, or the steward, MacIntosh.

"No, indeed." Cameron was all astonished affront. "I had no idea. But once I learned of the irregularity—the housekeeper…"

"Mrs. Peddie?"

"Ah, yes—Mrs. Peddie felt it her duty to inform me—I wrote straightway to those careless friends of Ewan's in Edinburgh to ask them what they meant by sending him to us like that. But after their original word of his death—nothing. My inquiries have fallen on deaf ears and idle pens—they have made no reply."

Greer was astonished into taking a page out of her mother's book of ladylike tactics. "How irregular." It was not helpful that her own missives to Ewan's friends had also gone unanswered.

The cold puddle of doubt and dread and guilt swilling up her insides expanded into an icy loch of misapprehension. She had been so sure the malice toward Ewan stemmed from Crieff, not Edinburgh.

"Have you met any of those friends?" she asked. "The *quadrumvirate,* Ewan used to call them."

"Disreputable is what I call them." Cameron's tone was curt. "The worst sort of people, libertines all, gamblers and fornica—" He stopped himself. "Forgive me, but I get so irate thinking of them. To answer your question, I did meet them once or twice in Ewan's company, but I never thought them suitable companions for a man with my cousin's responsibilities."

"Gracious," was all she could think to say again. Cameron's description was such a contradiction to the picture Ewan's years of correspondence had painted of his relationship with his friends, she did not know what to believe.

Only one thing was very clear—one way or another, she had been lied to.

Lady Greer Douglas
Dalshee House
Perthshire

16 April, 1790

My Dearest Lady Greer,

I stand rebuked. And rightly so. I fear I had some of the zealotry of the convert in my last letter. I hope you will forgive my fervor for agricultural improvement, for which I suffer great abuse from my friends, who all pursue far more classical intellectual studies—Alasdair reads Latin and history in preparation for the law and government, Archie pursues the written word as if it were game, and Rory refines his already exquisite taste with more study of medieval art and architecture, while also adding some elements of the up-to-date science of chemistry for reasons none of us understand. All of them disparage my agronomy as dirty and grubby but have little understanding of all the science—the breeding of strong seed and stock alike—that will revolutionize farming, which I esteem as the backbone of all Crieff's estates.

I do realize it is more than a little ridiculous to study farming from the ancient, medieval halls of the university, so far from any actual fields, but I must hope that the base of knowledge being pounded into my thick skull will eventually see me in good stead upon my return to Crieff.

I hope this letter finds you and your family in good health and good spirits, and that your spring lambing season goes well. Pray do keep me informed so I may have the benefit of your practical advice to weigh against the latest theories. You shall keep my feet upon the ground far more successfully that any of my friends.

As a token of my penance, I send with this letter all my esteem and devotion, along with an armful of Scots kisses—less refined, you may assume, than the Italian—but all the more passionate in their honesty.

I remain your devoted friend, EC

CHAPTER 19

Greer kept her thoughts to herself, and her breath to cool her porridge for the remainder of the ride to Dalshee, where Greer was chagrinned to find her father anxiously awaiting her in the stableyard.

"Greer, dear, there you are." Though he gave her a pointed parental look, he mercifully held his questions to himself. "Your Grace." Papa bowed and shook the Duke of Crieff's hand. "I hope you and Greer enjoyed your ride."

"His Grace met me at the edge of the southern forest path," Greer clarified, lest Papa get the wrong idea. "And was kind enough to insist on accompanying me home."

"For her safety," His Grace of Crieff reasoned. "We've reason to think there may be a miscreant—a madman—loose in the hills."

"A miscreant? Do you mean a poacher?" Papa asked, though neither he nor his gamekeeper had ever been overly strict about the taking of small game on Dalshee lands. "My dear young duke, there are rabbits enough to go around. No one on Dalshee ever need starve for the lack of food when there were rapacious rabbits eating my farmer's crops. Think of it as a service rendered at no cost to the estate!"

"My moorkeeper fears something more, my lord," Cameron answered, although Greer had seen nothing of concern in Dewar—indeed if anything, she hoped Dewar had steered Cameron toward the narrow southern glens on a goose-chase to keep him away from the bothy under Glas Maol. "And why I insisted on seeing Lady Greer safely home."

"Insisted, did you?" Papa cast a sly wink her way. "Why, she's safe as houses out there, my lass. Practically raised on the moorside, she was." His voice was full of amused pride. "Knows it like the back of her hand. But now that you've come all this way, come into the house, do, and take some refreshment. We're expecting guests, but Lady Shee will be glad of a visit."

Greer would be glad only of Cameron's departure, but she could not say so to her father. She could not share the revelations of the day or ask any of the questions lined up in her head like pistols on a table, primed and ready to be shot off. Ewan was alive, and every moment that she was not with him—was not actively helping him—felt like a dangerous waste of precious time.

But there was nothing she could do at that moment, so she used her considerable thwarted energy to hold her wheesht, pouring the coffee and tea her Mama had waiting for their arrival, and setting herself to be the dutiful, attentive daughter, while Malcolm Cameron spoke to her father in a low voice that she perhaps wasn't meant to hear.

"I am glad to have a moment to speak with you, sir. There is also the delicate matter of the small piece of business I wrote about?"

"Ah, yes, the parcel along the upland loch." But Papa, being not as delicate as His Grace, answered in a voice loud enough for them all to hear, and looked to her. "Greer? What say you?"

"Lady Greer is to be consulted?" If Cameron—for *she* refused to even think of him as His Grace—was discomfited, he hid his feeling behind mild, polite surprise.

"Greer is my firm right hand here at Dalshee, Your Grace, as well as my strong legs. I sent her up to have a look at those fields. I consult with her on all matters of the estate which she will someday inherit."

"Ah." Cameron acknowledged the logic with a nod in her direction. "How progressive."

"Indeed." Papa was unapologetic, turning his attention to her. "Did you get a good look at the property in question, my dear?"

"I did," she confirmed with just enough overly-polite smugness in her voice to please herself without being offensive to His Grace. "And I find it well worth buying, for it will increase our frontage on the loch considerably—almost entirely, depending upon how the boundary lines are re-drawn. But before I advise my father *for* the purchase, I feel I must advise you, as your neighbor, Your Grace, *against* its sale."

If she had another reason—wanting to preserve the hectares for Ewan—she kept it to herself.

Now Malcolm Cameron did look discomfited—heat reddened his cheeks. "Indeed?"

"Because you have asked for my advice on other matters relating to the estate, I feel it incumbent upon me as you neighbor, to advise you so—the price you ask includes the market value of the crop as well as the land, but if you sell Dalshee the crop, what barley will you have for Crieff to distill?"

For a moment Cameron said nothing, his mouth sealed in a tight controlled line. And then his hauteur gave way to chagrin. "You have the better of me, again. I had no idea of the crop—barley, you say?"

"Aye," her father agreed. "I wonder your steward did not advise you thus."

"Indeed. I shall remonstrate with him directly. I am more than thankful for your principled advice. Yet…" He stirred his coffee for a long moment. "I still needs must sell what land I can. Crieff must…" His voice dropped to a murmur, as if he hated to admit such news "…retrench."

Papa, bless him, got a rather particular glint in his eye. "If I may be so bold, but as your neighbor and your elder, with the benefit of years, might I enquire why Crieff's finances needs must be retrenched?"

"It is no great concern." Cameron frowned and smiled all at the same time, managing to look unconcerned about the very problems he had been hinting at. "Crieff is as sound as ever. However, I seek a more…prudent, careful hand on the finances, shall we say. I dislike extravagances and waste— thousands of pounds foolishly spent on silk draperies from France—and have undertaken a stricter course of action to make sure Crieff can continue on as a going concern for years to come."

A very, pretty speech, she supposed, though it stung like a skelp to hear of the room Ewan had so thoughtfully designed for her called a foolish extravagance. She knew the room had been extravagant—wonderfully, sentimentally so. But that was when she had assumed Ewan could afford the extravagance.

And yet, while the facts supporting Cameron's course of action might have been correct, the execution was sadly lacking—staff, who would need to find employment else- where, had been let go, burdening the village. Crops were being mismanaged to the detriment of Crieff's long-term financial health. And Ewan's reputation was being tarnished to no good end, while he could do nothing about it.

That Ewan was a good man still, no matter his injuries, she did not doubt. But her mind could not help but whisper that perhaps his injuries were the result of the extravagances and debt? Perhaps he had become indebted to the wrong sort of people in Edinburgh?

It was all so curious and confusing and contradictory, she did not know what to believe of Malcolm Cameron. How could everything he said be the truth? How some of what he said *not* be true?

She wanted a long, candid talk with her parents, but Papa was walking Cameron out with one hand over His Temporary Grace's shoulder, keeping him close in conversation, as if he sensed that the business of buying the acreage in question at an advantageous price would be concluded more swiftly if Cameron were brought to the bargain *man to man*—without a daughter's interfering hand.

So be it. She was practical enough to know the result was what mattered, not the way of obtaining it. And once she and Ewan were finally married, the two properties would for all intents and purposes be one.

If she and Ewan were ever married. If he remembered her.

Greer swallowed her bitter worries with her tea, until her thoughts were interrupted by the jangle of harness and crunch of carriage's wheels upon the gravel drive. "Are you were expecting other guests?"

Her Mama raised one elegant eyebrow. "You would know the answer to that question if you had spent more than a fleeting moment with us in the past two weeks. You're off at all hours, roaming the moor. I know you are still grieving for Ewan, Greer dearest, but as always, too much is too much."

"I'm sorry, Mama." But she wasn't sorry, really. "But the most extraordinary thing has happened. Today—"

But Greer didn't finish because the second most extraordinary thing of the day happened before she could say another word—Malloch, the butler, announced their guests.

"My Lady, the Marquess and Marchioness of Cairn, and the Honorable Mr. Archibald Carrington."

A tall, imposing, ginger-haired man and an only lightly less imposing woman, along with a dark-haired man, made their bows. "My Lady Shee."

"Lady Cairn." Mama made them a very graceful curtsey. "My Lord Cairn. You are all most welcome to Dalshee. May I present my daughter, Lady Greer."

"Lady Greer." The Marchioness of Cairn came to Greer in a rush, taking up her hand in a heartfelt gesture of support. "We came as soon as we could."

"But of course, my lady." Greer made her curtsey to both her and the marquess, though she was impatient with all the polite formality. "Please call me Greer."

"Absolutely, and you must call me Quince." The Marchioness of Cairn clasped Greer's hand with what Greer could only call sympathy. "I've heard so much about you."

Greer hardly knew what to think, or which one of the questions careering through her mind to ask first. "Some of it good, I hope?"

"All," the marchioness declared. "So much so, that I suppose I felt I already knew you, and wanted to be your friend. Which is why we felt we had to come."

"I am glad you have. I, too, felt that way from Ewan's letters about you all. And you must be Mr. Carrington." Greer turned to the dark-haired gentleman waiting quietly behind Lady Cairn. "You are also most welcome to Dalshee."

"My lady." Carrington bowed over her hand. "Call me Archie, please. It is an honor to meet you at last, thought I must admit to wishing that it were under very different circumstances."

"Indeed." Especially as the circumstances seemed to be changing hourly.

The marchioness—Quince—sat beside Greer. "Please allow us to offer you our most heartfelt condolences. We must thank you for writing to Alasdair and Archie, else we never would have known of Ewan's death."

But Malcolm Cameron had told her *he* had written them.

"Aye," Alasdair, the Marquess of Cairn, added from behind. "We had been in happy expectation of Ewan's word of your marriage, and so your letter, when it finally reached us in London, came as quite a shock."

"I am sorry to have been the bearer of such bad news." Though Greer would have better news for them directly, she hoped—as soon as she understood their place in this awful charade. "But I had—and still have—so many questions."

"As do I," Alasdair answered, just as Papa and Malcolm Cameron returned to the drawing room, and Greer was obliged to be patient through another round of introductions, though her curiosity was all but burning a hole through her tongue.

"But of course, you've met before."

"No," Alasdair answered. "I've not had the pleasure." He inclined his head to Cameron. "Your Grace. My wife, Lady Cairn."

Greer sharpened her gaze on Malcolm Cameron, waiting to hear what he might have so say, now, when the people he had spoken to her about were in front of him.

But Cameron said nothing to rebut the marquess's assertion.

"Your Grace." Lady Cairn made a curtsey perfectly calibrated to show just enough deference to Cameron's rank without any warmth.

The taut tension in the room was palpable. Archie Carrington made no more than a barely civil nod in Cameron's direction—no love lost there. If it had pained Greer to address Malcolm Cameron with Ewan's title while the latter was forced to hide in a remote bothy, she could see by their sudden stiffness that it was doubly harder for Ewan's dear friends to bear. And they certainly had not her solace in knowing Ewan was alive.

Mama offered their guests refreshment, but Greer was too aware and too curious to wait until all the social niceties had been completed to set a cat amongst the pigeons to see which one took flight. "But I thought that you all had met before? His Grace was just saying—"

"That I had not had the pleasure," Malcolm Cameron averred.

This was such a direct contradiction of what he had said only that afternoon that Greer could not but object. "Nay. You said that—"

"—that Ewan had spoken so eloquently of your friendship in his letters." Cameron frowned at her in concern. "Surely you remember—we spoke of this on our ride here?"

What she remembered was entirely different. And it never occurred to Greer that Ewan might have other correspondents, especially his cousin, whom he had never mentioned in four hundred and twenty-six letters to her.

"But you came"—Greer covered her confusion by redirecting the conversation with a question for the marquess— "you said, from London?" That might account for the delay in their answering her letters—she had written to Cairn in the marquess's case, and Edinburgh in Mr. Carrington's.

"Your letter was sent from Cairn to London," the marquess answered. "Upon its receipt there, we immediately made for Scotland to condole with you."

"I thank you." Greer felt a new stirring of hope. "It is very heartening to meet friends who knew Ewan so well." But first, there was Malcolm Cameron to try to suss out. "Indeed," she continued, "His Grace and I were just talking of you all this afternoon, and saying—"

"—what a very sad business my cousin's death has been. Very sad, indeed. But a business which, unfortunately, requires my immediate attention," Cameron answered. "And so I must take my leave. It was a pleasure." He bowed to each of the guests, and then Mama. "My Lady Shee. My lord." He bowed and shook Papa's hand. "We'll conclude our business some other time."

And then he took his hat in his hand, and left them. Like a man fleeing the scene of a crime.

Greer was sure of it.

Lady Greer Douglas
Dalshee House
Perthshire, Scotland

2 May, 1790

Dear Lady Greer,

I am reprieved at last and find myself at last at liberty to head home for the term break. I am therefore more than eager to see if we might finally—<u>finally</u>—arrange for our meeting upon Glas Maol. Grandfather has hinted in his letters that he should like to arrange for a more formal visit of your family to Castle Crieff, but I should prefer our meeting to take place on our terms and not in front of others' watchful eyes—I daresay neither my grandfather, nor your father, would allow me to kiss you the way I want, and the way you deserve for waiting so patiently for me these many years.

I also bring home the most delightful collegiate companion—a spaniel dog puppy out of Alasdair's superb bitch Meade. The dog is the honey-gold color of his dam and puts me in mind of another person who is said to have honey-gold hair—you. And so, I entrust to you the naming of his merry wee fellow who shall, I hope and trust, in future years be our companion at Crieff. Already he is my steadfast and most loyal friend, and my reminder that someday soon, I shall be back at Crieff for good, where we can all be happy and together.

Pray let me know at Crieff, where I shall await your answer from Thursday next, when I arrive at last at home.

In expectation of your word, E

CHAPTER 20

"TELL ME something," Quince Cairn asked in a low voice once Greer's parents had left to escort Cameron out. "What do you think of Malcolm Cameron?"

"Very little," Greer answered candidly.

"Hmm." Quince narrowed her eyes and looked up at the ceiling. "I thought I detected a decided frisson of..." She pleated her lips and scrunched up her nose. "...let us call it admiration for you, from His Grace."

"*From*, I hope, not *for*," Greer was quick to correct. "His Grace"—she strove to stay civil in light of all that she now knew—"has been overly desirous of formalizing a new alliance between Dalshee and Crieff."

"Marriage? Do you mean he sought to take up where Ewan left off?" Quince's eyebrows rose. "By jimble, that is bold. One almost has to admire his dispatch."

"Almost." Greer muttered.

"Ah." The marchioness made a most un-marchioness-like sound of assessment. "Do you like him?"

"Malcolm Cameron? As a suitor? Gracious, no." Greer

could not keep the hot outrage from her voice. "I don't want you to think I am not entirely devoted to—"

"—Ewan's memory. Not at all. But I'm asking something else." Quince rephrased her question. "Do you like Malcolm Cameron as a person?"

Greer was still not quite sure what Lady Quince Cairn was asking. "I've tried."

"Ah." Quince's nodding smile was all satisfaction. "Then the answer is no."

"I don't dislike him," Greer tried for what Mama would want her to say.

"No." Quince held up a hand to stop her. "None of that. Trust your gut."

"My what?"

"Your instincts—I see now that you're much too learned and worldly for *guts*." Quince laughed. "And we will talk someday about your Grand Tour as they call it, for I am wildly jealous. But for now, I want to know what your instant reaction was the first moment you met Malcolm Cameron? Tell me quickly—like or dislike?"

"I didn't like him," Greer admitted cautiously. "Mostly because he wasn't Ewan."

"It doesn't matter why—that's just logic and custom and bloody *manners* trying to talk you out of something you already know. Don't listen."

Greer could only smile at such outrageous advice. "My mama says I am a great deal too apt not to listen."

"I'm sure your mama means well," Quince said. "So did mine. But it is my experience that a woman's instincts—her first impressions—about men are nearly always right. You've lived in the world—you know what men are like, how they think, what they do when they think they can get away with it. Trust yourself, Greer. I would stake my life on my instinct. I have done, and I must say it's worked out rather well."

Greer's instincts had been what had led her to Ewan. But her instinct also warned her that she—and Ewan, and their future—were on a knife's edge, poised to go either way. But both choices seemed equally dangerous. "So you think I should distrust Malcolm Cameron."

"Ah, so it is *distrust* now, rather than dislike, is it?" Quince leaned in. "Better and better. And for what it's worth, I don't like him one bit either—I shouldn't even trust his skinny arse with a fart."

"Gracious!" But Quince's plain talk inspired Greer's trust in a way that Cameron's flattery had not.

"If you are through shocking everyone, my dear?" The marquess's dry remark reminded Greer that they were not alone. "My wife asks, because your letters set up a great many questions. But the unhappy fact of the matter is that we know less about Ewan's death than you."

"Were you not with him? In Edinburgh?"

The marquess shook his head. "I was not, though Archie saw him there. But I saw him last at Cairn, a little more than a month ago. He was on his way to Edinburgh, on some legal matters, as I recall." His gaze went from Greer to his wife. "Strengthening Crieff's entail in favor of the children he hoped very soon to have."

Children. It was something Greer had thought of in the abstract—something that would occur eventually after her marriage, someday in the future. But Ewan had been making concrete plans for that future, making room for a family of his own, while she had not thought beyond the two of them being alone, together at last.

But they were plans he would no longer remember.

The enormity of her loss—the seemingly endless tumble of grief—knocked the wind out of her. She knew she ought to be rejoicing that Ewan was alive. But if he was not the same Ewan that she had known— If he didn't know her—

The thought was enough to break her fractured heart into a hundred tiny, aching pieces.

But whether he remembered her or not, he still need her help. "And so you were not with him, in Edinburgh, or when he was attacked." Greer forced herself to be logical. "But 'those disreputable friends,' Malcolm Cameron said. He said he received word from them. I'm sorry, but I thought it must be you—for he spoke of no others, Ewan did."

"Nay." Archie Carrington shook his head. "I can't imagine there were others. I did see Ewan in Edinburgh. We shared a dinner together at the New Club there and drank a toast to his good fortune and happiness in marriage. And I saw him home—we walked together—before I returned to my own house, some streets away. He made no mention of any plan to go out 'carousing,' as your letters to us said, but only to go home to Crieff and be married."

"Then does no one know what happened to him that day by the Shee?" Greer could not keep the surge of fresh grief and outrage from her voice. "Was he all alone?"

"What do you mean?" Alasdair's voice turned sharp and prosecutorial. "That day by the Shee? Your letter said Edinburgh. And you just said attacked, when your letter stated that Ewan's death was an accident."

"Aye, but I know differently now." Greer drew in a deep breath and looked them in the eyes, one after another, before she could decide whom to trust.

And she trusted Ewan, even if he didn't trust himself. And all his life, Ewan had trusted these men, who had demonstrated their devotion time and again, most recently by hieing all the way from London to speak to her of their concerns.

Trust your instinct as a woman, Quince Cairn had just said.

And so she would. "Ewan isn't dead."

There were gasps—of horror from Mama, who had just returned, and avid interest from Quince Cairn. "Really?"

"Greer! This is not the time for a flight of fancy." Her father said from the door with his long-suffering, cautionary tone, only to be superseded by the Marquess of Cairn, whose steely tone took command.

"Lady Greer, you interest me. Tell me more."

"Now, Greer," her father tried again, "You mustn't let your feelings lead you to make foolish—"

"Pray hear me out before you dismiss me." Greer spoke over her father for the first time in her life. But she was done with censoring and distrusting herself. "I am more than rational enough to weigh the evidence I have seen with my own eyes. Which is that Ewan is not dead—he *is* the man we found on the road to Crieff. But," Greer cautioned, "he doesn't remember what happened—Ewan can't tell me how he was injured. And" —she hesitated only a moment before trusting them with the whole of the truth—"he doesn't remember himself as Duke of Crieff. The beating injured him badly—broke his nose and his ribs—and gave him a…brain commotion, is what he called it."

The marquess went deathly still. "Do you mean he's lost his faculties?"

"He has lost some." This was the awful truth she had not wanted to accept for herself. "His memory has returned slowly, in fits and starts. I took him to the village this noontime in the hopes that something might jar his memories— which sadly did not happen—but an ostler from the Inn at the Bridge over Shee Water recognized him as the Duke of Crieff, so it's not my foolish fancy, Papa." She could see her father wanting to break in to object. "It's true."

"Where is he now?" Alasdair was on his feet, as if he would charge up the moorside that very minute to find his lost friend.

"I don't rightly know," Greer was forced to admit. "We parted in the village. He was staying in a bothy hidden in the glens on Crieff land. I tried to get him to come here, to be safe. Because the potential poacher—the "mad miscreant" Malcolm Cameron was talking about seeking," she clarified. "I fear he means Ewan."

"Does Malcolm Cameron know his cousin lives?" Alasdair asked.

"I pray not," she said. "Ewan has been hidden away so completely, but when I met Cameron at the forest gate, he said he was investigating some report of a stranger in the village." But even as she said the words, Greer knew they could not be entirely true—whoever had seen Ewan must have also seen her, who was no stranger to the village. "And Cameron also said he feared something was amiss with Ewan's burial. And there was"—she looked to her parents for confirmation—"because the coffin was buried before the service. But he blamed that on you, or at least on Ewan's 'disreputable friends in Edinburgh.'"

She tried to weave the tangled threads of what she knew into some logical line of thought, but there were too many loose ends, too many questions still unanswered.

"And are you on good"—Alasdair paused—"or friendly terms with him, my Lord Shee?"

"Neighborly terms," Papa supplied diplomatically. "We were just negotiating an agreement on the sale of a small parcel of land."

"Unentailed land that might raise cash?" Alasdair asked boldly.

"Aye!" Greer answered before her father could shush her. "Why do you ask that, in particular?"

"Because, not only have your questions become ours," Archie Carrington said. "But we've more questions of our own, especially in light of a conversation I had with the last member of our foursome—"

"The *quadrumvirate*, he called you."

"I don't think that is even a real word." Alasdair sent a fond smile to his wife before he added, "Shockingly unscholastic, our Ewan, in matters other than agricultural."

Greer could hear the dry humor and true affection for Ewan in Alasdair's voice. How strange—and wonderful—it was to meet the men Ewan had described so perfectly. How wonderful it would be for Ewan to have them back to resuscitate his memories.

"But our fourth member," Archie explained, "Rory Cathcart, is employed as an expert in the appraisal of art at Mr. Christie's auction house in London. Your letter, Lady Greer, had not yet reached him when he first contacted me in some alarm." Archie leaned forward, eager to share his confidences. "Because he had been astonished to find that the auction house had received a consignment of particular paintings from Crieff—paintings we knew Ewan had collected. But more importantly, he found that the consignment had come from His Grace, the Duke of Crieff, Lord Malcolm Cameron. Which meant that our friend, Ewan Cameron, must be dead. And yet, we none of us had heard anything—no notice had been put in the paper, no letter from this Malcolm Cameron, of whom we had never heard anything beyond his being a nuisance of a spendthrift cousin."

"Spendthrift?" This was an entirely new characterization of Cameron—one entirely at odds with his own memorable statements regarding Crieff's solvency.

"Ewan had, over the years, shared some concerns regarding his cousin with me," Alasdair clarified. "So when Rory aired his concerns, I wrote Malcolm Cameron directly. But I received no reply. You, Lady Greer, were the one who wrote instead. And that your questions squared so completely with mine, saw me resolved to come to Dalshee with all haste."

"I am sure, His Grace, Malcolm Cameron, would have answered, in time, but…" Mama tried for her usual diplomacy, but even she had to cast about to excuse Cameron's behavior. "His Grace has been rather beleaguered by his new duties."

Alasdair raised one sardonic eyebrow. "Not so beleaguered that he didn't immediately crate up, and ship to London for immediate consignment, more than a dozen important paintings that Ewan had collected over the past eight years."

Greer's heart began to gallop as if she were running upstairs, trying to keep up with her racing mind.

"There is worse. Or at least more," Archie Carrington said. "After consultation with Alasdair, we recalled that Ewan had mention his cousin was rather fond of horse racing."

"'Making alarming bets with dangerous people,' was actually what Ewan said," the marquess clarified.

"Exactly," Archie agreed. "So spurred by your inquiry, Rory's consignment, and Alasdair's memory, I made my way north from London along the horse-racing circuit, during which I established that Malcolm Cameron is heavily in debt."

Greer let out the breath she didn't realize she had been holding. "Personally in debt—debts of honor—and not debts as Crieff?"

"Indeed, accrued before he came into the title, I reckon, and therefore personal debts of honor, as you said. But you will be more astonished at the amount," Archie vowed. "Malcolm Cameron is in deep waters, not only with money lenders in London, where he kept an expensive bachelor residence at Albany until recently, but at nearly every town with a race track the length of the countryside. Grahambury Park, Newark-on-Trent, Doncaster, Leith—the list is comprehensive."

"And all of the debts outstanding?" She wanted to be very clear. "None of them settled?"

"To my certain knowledge," Archie pledged, "nary a one. He has yet to raise the necessary funds."

"Gracious." She sat back in her own chair to think of the ramifications. "No wonder he is selling off anything that is not tied down to the entail." So many new questions arose in her mind that she couldn't quickly sort them all. "What is to be done?"

"Well, to begin with, Rory has made a bureaucratic sleight of hand, and bought up Ewan's paintings on our accounts before they could go to auction—but for considerably less than what we now know Malcolm Cameron owes. So while Malcolm Cameron will be able to pay at least some of his bills, Ewan's legacy will not be entirely lost."

"Thank you. That is very generous of you." It was an elegant and practical solution, but did not quiet the alarm clanging like a kirk bell in her brain—the alarm that told her it was mighty convenient that a man so heavily in debt should come into a dukedom capable of providing him with ready money to pay such bills.

The alarm that grew louder and louder at the realization that Malcolm Cameron might be actively seeking—nay, hunting—Ewan because someone in the village might have recognized him.

Questions and alarm that her three guests seemed to share and might help her in answering. "Please, you must help me find Ewan, and return him to Crieff."

"Most assuredly. We stand ready to assist you." Alasdair added. "We should be glad of the company and conversation of people who knew Ewan in a different way than the rest of us. I should think you knew him far better than the rest of us, Lady Greer, for he shared his thoughts with you."

The compliment was bittersweet—for those thoughts might be forever gone.

"He talked about you often, you know," Alasdair went on. "His lucky penny in his palm, he called you. Always made time for his letters home, as he called all of them, no matter where they went. He knew, even when we were young, that you were his home."

The heat in her throat made it hard to speak. "Thank you." Greer did not bother to hide the stinging tears slipping out of the corner of her eyes. "We must do all we can to find him as quickly as possible and bring him home—before it's too late."

Lord Ewan Cameron
Castle Crieff
Perthshire

12 May, 1790

Dearest Ewan,

My heart is crushed with disappointment. I am fit to stomp my feet in agitation. We are obliged by the death of Mama's mother ~ my dear grandmama the Countess of Kirdsay ~ to travel to the Northern Isles for her funeral. While I am excited about the prospect of fresh travel ~ first north to Inverness and Caithness before sailing for Wide Firth on the north side of Orkney Island ~ I fear I will not be able to meet you at Glas Maol, for unfortunately, we must leave this very morning.

But I do delight in the honor and pleasure of naming your dog. After much thought, and careful consultation of various texts available to me here, I have decided not to take anyone else's advice, and to consult only my own fancy. And I fancy he shall be named Gent in honor of his most gentlemanly and thoughtful master. Let me know if you approve of such, for I am sure, if pressed, I may come up with another name, though I should not like it nearly as much as I like Gent. And you must rub Gent's head, and tell him what a good lad he is, and assure him I, too, look forward to the day that we three, along with my older lasses, Milk who is creamy buff-colored cocker, and Honey who is copper gold, will take a gambol up the hills at Crieff. We will all be the best of friends. I smile so to think how cozy we shall be.

I wish you all the enjoyment of your stay at Crieff, and all the best for your end of terms exams. Pray save those kisses for me—I am sure I have just as many waiting for you.

Yours, Greer

*E*WAN WATCHED from a distance as Dewar crept toward the bothy in the thin illumination of moonlight. "Lad," the moorkeeper called into the velvet darkness. "It's me."

"I'm here." Ewan had been awake and on alert since his return from the village, and in expectation of Dewar since the moment the dog Gent first heard the auld keeper's approach across the moor.

Dewar swiveled toward the sound of Ewan's voice where he had hidden behind the stonewall. "Good lad. Clever. Though it be as dark as the Earl of Hell's waistcoat, we've tae shift ye out of here."

"Aye," Ewan answered. "I saw you, and the men you were with, riding through the forest this afternoon, and heard their talk. I've packed up my gear." He passed the bundle of goods over the wall to the moorkeeper. And saw that Dewar held a gun—a heavy hunting piece, primed and loaded. "Has it come to that?"

"Mayhap." The auld man shook his wizened head. "If ye saw 'em and heard 'em, ye know they're as nervous as a tinder box. Some biddy in the village swore she saw the old laird—an' what in the devil possessed ye tae go down there in the first place?—an' some other bloody busy-body, who don't know how tae keep his filthy trap shut well an' tight, sent word tae the castle. An' that Gow—that was yer cousin's man I rode with—come tae fetch me out tae track ye down."

"Do they know it's me?"

Dewar stopped on the path to peer at him. "An' who the devil are ye?"

"Ewan Cameron, Duke of Crieff." He was sure of it now, even if he wasn't entirely sure what it meant.

"Devil douse the fire." Dewar exhaled his relief. "Yer back. That changes things—"

"Not entirely." Ewan gave voice to his own misgivings. "I'm remembering more and more—Cat Sìth. He was riding my horse, wasn't he?"

"Aye."

"Damn him. But I did remember my friends Alasdair and Archie—but I haven't remembered everything. I can't remember how I got clouted over the head, or who the devil did this to me." He had spent the better part of the night trying in vain to sort out the spate of new images that had taken up residence in his head and reckon whom he might trust.

Dewar made a sound of disappointment between his teeth. "Ah, weel, more is more, and the rest will come. But first we'll get ye someplace safe tae do the remembering."

Another memory came unprompted. "Greer said I would be safe at Dalshee."

"Did she now? Clever enough lass, then." Dewar began to lead the way up the burn toward Glas Maol. "Come on wi' ye. I ken a spot. That Gow be a canny, suspicious man, and like as not, he'll be up here, putting his nose where it's no' wanted on the morrow," the wee auld fellow groused.

"Aye. I didn't like the look of him—" Something else about Dewar's news made his awakened brain pound like a blacksmith's anvil, beating out an alarm. "What do you mean, *my cousin's man?*" The hot question burned like an ember on his tongue.

"Aye, the devil's in the details, isn't he?" Dewar stepped close so he could look Ewan in the eye. "Aye, lad. The other man who rode Cat Sìth—did ye no recognize 'im? He's yer cousin."

A cousin was family, someone to whom he was related and upon whom he might rely. "Nay. There was only one man with you."

"Yer cousin must have gone off wi' her ladyship of Dalshee by then."

Another hammer of alarm nearly deafened him. "Lady Greer? *My* Lady Greer?" Even he could hear the acid leech of jealousy in his voice.

"No other. Though I may say, she's got gumption, that lass —led him off pretty as ye please, though she looked none too happy. Did so to keep him away frae ye, I'm reckon. Mayhap I've been wrong about 'er. Mayhap she's a good'un—she did gie ye yer dog back."

A different kind of relief warmed Ewan through. He had been right to trust her—she was trying to help him, though he had acted like a dunderhead in handling the revelations from the ostler. But he couldn't seem to think fast enough to keep up with what was happening. "So Greer went with my cousin? And we're to go to him? To Crieff?"

Ewan wished he'd had a look at this cousin, for he'd surely not liked the look of his cousin's man, Gow.

"Nay." Dewar was adamant. "I can't like it, lad. There's something crafty about the man. Something dangerous. Best tae hide fae a bit longer, until yer braw enough, and ken exactly who did this to ye."

It had already been a long, wearying night, and Ewan's patience was growing thinner with every hour. "I'm sick and tired of hiding—I can't find the answers I'm looking for by hiding in a bothy like a wounded stag in the forest. If this man—this kinsman of mine—has done me wrong—"

"Lad—"

"I'm not a lad, so why should I hide like one?"

"Hell mend ye." The auld man seized Ewan up by his shirt-front in a surprisingly strong grip. "What good has going out there, into the world, done ye? Ye've stirred up a viper's nest 'o trouble, or did ye not understand that those men today meant ye no good? Are ye ready tae act? To protect yerself? Are ye? Yer no good tae us—to Crieff, nor Dalshee, nor that lass ye fancy—if yer no' yerself. Ye need mor'n just yer understanding of the past, lad. Ye need yer full wits so's ye can see in tae the future. Ye need tae be able tae lead the way, not just follow yer scanty remembrances, and ye can't even remember yer own cousin, nor yer own damn dog." Dewar let go of his shirtfront and poked a hard finger into his chest. "Look around ye—these are wild, unforgiving hills, lad. The mountains have ears as well as eyes. No' for the faint o' heart, nor the feeble o' mind."

There it was, said out loud—his greatest fear laid bare.

He was feeble-minded.

Not just forgetful or injured or temporarily crack-brained. Feeble.

And likely to stay that way forevermore.

He felt gutted by the possibility.

"Ye'd do well tae think on what I've told ye, lad," Dewar intoned like an oracle. "Until ye ken—until ye understand tae the back of yer bones—what it means tae be Crieff, ye'll do well tae stay put and do as I say."

"Aye," was all Ewan could manage. "Come, Gent." He patted his leg, and the dog came without question, loyal to him no matter the diminished state of his mind—loyal even if he seemed to have forgotten the wee creature's place in his prior life.

They made their slow, careful way across the dark moor to fetch up at a high mountain bothy in the wee small hours of the morning.

"We'll rest now," Dewar ordered. "And in the morn, I'll see what's what."

"Aye." Ewan dutifully laid himself down on the pallet, but he got little sleep and less rest. His mind would not stop whirring like a broken clockwork, aswirl with shifting images and words. And behind the turmoil was the looming fear that he was never going to be able to recover himself fully enough to meet Dewar's requirements to resume his responsibilities. That this half-life, this shadow existence on the moor, was all he could expect.

That he would never again be himself—the man he was supposed to be. The man who could woo Lady Greer Douglas for his own.

He took what little comfort he could in the warm famil-iarity of the soft sleeping dog curled up against his side, and stared at the low ceiling until dawn, which came blistering pink over the mountains to the east.

Dewar woke soon thereafter, and as if sensing Ewan's bitter frustration, took a more hopeful tone. "You sit tight, lad. We'll see this through, see if we don't. Sit tight and take the day as it comes."

Ewan intended to do as he was told. But as daylight came, the forced idleness was more than either he, or the wee dog, could bear.

"Come, Gent." Ewan took a tall walking stick with a horned handle, as well as a collapsible stalking spyglass from the peg next to the door and headed up the nearest peak to exercise his frustration and keep his broken mind occupied with something other than its failures.

He was already so high up on Dalshee's mountains that the way quickly grew progressively rockier, until there was nothing underfoot but the granite tor. With only the stick for purchase, he was obliged to crawl, taking to the steep rock face on hands and knees as low and stealthy as if he were stalking a stag. Just as he had done countless times before—the corridors at Crieff were lined with antlers mounted on plaques that told the story of where each stag was taken and when.

He closed his eyes to see them high on the walls—the inscriptions written in ink in his grandfather's hand. The trophy at the end of the corridor with his own name, and the date he had taken his first stag at the age of fourteen. The same year he had gotten betrothed.

But to whom remained a devastating blank. All he could see, when he thought of a woman, was his lass, his Greer.

He could see no other.

Ewan gave into the press of gravity and lay flat against the solid foundation of the rock, letting the wind-roughened granite bite into his skin, trying to force his mind to go where it clearly did not want to venture. He sprawled there so long that Gent was impelled to scratch his way up to burrow beneath him and lick his face into some semblance of liveliness.

And there it was—the memory was like a raindrop sluicing under his collar, making him squirm with the knowledge. This was his dog—gifted by his friend Alasdair as a puppy when he had been at St. Andrews, and lonely for home, for the open moorland of Crieff.

He had forgotten his own dog.

Devil take him if he had forgotten a wife.

Ewan clutched the wee dog to him and fought against the

unsettling vertigo of another piece of the puzzle that was his life falling into place without revealing the picture it painted.

Dewar was right—for all his protests that he was a man grown, he was as helpless as a newborn babe. But a babe could learn—for Crieff's sake if nothing else.

Ewan put the spyglass to his eye. In the misty cool of the early morning, the Dalshee bothy they had slept in looked small and unsubstantial—as diminished as he felt. He swept the glass to the east where he found the low, regular chimney tops of a Palladian estate, all balanced symmetry and peaceful refinement—Dalshee, where his lass lived and where she had asked him to go.

But how could he? Of all the unanswered questions and problems with his past, the one that loomed larger than all others was that he had told the ostler he was about to be married—an event, and a person, of whom he had no recollection.

All he could find in his mind's eye of the day he was set upon was the image of the penny in his palm—and he still had no idea what that meant.

Ewan turned the glass to the south, toward the long, cool slice of the upland loch and the silvered curve of the glen under Glas Maol, where a rider picking his way toward the bothy he and Dewar had abandoned only last night.

It was not just any rider. And not just any horse—the big black stallion with the star on his chest the ostler had mentioned so particularly. Cat Sìth.

Recognition was like a punch to his chest—a furious mixture of rage and pride and longing. That was *his* horse. Being ridden by the man who had ridden with Dewar yesterday—Gow. His cousin's man, doing exactly as Dewar had predicted—putting his nose where it wasn't wanted.

Possessiveness kindled a low, smoldering rage—that was *his* horse. And hell mend him if he was going to sit obediently and wait and watch another man take anything more of his.

He refocused the glass to follow the man's slow, uneven progress up the glen. Gow was working like mad to keep Cat Sìth in check—the normally biddable horse was everything fractious and ill-behaved, sidling and jibing under Gow's heavy hand and heavier spurs.

Ewan felt the unfamiliar hand of anger take hold of him— his breath grew tight and sulfurous. He wanted to throttle the bastard for such abuse.

So after Gow had picked through the empty bothy, and remounted to turn westward into the heart of Crieff land, Ewan rose and followed, drawn down the mountainside as if he were strung upon a pulley and Cat Sìth were the counter weight. Where they went, Ewan was compelled to follow.

Compelled to find what else was his.

Ewan took the descent at a run—pausing at the Dalshee bothy only to bid the obedient dog to stay, before he headed west across the moorland. Even at a low run his legs burned and his lungs were straining for air—repairing the wall had recovered some of his strength, but the devil would have taken him straight down to hell if he had had to run up the moor instead of down.

He stalked Gow as if he were the deer, following him at a distance, until at last, Gow manhandled the stallion over a rise. And there, at the foot of the hill was a grey, crenellated stone castle that rose like a cliff out of the granite hillside.

Crieff.

Exactly as Ewan had seen it in his mind's eye. If he closed his eyes now, he could see the view from the battlements and feel the wind blowing up the glen on his cheeks. His grandfather would take him up there to show him the lay of the land —how the burn that flowed past the castle nourished the farmland that spread out like a patchwork blanket across the strath below, and how all this—the burn and the brae, the moor and the glens and the widening strath—was Crieff.

His home. His—*he* was Crieff.

Loss and longing fought with his fear. Fear of what he would find there. Fear of what—and whom—he had forgotten. Caution kept him hidden amongst the tall fir trees until Gow marched away from the stable, and the place descended into a calm quiet. But still, Ewan took care to make haste slowly, approaching the stable yard by stealth, pausing to listen for any unfamiliar sound.

In the wide doorway, the sweet scent of horse and leather and hay rushed at him like a friend, bringing memories with it—there on the right was his first pony's stall. And above, in the loft, was where he had sneaked his first cheroot—not thinking of the danger of the flammable hay—only to be tanned to within an inch of his life by the stable master as his grandfather looked on.

And there, at the end of the stalls, with his tall, proud neck arching over the door, was Cat Sìth. His horse. *His.*

Ewan walked toward the stallion as if he were in a fever dream, the images and sounds and experience coalescing into memory, into the very fabric of who he was. The station tossed his head and stamped his great hooves when Ewan drew near, but in another moment the animal lowered his head to take a deeply suspicious snort of air.

And then the great wee beastie let out a low, plaintive nicker, as if to chide Ewan for ever having left him.

"I know, lad. I know." He buried his face in his animal's broad neck, leaning into the comforting breadth of his chest, soaking up the stallion's power and strength and remembrance as if it were a balm that might heal him through.

"Fuck me blind." A groom—Angus, Ewan recalled with sudden clarity—appeared in the aisle and crossed himself. "Is it really you then, Laird?"

Caution warred with pride and longing—longing to be remembered. Longing to be at home.

But there was nothing he could give but the truth. "It is."

"Then yer no' dead."

"Nay," he answered quietly. "I never was." But dead or not, home or no, the place felt dangerous. Ewan wanted the comfort and protection of the open air. "I'll walk him cool," he said, referring to his horse, whose sides were still marked with sweat and the chafing of Gow's heavy spurs.

But he had still not discovered what he had come so far to find out. "Who—" For the first time in what felt like ages, he struggled with the words. "Who is living here, now?"

"Hisself, Malcolm Cameron, Laird Ewan."

"And my wife?"

Angus's wide face was blank. "Ye died afore ye could be married to the heiress of Dalshee, Laird."

Ewan's skin went hot with a blistering bolt of hope. "Dalshee? Lady Greer of Dalshee."

"Aye, Laird."

The rush of relief was like whisky in his blood, so strong and so intoxicating he could barely feel his feet upon the ground. He took the lead rope from the groom's hand, as well as a towel to rub the beastie dry, and led Cat Sìth out of the stable as if he were walking upon the mist.

"What'll I tell 'em, Laird?" Angus called after him.

He didn't care. It was too late to make haste slowly—he had come before he was ready to face all the consequences but one. It didn't matter what happened, as long as he could get to Greer—his lass. "Tell them whatever you think is right —but if you can, do it as slowly as possible"

In the yard, Ewan buckled the lead onto the stallion's halter, and vaulted himself up onto Cat Sìth's high, bare back, and set off at once, too ill at ease to even do as he had said and cool the animal. But he wanted the powerful feel of the stallion between his legs. He needed the sense of movement and control to combat the unease that he had pushed the situation past the point of control.

Ewan gave the horse his head, letting him range up the forest path and stretch his long legs as he willed before he gathered the stallion back to an easier pace, conscious of not over-working him—he'd already been ridden up the glens at dawn by bloody Gow. Ewan stroked the animal's broad neck, praising him in turn, while exulting in the glorious feeling of unity with his own wee beastie.

Devil take him, but it felt good to feel to be in control of even one small part of his destiny again. To feel that he was actively reclaiming what was once his. To collect up the forgotten parts of himself so he could be worthy of her. So he could win her for his own.

He guided the stallion beneath the sheltering canopy of the woods running east to where the mountain burns would join together into the Shee Water, and made his slow, deliberate way toward the Inn at the Bridge over Shee Water.

It was nearly mid-afternoon when he arrived.

"Yer lordship." The ostler he had met in Crieff village came running out as Ewan dismounted. "Ye've yer wee beastie back."

"Aye, lad. I thank you." Ewan's hand went to the pocket of his coat for a vail, before he realized he was neither wearing a coat, nor had any ready money to tip the ostler. "I'd like to have a quiet chat with your landlord."

"Aye, yer lordship." The lad went at a trot for the kitchen, while Ewan took the moment to take a long look around the whole of the yard, finding it familiar.

He remembered being there before, numerous times when taking the road to the south. He turned back to survey the building—the landlord would come out of that door, there—

"Yer Grace," a suet-faced man bustled into the yard, greeting Ewan as he came, reaching for his hand to pump. "Praise be! We thought ye were dead."

Your Grace. Aye. He was not *nobody*—he was somebody. He was Crieff.

"So I've heard, Boscowan." The landlord's name careered into his head. "I'd like to ask about the day I was here last."

"Aye. I've thought about it often, Yer Grace." The fellow wiped his palms on his apron as if it would clear his mind along with his hands. "Ye were on yer way tae Edinburgh, as I recall. Ye stopped, and took a pint of ale, and then ye continued yer journey on."

Ewan braced himself for the assault of the images flooding into his mind. But nothing substantial came. "But I'm told my horse came back, riderless," he prompted, nodding to the ostler in thanks for his earlier information.

"Aye," the landlord confirmed. "But that were later—four days or a week or so after." He licked his lips again. "The reins were unbelted—one was shorter than t'other, as if th' animal had stood on 'em an' snapped the leather."

"Was he in distress?"

"Some," the fellow acknowledged. "But not overly lathered. He were dry."

"Was there any blood on the animal?" Ewan pressed.

"Nay, Yer Grace." Boscowan shook his head, sure of his memory. "Nay. No sign of foul play, beyond the broken rein."

Ewan's ears pricked up—the anvil in his head pressed heavy in alarm. "Were you looking for some sign of foul play?"

"Aye, Yer Grace. For a mon I didn't know came afore the horse. 'E said as ye were dead"—the landlord's Adam's apple bobbed uncomfortably—"and as 'ee was going tae Crieff tae tell 'em, I should be on lookout fer th'horse, His New Grace's mon said."

Ewan's hands went slick as he clutched his reins. "Gow. When?"

"It were a'fore dusk. I sent out some lads tae look, for the mon had given me a gold guinea, and it only seemed right as evenin' was falling. But th'horse come back on his own in the night."

The image of darkness closing in over his head returned. Ewan forced himself to breathe, to draw air in and push it out of his lungs. To remind himself that his ribs were healed and he was no longer being suffocated by the black pain. "And then?"

"And then I sent word tae Crieff that we'd found th'horse."

"And then?" he prompted again.

"The mon came back for th'horse. And promised me another gold guinea to keep quiet about it." Boscawan shook his head like a bulldog trying to set himself to rights. "I took it, I'm ashamed to say, Yer Grace."

"No harm done, Boscowen. Thank you for seeing to the horse." Clearly the landlord was a man who knew how to hold his tongue. "And though I've no guinea to give for my thanks, I would ask you to keep my visit as quiet as possible. For I am a man caught in a damnably precarious position." A man still unsure of whom he could trust, besides his Greer.

"Aye, Yer Grace," the landlord pledged. "I should'a reckoned there were some great mischief afoot, for here ye are, and praise be. We're that happy tae have ye back tae us." He bowed his head, as if in contrition. "Ye can count on me—I'm yer man. I gie ye freely my fealty."

Fealty. Now, there was a word—a damned medieval holdover of a word that still, somehow, applied in this supposedly enlightened world.

But as it was all that he had, Ewan would gladly take it.

Lord Ewan Cameron
Castle Crieff
Perthshire

26 May, 1790

Dear Ewan,

I fear telling you that I make a fine traveler ~ every portion of our trip north, from our passage over the mountains to Braemar, and then east along the Dee before turning north for Inverness, has been a delight. The weather has held fine and the roads firm, making our trip swift and smooth. And such a variety of scenery and of people! Each inn along the road has yielded such a variety of personages I wish I were a better artist so I might capture their likenesses.

But our conversations in-between the stops have really been the most illuminating. I had not remembered that my grandmama, and now my aunt, inherited the title of Countess of Kirdsay in her own right, through direct lineage. It seems when the Earl of Kirdsay was created such, the title was made with remainder to the heirs whatsoever of his body, which means that the titles could be passed on through both male and female lines. What a sensible arrangement!

I should have very much liked it if I could inherit Papa's title as well as the estate. But instead my son shall have the title, along with yours, in time, if such a child were born. It gives one leave to wonder at the strangeness of life, does it not? Though I must say that I should so much rather spend more time in travel that in raising babies. They don't seem to be appealing wee things at all. And we had much better spend our time breeding better cattle than any children.

Pray do tell me if you are earnestly opposed to my views, for I suppose I had better revise them if that is so. (A hopeless task, for once my opinion is set, it is a trial to undo, but one I shall undertake in the name of domestic happiness if need be. And kisses, of course ~ I fear I should do almost anything for your kisses.)

I await your reply at Orkney.

Yours, G

CHAPTER 22

Greer slept badly, though it ought to have been a comfort to know Ewan's friends were there to help him. She had spent the night listening in vain for his arrival, still hoping that he might yet come to the relative safety of Dalshee—relative, because there were perils yet unknown that not even Dalshee could prevent.

The understanding that he could not remember her sat like a weight upon her chest, squeezing the hope from her. But that could just be her darling dogs, Milk and Honey, climbing atop the bed to rouse her out of her laziness to greet the gray day.

She dressed against the chill of the wet autumn morning in a warm wool redingote of muted heather-colored plaid suitable for a day searching the hills, and quickly made her way downstairs.

"Gracious, Greer," her mama admonished when she appeared in the breakfast room. "You've worn yourself to a candle stub these past few weeks, with little sleep and no rest. You would do His Grace no good to be charging across the moors on an empty stomach and with no sleep."

Her mama's tone was tart enough to brook no argument. "Now take some eggs before I allow you out upon the moor."

Greer did as instructed—but left her plate half-eaten to join the rest of the search party, including her father's moor-keeper, Jock Keith and his sons as well as their guests in preparing to head up the moorside. Time was of the essence.

"Now then," her father addressed the group. "Jock and I have decided it might be more efficient to split into different groups, to search the different paths and meet again at Glas Maol."

"I'm to come with you and Mr. Carrington, mileddy," young Lachlan said.

"Excellent." But Greer was too impatient for the slower pace of the lad's highland pony, and rode ahead, letting her surefooted mare Nicnevin find her swift way up to the tor in the hopes that Ewan would be found safe and sound in his bothy.

Archie Carrington kept easy pace with her, asking a few questions about the lay of the land, but mostly leaving her to her own thoughts, which were all for the urgency of making Glas Maol as quickly as possible.

But when she arrived at her special viewpoint down into the glen hoping to find Ewan, who should she spy instead but Malcolm Cameron, accompanied by his man, Gow, investigating the bothy—surely looking for Ewan.

Greer swallowed down the panic that gripped her and immediately dismounted, gesturing for Archie to do the same.

They took cover behind a boulder, while she shook out her spyglass. That the bothy was empty, as evident by the way Cameron sat unhappy on an indifferent mount, while Gow poked about with his riding whip and kicked what little was left to examine on the grass.

Greer felt her breath fill her lungs. "He's gone," she whispered, lest the contrary wind take her words down the glen.

"He's a canny lad, injured or not," Archie observed in a low voice. "We'll find him yet."

"I hope so." However worried she might have been for Ewan, he seemed to be at least one step ahead of Cameron and Gow, who moved north up the seam of the glen, and out of her field of vision.

She and Archie followed their own path on the Dalshee side of the ridge, descending until they met with the rest of the search party.

"Any sign of him—your Ewan?" Papa asked.

"No sign."

Papa gave her the same reassuring smile Archie had. "Well then, we can only hope he is safe for the nonce." He placed a kiss on her forehead. "The day is wearing on—the wind is picking up and the clouds are blowing hard from the east. We had best make the most of what good weather remains to us. What think you, Jock?"

"I reckon Crieff's moorkeeper, Billy Dewar, would know of the bothy in the upland meadow."

Greer had been there once or twice. It was close enough to the divide between the two estates that Ewan could have walked there last afternoon—if, and only if, he had heeded her advice that he would be safe on Dalshee land. "Would he trespass to make use of it, do you think?"

"Aye," Jock Keith decided. "He might at that, but I wouldn't call it trespass if 'ee did. Known Dewar all me life."

"Of course. The upland meadow it is," Papa confirmed. "We'll find His Grace for you, Greer. See if we don't."

She could not contemplate the possibility of them not. "Thank you. Let us gang on."

Her father led the way forward up the mountain. Greer followed, only to find the ghillies, Lachlan and Leslie, quickly ranging before and behind. "Lachlan Keith." She fixed him with a narrow glare. "Did my father bid you protect me?"

"Oh, aye, mileddy," the keeper's young son answered straightaway. "So's ye don't get too far ahead o' the rest o' the party, mileddy."

Greer saved her indignation to fuel her search, keeping her gaze on the crest of the hills—scanning the edge of her horizon, as if someone or something there were drawing her attention, like a midge dancing just on the edge of her sight.

Looking, in vain, she knew, for Ewan.

Several times the dogs set up large coveys of grouse that tempted her father's sportsman's eye, but they were out to find a man, not take braces of game. The dogs quartered back and forth, scenting and flushing out the wild brids, but a glint of something—the glimmer of light on the ridgeline over her shoulder—deflected Greer's attention from the field.

But then the cry, "Over," went up as another covey burst from cover and the ghillies reflexively followed the line of their flight.

And then there was another sound. Louder, thundering down the glen from behind with a roar that most certainly could not have come from one of the shot-loaded fowling pieces, or pistols the party carried. From a deer gun, rifled for longer range.

Her ears knew before the information could catch up with her brain and the deadly result unfolded before her eyes —her father's arm flew up and he fell from his saddle at the same time that young Leslie crumpled to the ground.

She was already flying from the saddle, running for her father when she heard her Jock's voice, roaring with savage fear, "He's hit!"

The Dalshee moorkeeper was instantly by his son's side, propping the lad up, pressing a wad of cloth to staunch the flow of blood blossoming from his shoulder and discoloring the dark tweed of his coat. "That's no birdshot," the keeper growled. "He's hit by a bloody, goddamn ball!"

"Good God," her father swore. "It grazed me before it struck him." His gaze lifted to search the party. "Who in the hell has loaded with a ball—"

Another thunderous shot burst into the heather nearby.

"Git doon, man," was the keeper's fierce instruction as he pulled his laird by his coattails into the cover of the heather. "All o' ye," he screamed back down the line. "Git doon!"

Greer ignored the good advice to reach her father. "Where are you hit?"

"Just grazed. It's nothing. Get down!" But a sludge of rusty red was soaking through his coat sleeve, and blood was dripping slowly from his fingers. "Get bloody down!"

She hunkered by his side. "Let me see," she insisted.

"Not now." Even shaken, his voice brooked no argument. "We'll see to the boy. We need to get off the moor and see to the him immediately."

Greer's gaze went back to the ridge line, to the outcropping of boulders on the far crest of the hill—Glas Maol. She knew the spot like she knew her own face in the mirror. It was more than familiar—it was all but bred into her bones.

And she knew it was the perfect spot to hide from the world, or lie concealed, and steady the kind of rifled long gun used for deer stalking. Only today someone was stalking people.

Fear coalesced like a hot stone in her belly—a hot stone that couldn't begin to heat the icy chill sinking into her bones. Malcolm Cameron's words came hurtling back in to her mind—*Accidents happen all the time, my lady. There are miscreants up there with guns.*

An "accident" had already happened to Ewan. And now an accident was happening to Papa. Had he been trying to warn her, Malcolm Cameron? What did he know about his cousin's attack that he hadn't told her? Was he trying to frighten her?

But she had just seen him ride in the opposite direction, back toward Crieff, and away from Dalshee's highlands. Could there really be another man—a truly dangerous, mad man, who had been the one to try and murder Ewan— roaming these moorlands?

At the far end of the group, Alasdair was all but sitting on top of Quince to shield her, and the rest of them were hunkered down in the heather, taking what cover they could, with their fowling pieces at the ready, though there was not much they could do at such a distance.

"I'm going to draw him off," Archie shouted from somewhere behind her. "And after the shot, you move—all of you —and get to better cover while he reloads."

And then he was off, running for the far side of the hill, hopefully drawing the shooter's eye away from the rest of them, who rushed or crawled at various speeds in the opposite direction, toward the shelter of the tree line.

Greer stayed exactly where she was, crouching in the scrubby heather. Waiting for some sign, some revelation, some movement from the ridge line above that would give her a clue as to what she ought to do next. Her heart was pounding in her ears, drowning out all other sound—she could not even hear her own breathing as it see-sawed in and out of her chest.

Off to her left, Archie reached the relative safety of the trees along the burn without another shot being fired—there was no other sound but the chill autumn wind screaming atop the heather. Nothing.

And so Greer took her courage and fear in hand, and began to stealthily ascend the moorside in the opposite direction of the rest of the party—toward Glas Maol, rather than away from it. Because every instinct—for good or for bad—told her this present calamity had to do with Ewan.

He was up there somewhere. Somehow. Either being harmed, or—God forfend—doing the harming.

Either way, she had to know.

Upward she crept, continuously scanning the ridge above, so intent that she paid scant attention to what was happening behind until someone was upon her, slamming into her the heather, knocking the wind from her lungs.

"Get down, lass!" Ewan, looking like God's revenge against murder.

His hard, whipstrong body rolled over and around her, tumbling them to the ground. "For God's sake, lass, are you mad? Stay down." His large work-roughened hand covered the top of her head, shielding her, while the rest—all twelve-odd, uncompromising stone of him—pressed her down into the humid earth.

It was the most wonderful thing she had ever felt.

He had come back to her.

They were all tangled together—his leg had insinuated itself between her rucked up wool skirts, and the hard ridge of his knee pushed her quilted petticoats against the inside of her thigh. His arms surrounded her, pulling her into him, while he curved his long body around her, cradling her with his strength. "Are you hit, lass?"

"Nay." She was too relieved, too happy that he was alive and had come back to her to say anything more. Instead, she pulled his mouth down to her and kissed him.

She kissed him with all the love and relief and hurt and grief and breathless wonder that she could channel into the bliss of her lips on his. She kissed him because he was alive and so was she, and they were together. She kissed him because she could.

"Aye, lass." He lifted his head enough to smile down at

her. "I'm that glad to see you in one piece, too. But we're in a hell of a fix. Best get to better cover before we can—"

"The bracken," she managed. "Along that little burn to the left."

He raised his head for only a moment before he said, "No time like the present," and sprang to his feet. Greer just managed to grab her fowling piece before he took her other in a hard hold and pulled her at a breakneck pace for an outcropping of rock alongside the burn where the bracken of fern grew thick and sheltering.

She lost her hat somewhere along the way, and they were both panting from the exertion and the frantic, sheer terror and excitement of being alive, but she had never been so happy in her entire life. She threw herself into his arms, pressing herself against the warm surety of his body. He was alive and so was she, and it was absolutely lovely.

"Aye, lass, I've got you." She felt his kiss against her hair. "I'll not let any harm come to you."

"Not me." She laughed to keep from crying against the warm leather of his jerkin. "I've been that worried about you."

"I'm all to rights, lass," he assured her. "We're safe enough here for a bit."

She buried her face against the warm crook of his neck and fisted up the linen of his shirtfront to hold him close, squeezing her eyes shut so the tears that she had held back might not spill down her cheeks.

"What's this?" he murmured as he tipped her chin up so her lips could meet his. He kissed her with such heat and tenderness that she was left in no doubt of his feelings about her. Just as she was in no doubt of her feelings for him.

There was so much to say, so many questions to ask, she hardly knew where to begin. But she couldn't stop looking at him—it was as if she were seeing him for the first time.

There was something about knowing he was *her* Ewan again, that warranted a longer, more intimate look than she had ever taken at her lost friend in the bothy. Her eyes pored over each feature, from his kind green eyes to his crooked, broken nose, memorizing every facet of his face, so she could never forget, never doubt that he was her Ewan again. "I can't tell you how glad I am to have you back."

"Aye, I'm back, lass." He kissed away her tears. "And I aim to stay." And because he was himself again, he pulled her close and kissed her.

He kissed her with such fierce possession and passion that all the grief and frustration of the long, lonely, wasted weeks disappeared. He kissed her as if she was what he had been searching for through the fog of memory. As if she was all he wanted.

But they were in the middle of the moor, hiding from a shooter, and something besides kissing had to be done.

Ewan turned his attention to the danger lurking above. "I'm going to try and circle around him along the shoulder of the ridge. You stay here."

"I will not! And neither should you." She clutched at his arm, her alarm a cold fist gripping her chest. "What I mean is that you should stay put as well. I've lost you once, I don't want to risk losing you again."

"You'll not lose me, lass, for I've a thick skull and a thicker hide. But I won't sit here while he keeps shooting at you until he hits you." He turned her hand and placed a tender kiss in her open palm. "I've been searching for you all morning. I thought you might come to the bothy and find me gone, but then I saw you come back over Glas Maol, and the two men following you—"

"Following me? Who?"

"Gow—I first saw him with Dewar, when they tried to track me up from the village yesterday. With my cousin."

"Malcolm Cameron?" All the dreadful fear and apprehension returned as swift as a kick. "I thought they were looking for you—but you think they were following me?"

"Aye, I know it—I watched them double-back toward Glas Maol. I reckon they might still be up there, but this storm's moving in..."

The light was fading fast as a damp enveloping mist settled around them, blown up the glen by the cold east wind.

Greer shivered, despite the comfortable enveloping warmth of his arms.

"Aye," Ewan agreed. "We've to get off the moor, and to shelter. How's your deer stalking technique?"

"Ingrained," she answered.

"Ye'll do, lass." He patted her shoulder in reassurance, before he changed his mind and kissed her. It was no more than a quick buss on her lips, but it was warm and firm and told her everything that he did not say—that she was important to him, and that he would protect her with all that he was. "We'll go together. Follow behind me. Slow and low," he said low into her ear. "Make haste slowly."

They were very nearly the most beautiful words she had ever heard. Her Ewan was back, and at that moment, crawling carefully over her like a great tortoise, until there was nothing for her to do but watch the soles of his feet disappear into the bracken.

She took his words to heart, silently repeating them in her head as she inched forward on hands and knees and elbows and toes, moving in his path up the moorside toward the high rock outcropping near the crest of Glas Maol as best she could manage without being seen.

But once he reached the top, she found their caution had been unnecessary—whoever had been there before had already fled. Ewan went ahead, and now stood alone between the rocks, staring at something he had found.

"What is it?"

"A Jäger rifle." He scowled down at a long gun left among a litter of papers. "My Jäger flintlock rifle—this is *my* gun."

She was confused. "Did you lose it, or did they steal it from the bothy?"

"No. I never had it in the bothy. I bought it in Hanover when I traveled there, a long time ago. I can see the gunsmith's shop as clear as day." He squeezed his eyes shut, as if he could see more. "Alasdair was with me, approving the purchase."

"He was there, searching for you, today. Did you see him?"

"Hell mend me," Ewan swore. "I never noticed him—my eyes were all for you." He bent down to pick up the gun, running his fingers over the engraved steel of the lock mechanism. "The pan is cold. He left some time ago." He studied the ground and picked up a wee fleck of thin paper. "His powder twists." He searched the area and found two larger twists of paper that had held the charges of powder. "He was well prepared to kill you."

His tone was so grim and bitter and full of fury, she hastened to correct him. "I don't think so. The first shot was at my father. I was well away on the flank." She was sure of it —two shots to the center of the line. "But if this is your gun, that means it came from—"

"Crieff." He took her by the hand. "Castle Crieff. My home."

"Yes," she breathed, relieved and happy for him—happy for them both. "Then you remember?"

"Not all, but most." He looked down at the gun in his hand. "I remember this. I remember that I used this rifle for deerstalking on these hills, in these glens. I remember where it was stored in the gunroom at Crieff, under lock and key that only the steward, the keeper, or I had. But someone else has that key now, and they brought the gun here from Crieff." His clear gaze sought hers. "The men who followed you here."

"Malcolm Cameron, your cousin." Thoughts were racing through her head tumbling one over the other in their haste to reach her brain.

Accidents happen all the time.

"And Gow," Ewan added. "He was the one who must have shot at you—Malcolm hasn't the skill."

"Nay. It wasn't meant for me." Greer was sure of it. "He shot at Papa." But what could Malcolm Cameron hope to accomplish by shooting her father? What could he hope to gain?

The realization hit her with all the force of a shot—her. Her hand in marriage. Her dowry. Her un-entailed estate.

Without a protective, canny father to object to his debts, Malcolm Cameron must have hoped to frighten her into accepting him. What he could not accomplish by so cleverly appealing to her vanities and ambitions, he had tried to gain by malice.

Aye, there was malice in these glens. And it definitely came from Crieff.

Lady Greer Douglas
Kirdsay Castle
Orkney, Northern Isles

1 June, 1790

Dear Lady Greer,

It seems we have, like two ships in the night, passed each other unseen. I am happy that you find delight in your travels and will hope with all my heart that you have safe and smooth passage to the Northern Isles. Please convey my deepest condolences to your lady mother on her loss. Thinking of the loss of your grandmother, I am happy to be at Crieff with my grandfather, who, thankfully, continues in excellent health despite his advanced age, which makes me more anxious than ever to use my remaining time at university wisely, and to Crieff's best advantage.

And speaking of vantages, I made the climb up the glen to the crest of Glas Maol, and I fancy that I found something of yours there—a wee GD scratched into the top of the rock. It was deep enough to give me the impression that you have dug it out during years and years of successive visits, each time making another cut. I hope you will be happy that I have done the same and started my own initials next to yours. If you are not happy, I will apologize for the impulse, but it is already done—etched in stone as it were—with no going back. Pray enjoy your travel but come back and tell me what you think of my work. And give me at least one of the kisses you have saved.

Your devoted friend, EC

Lady Greer Douglas
Kirdsay Castle
Orkney, Northern Isles

2 July, 1790

Dear Lady Greer,

We have made an impromptu visit to Amsterdam, as Rory was sent there by his father to purchase a painting. And as I could not see you at Dalshee, I went with him for the journey. I have purchased something else for you that is more in keeping with our shared passion for agriculture. Within this pot is a special tulip bulb, Tulipa marjollettii, bred by a horticulturist friend who recommended it especially. It is said to have delicate, pale lemon-to-cream petals that are touched at the edges with rose. I thought you should like it to experiment in your glass houses at Dalshee. Pray plant them in the autumn, as a November planting should yield a bloom by Easter, by which time I hope to be home to you for good.

Until then, I remain your devoted, EC

CHAPTER 23

BLOODY HELL, the lass was going to faint—her face went white as ash. Ewan gathered her to him, wrapping his arms around her slight form. "Easy now."

"No, I'm just shocked, is all," she breathed. "I knew he was in heavy debt, your cousin, and I knew he wanted to marry me, but I didn't think he was so desperate as to attempt something so…so villainous and malicious!"

"Marry you?" The jealousy Ewan thought he had quashed came roaring back. "My cousin?"

"Aye. But clearly he only wanted the money—my inheritance from Dalshee, which is not entailed." She let out a sound of disgust that was only muted by the rising patter of the rain starting up in earnest.

Her dismissal was emphatic enough to put paid to any residual jealousy. "Come, lass." He took her by the hand. "Let's get to shelter." He turned north leading her along the ridge, away from Glas Maol. "I know a safe place."

She came willingly, though she was wrung out by the shocking events of the day. He of all people knew, it was decidedly frightening to know someone wanted you dead

"I'm sorry," he said more than once as he led her higher up the moor, but he did not slacken his pace—they would both be soaked to the skin by the time they reached the bothy tucked high above the glens at the edge of a mountain meadow. It would be cold there, but safe—he had hidden Cat Sìth in the lean-to stable at the back earlier in the day.

They reached the bothy just as the last vestige of light was obliterated by the rain, plunging them in deep, impenetrable grey. Ewan put the flintlock rifle on the pegs over the door, and took her fowling piece, setting it carefully to the side—cares to be taken up later, when they were dry and his Greer was not nearly shaking from the raw cold.

He went to light the fire to warm her, but she was no delicate daisy, his lass—though she was soaked through and white-fingered with the chill, she came to her knees at the hearth beside him, feeding in the kindling until the blaze took hold and began to light and heat the gloom.

"I feel safer knowing we're on Dalshee land." She cast a glance over the room. "Is this where you hid last night?"

"I thought since you had invited me, you wouldn't mind."

"Not at all. I'm so glad you did. I hate to think of what might have happened if your cousin and his man had gotten ahold of you."

Ewan hated to think of it, too. So he turned his mind to more immediate, practical needs. "Best to have the wet things off, aye, to set before the fire to dry." He stood and began to unbutton his damp leather jerkin.

"Oh, aye," she agreed. But she did not move, save for her eyes, which swept around the sparsely furnished bothy, taking in the straw pallet with one tartan blanket.

He swept the tartan up and handed it to her. "At least it's dry and clean." And he turned his back to change himself out of his soaked shirt and breeches. But having her out of his sight somehow made his other senses stronger, and more acute. Because he could hear the soft sound of each button on her coat jacket popping free of the holes. And the whoosh and shush of tweed over silk as she shook out her soaked skirts and petticoats. And the stroke of her boot laces being undone, followed by the quiet fall of her soles against the floor.

His body stirred in rude appreciation, and he had to stab a hand into his short hair to chafe some better sense into his head, before he could move again. But when he bent down to pick up his sopping small clothes and leather breeks, he caught a glimpse of her clad only in her stays and shift and blouse, and he knew he had never seen anything lovelier.

By the time he had donned his only other pair of dry breeches and a linen shirt, she was seated in front of the fire, wrapped in the tartan with her bare feet poking out toward the heat. Far more like a ragamuffin than a lady. "I should have thought of filling the kettle before I took my boots off."

"We'll take off the lid and set the kettle out in the rain—it'll fill up soon enough." He took the heavy kettle and set it on the doorsill. "But I've something better than tea, lass. Whisky." He offered her the wee flask Dewar had left with him. "Have you ever tried the water of life?"

She swiped the flask from his hand. "I may not own my own distillery, but I'm two and twenty, and not, as I keep having to tell people, a green girl. And I'm Scots." She tossed back a goodly gulp. "Oh, gracious me," she swore on a deep inhale. "If that isn't strong enough to make an auld whore blush, I don't know what is."

He laughed and patted her on the back. "Keep breathing, lass." Ewan took his own swig, letting the smoky fire bolt down his throat and light up his insides in a way the fire never could. "I've some bannock cakes and honey left." He foraged in the cloth bag that served as his larder. "It's not a ham, but it'll keep us the night."

"Manna from heaven." She took the dried wedges of oats and barley and set them to warm on the hod.

They sat there in companionable silence, eating the warm oat cakes, and sipping whisky, until they had eaten all he had, and were warm from the fire. Her bright ginger hair had escaped its careful, orderly pins, and spilled across her cheek like dark amber honey in the moonlight. Glistening and shining and calling for the touch of his hand.

He reached out to where a long ginger strand fell across her shoulder, and let it slip, soft and silent between his fingers. And if the bright fall of her hair was so soft and wondrous, what would the living warmth of her skin feel like? He turned his hand and let the backs of his fingers graze across the high planes of her cheekbones and the pale cream of her skin.

He wanted to touch and see more of it, her sweet skin. He wanted to run his finger down to the soft spot beneath her chin, and along the slide of her neck, to the little hollow above the top button of her linen blouse. And over her lips, as smooth and sweet and inviting as a summer sloe.

Just a kiss, he lied to himself. While she was his, and he could protect her, and they were away from all other cares. While he had could give her something sweet and kind of himself.

"Just one kiss." On the corner of her mouth, where the smooth cream of her cheek gave way to the crushed berry of her lip.

"Maybe two," she whispered back. "Though I've saved far more for you."

He did not need to be offered twice. He kissed her, and they were exactly as he had dreamt, her lips—plush and giving, like ripe fruit. Exactly as he wanted.

How he had been so lucky to fall in love with the woman he was destined to marry, he did not know. He did not care.

With his lips upon hers, her eyes fluttered closed, but she gave him a slow smile of such welcoming warmth—exhausted and rumpled, and happy—that all his good intentions were incinerated in an instant. His poor, aching, abused brain abandoned all pretense to thought for the more immediate gratification of feeling.

And she felt marvelous—she sighed into him as he gathered her lithe body closer, a soft sound of pleasure and welcome, and he was lost to the wonder that was her. To the pleasure of her kiss.

It seemed the most natural thing in the world to kiss her again while she was in his arms and warm and so wonderfully willing to kiss him back. "Ewan," she whispered.

"Aye." He answered her kiss for kiss. He would have crawled over rocks and glass—he had crawled over half a mountain—to taste her like this.

He deepened the kiss, wanting her to open to him. But it was he who was opening—falling into the rightness of her, plummeting into the pleasure that came whenever he was with her, that grew ten-fold with her lips meeting his.

She tasted of the rain, slick and earthy—like water, and he was nothing but a salt bed, parched and dry. He had thirsted for her from the first moments he could remember, when he wanted her more that he had wanted the water that had eased his aching throat.

He pulled her closer, and her hand found its way along the line of his jaw. He turned into the sweet chafe of her palm, rubbing the rough texture of his scraggly beard against her like a mute animal trained to her hand—the near-growl of low pleasure that wound its way out of his chest was beast-like in its primitiveness. He felt primitive, crude and low, and not fit for the fine likes of her, but for this momment when she welcomed him, he didn't care.

He took her into his arms, lifting and turning her and

letting her down upon the low pallet. He felt clumsy and stupid as he settled his weight upon her, importuning her with his rude arousal. He tried to slow himself, to hold the clawing need at bay, so he kissed her carefully, making sure of his welcome, waiting for her to pull back again. To tell him they ought not, to put him back in his place.

But she was kissing him, her mouth rising to meet his, her breath heating and tangling with his. And he was falling deeper, pulled into her exquisite sweetness by the loop of her arms around his neck. She clung to him, holding him as tightly as he held her. And then her hands speared into his hair, cradling his skull, brushing through the short locks as she pulled him closer still.

He nosed his way behind her ear, where her hectic pulse beat under the fragile surface of her skin, where the scent of woman and crushed heather and rain mixed with the light perfume of soap.

And he wanted more.

He wanted to taste more than her mouth. He wanted to take her into himself and keep her there. He wanted her to be his in the most basic, most essential way possible. To bind her to him so that she could never leave him. Never abandon him to the emptiness that was his past, or the uncertainty that was his future.

He wanted to be such a part of her, that she needed him as much as he needed her.

He rose upon his elbows to feel the lovely curve of her lithe body beneath him, to watch as his hands roamed over her of their own accord, searching out every interesting nook and exquisite curve. He kissed her closed eyes, and the soft spot beneath her ear, and the long line of her jaw, and lower, down the endless cascade of her neck, where he plied his teeth along the sensitive tendon, nipping his way to her collarbone.

She shivered and sighed and arched her head back, all gasping concession.

His fingers stripped away the tartan, pushing aside the lapels of her blouse, working clumsily trying to undo the short row of buttons at the throat. His hands felt awkward, as if his brain couldn't send the message to his fingertips. "Am I doing this right?"

"I've no idea." Something about his ineptitude made her smile. "No one has ever undressed me before."

"Nor I. Or if I have, I don't remember." It seemed the sort of thing a man would remember.

"We'll learn together how to go on," she assured him. And she was helping him, shrugging one arm out of her blouse, putting her smaller, more nimble fingers over his to finish the unbuttoning.

He sat back upon his knees to watch her, unsure of what to do next, cursing the fickle fancy of his brain that told him he must get her bare, but not remembering how. But he could take his own shirt off, so his skin that craved the touch of hers would be ready.

He tugged the linen over his head, nearly ripping the strained seams in his haste, eager to return his lips to hers for another intoxicating kiss. He couldn't seem to order his thoughts enough to effectively disrobe either of them, but it didn't matter—as long as she welcomed him into her arms he was happy.

Her bonnie eyes were closed, but she was smiling, that soft secret smile he loved, so he kissed her there, along the curving seam of her lips. He angled his head to get closer, and kiss deeper. He was glad he was with her, and no other— glad he could not remember, or even imagine being with another. "Greer."

She sighed into him and all her sleek, strong, self-suffi- cient edges softened. She took his lip between hers, nipping and sucking lightly, learning the way of him until she grew bolder and closed her mouth around his, and took his tongue with hers.

His need became like a current running down the burn, tumbling over itself.

He speared his big hand into her hair, cradling her head so he could kiss her more deeply, pulling her into him as if he could absorb her essence, her very being.

She spoke, calling his name in little gasping pants of astonishment. "Ewan," she said with every kiss, as if she were trying to convince herself that he was real.

"Aye, my Greer." They were both alive and together at last, and there was nothing to stop them.

Nothing but several layers of useless clothing.

And he wanted them off. He wanted her to himself, completely and irrevocably. He wanted to taste her everywhere. He wanted to touch her everywhere. He wanted to see her everywhere. To leave no part of the wonder of her undiscovered or hidden.

He went at her stays with every last shred of his concentration, following the long laces wound around her waistband. "How?" was all he could manage from a tongue that felt thick with stupidity.

"Here." She turned and lay her hand over her shoulder to show him where the laces were tied in an efficient bow.

He wanted to rip them out—to pull the dirk Dewar had given him from his boot and slice the confounded things away until the stays fell to the floor and he could peel the shift away with his hands. But he didn't—he fished and fumbled with his fingers until he found the salient bit of the lacing and could slowly, painstakingly pull out the ribbons until the boned canvas stays fell away and she was clad only in her in the nearly transparent cutty sark the poems had conjured for him.

Her bared shoulders were washed pale in the moonlight, and she was the loveliest thing he had ever seen. Lovelier than light and sky and heather. As lovely as life itself.

She held the shift in place in front of her, not as if she were shielding herself, but as if she were waiting. Gathering her courage and herself into readiness.

Or mayhap waiting until he was ready.

By God and St. Andrew he was ready. He shoved his rough leather breeks to the floor to show her he was ready willing and able—his ruddy manhood stood out crude and proud.

"Oh," she said, in a tone he couldn't quite understand. Her pale cheeks shone pink in the silver wash of moonlight.

He didn't know whether he was meant to be abashed or amazed.

"Just kiss me again," was what she said. "Please, kiss—"

He obliged her. He kissed her with all the howling want and fear and rage that seethed like a caldron within at the very thought of her being shot at, or God forbid, hit. Kissed her with all the ardor of all the words he hadn't been able to say piled up in his head like a dam that was finally breaking. Kissed her because she was important and bonnie and precious, and he wanted more than anything for her to be his. To make her his.

He wanted to kiss her and kiss her until he fell off the heathered peak at the top of the world. Until he could not think or worry and had only to feel—to feel the incredible vibrancy of her body, and experience the more incredible pleasure brewing within. Until that wasn't enough, and he wanted more.

He wanted to see her. "Let me—" The words got all tangled up in his brain before they could make their way to his tongue. "I want—"

But it was easier to show her than to tell her. "Please," was the only word he needed to brush the gauzy linen shift from her shoulders to reveal the gloriously apricot-tinted peaks of her breasts.

He could only look at her, and marvel at the earthy perfection of her, this woman who had seen his need and pulled him back to life, to living.

The architecture of her bones was as beautifully perfect and natural as any sight in nature—glorious, colorful, and bonnie. He looked and looked at her, drowning in his wonder, until she grew shy under his gaze and reached to cover herself.

"No, please. Don't." He had to see her, mark this moment in his too-often clouded brain. To know that she was a gift to him. That he needed to give of himself in return.

He did so by taking her hands and spreading them wide, so he could see all of her. Her breasts were bonnie, her skin gleaming pale and silvered in the moonlight shivering through the window, washing across the cot long enough for the image to etch itself indelibly into his brain. Her nipples were the exact color of the wild campion flowers on the hillsides. And the exact same color as her lovely lips.

He began to kiss his way toward them—those lips as soft and ripe as a summer bloom. He kissed first the back of one hand, and then the pulse at the inside of her wrist on the other, working his way from side to side, from the sensitive joint of her elbow, to the exquisite hollow beneath her collarbone, until she tipped her head to the side, granting him unlimited access to the treasure of her body.

He kissed the soft, scented underside of her breast, and nuzzled his cheek along its sensitive peak, and only when she arched her back, raising herself up to him in silent plea, did he take the tight wildflower bud of her nipple into his mouth and suck lightly at her breast.

She made a sound of deep pleasure, like the warm wind

through the glen, that sighed through her and into him. He touched her again, learning the way of her, finding the way to her pleasure. And she helped, this clever, curious, courageous woman—her hands were in his hair, cradling his head, holding and directing him to the exactness of her want.

He returned briefly to kiss her mouth, the taste of her like the tang of strong Scots whisky—potent and intoxicating. Her felt drunk on her, on the wild abandon brewing up in his veins. And he wanted more. It was not nearly enough to see only her breasts—he needed to see all of her. He wanted to see the entire glory of her body.

But as he worked the shift down over the slide of her belly and the curve of her hips, he had his first glimpse of the vivid tousle of curls at the apex of her thighs. He all but froze, cleaved by need at the splendor of her body.

He must have been gaping like a dumb animal, for she was looking up at him with eyes pressed wide with concern. "Are you all to rights? Are you remembering something?"

"Nay." He didn't want to think of anything else. He didn't want to remember if he had done this before, with someone else. He wanted only now. "You're bonnie. More than bonnie —beautiful."

A rosy sweep of pleasure blossomed across her face. "And so are you. You're a braw, handsome man even if you aren't fourteen stone. Makes me wonder how much more handsome you were before."

"I don't care what I was." There was no before. There was nothing but what they could make this night together. "I only care what I am now. With you."

"Aye." She reached up to take his face between her hands, caressing his cheeks and jaw as she brought his mouth to hers.

The sound that tunneled out of his chest was something

in the space between a sigh and a groan. He felt buffle-headed. And extraordinarily alive.

And determined to get it right. For her.

For both of them.

She reached her arms around his shoulders, pulling him close, holding him tight, and kissing him. Kissing and kissing him while his body sought out the exquisite warmth within hers.

"Aye, lass. That's the way of it." She felt so bloody, bloody good, so wonderful, he couldn't think. He could only feel and want. And what he wanted was her. All of her.

He guided himself into her body, pressing himself within. Within the welcome embrace of her heat.

The rush of ecstasy felt so sharp and so raw he couldn't breathe, and he didn't need to. He didn't need anything but his lass, and the fiercely beautiful friction of her body, ever again.

Lord Ewan Cameron
St. Salvador's College
St. Andrew's, Fife

2 December, 1790

Dearest Ewan,

Your suggestion of travel has at last fallen on sympathetic ears! Papa declares that I am old enough and thinks it a very sound idea for us to travel to Paris in the spring. In fact, now that the idea has sprouted in his brain, he begins to expand the plan, and talk of taking me on to Italy as well, so I might have the benefit of studying the masters of art and architecture in person, to be a properly cultured duchess. And I must admit, the idea has found great favor with me as well. In fact, such favor that I am pressing that such travel be attempted now, before you are done with your studies. After all, I have said to him on every occasion I might, we are not getting any younger!

Your devoted friend, GD

Lord Ewan Cameron
St. Salvador's College
St. Andrew's, Fife

20 January, 1791

Dearest Ewan,

I have won the battle and hope to take the whole of the war! Papa is at last convinced in favor of travel, and we leave for an extended tour of the Continent, staying with such friends as he has made throughout his many years of foreign correspondence with other landowners concerned with animal husbandry and agricultural improvement. We begin with the long sail to Italy, stopping at Malta for some few weeks, and then on to Leghorn, or Livorno, as I'm sure you would properly call it. We shall see all the sights of Italy, but none of France, for Papa thinks the politics there too radical for safe passage. Papa assures me there are treasures and sights aplenty to be seen on the Continent outside of Paris. Still, I long to be in the city of your residence and walk its streets and parks in your footsteps.

I pack all my correspondence with me in the cleverest writing desk imaginable, so I might have the benefit of all your letters whilst I am away. I like to have them with me always, since I cannot have you.

I hope I am a good traveler on the longer sail to Italy (longer than the trip to the Northern Isles), or I shall never be able to complain after all my nagging poor Papa! If I am, I shall only tell you, who will understand my agonies. But, oh, I hope it isn't so, and that I might find the world just as I want it. You, I know are just as I want. And so I remain, always,

Your devoted traveling friend, G

CHAPTER 24

GREER CLOSED her eyes tight to hold back the cathartic heat behind her lids, and to shut out anything that wasn't the sublime feel of Ewan with her. Her world narrowed to the physical—to the strange and powerful sensations stirring within her body. She wanted to forget everything else—the danger, the fear and sorrow—and keep only this fierce joy.

This was what she wanted—this blissful joining. This becoming one.

She wanted to let the rest of the world go on without her, while she made something for herself with the man she loved —the man she had always loved. She wanted to give in to the heat and weight of him, poised above her. To the pleasure she knew lay just out of reach, waiting, beckoning her forward. Toward bliss.

She was no stranger to the ardor she knew could be made in her own body—she was two and twenty and not some child who had never explored her body's own potential to give pleasure. But while the pleasure was not new, the possession of his body—his heat and scent and strength surrounding her—was.

Hot, salty tears slipped from the corner of her eyes—tears of relief and release. The long years of waiting, the lonely nights of grieving were over. She could let the past go and concentrate on the future. Concentrate on making the pleasure grow into something more. More daring, more passionate.

She could hear her love's agitated breathing meld with her own, and all but feel the pleasure and excitement coursing through his veins. "Ewan," she said, because she had always wanted to say his name like this, in the breathy soft quiet of the night. She had dreamt of such a moment in the long years that had gone before.

She cupped her hand at the back of his skull—his dear precious fragile, hard head—to pull him down for another kiss. To rekindle the delicious hunger that had taken her this far.

She kissed him again, lightly tracing the indentations of his dimples with her tongue before she followed the angled line of his jaw up to his ear. "With my body I thee worship."

The words came unbidden, but now that she had spoken them, she understood herself—this was what she had wanted, this close intimacy, this physical manifestation of care and kindness.

Her heart was weighted with something deeper and more profound in the midst of physical bliss—a heart-wrenching, bittersweet sort of peace. This was the wedding night they should have had.

This was the sacred joining they had both long desired.

But they were both different people now. His ordeal was etched upon his body—in the taut line of his jaw, in the broken crook of his nose, but he was resilient. He had somehow absorbed the worst and come out so whole, he was a miracle.

It was a miracle that he was alive. A miracle that after everything—all the machinations, all the loss—he was still hers.

And, oh, sweet heavens, but he was a braw lad. His arms and torso were honed, as if everything but the essential man had been stripped away. His skin was tanned down to his waist, where the skin turned paler again. His chest was very lightly sprinkled with hair, as golden blond as his head. It glinted in the firelight, leading her eyes down, where the hair trailed lower to where they were joined in a fierce, joyous embrace.

She could feel heat flush up her neck and across her face. And lower, where the hot pulse of bliss stirred restively.

He didn't seem to mind her curiosity. He just looked back at her with that steady, contented smile. "It's only us, lass. Do as you please."

She ran her hands down his smooth chest and then lower, seeking his sex where it joined hers, to find the round weight of his stones.

"Oh, God, lass, aye," he bit off, the words deep and guttural with gratification.

He kissed her more deeply as her hand settled firmly about him, hungrily delving into her mouth with his tongue, until she felt the urgent press of his pelvis against hers, and he pushed her legs wider with his hands.

"Easy, lass. Handsomely now," he whispered into her ear. "Let us make haste slowly."

Her heart all but burst within her chest. Nothing he could have said or done—no stroke of his hand across her flesh could have touched her as deeply as those five words. This was her Ewan.

And so they did make haste very slowly indeed—for a

while. Until the slippery sensations of urgency began to slide under her skin, leaving her tingling with need for something more.

Her hands fisted in the rough wool of the plaid, and in response he covered her hands with his own, and smiled down at her, rubbing his nose against her cheeks, and kissing every part of her face. "Hold fast, lass."

He lowered his head to her breast and took her nipple into his mouth in a way that made her release her hold on the blanket and cradle his head to her chest. In a way that made her body move under his. Made her arch her breasts up to him in supplication.

"Aye, lass," he whispered against her wet skin, and it felt to wonderful, so glorious that she thought to do the same for him, running the flat of her palm across his chest until she could rub the nubs of his flat male nipples between her fingers.

He arched back, and his hands replaced his mouth at her breast, and Greer pulled his mouth back to hers, kissing him back, sliding her tongue with his, wondering at the taste, the smell, the feel of him around her.

Her body began to move of its own accord, her hips rising rhythmically beneath his. He pressed up higher on his arms, taking his weight off her, and flexed his hip muscles against her.

Oh, gracious heavens. It was bliss.

"Ewan." She breathed his name because he was everything she wanted everything she felt for him.

"Aye, Greer, that's it, lass."

She moved more purposefully in response, arching her pelvis toward him, and he nudged his hips against her again, and lowered his head to her breast, suckling her in time with the pulse of his body surging into hers. Greer closed her eyes and concentrated on the rhythm, and the wonderful, powerful sensations sliding to and fro under her sensitized skin. Her palms tingled with the need to touch him, to worship his body with the same abandon he was worshiping hers.

She ran her hands up the living sculpture of his sleek, taut arms, kneading the sinuous muscles there, before riding upward around his neck, over his shoulders, and down onto the lean line of his chest

He made an inarticulate sound nearer to pleasure than pain.

Greer opened her eyes to see him rising above her, his teeth gritted and bared in something too much like anguish. "Ewan?" She whispered her question.

"Keep on, lass."

"This?" She ran her hands across his chest again, slower this time, her fingers tracing over his nipples in imitation of the way he had touched hers.

"Aye. Like that." He rose higher upon his knees, pulling her tight against him before he let go of her hips, and molded his hands to cup her breasts. He flicked the tight rosy peaks with his callused thumbs.

A sound she did not know she could make—of carnal encouragement and need broke from her mouth on a cry. Her eyes crashed shut as she felt the first wave of pleasure push deep into her belly.

Ewan ran his hands down over her hips and around to her bottom. He traced the curve of the taut globes with his clever hands, cupping her flesh to draw her closer still. She opened her eyes to watch his hands round to her hips and pull her up high against him. She felt a jolt of such intense, joyous pleasure streak through her, and something inside, some last vestige of restraint came untethered and ran riot— a heady, insistent, intoxicating rush of bliss that rose higher still with each escalating thrust. His body surged into her, stronger and stronger, feeding the need, stoking the fiery heat that built where their bodies touched.

Greer felt herself slipping away, losing herself to the inexorable whirl of sensations. She clutched at his hips, his shoulders, his neck—anything to anchor herself against the relentless tide of pressure and pleasure.

Oh, she wanted. She wanted, she wanted.

She planted her feet flat against the blanket and angled her body higher, trying desperately to appease the persistent, insistent need. But then Ewan drove the breath from her lungs with the simple efficacy of lifting her legs flat against his chest.

The sharp, aching pleasure bolted back through her. She heard a high keening moan and knew it came from her, that it was a sound of approval as much as distress, because it felt so good—too good, a pleasure so intense it was almost pain.

But Ewan was relentless. He leaned into the strength of her legs and she watched him, moving above her with such strength and beauty that her heart constricted. She felt him, apart from her and yet in her all at the same time, and she knew in that instant what it meant to be undone—to let go of every last tie to reality and give way to the glorious physical wash of upending emotion that shot through her.

She closed her eyes and felt him stroke his hand down her belly, into the thatch of curls shielding the place where they were joined. He teased his fingers through the hair, then slipped his fingers lower, ever so slightly lower, to the sensitive, engorged flesh below.

Greer cried out and bucked up hard. It was too much and not enough all at the same time. He pulled her back against him, holding her hips still against him as he surged inside her. He held her just so, so that something changed and sharpened, and it felt good, so good. She felt like she was going to break into a hundred pieces of bliss.

And then she did.

Heat and joy and peace and relief cascaded through her body in rushing, tumbling waves, leaving the glorious serene warmth behind. And then, in the next second, it was he who tensed, and with a sound that was both joy and anguish, pushed himself into her, one last time.

Greer felt strange and weightless, as if she couldn't feel the blanket beneath her, as if all the feeling had drained from her body, leaving her pleasantly, gloriously numb. She watched with a sort of detached amusement as Ewan let go of her and sat back on his heels, slipping away from her body, and then collapsed by her side. He looked as dazed and disoriented as she felt.

The two of them were gasping for air as if they'd run up the moorside, winded and spent. She felt her mouth curve into a broad smile, heard the puff of laughter that blew across her lips. "Well, that was worth the wait."

"Patience is its own reward." She heard the wicked amusement in his voice as he slipped his arm around her waist and pulled her snugly against his chest. "My sweet lass," he whispered against her hair.

Greer smiled in wonder at the strange scratchy feeling of his chest against her back and closed her eyes in contentment. She felt so happy, so safe in his arms that she wanted to stay and savor the moment for just a while longer. She took a deep breath and felt his breathing slip into the shallow regularity that signaled he was already asleep.

She curled herself tight against him, and stayed awake for a long time, listening and feeling and thinking of the wonderful strangeness of the heat and scent and texture of the man surrounding her. It was overwhelming and yet perfectly right, knowing that this night was the start of the rest of her life with him.

She slept, and woke at dawn to find herself alone, but bundled in blankets.

"Ewan?" She stretched herself awake.

"I'm here, lass." He was coming in the door with more fuel for the fire.

"Of course you are, sweet man." She covered herself with the blanket and reached for her now-dry clothes from where he must have hung them before the fire, while he busied himself with stacking the wood. "And I think it best that we go immediately to Dalshee—your friends should still be there."

"Friends?"

"Alasdair Colquhoun, whom we spoke of before, and Archie Carrington. They will be most anxious to see you—they came to Dalshee in concern when they heard about your death."

"Oh, aye." His smile turned rueful. "Good thing I'm not dead."

"A very good thing." She laughed. "It's made things ever so much nicer for me."

"Aye. For me, too, lass." But the warmth was leeching from his smile. "I'll be glad to set them straight that their assumption was wrong."

"It wasn't just an assumption, Ewan." He had to understand the level of malice that stood against him. "Your cousin held your funeral. It was awful."

He scrubbed his hands through his hair as if his head pained him. "Devil put me in hell," he muttered. "I knew someone tried to kill me, and I understood I needed to stay hidden for my own protection, but I didn't know anyone thought me dead and buried."

"Oh, yes. I don't suppose it occurred to me to tell you, you were dead." She tried to joke, to return them to their cozy happiness, but it really wasn't even remotely funny. "But then again, I wasn't sure who you were when I first met you on the moor."

"I'm Crieff. I understand that now."

"Aye." She was so grateful to have him back. "My Ewan—fifth Duke of Crieff, sixth Earl Beinnàigh, and a host of other lesser titles and honors that I had once memorized but have thankfully forgotten."

"Aye. I went there, to Crieff, this morning," he told her. "I went there to find my horse—to get Cat Sìth, that the ostler told us about. He's here—Cat Sìth, not the ostler—in the lean-to out back."

"Oh, gracious. Your cousin won't like that." Perhaps the search to reclaim such a valuable horse was what had spurred Cameron and Gow's search of the glens—even if Malcolm couldn't ride him, the stallion was a valuable asset he could sell. "I'm glad you've got him safe."

"I rode to that Inn at the Bridge of Shee," Ewan went on. "And I recognized it, the bridge. It brought back new memories—images of grey stone and mortar speckled with moss. And blackness at the edge of my eyes. Water. And wanting to close my eyes against the pain of the light—which must be part of someone trying to murder me."

Greer's normally strong legs suddenly felt unsteady, as if the mountain had shifted beneath her feet. She braced herself to hear what she was sure she already knew. "Do you remember who?"

"Nay. If I remembered that, I wouldn't be hiding up here in the hills, would I?"

"Nay, I suppose not," she agreed. "Can you remember anything else of your assault? Anything at all?"

He closed his eyes as if the very act of remembering made his head ache, but he swallowed and spoke. "It's like everything else—it comes in bits and pieces. In snatches of memory that come and then go before I can recognize what they are and what they mean. When I went to Crieff I remembered it—the castle and growing up there. My grandfather. Eating in the long dining room, when he had guests to stay, listening to them talk. Listening to him tell me what it meant to be Crieff."

"I'm glad you remember him—he was a grand gentleman. He came to Dalshee once, for dinner, and spoke to me very kindly as if he really were interested in whatever a ten-and-seven-year-old lass had to say."

Ewan smiled at the characterization. "I remember dinners with him like that, too. Just the two of us, which was different from what I was used to."

"From traveling with your friends?"

"Aye." He narrowed his eyes, as if that helped him see the past more clearly. "Alasdair, Archie and…Rory, in a wretchedly ill-built set of rooms in…Spain, I think."

"Italy." Greer could only marvel at the swiftness of the returning memories, and pray they continued. "Rome—on the Piazza di Spagna, number seventy-four."

"Oh, aye?" But the pleasure lighting his face was not of remembrance—it was discovery. "Fancy you knowing that."

Something about his tone—the offhand amusement—chilled her. Doubt crept up her spine like a spider. "But I wrote you there."

"Did you?" He frowned and shook his head, again, as if he could not think of why any letter might be important. "I don't remember that."

Doubt was replaced with dread. "Aye, I did. I wrote often. Many letters over the years."

"Really? I don't recall at all. But we were betrothed, were we not? You are the heiress of Dalshee, or is there some other flame-haired lass I've lately fallen in love with?"

"Lately?" Her fear made her voice shake. "Aye. I *am* Dalshee, the same way you're Crieff."

"Aye, I see that now."

Seeing was not the same thing as remembering. "We were in love. Before. We were to marry because we were in love."

The look on his face told her everything the words he did not say did not—he had no idea. He did not remember. He had no recollection of her.

The thought was sickening—scorching heat tightened her throat. "Oh, dear God. You don't remember, do you? We were to be married—the two of us. *I* was the one you told the ostler about and asked him to wish you happy. We were to be married at Crieff and be happy. How could you not remember that?"

How could he have come back to her, and still not be hers? How?

Lady Greer Douglas
Dalshee House
Perthshire, Scotland

10 March, 1791

My Lady G,

I write to tell you the happy news that at the end of a month's time, my studies will be at an end. I am throwing books and bats into my trunks as fast as I may, to head home to Crieff. Though I will miss my steadfast companions who have been with me these past six years—the quadrumvirate of Alasdair, Archie, Rory and myself—I know it is time to be home and put all I have studied and learned into practice. And I will venture to say that I also look forward to your return.

But I will in the same breath pledge to you that you shall have all the time in the world that you want to finish growing up and traveling to your heart's delight. I shall not begrudge your time spent in happy travel, even if I never found it so myself.

I shall content myself in a smaller travel—up to the crest of Glas Maol, there to patiently await your return, as you so patiently awaited mine.

Ever your servant, EC

Lord Ewan Cameron
St. Salvador's College
St. Andrew's, Fife

6 April, 1791

Dear Ewan,

I am happy to report that I am a stout, and even hearty sailor. I am enchanted by every facet of the sailing from the positioning of the sails to the turning of the wheel. I am on deck as much as possible, for nothing is lovelier that the feel of the wind off the sea. I hope you don't think I write to mock you and your mal de mer! I should never forgive myself if you thought so.

Our course takes us south along the Coast of France around through the Straits of Gibraltar. Our sojourn on the 'Rock' as it is called, has been short but pleasant ~ it is the loveliest of towns with fine shops and a glorious climate. On to Malta, which was even more charming a town that Gibraltar, and which Mama liked especially, and from there to Leghorn, or as you and the locals would have it, Livorno.

We are at a very nice inn here for the few days that Papa says will take to arrange our travel onward through the country. I expect to be gone from here but will write to tell you our direction soonest. Until then, I remain,

Your intrepid Greer

CHAPTER 25

GRIEF WAS A hellish hole she kept stepping in, no matter how carefully she tried to place her feet.

"Lass." She could hear the apology in his voice as he came toward her with his arms spread wide to sweep her up into his embrace.

As if that would put everything all to rights again.

"Don't," she said, stepping away. "Please. It was foolish of me—" She closed her eyes so she wouldn't see the rumpled pallet, still warm from the heat of their bodies.

"Foolish?" It was his turn to be hurt by the cut of her words. "I thought what we did was beautiful. And I'll not regret it."

Greer knew she had spoken too rashly. "I don't want to either." Her voice was cracking from the hot pain of trying to hold her emotions in check. But it was too hard. " I thought that you knew me, the way I knew you. But you don't even *really* remember me."

"Nay," he finally admitted. "Not from before. But I remember every moment that we have spent together since we met—every help, every kindness, every kiss."

"But when the ostler told you that you were to be married, you said a man would remember something like that." Her voice cracked. *"Someone so important."*

"Lass—" His voice was full of regret, but it was not enough.

"My name is Greer." She dashed the useless tears from her eyes. "I'm not just some *lass.* I am someone so important that you *should* remember my name."

He took her rebuke like a man. "Greer, I am sorry," he apologized. "I remember your name—I will never forget it."

"But you already have."

"I'm that sorry, Greer." He spread his empty arms wide in a gesture of frustrated futility. "But I've no control over what comes back to me. I've only just discovered who I am, and I've hardly had time to reckon what in God's name I'm supposed to do about that. I've been beaten within an inch of my life and left for dead—and said to be *buried,* so there's even more mischief afoot in *that*—by people I can't remember, and I have no bloody damn idea why." He scrubbed his hand into his cropped hair, fisting up the short lengths as if he would pull the information out of his thick skull. "And if that's not also important for me to remember, I don't know what is."

She was almost too hurt to admit the right of his words. Almost.

"I know you are right." But his omission hurt all the same. And yet, loving him was a habit she could not, and would not, break. Especially not now. "If you are to remember anything more, I think it best we go to Dalshee. Your friends are there—Alasdair and Archie—and they can help you."

"You have helped me." He reached for her hand and held it, her fingers cold in his warm palm. "Every time that I am with you, I remember something more. Your presence, and your confidence, have helped me more than you know."

She didn't feel very confident now. But his sincerity soft-ened her. "I am glad to have helped. So let us see if we can do more. Let us go to Dalshee."

"Greer, lass. I know I've disappointed you—I've disap-pointed myself. I wish to hell I could remember everything—don't you think I want to?"

"Aye." She knew it wasn't his fault. But that didn't make the knowledge any less hurtful or easier to bear. "We'll just have to scrub along as things are."

"We will."

She couldn't tell if he were repeating it for her benefit or his own, but he took her hand in a gesture of affection and affinity that could not help but give her hope that even if he hadn't remembered her, he might yet.

"Come, Greer, lass. We've a long road ahead of us—and not just getting off this moorside. And Cat Sìth's been waiting all these years to make your acquaintance."

"But—" She swung back to him. "But how do you know that unless—" Unless he really did remember more.

The realization brought a quick smile to his face. "That's how it comes—fits and starts that I don't always know the meaning of. But I will, I promise. But now come, meet my wee beastie."

Wee beastie, indeed. She put out her hand for the great goliath of a horse to whuff gently at her fingers with his bonnie black velvet nose and nuzzle against her as if nudging her closer to Ewan, who took advantage of his wee beastie's assistance to lift her astride Cat Sìth's broad back.

He swung himself up directly behind her. "That's better." He tucked her snug against his chest and urged the animal on. "Tell me more about Dalshee, and who we'll meet there."

"My father and mother, the Earl and Countess of Shee. I think you may have met them before, when you were young

—when the betrothal was first being discussed between Papa and your grandfather."

"Ginger-haired, rangy fellow, your father?"

She couldn't help but smile at such a description. "Aye. Gone white now."

"Aye." He smoothed a fly-away hair out of her face. "You favor him."

"In coloring, but I'm told I also look like my mother, who is more petite."

"Oh, aye?" His agreement rumbled through his chest and down her spine. "Dark hair and an oval porcelain face?"

"That is she." How strange that he should remember her mother from years and years ago, but nothing of her and their betrothal. But life wasn't very often fair. "Though she too has some white at the temples, she's as beautiful as ever."

"Then you do take after her." He pressed a warm kiss to her temple to seal his words.

He was such a man—a good, honest, true man that she wished with all her heart that his not remembering her didn't hurt. But it did. And as much as she wished and hoped and prayed that something better—some remembrance—lay ahead of them, there was no way to be sure.

There was no way to face the future but to go to it.

They approached Dalshee House from the rear, winding down from the hills. Greer half expected her father to be out on the lawns searching for her, but they wound their way through the wilderness garden with no interference.

But now that she was home, and the idyll in the bothy was well and truly over, Greer began to get nervous—a cold lump of dread and guilt settled like day-old porridge in her belly. "I hope my father's all to rights. And the lad."

"I hope so, too," Ewan answered, but he kept his voice low, too, almost as if he felt the same sense of dread.

The enclosed stable yard was empty and quiet—Cat Sìth's

hooves echoed off the stone walls—even though a number of traveling coaches were parked nearby.

"My father's guests. That one is the Duke of—"

"—Cairn's," he finished. "Alasdair's. Aye. I've ridden in that carriage." He drew rein, but did not dismount, waiting for something—anything.

Robbie, the groom, obliged them by coming out of the stable, followed by several others. "Mileddy." He came forward but didn't take the stallion's bridle. "There was a rumor said as ye was kidnapped."

"Who would say such a thing?" Surely not Lord or Lady Cairn, or Carrington. And certainly not her parents. "I was not kidnapped—as you see." But her own trials were nothing to others'. "But how is Leslie? How does he fare?"

The question seemed to prompt the groom out of his unease. "They had the medical man up frae Crieff. 'E's still there, up the 'ouse."

"And my father?"

"Fit enough tae be out 'ere last night, pacing the yard, waiting fae ye, mileddy."

Guilt might have painted her cheeks a riddy red, but it could not compete with the relief that lightened her lungs. "Excellent. Thank you, Robbie."

By now there was a collection of people, some from Dalshee, along with others she did not know.

Ewan surveyed the little crowd before he dismounted, and then reached up to hand her down. "Robbie, see to my horse, if you please. Keep him away from the mares, if you don't care to have the stable come down upon your ears."

The lad took the reins. "Aye, sar. Laird. Yer Grace."

"I told ye." The young ghillie, Lachlan Keith, spoke up from the stable door. "Saw 'im myself, I did. Told ye he weren't a ghost. And 'ee couldn't'a stole an 'orse that were 'is own."

Ewan stopped to face them all. "Who said I stole my horse?"

The lads looked back and forth at each other, as if loath to be the one to tell.

"Lachlan?" Greer prompted.

"Just a rumor, mileddy, that Laird Ewan— Weel, they was sayin' down the village as himself's an impostor—a mad mon, ravin' up and down the glens. And stole the 'orse."

Ewan's reaction to such infamy was far more sanguine that hers. "But you know me," he suggested reasonably, looking to some of the older members of the small crowd. "I'm no impostor."

A coachman in Cairn livery stepped forward. "Aye, Yer Grace, I ken ye."

"Good man, Cowrie." Ewan's relief—and surprise at what was clearly a sudden memory—were evident as he nodded his thanks to the Cairn coachman. "How's that new bairn?"

"Growin' like a wild carrot, my lad is, Yer Grace."

"Excellent. Good to see you in good health. See my wee beastie gets some oat mash, if you please, Robbie." He flicked a fond glance at the horse. "He had to spend the night in lesser accommodations than these, and he's not overly fond of standing in the rain."

"Aye, Yer Grace." Robbie knuckled his forehead and bowed himself away.

Ewan smiled at the others, and then turned and offered Greer his arm, as if he were a brocade and velvet-clad courtier, and not a mad, bad impostor wearing second hand clothes and sleeping on the moor side. "Shall we?"

"Let's." She took his arm, and together they went into the house.

"I should have listened to you days ago," he admitted. "And come here then. But then if I did, I wouldn't have Cat Sìth."

"Nay." She hurried along, anxious to get to her mother—kidnapped indeed! Her poor mama must be beside herself with worry. "But I can't like these rumors—there seems to be some great maliciousness at work there."

"Well, I did take Cat Sìth from the stable. And if the villagers thought I was dead, seeing me ride him to the inn…" He shrugged and smiled, everything kind and reasonable in explaining people's behavior while she was bristling with judgment and suspicion.

"But this supposition that I died and was buried—I'm not dead, so who is buried in my grave?"

"Indeed. I have no notion—I never did see the body. They buried the coffin before the service. Mrs. Peddie was beside herself at the impropriety of it all." An impropriety that Malcolm Cameron swore he knew nothing about.

"Aye. Mrs. Peddie—Crieff's housekeeper. Aye, of course." He nodded as if he were matching the name to the face in his mind's eye. "But my cousin has seen to the estate in my absence? He's protected Crieff at the very least?"

"Ewan, I fear not." She touched his arm to stop him—to warn him against that dangers she was sure still lay ahead. "Your cousin has been doing all he can to sell off Crieff's unentailed assets to pay his personal debts of honor—racing losses mostly, which, according to your friend Archie, are considerable—though Malcolm has claimed the sales are retrenching due to your financial mismanagement."

"Hell mend me." Ewan drew in a long, tense breath. "So he's to blame me for…mismanaging Crieff? Stealing a horse I already own? Shooting your father, most certainly, as they used my own particular gun, and left it to be found?"

"Mileddy!" Greer's lady's maid, Morna Beale, came running toward them.

"Ah, Morna." Greer let go of Ewan's arm to peel off her gloves. "How is my father? And where is my lady mother?"

Morna bobbed a belated curtsey. "Weel, mileddy. Doctor patched 'is lordship up straight away, and yer lady mother's in the drawing room, an' that anxious fae word o' ye."

"Thank you." But her relief was only a temporary thing. "And Leslie Keith?"

"Doctor saw tae 'im first, mileddy, as 'is lordship insisted."

Of course. Dear Papa. "As he would."

"Aye, mileddy. I'm that glad to see ye, I am. They've been talkin' aboot ye somethin' fierce in the drawing room." The maid sent a half-fearful glance at Ewan. "There was rumor flyin' up an' down the glens that ye were kidnapped by a horse-thievin' mad mon."

"I suppose I ought not have taken my horse." Ewan smiled, charming the maid with quiet humor, much as he had in the stable yard. "But he is my horse, and I had need of him, and didn't have the time to tell my cousin that."

Morna's mouth opened in a little moue of astonishment. Doubtless, she would carry this fresh intelligence straight to the servants' hall for dissemination throughout the glens.

"Thank you, Morna." Greer turned the lass by the shoulders and set her off in the right direction, before she squared her shoulders. "Best to get straight to it."

To say they made a dramatic entrance was putting it mildly—there was a collective gasp, and Mama's hand went to her mouth in tense relief. Greer went immediately to her mother, who clasped her hand with nothing short of maternal devotion. "Thank the Lord you're all to rights."

"I am. And I see Papa is as well." She kissed her father's cheek. "But the boy, Leslie—how does he fare?"

"He'll live," Papa said as if he still wanted convincing. "It was not so bad as we thought—the ball passed through the shoulder, missing the collarbone. Nothing broken, no internal vessels unduly disturbed. Since then, our concern has been all for you."

"Archie and Alasdair went back and combed the glen for some sign of you," Lady Cairn supplied, "but could find none. Not even your gun. Which I told them meant you'd kept it."

"Indeed I did," Greer confirmed. "And we found the other gun, Ewan and I—the rifle that was used to shoot Leslie, though the perpetrator had long since cleared out."

The Marquess of Cairn took Ewan's hand in a tight grip. "Good work, old man."

Carrington also came forward with words of greeting and fond abuse for their dearly un-departed friend. "I knew you couldn't be dead, you thick-headed old goat."

"Good to see you too, Archie, auld man." She could hear the smile in Ewan's voice.

Arms were thrown around each other, backs thumped and introductions made.

"I'm Shee," her papa introduced himself. "It's been quite some time. And I must say it's grand to have you back my boy." He extended his hand. "Grand."

"Very good to be back, my lord," Ewan said as they shook hands. "It has been a very long time. I am glad to find you so well."

Papa beamed his pleasure. He introduced Mama, "My lady wife, Flora, Countess of Shee."

"My Lady Shee." Ewan bowed over Mama's hand. "A vast pleasure."

"Dear lad," Mama said, while she also reached for Greer's free hand and brought it to her lips to kiss in love and gratitude for her safe delivery home. "We are all together, at last."

Indeed. Almost all of the people important to Ewan were in the same room.

Only one was missing.

But if the jangling of harness and scratch of gravel on the drive was any indication, the missing miscreant was about to arrive.

A cry came from the entry hall. "I must see Lady Greer, at once!"

She must have stiffened because Ewan asked, "Who comes?"

"Your cousin, who I fear is the author of all this malice." Greer's fingers tightened on his hand. "I'm torn between wanting to hide you away from him and wanting to prove to him that you are not, in fact, dead, or an impostor, or a madman raving in the glens."

"I'm done with hiding," Ewan said. "I am among friends. Let him come. We will know the truth."

Would they? Greer herself was buffeted by contrary doubts—every time she thought she had discerned the truth, she learned something else to contradict her theories.

"Perhaps it were best," Alasdair said to Ewan, "if we stood back, to give Mr. Cameron some room to…speak. The door to the music room might provide some concealment, perhaps?"

What he mean was room for Malcolm Cameron to incriminate himself. "Oh, aye."

At her encouragement, Ewan complied, moving to the open doorway to the music room with Alasdair, as rapid footfalls echoed in the reception hall and sounded at the door of the drawing room, which was flung open by Malcolm Cameron.

"I came as soon as I heard the news that Lord Shee had been shot!" He came straight toward Greer, with his hands outstretched, as if he meant to comfort her. "Is he dead?"

"Pray do not alarm yourself so, Your Grace." Beside her, Mama was all gracious composure. "My lord is recovering, as you see."

"Indeed." Papa stepped forward into Cameron's line of vision to offer himself as evidence. "It is the young ghillie for whom we are most concerned."

"A ghillie?" Malcolm Cameron managed to look interested and baffled at the same time.

"Yes, the son of our moorkeeper, Jock Keith—a boy named Leslie," Papa clarified. "He has been seen by a reputable local man, but I've sent to both Edinburgh and Inverness for the best surgeon available to see to the lad."

"That is very good of you, I'm sure, to go to such expense." Cameron took up Greer's hand, as if you would kiss it. "My dear Lady Greer, how frightened you must have been."

"Indeed," she agreed, though she took her hand from his possession. "It is never pleasant thing to find one's father being shot at." She could barely contain her contempt for the man. "But what were you doing up on Glas Maol so close to the time of the shooting?"

"Me?" He laid his hand to his chest in that well-remembered, and perhaps well-rehearsed, show of innocence. "You must be mistaken—though it is hardly to be wondered at after your ordeal. I heard the most alarming report that you had been kidnapped—taken away on the moor."

"Not taken away," her mama insisted. "But here, safe and sound with us."

"Well, I must say." Cameron paused for breath. "Taken alongside the reports that there is a man—a mad impostor—roaming wild on Crieff land, you can see why I was doubly concerned."

"An impostor?" Greer tried hard to keep her emotions—her distrust and anger and fear—from showing in her voice. She would be as serene as a swan, even if beneath her surface was all determined paddling. "Posing as whom?"

"I hate to say, as I know it will upset you to hear, Lady Greer." Cameron was the picture of reticent concern. "He's already vandalized a bothy, broken into Crieff and stolen a long gun, as well as a valuable horse. I fear it likely that he is the man who tried to kill you."

Greer firmed her voice. "Posing as whom?" she asked again, though she already knew the answer.

"Forgive me." Cameron tried to justify himself while at the same time not answering. "I only say that because I fear for my moorkeeper as well—that old fellow Dewar. I sent him up to track this impostor—this madman saying he is my dead cousin—and now he's disappeared as well, Dewar has. I fear this madman may have murdered him as well."

"Murder is not a charge to bruit about a drawing room like gossip, Your Grace." Alasdair spoke quietly from the music room doorway. "Based on what factual evidence?"

"I'm sorry." Cameron's tone was sarcastic as he turned to this new inquisitor. "Am I now in a court of law, my lord?"

"Alas." Alasdair made the vaguest impression of a leg. "Force of habit, I'm afraid as I serve as Home Secretary for His Majesty's Government. But it is always a good thing to have one's facts straight. Wouldn't you agree, Carrington?"

"Aye." Archie raised his chin in greeting instead of lowering it, in a show of indifference to Cameron's elevated rank.

"We were all very great friends—" Alasdair began smoothly.

"Lifelong friends," Archie added.

"—of your late cousin. We were all very close."

"In each other's pockets," Quince, Lady Cairn chimed in.

"And we'd know him anywhere," Archie said.

"Even on the top of a moor," Alasdair followed, never once raising his voice.

"While getting shot at." Archie smiled like a fox—all keen eyes and keener teeth.

Oh, they were marvelous, fierce friends, these people. She envied Ewan their devotion. But then again, she shared that devotion—ten years' worth of steady adoration. Because no matter what Malcolm Cameron had tried to insinuate, Ewan *was* worthy of adoration.

Malcolm Cameron stared at the three in horrified surprise. "I don't understand your point."

"You should," Alasdair advised. "And as a magistrate and a member of His Majesty's government, I should caution you to be very careful to have evidence before you start talking murder. Someone might take you very, very seriously."

Lord Ewan Cameron
Castle Crieff
Perthshire, Scotland

28 May, 1791

Dearest Ewan,

I write from glorious Florence! We have the lease of a splendid villa in the hills overlooking the city from which to make our expeditions into both the city and the countryside. I myself am most taken with the Renaissance delights you once described to me.

The Baptistry! The Duomo! We climbed to the very top this morning to see the city laid out like a patchwork quilt, the roofs and piazzas all burnt orange and gold, beneath us. The Monastery of San Marco! The frescoes of the Annunciation! Such sublime art. Such extravagant architecture. Every day is a revelation. I exist in a constant state of wonder, astonishment and curiosity. And we have but just begun our trip! How on Earth did you survive nearly two years of such sumptuous living? Such food! Such flavors! It is as if the very air leaves me intoxicated!

I must go, for Papa and our trusty guide, a Jesuit priest who does not object to educating females about such art and architecture (although he accepted the commission, Papa tells me with a laugh, only after being told I am a 'great heiress' who will one day be a duchess), are calling me to the carriage to make our studies for the day.

I will write again soonest, but remain,

Yours always, G

CHAPTER 26

"You mistake me, my lord," Malcolm contradicted Alasdair. "I made no accusation of murder."

His cousin's voice was so familiar, memories began to stack up in Ewan's mind's eye like cordwood—Malcolm, as a child, standing in the library next to Grandfather. Malcolm walking beside him in a wood. Malcolm hailing him on the street in some city.

"But I am glad to find everyone is, thus far, unhurt," Malcolm went on. "Especially Lady Greer, who must of course be suffering from her ordeal. And being out all night. Alone."

Rage was an unfamiliar rush in Ewan's blood, but he wanted nothing more than to wrap his hands around his damn insinuating cousin's neck and choke the snide implied slur to Greer right out of his mouth. There was nothing his lass could say that would not call her character into question.

Or was his cousin angling for answers? How could he know that she had not been home with the others? Unless he had been watching?

Ewan's recollections of his cousin were becoming clearer by the moment—there had always been snide insinuations and accusations. There had always been lies and debts of honor. There had always been spying.

"Now see here," Greer's father began.

"She was not alone." Ewan stepped out from behind Alasdair. "I was with my betrothed."

Malcolm Cameron looked exactly as Ewan would have expected him to be—tall and handsome, with their grandfather's almost white-blond hair. "Malcolm." He made himself smile at his cousin. Made himself control the rage and fear seething within him. Made himself remember Malcolm was his family.

Malcolm's reaction was everything controlled, though his skin went so pale it almost matched his hair—his face lit in a perfect show of amazement, and his eyes went shiny with unshed tears. "Ewan." Malcolm looked down at the hand Ewan had stretched out as if he didn't know what to do with it. "You're alive."

"Aye." Ewan kept his own smile firmly in place, like armor. "I assure you, I'm not a ghost."

"It's a miracle," Malcolm stammered over his smile. "I don't—"

"Aye, I don't quite know what to say myself." Ewan remembered enough of his cousin not to let him direct the conversation to his advantage. His grandfather's sage advice echoed in his ears—*When he uses words as weapons, flattery is the most effective shield.* "Except thank you, for seeing to Crieff in my absence."

"Well, of course." Twin spots of color rose on Malcolm's cheeks.

"And so we may at least solve the mystery of this mad impostor." Alasdair's gaze leveled on Malcolm Cameron.

"For clearly he is no impostor, but himself, our good friend Ewan Cameron, Duke of Crieff."

All eyes were on Malcolm Cameron, but it was Ewan who spoke. "I fear this must be partly my fault, for so glad was I to see my horse, Cat Sìth, when I discovered him in the stables, that I rode him off straightaway, all the way to the Inn at the Bridge over the Shee Water." He very carefully did not mention the allegedly stolen Jäger rifle—that was a piece of the puzzle he wanted to keep hidden until he could learn more.

"Oh, then it was you?" Malcolm shook his head in chagrin. "That was my mistake then, of course. Because how —" He broke off as if his feelings prevented any further speech and seized Ewan up in a rough embrace. "How did you survive? They told us you were dead."

Ewan turned to his lass and clasped her hand. "Greer saved me." Let Malcolm see that they were united, though they were not yet wed. Let him see that she was protected.

"Lord, yes," Lord Shee rejoined before Greer could make any response. "Saved by her persistence, I should think. You were right all along, my dear," he told her. "Quite right at that."

"Then I must thank you for finding my cousin." Malcolm said to her with seeming emotion—his eyes were still glassy with unshed tears. "And returning him to Crieff. But why did you never tell me this whole time?"

"I did, actually." Greer kept her gaze level with Malcolm— the way one kept an eye on a snake. "That very first day— that awful day—when we came to Crieff for the wedding. We talked in the wood beyond the forecourt. I asked Dewar after the injured fellow that we had found, for his presence in the road seemed too much of a coincidence to me."

"Dewar?" Cameron was all curious bafflement. "But he said the lad was dead."

While Dewar's subterfuge was news to Ewan—and explained some of Greer's surprise at finding him at the bothy—it did not surprise him. Dewar was a canny, crafty auld coot—how better to make sure that Ewan was left alone to heal than to tell people he was dead.

"Yes, he did," Greer acknowledged. "But happily, he was wrong, and Ewan recovered."

"My thick skull at last came in handy," Ewan joked, mostly for Alasdair and Archie's benefit. Yet while they laughed and patted his back, unease slid down the back of his neck like a cold raindrop. "But what has happened to Dewar?" he asked his cousin. "Where is he now?"

"He is gone." Malcolm shook his head in bafflement. "Nowhere to be found. I had thought that whoever was stealing horses and making an impostor of themselves might have gotten ahold of him." He held out his hands, all open astonishment. "But since we now know it was you, not an impostor, I am more confused and concerned than ever. I sent Dewar into the hills to track whoever it was who attacked my cousin and shot at the earl, so I wonder what could have become of him? Though he did say these moorland glens were wild and dangerous—one misstep could kill a man."

"Not Dewar." Of this Ewan was confident. For a man who looked half as old as the hills, Dewar was as canny and spry as a young spaniel. The man was ageless.

"But now," Cameron went on, "it makes me wonder why Dewar should tell me my cousin was dead? Why he should want to keep Ewan apart from his family?"

"I asked him to." Ewan gave way to a small falsehood to defend Dewar, who had been nothing by loyal. "As I could not remember how I came to be injured. But you said I was attacked? How did you know that?"

"I inferred it, of course." Malcolm held out his empty

hands again, as if to show he had no cards up his sleeves. "And you look, if I may say so, not entirely yourself."

Ewan felt himself forced to more honesty than he might like in dealing with his cousin. "I did suffer a grievous injury —a brain commotion, Dewar called it. And though Dewar knew me, he feared for me. Feared what might happen to me if my murderers found out I was alive."

This admission was met by shocked silence—the Earl and Countess looked to each other, and then to their daughter, while Alasdair and Archie exchanged a worried look.

Beside Ewan, Greer gripped his hand in a clasp that would have done a gunner proud. But he was not afraid of the truth, however vulnerable it might make him seem. The real vulnerability was in not acknowledging what had happened to him. In pretending and blustering his way forward instead of making haste very slowly indeed.

"But in your injured, confused state, can you really be sure about Dewar?" Cameron put his own hand on Ewan's shoulder to ask. "If he was so concerned for you, where is he now? Why is he not with you, protecting you now?"

"I have not asked him to do so." He mirrored Malcolm's concerned smile and asked his own question. "But why should I need protection among my friends and family."

"I wonder," Malcolm suggested with a thoughtful frown. "Now that he knows you are returned to your family, I think it more likely—and a proof of his guilt—that the man has absconded."

"No." Ewan was quietly adamant. "Dewar is my man— loyal to Crieff. Loyal to his core. It cannot be."

"I agree," Greer said, before she asked Malcolm. "But why did you think that Dewar had been murdered? And that Ewan had murdered him?"

"No, no. You misunderstand and draw the wrong conclusion." Malcolm waved the suggestion aside. "I was only acting on what I knew of Dewar—that he hasn't been seen in some time."

"But you said that you sent him up onto the moor to track this mad impostor." Quince Cairn asked quietly. "Is it not safe to assume he's doing just that? Because someone did attack His Grace and shoot the earl."

Pray God that was what Dewar was doing—calmly and competently going about his own business while the rest of them wore out Dalshee's carpets with their talk.

"Well, then let me take you home, so we can find out." Cameron was all familial bonhomie. "I pray we will find him safe and sound at Crieff. But as it is, we will kill the fatted calf to have our prodigal son returned to us."

The memory came, so swift and disorienting, Ewan half-thought he must be making it up. But there was the image of his grandfather standing at his desk in the comfortable, walnut-paneled library, looking down at a pile of markers— notes that Malcolm had written to cover his debts in the belief that his grandfather would pay them.

"But I am not the prodigal," Ewan said with quiet conviction, "am I, Malcolm?"

"Of course not, of course, you misunderstand me." Malcolm was all happy, smiling confusion. "You have no idea what kind of a relief it is going to be for me to turn the reins back over to you."

"Then I am sorry that I shall have to postpone your relief." Ewan felt himself poised on a precipice—balancing between his past and his future. Balancing his suspicions and instinct against his better hopes. Against his conviction that the best way forward was to make haste slowly, methodically, with surety and proof.

And as his mind would not yet reveal either the truth or the proof, what he needed was time. "For as I said, my memory is not what it once was, or what it should be, to have the full responsibility of an estate like Crieff. Might I impose upon you to continue on as you are?"

This appeal met with stunned silence from all corners, until Alasdair said quietly, "We would have helped, old man. You had but to ask."

"I thank you, Alasdair, but you have your own responsibilities at Cairn, and in the government. And I have my family to help me." Ewan waited to see how this appeal would work on his cousin—if it would keep him at Crieff long enough for Ewan to sort through the past so he might look to the future. Malcolm was many things—greedy, in debt, and a practiced liar—but he was *family*. The ties that were bound in blood could not—ought not—be easily broken.

Malcolm took the bait. "Aye." His smile was bright with some turbulent emotion Ewan could not decipher. "I should be honored, cousin." He clasped Ewan's hand as if he would draw him along with him. "Let us go there now. My—your—carriage awaits."

Before Ewan could voice the arguments he had ready against such plan, his friends stepped firmly forward to his rescue. "But we must have you with us," Archie Carrington objected.

"So much to catch up on," Alasdair seconded.

Greer tried a softer protest. "But dearest, you promised me that we wouldn't be parted. Please," she mouthed as privately as she might with so many others around, all the while gripping his hand as if she wanted to say more. "Just stay."

"Aye. Of course," he answered immediately, before he turned to her lady mother. "If I may impose upon your hospitality, my lady."

"But of course, Your Grace. Nothing would give us more pleasure." The Countess was gracious enough to include his cousin. "And Mr. Cameron, please do join us as well. We'd be happy to have you join us at dinner."

If *Mr.* Cameron rankled after having become used to *Your Grace*, Malcolm hid it well. But then again, he always had. Ewan could hear his grandfather's baritone as if he were standing beside him in Crieff's library. "You will have to learn to be cautious of your cousin, lad, even as you help and protect him, for he lies as easily as he breathes."

"I thank you, my lady." Malcolm's manners were as smooth as a loch at sunrise. "But there is much to be done at Crieff to prepare for my cousin's return. Much to celebrate." He smiled at Ewan. "Are you sure you can stand to keep away from Crieff after so long a time—perhaps after such an early dinner, I can persuade you to return with me to Crieff."

Greer almost spoke—she opened her mouth to make some excuse—but her lady mother laid a hand upon her arm, and said in a quiet voice, "His Grace can surely speak for himself, Greer."

So he could. Ewan lifted up their joined hand and placed a kiss upon his betrothed's rather white knuckles. "I'm not going anywhere—you can let off strangling my hand now."

"Oh, gracious." She had gripped him so hard both of their hands were white. "I'm so sorry."

"Don't be," he assured her. "It felt good—mostly," he joked to relieve the tense look on her face. And on Alasdair and Archie's faces as well—clearly they wanted him to stay. For just as clearly, they did not trust his cousin.

That made four of them. But while Malcolm had always been a liar and a cheat, his cousin had never shown any tendency toward violence of the kind that had kicked in Ewan's skull and broken his ribs.

And family was *all*, Grandfather had always admonished him.

Until Ewan was sure—until the memory came fully back —he would bide his time and make no hasty accusations.

"I'll see you out," he said to his cousin. "If you're sure you can't stay."

"No, I must go," Malcolm insisted. "You know how much work must be done to keep Crieff running smoothly— enough that I shall be glad to turn it all back to you."

"All in good time. First I must solve my own murder."

And Dewar's disappearance. And ask Greer to marry him. And then he would deal with Malcolm selling off Crieff's un-entailed assets to pay his debts—surely Malcolm could not cart off the entirety of Crieff's patrimony in one evening.

Another night could not matter.

There it was—another image, sharp and clear of Malcolm standing in front of him somewhere—somewhere dark and grey and stony—perhaps the outside of Castle Crieff, perhaps somewhere else, pleading with him about something.

The image faded before Ewan could decipher its meaning or recognize anything more substantial that the feeling of being imposed upon by his cousin. But perhaps that was just a natural feeling for him, who had felt imposed upon and disconnected from his true self for the better part of the last month. "I'll see you out."

As if they were all loath to let Ewan out of their sights, Greer, Alasdair, Quince and Archie all accompanied him to the entrance hall, where his cousin took his reluctant leave.

"Are you sure I can't convince you to come back to Crieff now?" Malcolm asked one last time. "I should—"

"Not a chance," Alasdair said jovially, but Ewan heard the steely finality in his voice. Clearly his friend had his reasons.

"Until tomorrow," Ewan told his cousin. Tomorrow was soon enough.

"Well," Alasdair said, clapping Ewan on the back as the

coach wheeled out of sight. "I thought the soaker would never leave."

And there it was, another memory, as clear as if it were yesterday. "That's what we called him." It was more of a question than a statement, but Alasdair and Archie seemed not to mind—they looked at him with what he could only call fondness.

"Aye. Always touching you for one debt or another," Alasdair claimed.

"You were the soul of patience with him," Archie added. "I'd have sent him away with a flea in his ear ages ago."

It was deeply heartening to hear his friends' good opinion of him—it made Ewan feel at home, even if he wasn't at Crieff.

He turned to the Countess. "My lady, if I may be allowed the hospitality of Dalshee, I should very much like a chance to make myself presentable before dinner."

"But of course," Lady Shee answered. "Greer, why don't you show His Grace up?"

"Of course." Greer led them toward the stair.

"If my wife will forgive me—" Alasdair began.

"Of course—" Lady Cairn rejoined. "I've forgiven worse."

"Excellent spouse." Alasdair kissed his wife's hand and turned to Ewan. "Come, let us repair with you to your chamber and see if we can make you into a gentleman. Shall we, Archie?"

"Have we got baling wire and a scythe handy?" Archie joked.

"I put myself in your more than capable hands," Ewan returned. "As long as you don't start drinking."

"Too late, my friend. Too late."

They went up the stairs in companionable bonhomie. It wasn't home, but damn, it felt good to be back.

Lord Ewan Cameron
Castle Crieff
Perthshire
Scotland

1 June, 1791

Dearest Ewan,

Rome! My delight knows no bounds, but Rome, the Eternal City, gives me more pleasure from having had you in it before I came. I fancy I can see your likeness in the students clamoring down the narrow streets surrounding the Piazza de Spagna. I love it all, from the cobbles to the plazas with their gorgeous fountains. We are fortunate to be the guest of my father's friend, the Conte d'Aguirre here as well, in the old part of the city, the Pincian Hill. But I am sure you, who know Rome far better than I, know this. I must say, I grew up thinking Dalshee a fine, bonnie house, but it is nothing on the Baroque exuberance that is the Villa Aguirre. Mama and Papa are more reserved in their praise, for Mama says exuberance has its place, and restraint is the harder art.

Papa says something entirely different apropos our travels ~ that he no longer wishes us to visit France at all, for the great unrest brewing amongst the people and what he calls the agitating classes is growing ever more fractious. Accordingly, we will travel south to Naples and the wonders of the buried city of Pompeii before jour-neying on from Rome north to the lakes, and from thence to Venice before traversing the Alps to Geneva in Switzerland, and then on to Salzburg in Austria. Though I am vastly disappointed not to visit Paris and see the city for myself, I content myself that I have already seen its beauty through your eyes. And I suspect that I will spend the majority of the coming days as I am this moment ~ goggle-eyed with all the wonders there are to see.

But though I am grown more worldly, I still keep all my kisses safe for you, and remain as ever,

Your devoted G

GREER COULD BARELY stand to let him out of her sight—her hand felt empty without his to hold. But *some* proprieties had to be observed under her parents' roof. She made use of their time apart, dressing with more care than had been her want of late, for it was not every day that Dalshee played host to a fashionable marquess and marchioness, as well as a lost duke—a duke she wanted desperately to impress.

She chose her favorite redingote-style gown of cherry-red, embroidered striped silk she had purchased in Italy, in the hopes that it would help her feel worldly. As if a dress might help a duke with a faulty memory somehow remember her.

But the moment he came down the stairs, she knew all her efforts to impress him had been for naught. Because he was nothing short of magnificent.

This man could never have been taken for a ghillie—he was tall and imposing and everything aristocratic and gentlemanly. Alasdair or Archie must have loaned him a fine suit of clothes, and he had shaved off the scraggly beard. The clean line of his jaw and high cheekbones were enough to make her gape at him like a shopgirl.

Her cheeks went hot with some awful mixture of attraction and trepidation.

"You *are* beautiful," Mama, bless her perceptive heart, murmured, much as she had the first time Greer had been about to meet Ewan.

Her words made Greer feel less ordinary, less sharp-jawed and flame-haired, and reminded her that she was deeply loved. So loved that Mama had seated her on the opposite side of the table from Ewan, so she could look her fill without being rude.

"To Crieff and Dalshee," Papa toasted. "Long may they prosper in harmony."

"Hear, hear."

They tucked into the *filet de boeuf en croûte*—for Greer was not the only one to bring worldly things back to Crieff from their travels—before Ewan addressed her father. "Speaking of the special relationship between Dalshee and Crieff—if I may be so bold, sir, I should like to know more about the circumstances of the betrothal. My memory is spotty and incomplete at best. Alasdair and Archie have been kind enough to help me with remembrances of some of our times together—"

"Many years' worth," Archie interjected. "Though not much of that is respectable enough for dinner conversation."

"Thank you for your discretion," Mama demurred.

"Aye," Ewan agreed politely. "But I should like a better understanding of something so important to me. And to Greer." He met her eyes across the table, and she felt her breath tighten in gratitude—he wasn't perfect, but he was hopefully hers. "The contract was of long standing?"

"Aye, twelve years." Papa took a sip of claret before he answered. "When it became apparent that Lady Shee and I would have no male heir, I naturally sought to secure the future of both Dalshee and my dear daughter. I approached the late duke, your grandfather, as I esteemed his counsel. It was he who suggested you as a possible bridegroom. With your father's early death—God rest him—your grandfather was as concerned for the future as I."

This was history that Greer knew by heart, having asked question after question of her parents when the idea was first presented to her so many years ago, but it was mortifying to think that the others would soon discover what she already knew—that Ewan remembered nothing of the betrothal. Or her.

"And so you betrothed us?" Ewan prompted.

"Not straightaway," Papa collected. "There was the question of character, and you young people's feelings to consider. We wanted to act prudently—we wanted, as your late grandfather used to say, to make haste—"

"—slowly," a chorus from around the table rejoined with her.

"He used to adjure me with that all the time," said Ewan with a fond smile.

"And so did you adjure us," Alasdair reminded him.

"And me," Greer added thinking of their correspondence, before the vivid recollection of his whisper in the dark of last night sent a wave of mortified heat streaking up her neck. "In your letters."

Ewan's gaze found hers across the table, which sent another flash of unhelpful heat scorching her cheeks and tingling under her skin at the very thought that he was thinking of their tryst in the bothy, too.

Her father, thankfully, took no notice. "We thought it best to formulate a plan of education to make you fit for each other, to make sure that the qualities needed for each of you to become a duke and duchess were not lacking. To form you for the future, and for each other."

Greer had heard this talk, but it struck her for the first time that despite such guidance, and formation, their affinity for one another had been wholly their own creation—she and Ewan had chosen of their own accord to trust, confide and support each other. To suppose otherwise would be dismissive of her own free will.

A free will she wanted to exercise now—the past could not be changed, but the future could. "Perhaps we might also turn our well-formed ducal characteristics"—she cleared her throat to keep her voice from betraying her feelings, or her desperate sense of urgency—"to the more immediate problem of who it was that tried to murder both you and Ewan, Papa? And who is buried in Ewan's grave? And what has become of Dewar? And why Malcolm Cameron is such a skillful liar?"

"Greer—" Her mother was aghast.

"Nay," she answered. She was done with politeness and manners for manners' sake—someone, who was still out there in the world, waiting, had tried to kill both her most beloved friend and now her father. She'd be damned if she would sit idly by out of politeness.

"I know it is unladylike in the extreme, and that I have no proof of my assertions, and that one is supposed to give others the benefit of the doubt. But I have been *formed* to think for myself, and *I* think that the situation is dangerous. And I think Malcolm Cameron is dangerous. And I think that, at the very least, word ought to be sent to Crieff to make sure that Malcolm Cameron is not crating up and shipping off everything and anything he can haul off to sell!"

"Hear, hear," Quince said. "We have reason to believe his debts are so considerable—"

"He won't go." Ewan's voice was low but carried like a

shout. "It would be best—easier, at least—if he did just disappear. But greed will keep him—he will stay because he thinks he can get more money yet out of Crieff. He will stay because he likes having his way. And he will stay because he cannot resist the temptation that I might not be fit to lead Crieff."

"Ewan?" Alasdair asked carefully. "Did you purposefully lie, and tell him you couldn't remember enough to have the responsibility of Crieff, so he would believe he could continue to take advantage?"

"I might have done, though it wasn't entirely a lie. My ability, or lack thereof, is a real concern for Crieff."

Greer's heartbeat leveled out to a less lively throttle. "But you understand and admit that Cameron is dangerous?" she asked to bring the discussion back to the important issues.

Ewan wouldn't agree. "Mostly to himself."

"Ewan, please don't be 'too kind' or too noble now," she begged. "Not when you might embolden him to try to kill you again again—he's already tried to shoot Papa."

Her father pushed back from the table in alarm. "As the marquess said, Greer, I should be very careful if I were you, to have evidence before you start talking murder. Someone might take you seriously."

"The gun came from Crieff, Papa." Greer laid out her evidence. "It was Ewan's particular deer rifle—"

"That Jäger from Hanover," Ewan confirmed with a glance at Alasdair.

"Ah."

"—left there for us to find to implicate either Ewan, himself, or this 'imposter,' I suppose, even though that doesn't make much sense." She closed her eyes for a moment to force herself to concentrate and reason it out. "It's almost as if he's... As if Cameron is lying as he goes along—and making accusations as he goes." She was thinking out loud now, but the ideas were coming too fast to stop and think through. "Accusing others of the things that have happened before he might be accused. Accusing Alasdair and Archie of getting Ewan into trouble and being responsible for his death. And then accusing them of burying the body improperly. Accusing Ewan of racking up debt. Accusing the mad imposter of poaching and reeving and shooting Papa. And then accusing Dewar of the same, the moment Ewan was proved to be alive."

Papa sat down abruptly, as if his legs had gone from under him. "Good Lord. My own neighbor shot me?"

"Nay," Ewan disagreed. "That will be Gow, I reckon, who shot at you. He was a military man, I begin to recollect for some reason, well versed with firearms, while Malcolm's shooting and stalking skills always left a great deal to be desired—he doesn't like the moorland. Doesn't like the damp and dirt. Prefers the pavements of London, though a damper and dirtier place I've yet to find."

"Cameron can still get up to a great load of mischief in the clean, dry castle," Greer insisted. "He's dismissed staff and sold some of your paintings in order to pay his debts, as well as trying to sell the barley fields by the loch." Greer ticked the charges off on her fingers.

"He can't sell those fields." Ewan looked baffled. "We'll have no malt to make whisky."

"Ah." Alasdair's tone was as dry as his wit. "You've not forgot Crieff's distillery."

Ewan smiled even as he frowned. "Impossible to forget, I'm glad to find. And far superior to yours. But all the arable land is entailed to the estate. He simply can't sell." But Ewan put his hand to his head, as if all the thoughts and accusations were making it ache.

Alasdair took a long look at his friend, as if he were weighing his next words very carefully. "As much as it may pain you, Ewan, I think the two things—your attempted murder, and his debts—must be inexorably related. You must consider that Malcolm Cameron had the most to gain from your death—his preservation against insolvency."

Ewan put his hand down, and sat back, but his face was carefully, almost unnaturally blank. "Why would I not just give it to him? Do I not have the money?"

Alasdair considered this. "Given your generous nature, and the fact that you have done so—paid off his debts—before, I cannot say. But his debts are enormous."

Ewan still shook his head, like a dog with a bone. "But before I can accuse him of anything beyond imprudence, I have to remember what happened." He closed his eyes. "But I can't remember. I've tried—"

"Can't?" Alasdair's voice was quiet, but as insistent and unbending as steel. "Or won't? Because it is too horrific to think of such a betrayal?"

Ewan's head went back as if he had been struck. "He is my cousin. My family."

"He is," Alasdair confirmed. "But your cousin is also lying, not for the first time. Think back on your youth, Ewan. We— Archie and I—have often heard you speak of the difficulties and problems you had with your cousin."

"Did I?" Ewan admitted. "But we were no choirboys, either, we four. And murder is…" He trailed off, unable, or unwilling to complete the thoughts. "Lying is wrong, but it is not murder."

It was too much for Greer. "So we are to do nothing but wait? Wait until someone else is shot at or turns up dead? Wait until we find Dewar, who—because Cameron just accused him of being the shooter—is likely to be the next one found bleeding to death on the moorside?"

The silence was nearly deafening. No one else moved— Papa stopped with his wine stem half-way to his mouth. No one else spoke—though their eyes shifted from one to the other. All looked at Ewan. Because only he could really answer.

"Aye," Ewan finally decided. "We wait. And hope that he goes."

Greer's disappointment turned the food bitter in her mouth. "And hope you haven't signed Dewar's death warrant. Or your own when he's out of money and comes back to try to murder you again."

"Greer," Mama's caution was cutting. "That is quite enough. Listen to yourself."

"I have." Greer refused to apologize—she was *done* with polite caution. "I wish someone else would. What do you think would have happened to me, if I had succumbed to his flattery and blandishments, and married him? Once he had hold of Dalshee's monies? Do you think we would have scrubbed along in perfect harmony? Or do you think I would have ended up dead in a glen, or on Glas Maol, from an errant poacher's shot?"

"We do have one thing in our favor," Quince asserted into the tense quiet. "We have the consolation of knowing he's really not very good at it—murder—is he? Ewan is not dead, and neither is your father. So there is hope for Dewar."

"And Dewar is a canny, crafty auld soul who will see Malcolm coming for miles," Ewan swore.

"So we leave Malcolm to wreak his havoc on the rest of the estate and its people, until you can remember enough to say one way or another?" She had to say it—though the words were like hot ash on her tongue, it had to be said. "What if you never remember? What if your mind doesn't recover because the wound and the hurt are too deep?"

Another heavy silence descended.

Ewan ran his hand through his hair, and then abruptly stood. And reached for her hand.

"I want to talk to Greer. Alone."

Greer did not look to her mother for permission—she was done with accepted modes of ladylike behavior when so much was at stake. She took the hand Ewan offered, and led him to the only place she was assured of being left alone for as long as necessary–her private sitting room adjacent to her bed chamber.

She locked the door behind them and tried to be patient as he silently prowled around the room looking and thinking, clearly trying to either remember or make up his mind about something.

He came to stand before one of the windows facing west over the gardens and lawns. "All this is yours, then? The estate and house will not be entailed away from you?"

"Nay." She could not quite place his tone. "There is no entail away from the female line. I am my father's sole heir."

"So you don't *have* to marry."

"Nay," she said slowly, still not following his line of reasoning. "Not to secure my future. And not"—in case he needed more about the betrothal explained to him—"if I don't want to."

"Even to me?"

"But, I—" She made herself stop, and shunt aside the sting. Made herself put aside her own misgivings to listen to his. "Do you mean if I had said, at any point, that I didn't want to wed you, would my father, or your grandfather, have insisted?"

"Aye." He scrubbed his hand through his hair in that familiar gesture of frustration. "I should have asked such questions before, but I didn't know what I didn't know, if that makes any sense."

"Aye." She sat so she could discuss the topic calmly, without betraying her clammy palms or weak knees. "I have read the betrothal agreement—several times. My father insisted I do so, first when I signed the formal agreement as a young lass, and most recently when I came of age. The betrothal was predicated—depended upon—our consent and agreement. Which I gave."

"Because?"

Greer felt her chest tighten, and her skin grow chill and taut with dread—this was the heart of the matter, the compact between the two of them. "Because I felt I knew you."

"From before—before you found me in the road? We had known each other for a long time?"

She set aside her own hurt enough to see how much this gaping hole in Ewan's memory hurt him, as well. "Not exactly—we'd known *of* each other. We had never met in person, you and I. You'd gone away, to school in France, and traveling, and then university. And then I went away to travel and be educated. That's why I didn't know who you were, that day we found you in the road, though I think even your own grandfather might have been hard put to recognize you, so bloodied and beaten were you. And Dewar, who was, I suspect, trying to protect you, did not say who you were. But when I met you up on the moor, there was something about you. About your—"

"Madness?"

"About your character," she insisted. "About how kind and upstanding and gentle you were, even injured, that moved me to trust you. And I was honored that you trusted me even when Dewar told you not to. That you were, despite not knowing who you were, *yourself*."

"But I am not myself." He was just as insistent. "I am not the man I was. All those hours of study, all those years of learning are gone from my mind as if they never existed." His voice was an agony of doubt. "I am diminished."

Her despair vanished in the face of his. "But it may come

back. Surely it will. Every day you remember more and more."

"I remember some of the things I've forgotten. I see glimpses of others." He gripped his head as if he were trying to keep it from falling apart. "But talking to Alasdair—my God, what a mind—and Archie—so brilliant and incisive—has made me realize just how much I have lost. Just how far and how much I have to gain to be Crieff again."

The pain and frustration in his voice tore at her heart.

"You *are* Crieff. There is no *not* being Crieff, no matter how much you know, or do not know. You aren't worthy of Crieff because of how much you know. You are worthy of Crieff because of how much you are willing to learn."

He looked at her, his green eyes so clear and vivid and vulnerable. "And what if I can't learn it?"

"Ewan, I assure you—" She tried again to rally him. "Listen to what I just said—"

"Listen to me. Please." He took her face in his hands so they were eye to eye, heart to heart. "You don't think Malcolm is worthy of Crieff, do you? You don't think he has the character or the learning for all that responsibility."

"No," she admitted. "I don't. He has neither character or learning. But you have character. So much character that I am ashamed by how little I have in comparison." She took another deep, steadying breath to quench the stinging tears forming in her eyes. "But you have something else Malcolm doesn't have and will never have—you have me. *I* have the learning. Everything you studied, I studied, too. My father and my governess made sure of it. I am Dalshee"—she laid her hand over her heart—"in the same way you are Crieff. I can help you. If you let me."

She could not tell if he was relieved, or stunned, when he asked. "Would you marry me, knowing I may never recover myself?"

Everything within her stilled and came to livid attention all at the same time. It was the question she had hesitated to ask herself. It was the question she did not want to answer.

But if she quieted all cacophony of questions and ignored every shred of evidence and listened only to her instinct—to her heart—she would find the answer. "My heart has belonged to you since I was a lass, Ewan. And I fear it is far too late to change now. You are, and always will be, that man I loved, even if you don't believe it."

He came closer. So close she had to look up to see the clear green gaze that poured over her like water. "But that's not an answer, Greer lass."

"Aye, it is." She knew it was true. "My heart belongs to you and no other. I love you and no other. I can marry no other." She waited while her heart was beating so loud she could barely hear her own words. "And you?"

He touched his palm to the side of her face, slowly, carefully as if he were measuring both her and the moment before he could speak. "For me, lass, there has only ever been you, and no other." He cradled her face in his hands. "But would you love me, if I were not Duke of Crieff. Could you keep with me, if I decide that I am not worthy of Crieff?"

It was an impossible choice. And a surprisingly easy one. "I lost you once before, Ewan. I could not bear to lose you again. I don't want to live my life without you."

Lord Ewan Cameron
Castle Crieff
Perthshire
Scotland

8 July, 1791

Dearest E,

No post has reached us this four-week, which I put down to our rapid progress across the continent. Italy is a revelation, and the beauty of the northern lakes simply stupendous. But lest you think that I will forsake our own dear loch for the more polished gems of the lagos, fear not. Though they may shine crystal bright in the sun, I shall always prefer our loch as a diamond in the rough.

And while we are speaking of diamonds or other, lesser gems in the rough, I send you the enclosed present. It is, I know, not perhaps so fine as your portrait by the esteemed Madame Vigée-Lebrun, but it is a fair likeness by a female painter much in favor here in Italy, Angelica Kauffman. I hope it shall afford you some pleasure, or at least the same pleasure and comfort I take from your miniature, which I carry with me always. I hope that Papa, or some person, did warn you that I am a ginger, but I fear that it is too late if you find red hair anathema. I can always try to bring the fashion for white powder back. I do hope this missive will find you safe and well. I miss you, somehow, in a way I cannot explain, but hope time will rectify, when we become one.

I remain your devoted, G

La Signorina de Shee, Greer Douglas
Villa Charlotta
Lago di Como, Italia

24 August, 1791

Dearest Greer

I received with abiding pleasure your gift of your miniature. At last, I have your bewitching smile to look at when I read your words and imagine your cheerful voice speaking to me. And I will tell you for your relief that I am <u>very</u> partial to gingers and find red-haired Scotswomen more bonnie than any other on the Earth as a result. So pray, do not invest in hair powder. We will scrub along in perfect harmony without it.

I will treasure your gift and keep it with me always until I have the real person in front of me at Crieff. I miss you, too.

I remain your devoted but patient admirer, Ewan

CHAPTER 28

$\mathcal{E}$WAN KISSED HER. He kissed her with all the worry and fear and sheer terror of wanting someone he wasn't sure he could keep. And all the joy and relief that she loved him despite himself.

He kissed her because it was the only thing he knew he could do without thinking. Without wondering or worrying, because this he remembered—this need, this desire. He had felt this need and desire for her, his lass, and it had been utterly, cataclysmically brilliant.

And he wanted to do it again. Now.

He wanted to spare no thought for the impropriety of the situation, or the others left downstairs, and lose himself for those few, fleeting, heady moments when his body triumphed over his battered brain. He needed that oblivion. He needed it now.

But she was taking her time, kissing him sweetly. As if she had no idea what she meant to him. What she did to him.

He would leave her in no doubt. "I want you, lass. Fierce-ly." He dove into her kiss like a man parched for water, his life a desert without her.

She pulled back, and stared at him, as if she couldn't tell if he'd gone mad. And then she took his hand and led him into her bed chamber, turned the lock, and leaned back against the door. "Then you shall have me. And I shall have you."

He was on her, against her, kissing her, pressing his body into her, wrapping himself around her. It felt tight to have her in his arms. It felt good.

Better than good.

And better than best was having her lips upon his. Her sweet ardor pressing upon him. Her tongue questing and playing with his. Making his heart and his blood sing the same lively tune.

She looped her arms around his neck and held fast. Kissing him back as if *she* thought it better than best. Her hands speared into his short hair, tugging and pulling her way around his scarred skull, and down his neck to his jaw. She slid her palms along his jawline, exploring the feel of his freshly shaven chin.

He wanted to turn into her palm to rub himself against her like a dumb animal. Better yet, he wanted to rub against her, flesh to flesh, heart to open heart, like a sentient being instead of a dumb animal. To be like a man, not to overpower her like a dumb brute.

"Take me to bed."

Her words were all the encouragement he needed to wrap his arms around her and pull her tight to his chest and hold her as if he would never have to let go. She was safe and in his arms, and at that moment, nothing could harm them.

He picked her up, and she came readily, clasping her legs about his waist, her lips never leaving his. He pulled her flush against his chest with his hands around the firm curve of her rump. She was a well-made lass, with long legs that could wrap around him like a present. Strong well-muscled legs and thighs made stronger from all that walking and riding up and down the glens.

No remote drawing room duchess, his lass, with her lips pressed ardently to his. And there it was the flash of an image in his mind—a drawing room, all tartan-covered chairs, antlers on the wall and turkey carpets lining the floors, dark and beautiful. Crieff.

But he didn't want to think about Crieff now. Not when there was a bonnie lass, holding on to him as if he were shelter in a storm.

And there was a storm inside him.

He set her down next to her high bed and went at the buttons of the velvet tartan waistcoat Archie had loaned him so he might look the part of a Scots gentleman. "Gie it laldy, lass. You're falling behind."

A magnificent pink blush painted her cheeks as she watched him with what he took for admiration, before she went at her own buttons of her own redingote gown, peeling it off until her stays and chemise were revealed.

He shucked off the velvet breeks in record time. "Your turn, lass."

The swath of pink spread up her neck and down across her collarbone.

"Mayhap we should kiss again," he suggested. "You didn't look so worried when we were kissing."

"No. I wasn't worried." She gave a little silly, endearing smile. "I mean, aye. Please. Kiss me."

He took her face in his hands, cradling the sweet line of her jaw, and teased her lips open while she let her skirts and petticoats fall to the floor in a pool of fabric at their feet. "And my shoes," she whispered against his lips. She leaned into him to toe off her heeled slippers. "What about yours?"

He sat on the edge of the bed and pulled her onto his lap,

so she was sitting sideways, and he could still get after his borrowed buckled shoes. "But I can still kiss you."

"Aye," she agreed with that same breathless wonder that made him so bloody glad to be alive, glad to be here today to be kissed by her.

And when their shoes had dropped to the floor, and she had peeled her stockings off as well, her arms went around his shoulders. It seemed the most natural thing in the world to lean back and carry her down to the bed atop him. The most natural thing in the world to lay her lovely, curved body along the length of him and let her legs tangle and entwine with his.

She looped her arms about his neck and pressed herself to him, her lips hungry for his. And he was happy to oblige her.

Her lips were as soft and sweet as her opinions were tart, and he liked that. Liked the tart, unpredictable nature of her. Liked that while they had been formed for each other, they had formed themselves so very differently in many ways. And not so differently in others—judging from the pleasurable ache in his own chest, at the near contact of her skin.

But there was the solid impediment of her corset. "Your stays."

"They still lace in the back," she instructed on a whisper at his ear.

His hands immediately tried to make clever with the ties but were easily confounded.

"Poor lad." She kissed his lips before she pushed herself to sitting, straddling his waist.

His mind blanked at the sudden feel of her naked thighs and the bare skin of her bottom pressed against the taut flesh of his stomach. Poor lad, indeed.

"First, I have to—" pluck at the ribbon that wound around

her waist and was tied in a bow at the front. Like a present he hastened to unwrap.

He sat up, urging her to lean forward so he could look over her shoulder to expedite matters, while she took a more leisurely meander, kissing her way from his lips to his ear lobes and back down the taut sinews of his neck. The feeling was so bloody good that he was having trouble concentrating on what he knew he ought to be doing.

He ought to be finding her secret places, the hidden swaths of sensitive skin beneath her collarbone. He ought to be rounding her sweet rump in his hands or scooping his fingers under the edge of her stays, touching her there, at the very edge of her nipples, making her skin heat, and her knees clench and her heart beat too fast beneath her pink hued breast.

But it was *his* skin that felt new. *His* knees knocking together beneath him. *His* heart that beat a wild tattoo within his chest.

Because she was making love to him. Pressing closer when he leaned back. Taking action when he lost his way and faltered, when his fingers had grown clumsy and made a tangle of the laces.

"Let me." She put her cool palms against the heated skin of his chest and pushed him flat on the bed. He lay back and watched with something more than fascination as she put her arms behind her back to slowly and methodically pull out the lacing.

Her back was arched, and her head tipped back, and he reached up into the glorious copper coils of her hair to pull out the careful pins and let the bright ginger strands cascade through his fingers.

And there it was, sliding into his vision like a mirage—the unbidden image of something bright and metallic shining in his palm. His lucky penny.

But the mirage was banished in an instant, when at last the stays were loose, and she pulled the stiff linen garment free and let it fall to the floor with a silent crash that shook him to his bones.

Because there before him was her delicately formed body, screened from his view by only the nearly translucent linen of her shift. But what he saw of her was exquisite.

He wanted to hold her, to wrap her in his arms and hold her tight against his naked skin. He wanted it with a hunger that felt as if it might eat him alive if he did not give in, and grip the delicate rounds of her shoulders, and take her nipples with his mouth.

But lightly. Slowly. Slowly enough to demonstrate that he wanted this slow death by delight, this slow teasing march toward bliss, as much as she. That he wanted this excoriating brush of her peaked, linen shrouded nipples against the bare skin of his chest. That he wanted her with every breath of his body, and every fragmented thought left in his mind.

She wanted, too. "Oh, aye, Ewan, aye." Her voice slid away into irregular breathing. "Gie it laldy, indeed."

And now he was having as much trouble breathing as she—his breath began to saw in and out of his chest as if he were running a race to the top of the moor. To the top of the world.

"Aye." She breathed her urgent agreement into his ear. "It's like that, isn't it?"

It was. But he wasn't going to waste the breath to tell her so, when he could show her with his fingers, running down the outline of her body. With his lips, kissing his way from her fingertips to her shoulder. With his care and restraint in slowly lowering her chemise so he could at last see what he had mapped in the sacred dark of the bothy last night.

He kissed his way from her collar bone up the sensitive

slide of her neck, to her lips, and then down the other side, going past her collarbone, to the perfect peak of her breast.

She needed no more encouragement to arch back, to let him kiss and worry her glorious pink nipples into tight, needy peaks.

"My God, lass," he murmured against the soft sweetness of her skin. "You make a man glad to be alive."

Her face softened, and she smiled—that warm, open guileless smile that slayed him, and shot him clean through with heat and need and torturous bliss.

His arousal was rude and proud between his legs, and his breath slammed against the cage of his ribs, straining to be let loose. But not yet. Not until he gave her all the pleasure and kindness she had given him. "What do you want most?"

Her answer was as quick as it was satisfying. "I want to kiss you again."

He obliged her by closing the distance between their lips and set his mouth to hers. It leapt between them—the need, and heat and desire—like an arc of electricity jumping between poles, the moment her lips touched hers. He was jack-knifed back into arousal by nothing but the push of her plush lips against his, and the soft breath of her satisfied sigh whispering against his cheek.

And her hands were everywhere upon him, kneading his shoulders and circling around his neck so she might pull him close. He eased back onto his elbows and allowed himself the satisfaction of letting his hands grip her by the waist. He resisted the urge to pull her against him, forcing himself to wait for her to lay her sublime body flush against his, to press her sweetly rounded breasts into his chest.

Only then did he allow himself the pleasure of opening his mouth to her kiss, to tasting her heady sweetness, of exploring the plush tartness of her tongue and mouth.

"Aye," she whispered, and he took that encouragement for

the permission it was, to draw up her shift as they kissed, teasing her with his tongue and his teeth, nipping and sucking and tantalizing her with new sensations. With more delight, if only she chose to come and follow his lead.

She did. She pushed forward as he leaned into the cushions at his back, never breaking their contact. Never letting her lips part from his for more than the time it took to change his angle of approach, or take her lower lip delicately between his teeth, and sweetly bite down with just enough force to send a jolt of unholy arousal careering through his gut. "Greer."

Her name was both a groan of entreaty and a plea. A plea for more of the wickedly divine caresses that spanned the divide between pleasure and pain so neatly, he was nearly poleaxed by the force of his response. By the force of his need.

His need for more of her.

He widened his knees, and pulled her closer, so that the delicate heat of her body would press directly against his arousal.

But she was moving faster than he. She spread her knees wider on either side of his legs, and moved against him, while her hands speared through his hair, fisting and tugging the disordered strands. He leaned his head into her palm, and let her roll his head in her hands, trying desperately to exhaust the itchy need for skin to be against skin.

She kissed him again, filling him full of urgent, insistent need. "Ewan. Ewan, please."

His name was like a spur to his own hunger, urging him on. Her clothing was a bunched impediment between them, but he could not bear to set her away from him, even to bare her porcelain, pinked skin to his touch, and to his greedy gaze.

He crumpled up her shift, and drew it up, up the length of

her body, taking his time, dragging the soft muslin slowly across her skin in a precursor to his touch.

The action broke the kiss, but Greer didn't seem to object. Her head fell back, and she groaned her approval to the canopy over their heads. Ewan tortured them both by drawing the neckline up in his fist, so the thin material pressed tight against her skin. So he could tongue her breasts again through the veil of the fabric, kissing and sucking and laving her harder, showing her his hunger and need.

"Ewan," she called to him, her breath full of insistence. She was the one to pull the chemise off, to yank it over her head, and collapse against him, so that at last they were flush against each other, skin to skin, heart beating against heart.

He plied his lips to the hollow under her ear, kissing and nipping his long way down the sensitive side of her neck, learning that a wealth of sensation could be evoked from thorough attention to this lovely swath of skin above her collarbone. All the while his hands were stroking up and down the curve of her waist, his fingers fanning across the sweet curve of her back, his thumbs making light sweeps against the side of her belly.

He urged her closer, rounding his palms over the taut flesh of her bottom, cupping her sweet arse, and pressing her against his achingly erect arousal. He appeased his fingers' need to touch her sweet sex by raking his hands through the soft ginger curls at the entrance to her body before he delved into the warm heat of her body. He cupped her, pressing the heel of his palm against the edge of her cleft, rubbing just enough so she gasped, and pulled herself tight against him, and just as quickly levered back, so he could continue to touch her so intimately.

She made a sound of excitement and encouragement, and tightened her grip on his shoulders, so he spread her legs wider, pushing her open, laying her bare and vulnerable before him. She was light, and heat, and soft slippery need, encouraging him with her breathy sounds of frustrated delight.

His own heart was hammering away like an anvil inside his chest, when he eased his fingertip along her delicate folds, and was rewarded for his patience with the slick feel of her sex. He slid his finger into her tight sheath, exploring her, watching her face for her reaction, but she closed her eyes, and buried her head against his shoulder, but made not a sound.

"Greer, lass. My lass."

She kissed the edge of his ear, softly gently, and then with more force as his fingers played upon her, and her body began to understand its rhythm. She rocked against the insistent pressure of his hand, enough that her body pressed itself forward, grazing against his cock, straining to be within her.

He slid another finger inside her, exploring her, letting his thumb graze the nubbin of her desire to stoke the flames higher.

"Aye, Ewan, please."

He wrapped his other arm around her nape, and pulled her mouth down to his, kissing her with all the heat and urgency and need he no longer wanted to hide. He kissed his way along the line of her collarbone, across the hollow at the base of her neck, and out again along the straight line of delicate bone, until she arched her back, and scored his chest with the soft pebbled peaks of her breasts.

"Aye, lass." The word was an exhalation of encouragement through his teeth, but he could barely hear it for the sound of his heart in his ears.

She was there, open and pink and bare and his. Waiting for him.

He slid his hand out of her and grasped her as gently as possible by the waist, because he didn't feel gentle. He felt tense and taut, and on the very edge of something bigger and more powerful than desire. He felt as if he couldn't breathe, and didn't need to, because his arousal was pushing against the lush, slippery warmth of her entrance, and easing into her sweetly tight body.

He made himself take a lungful of air, and then another, and he could hear the harsh cadence of his breath, and he tried, tried to go slowly, and ease the way. But he was going mad with the need for her, with the need for the tight friction of her body gripping him in the most intimate way, and the sweet bliss of the joining of their bodies, that he could no longer think.

He could no longer watch her carefully, or touch her gently, or take his time. There was no more time. There was only now, and the pleasure that ripped him in two when she rocked her hips to seat his cock inside her.

She gasped, and went still, and he kissed her open, gasping mouth, and kissed her tightly shut eyes, and pressed his care and concern and love against her pleated lips.

He was babbling again, crooning the harsh Scots into the delicate shell of her ear, kissing and stroking her to stoke the embers of her pleasure back into flame.

But it was working. She drew in a deep shaky breath, and then another, and kissed him back, just a little. And then a little more. And then more still when his hands stroked up her sides to cup and fondle her breasts.

He pushed her away from him so he could see—see everything from her flushed face, all the way down the pale, pinked slide of her body to the triangle of golden ginger hair that hid the joining of their bodies. So he could see her crush her lower lip between her teeth. So he could see her nipples crest into tight, pink peaks. So he could see the softening of her belly when she finally relaxed, and began to move against him.

And then he wanted to see it all, and feel it all, as she slowly began to undulate in a sweet, sinuous motion, sliding her body against his, sending him rocking against the hard edge of his pleasure, over and over, and over again.

He grasped the glorious round globes of her sweetly rounded arse, and quickened her pace, helping her move, adding force and strength to the dance of her body upon his. "Aye, Greer, aye. Just like that. Just like—"

Like that.

Heat and light and pleasure and pain and bliss burst behind his eyes and blinded him with the bright force of her love. And he was gone.

Freifräulein Greer Douglas
Schloss Berend
Köpekestrade
Dresden, Saxony

16 November, 1791

My Dear G,

It is with the heaviest heart that I must inform you that my grandfather passed away Tuesday last. He slipped way in his sleep, as only the righteous can do, but his loss is immeasurable, though he left the estate and all his affairs in such precise shape that there was, and is, nothing more for me to do than follow his excellent example.

I have accordingly returned to Crieff, but there is no account for you and your family to cut short your travels to return—his wishes were for a simple funeral and burial, which have been accomplished, thought simple is not exactly the right word to covey the sheer number of people from all of Crieff and the Highlands who came to pay their respects to such a great man. I carry him in my heart, and on my hand—his ring, an onyx signet with the seal of Crieff, weighs heavily on my hand, reminding me of who and what I ought to be—a person like him, fair-minded, kind and patient in all things.

And so I urge you to carry on your travels with the knowledge that he delighted in being read your letters, and that your happiness in exploring the world gives me comfort and ease as well.

With sorrow, and some fresh joy, I sign myself for the first time,

Your Crieff

His Grace, Ewan Cameron, Duke of Crieff
Castle Crieff
Perthshire
Scotland

18 December, 1791

My dearest Crieff,

My heart is heavy for your loss, and there is nothing more I wish than that I were there in person to offer you some solace. We send you our most sincere condolences. We mourn the passing of your grandfather with you. My papa, in particular, feels the loss of his friend and neighbor most particularly. He has told me, with tears in his eyes, of the day long ago when your grandfather and he decided upon the pledge between us, and swore to raise us up, one for the other.

Oh, how glad I am that they did. How glad I am for their care and carefulness in making us fit for one another.

In that spirit, I will promise to continue my travels as you wish, educating myself and learning all that I can for Crieff and Dalshee and our future life together.

Always, your Greer

CHAPTER 29

*E*WAN AWOKE in the night to find the room as dark—as his grandfather used to say—as the Earl of Hell's waistcoat. The fire burned low, giving enough glowing light for him to take stock, and wonder at the impropriety of bedding his lass under her father's roof.

No matter—it was her roof, too. And they were well and truly betrothed—she had chosen him just as surely as he had chosen her. It only remained for them to decide how and when to go about it—how long they would wait in the hopes that his muzzy brain would heal enough for his memory to return. Or not.

Hell mend him, but he wanted it more than ever—because he wanted more than anything not to disappoint her.

Ewan reached toward the clock on the small table next to the bed to see the time, to calculate the hours that he might spend holding her before daylight forced them to face the future. But instead of the clock, his hand found a packet of letters tied with a faded velvet ribbon—letters addressed in a familiar hand. So familiar, he was prodded up and out of the warm bed, and closer to the fire to decipher the direction written in a firm hand across the back page of each and every letter—Lady Greer Douglas.

This he knew as well, these slanting letters, this carefully memorized direction—Dalshee House, Perthshire, Scotland. He could see his own hand before his eyes, dipping the quill into the ink, touching it to a second paper set to the side, so he might not make a blot. He could hear the scratch of the nib against the paper. He could all but feel the quill in his hand.

He carefully untied the packet and unfolded the first one he came to read—*Dearest Greer*.

One by one, letter after letter, he read them, going back to the drawer to find more letters—hundreds of them—before returning to the fire and building it up so he could continue to read. To learn and remember and see the scenes unfolding from his memory. The stony grey and lush green of Crieff, the stormy passage across the Channel, the dusty lanes through the French countryside, the beautiful house on the Rue Malebranche. Ancient Rome and Renaissance Florence and sunsets over hill forts in the Italian countryside. A sunrise over the Italian lakes. The dark medieval stone arches of St. Andrew's and St. Salvador's College.

And then other things that were not written down—Alasdair, Rory and Archie laughing uproariously. An evening getting viciously, cat-spittingly drunk. The empty, lonely silence after his grandfather's funeral.

Memory after memory crashed over him. Waves of incidents and accidents and life and bloody living. All the lost years stretching back through his mind. All the feelings that had made him into the man he was supposed to be.

"Ewan?" Greer's voice was fretful in the dark.

"I'm here." But he was not—he was thousands of miles and years away in the past, searching for her.

"What are you doing on the floor?" Greer dragged a blanket from the bed to cover her nakedness. "Those are your letters." She came to quietly take one of the precious folds of paper from his hands. "I know them by heart."

"I'm learning them by my heart, as well." He reached to pull her down to his side, though he still looked intently at the sheaf of letters he had not yet read clutched in his hands. "These are *my* letters. I remember these things. I can see this"—he poked one of the letters near the top—"house in Rome, painted that awful hot rusty pink. And the sublime view out the window up the long line of white marble steps."

"The Piazza di Spagna, number seventy-four."

"Just so—we talked of it earlier." He felt as if he were finally in control of fitting the puzzle pieces together, pushing them forcefully into place.

She placed a sleepy kiss on his bare shoulder. "They've helped you remember."

"Aye. Some. A great deal." So many images flooding his mind's eye. But still there was a void, an emptiness where she should have been. "These words bring the images to my mind—these places—and the faces of these people. But…" He probed his memory, pushing against the impenetrable wall that kept him from any memory of her.

"But?" She was still smiling, still waiting in happy expectation of his moment of clarity—the moment when it all came back to him.

But it hadn't.

"I'm sorry," he began. "I just can't seem to remember anything more."

"Anything more about…?"

"About you."

The pain in the liquid depths of her beautiful brown eyes gutted him. But he had to be honest. He could not lie about this, that was so important. "I am sorry, my love. I know how much this means to you."

"It does." She did him the honor of not hiding her disappointment, though she was clearly holding herself very carefully in check. Her gaze went to the letters still crushed in his hand. "There are still some more you haven't read that might…"

"They might. I hope they do." He pulled her close to kiss her forehead, but she eased away. "I want it more than I can say. But I must also say that I am sorry they have not yet."

"Please don't apologize for something that can't be helped." Her answering smile was over-bright. Carefully considerate of him. "I do want you to know how much I loved—and still love—these letters. You taught me so much and shared so much. You sent me books, and paintings, and we wrote of…everything. Poetry and dogs and parents and travel and philosophy and kisses…everything."

"Kisses that you saved for me."

"I did. Every last one." She took a deep breath. "It was exceptional, our communication. Our openness. Quite exceptional." Another quick exhalation, before she took his face between her hands. "But you *are* exceptional still. You are remarkable all to yourself, without any of this. You asked me last night if I would love you if you were not Duke of Crieff, and my answer is, and always will be the same—I love you. I love your kindness and your sly wit and your honor. No other man would even consider if he was worthy of his birthright, and *that* is why I love you. Because you are a man for others—a man who will always put others' needs before your own. You always have and you always will, no matter what you remember and what you forget."

"My God, lass. My lass. My Greer." He pressed kisses into her palms and pressed his cheeks to her hands as if he were swearing fealty. Because he was. "I can promise you one thing—and this is that I will never forget you again. Ever. You are a part of me now—a part I will never forget."

She kissed his cheeks, one to a side—a solemn benediction and sweet forgiveness all at the same time. "You will so long as no one ever hits you over the head and hurts your brain or tries to murder you."

He could see the unspoken fear shining in her eyes— what both she and Dewar and his friends feared—that whoever had been unsuccessful in killing him would try again.

"There is no guarantee of anything in this life but death, and I have already cheated that once," he assured her. "My memory may never come back. I may never be fully fit to be the Duke of Crieff again. But I will pledge myself to try. For you I will dare anything."

"Not for me," she disagreed with that quiet smile. "For Crieff. You always remembered Crieff. Right from the beginning, then it was the only word you could say—Crieff. Crieff belongs to you, just as you belong to Crieff. You belong there." She gripped his hand as if she could impress her surety upon him. "You are Crieff. Nothing, no memory or lack of memory, can change that."

I am Crieff.

He had to remember. He had to remember for her. He had to remember *her*—it felt important to see her, to place her into the puzzle of his past in order to find his way into the future. He felt incomplete without her.

Ewan returned to the letters scattered across his lap. "So you wrote back to me—answered all these letters?

"Every one. Except the last." Her quiet smile warmed the corners of her eyes. "The last, I meant to answer in person."

"Then they will be at Crieff, your letters to me?"

"Perhaps." She did not look hopeful. "Perhaps you saved them. Or perhaps not. Though I should hate to think they were lost or destroyed. But perhaps I have grown sentimental."

"Nay. I would have kept them." He was sure of it. He was a thoughtful, methodical man—his friends, as well as his own best understanding of his character, had told him so. "I'll go there, tomorrow, to look for them along with everything else —and Dewar." He couldn't forget the man who had done so much for him.

"But we should all go with you," she cautioned. "We should be with you in case…things don't go according to plan."

In case he didn't remember. Because that was his only plan—to hope that his memory would come to his reuse and lead him home.

But not this moment. At this moment he was going to gather his lass up and take her back to bed where they could nestle until they were warm. "I'll find them lass. I'll find you," he swore. "I promise you."

EWAN WOKE before the first dim rays of dawn, haunted into wakefulness by the images and lessons of the night. The images and lessons that forced him to confront the fact that while it would be easiest if Malcolm simply slipped away, it would not be right. Not for Crieff.

And so he kissed his lass and tiptoed back to his assigned room before they might be discovered together, and make the impropriety of disappearing from the dining room table together any greater. But he could not rest. He could not sit. He could not wait one moment longer.

If he was Crieff, he owed it to Greer, to himself, and to Crieff, to *be* Crieff. Now. No more waiting.

So compelled was he to get to Crieff as soon as possible,

that he wore his borrowed velvet evening suit rather than take the time to find more suitable clothes. So compelled was he that he did not wake the stable boys or grooms, but slipped a bridle over Cat Sìth's head, found a suitable saddle and mounted alone, following the drive that wound away from the house.

He took the main road that followed the course of the Shee Water south as it carved its way down glens and across the middle of straths. The sky had lightened to a bony, whitewashed grey by the time he drew rein at the Inn at the bridge, pausing only long enough to water the horse, before going on toward the bridge itself, rather than going west toward Crieff.

His hands went suddenly clammy, and his skin chilled with the uneasy, eerie feeling that crawled up his neck when he crossed to the center of the narrow stone bridge.

He had been there before—stopped in the middle of this bridge.

Ewan dismounted to try and stop the disorienting feeling of vertigo that came from being atop his tall mount on the narrow span suspended a hundred feet above the river. But perhaps that was what had happened—he had become disoriented and fallen, hitting his head on the stone.

The feeling of falling was so overwhelming, he could see it in his mind's eye, the tumbling spin of grey stone, blue sky, and green leaves that had been swallowed in enveloping, cold blackness.

He straightened his shoulders to shake off the feeling and walked back to the wide solidity of the roadway on the north side of the bridge. He had to stand there for a good long minute, peering hard at the steep banks of the river. Imprinting into his mind the sight of the granite boulders glistening at the water's edge. Waiting for memory to prompt him into action before he remounted and headed west along the branch of the Shee Water that flowed slowly south by west, letting the morning sun warm his back as he made his way along the road. Letting the babble of the water drown out the blether of doubts and uncertainties clamoring in his brain.

But then the burn was telling its own tale—buoying him up and carrying him along like a boat, except that he was the boat, and the water chilled him to his bones so completely he was numb even to the pain. But not to the knowledge that he was dying.

That was it—he had fallen into the water because he was dying.

The awful knowledge of how close he had come to death —how close he might yet come again—made him restless to take some action. Anything to chase the chill from his bones.

He spurred Cat Sìth to a dead run, letting the stallion's gallop eat up the miles. Ewan spared no eyes for the road— he kept his eyes on the burn, trying to keep that strange feeling of suspension for as long as possible, letting his battered brain find its own way, winding like the course of the water toward the raft of memories floating just out of reach.

Ewan finally drew rein at the last turn of the burn, where it veered north toward the village. There at the bank, an eddy of water formed a shallow pool that caught flotsam, like logs and leaves and tree limbs.

And men—the eddy had caught him. That strong swirl of water had saved his life, tossing him into the bank, forcing him to crawl onto the warm land as the cold numbness of the deep water wore off.

He had used the reeds and bracken as hand holds to push through the mud and leaf mold and pain that nearly took his will to live, to reach the roadway. He had staggered to his feet for a few paces before the pain and blindness and blood loss made him collapse in the middle of the road. Here he had fallen.

And she had appeared above him, a bright, golden angel of mercy. A last chance for redemption. A way forward, but not back.

He slowed Cat Sìth to a walk as he approached the village, wanting to go it slowly up the high street, to glean as much information as possible from each and every moment, each and every piece of knowledge that might make the journey onward easier.

The world seemed to be waking up around him—doors and windows were being pushed open. Shopkeepers stood on their stoops, gawp-faced and slack-jawed at the sight of His Late Grace, the Duke of Crieff, alive and in breathing in their midst.

The village looked different from his newfound memory —the orderly disorder of buildings, homes and shops that made up the fabric of Crieff village looked a little scaffy and shabby, down at heel, as if the Scots' pride that kept the village neat and tidy had taken a turn for the worse.

Here and there a fellow spoke. "My Laird," or "Yer Grace." On a corner a merchant's wife dropped into a low curtsey, while at another, a lad bearing a bushel of apples, set down his load to knuckle his forehead in respect.

Ewan nodded in acknowledgement to those he thought he recognized as well as anyone who looked him in the eye. *Aye, I'm back*, he wanted to say. *I never did leave. I never would.* This was his home—this glen, with this village and these people. He served them just as assuredly as they served him.

He was tempted to stop, to take their assurances to bolster his confidence, to put off the moment of reckoning at Castle Crieff as long as possible. To keep from the awful moment of discovery, or lack thereof. To hold back the uncertain future for just one minute more.

To keep him from feeling diminished.

But he could not stop, could not slow the press of time, though he dismounted when he reached the tall stone pillars of the gates of Crieff, and pushed the ancient wrought-iron gates wide. He took his time, walking up the long arching avenue of lime trees his grandfather had planted in his youth. *"Look forward into the future, my lad,"* the grand old gentleman used to say. *"Plant trees for your grandsons and make gardens for your granddaughters."*

Ewan looked ahead to the right to see that garden—nine walled acres with blossom-filled borders surrounding a long pond made for curling in the winter. He could feel the heavy weight of the polished granite rocks in his hand and remember the blissful slide of the ice beneath his feet as the rock slid home.

Home was more than the magnificent grey stone keep rising out of the granite ledge at the edge of the home loch behind. Home was this experience, this confluence of past and future. This knowledge. This belonging.

Ewan gave in to the urge to remount and come to Crieff like a laird, instead of the prodigal he felt. Beneath him, Cat Sìth crossed the wide gravel forecourt in a trice, the crunch of his hooves keeping time with the mad tattoo of Ewan's heart.

Come what may, this was his home. This was where he was meant to be. Hell mend him if he let anyone take that away.

*The Lady Greer Douglas
Engelshuis, Vaarstraat,
Antwerp, Belgium*

6 June, 1792

Dearest Greer,

Thank you for your wonderful descriptions of places that I am happy you are enjoying far more than I ever did. I am a man for home, happiest at Crieff with my dogs and my friends and my people. I am settling in to fill grandfather's well-worn boots, though there are days when the task seems too great. But as the great Sir Isaac Newton informed us, to see further, it behooves us to stand on the shoulders of giants.

And so I do. Crieff was more than just Grandfather—it is the living memory that is MacIntosh, the steward of the estate, stoic and reliable, and Dewar, the craggy old keeper who, despite his wizened size and age bestrides the moorside like a stag. It is Mrs. Peddie, the housekeeper, who was raised at Crieff and has worked all her days at our castle, with her intimate knowledge of each and every room, as if her head held a catalogue of all of the castle's precious and rare objects and works of art. They are the giants of Crieff.

I am off to the moor with Dewar, and hope that after our business in assessing the timber and checking the grouse count are done, I may make my way to Glas Maol, there to work on etching my initials more deeply next to yours. And thinking up something more to do with you, besides just kissing.

Imaginatively Yours, E

His Grace of Crieff Ewan Cameron
Castle Crieff
Perthshire, Scotland

18 July 1792

Dearest Ewan,

Oh, how I long to be home this very moment and help you exercise your imagination! I am all afire to discover what you have in mind besides kissing and kissing and kissing. I long to have secret looks and private smiles that are for you, and you alone. I am meant to be visiting the Rubenshuis, the home and studio of the great painting master, Rubens, but my cheeks are hot and my breath is all bottled up behind my stays for thinking of you. Today I am done with travel and education and erudition. Today I want only you.

Your adoring, impatient G

CHAPTER 30

GREER CAME INSTANTLY AWAKE with the certain feeling that something was wrong—that she was already too late. The flat light of a grey, windy day showed it was already well past dawn and into the morning.

She hurled herself out of bed, into the first clothes that presented themselves in her wardrobe, and down the hall to the green bedchamber—the bed was cold, the bedclothes entirely undisturbed.

He had never slept there.

She flung herself down the stairs to find the others. "Where is Ewan?"

While Cairn, Carrington and especially Mama and Papa hardly knew where to look or what to say in answer, Quince simply smiled. "We—well, I—assumed he was with you, sorting out your…difficulties, as it were."

"We have no difficulties. Or we would not if he had only waited for help—I fear he has already gone for Crieff without us."

"Oh, by jimble," Quince swore. "Men."

"Aye," her husband rejoined, as he put down his cup. "So very like women. Let us go then at once."

"Aye. I'm for Crieff." Greer ran for the stable.

"Not alone." Her father's command was like thunder. "There's been altogether too much time alone together as it is," he muttered, before he fixed on Greer a stern paternal glare. "You will take your own best advice—we all will—and go together, in an organized fashion. I will take the road in the carriage." He moved to ring for Malloch.

"I'll go over the moor on Nicnevin." Greer was wasting no time on embarrassment. "Ewan may be searching for Dewar, but I fear that Gow may be searching for them both. And as little as I like Malcolm Cameron, I like Gow even less."

"So noted," Quince said. "I'll go with you."

"As will I," her husband added. "Whither thou goest."

"Is there some other path I ought to take?" Archie Carrington asked Papa.

"I'll send Jock Keith to guide you on the path to the south toward the village of Crieff. In fact, I'll send out all the ghillies to fan out across the land looking for them both."

"And I shall stay here," Mama finished. "And pray that all this is only a tempest in an impulsive teapot, and His Grace will return here, chagrinned to find you all gone in search of him."

"Thank you, Mama." Greer pressed a fervent kiss to her mother's cheek. "We can only hope you are right." But she feared not. She knew not—her chest was a fisted knot of dread.

Ten minutes, and a short stop in Dalshee's gunroom to equip the party for all eventualities, and Alasdair, Quince and Greer were climbing the moor for the high lookout of Glas Maol.

Two hours of pushing their mounts hard up the hills brought them to the rocky ridge, from which they could survey the bothy in the upland glen and see across to a larger portion of Crieff's moorland. The bothy was still dark and empty, and Greer could discern no movement save the occasional sheep grazing in the lowland pastures.

"Anything?" Alasdair asked from behind his own glass.

"Nothing." Greer didn't know whether to be relieved or worried—both Ewan and Dewar could be hiding in a thousand and twelve places they would never find. The distances were too far, the estates too vast to comb carefully. All she had to direct her was her intuition. "Best push on toward Crieff."

They did so apace, easing their mounts as quickly as they dared on the downhills, winding across the ridges, glens and brae side, until Alasdair called a halt. "Back there. Down the hill. Did you see that?"

Greer followed the line of his arm, scanning the forest edge where the fringe of trees cut across the moor until a flash of movement—the stony gray of a pony's hide—caught her eye. And there, leading a pony with a body trussed over the saddle was the old moorkeeper, striding stoically for Crieff.

"Dewar!" Her cry carried down the glen, eventually reaching the moorkeeper, who stopped and waited the long minutes for their approach.

It seemed forever for Nicnevin to pick her way down the steep brae until Greer was close enough to ask. "Who is it? Is it Ewan? What happened?"

"Dinna fash, mileddy." He turned the pony to show the trussed man's head. "It be the mon Gow, mistress."

"Gow?" Relief made her too giddy to recognize the fellow. "What went on?"

Dewar touched his cap as Alasdair and Quince made rein beside her. "Milord and leddy. Yer mon bid me take 'im up the glens, but he were naught but cutty-eyed the whole trip. I reckoned he were up tae no good, an' meant tae kill me, same as he tried tae kill our lad."

"Gow?" Alasdair asked. "Not Malcolm Cameron."

"One or t'other, makes all the same—one tae gie th' order an' t'other tae make it so. Thick as thieves, them twa."

The satisfaction of having her feelings confirmed made her imprudent. "I never did like him."

"Reckon the feelin's mutual, mistress, wi'im likely the one as shot at yer father, the earl, an' ye up the glen. Right comfortable with 'is guns, was our Gow." Dewar held out an ancient but very well-kept rifle cradled alongside his own smaller fowling gun.

"That's a Ferguson breech loading rifle of the last war," Alasdair claimed. "Ewan said he thought this Gow was a solider."

"Aye, milord," Dewar agreed. "Stands tae reason. A good shot, but no hill craft tae speak of—caught 'im in a man-trap. T'weren't much of a job tae steer 'im right intae the snare. He's a fair shot wi' a rifle, I'd reckon, but he's no' a man o' the moor to ken where tae put 'is feet."

"Is he dead?"

"Nay. Savin' 'im for the hangman, as it should be, mistress. Though, 'ee'll have hisself the devil o' a loupin' head when he wakes up." Dewar gave her a craggy wink. "I may have skelped 'im good wi' the butt of me rifle while 'ee was danglin' there in me snare."

Greer's relief at having one of their miscreants accounted for was only temporary. "What about Ewan? Have you seen him?"

Dewar shook his head, all grumpy annoyance. "I've no' seen him these two days now, mistress. Told 'im no' tae go haring off to one place or another, but tae keep tae himself 'till he remembered who it was tried to kill 'im."

"Perhaps he has." She could only hope Ewan had enough

craft not to go walking into a snare unawares. "I fear he's gone for Crieff. I feel it in my bones."

And the feeling was that something had gone very wrong indeed.

~

OVER THE ANCIENT oak door of the keep were the words inscribed in the stone by a mason in medieval ages past —*CUIDAM TOLERANDA EST*. One must endure—the motto of Crieff.

If Ewan had wanted a signpost from a helpful God, this would have sufficed. Because that was what he had done—he had endured. And he would endure longer still to make himself worthy of Crieff, and of her, his lass, his Greer.

A shining face—perhaps a clock dial, gold and gleaming— swam across his brain, but he pushed it aside, and concentrated upon the reality before him. He urged Cat Sìth up the paved steps of the keep, letting his mount's big hooves clatter like drum beats on the stones until he was directly in front of the door.

"À Crieff," he bellowed against the high stone walls that echoed his name and passed it back through the ancient courtyards, guard towers and turrets. "À Crieff," he boomed again until he was sure every window pane rattled and every person that belonged to the house had heard.

Crieff was back, and he wanted his house. His home.

They poured out of the building, his people, throwing back the massive oak portal of the front door, hurrying out of lesser entryways, throwing up windows, and running down the drive from the stables.

He waited atop his horse, like some medieval crusader come back after years and years away as they gathered around him, waiting for their own sign that he was not in fact a ghost, but a real flesh and blood man, returned to them from the dead.

"Your Grace," MacIntosh looked thinner and more severe than ever, as he made his careful, measured way through the throng. "Welcome back, Your Grace. I trust you had a good journey?"

As if he had only been out for a morning ride around the loch, and not hauling himself out of the Shee and fighting for his life for the better part of the last month. Trust MacIntosh to be as true as a tall fir, bending to the wind but never relenting his grip upon the solid earth.

"A long journey, MacIntosh. A very long journey, indeed." Ewan dismounted and took his steward's hand in an overlong clasp. "It is good to be back. And to see everyone." He acknowledged the thinned rank of servants he knew better than his own face. "But where is my cousin?"

"I am here." The way parted to reveal Malcolm standing in the wide doorway. "Welcome, cousin. Welcome home so you may begin your recuperation. I've sent for a doctor—a specialist from Edinburgh to help you regain your faculties, but for now, come home and let Crieff rejoice in your rebirth, as it were."

There was something too pat, too rehearsed, in his cousin's otherwise fine manners—something of the underhanded child who had delighted in besting his younger, but already taller, cousin. Something that Ewan didn't like and felt sure he shouldn't trust.

It was doubt—doubt that made the smiles and looks of wonder ebb from the faces of Crieff's people like the retreating tide, washing all comfort away. The doubt that he was capable of being Crieff.

He hated it—however true it might have been.

Ewan met his cousin's eye, and prickles flashed across his palms and up the back of his neck in warning—pride rearing its stubborn head. But his pride was all he had left of his own. "I am Crieff. And I am here to stay."

He would be Crieff, whether he was worthy or not. He would make himself worthy.

"Of course." Malcolm smile was easy and bright. "As long as you are able, and your mind holds."

"Aye." His changeable mind did need to hold. But he could see that he also needed to hold the line with his cousin, who was as insinuating as he was openly amiable.

"So remarkable, your return. It's as if you've come back over some otherworldly bridge to us."

The memory slid into Ewan's head like a granite curling rock, heavy and substantial, and polished to a shine—Malcolm waiting for him on the bridge. "We met."

"Yes, of course." His cousin was all familial agreement. "Many times. We are cousins, of course."

"Nay. On the road home from Edinburgh. At the bridge over the Shee Water."

"What?" Malcolm's smile never faltered, though he shook his head and creased his brow into a bewildered frown as if Ewan had taken leave of his senses. "No. You must be mistaken. Although I understand you had a grievous injury to your head. Your brain has no doubt been disordered."

Had he told Malcolm what happened—that he indeed had a grievous injury to his head? Or only that he did not remember what had happened?

"You are mistaken," Malcolm repeated, surer now. "I went to Edinburgh to meet with you there, but you never came. I went to your house, where we were to meet, but your people said you had gone missing."

Nay. The image in Ewan's head grew stronger, and more clear. "Your man was there, too." The pale face of the man standing as still as a stone behind Malcolm came into focus, stark against the vivid green of the trees. "Gow. And not in Edinburgh."

"Gracious, cousin. Such fanciful ideas you've dreamt up." Malcolm smiled at Ewan before he turned to the steward. "That's enough theater for the day, don't you think? MacIntosh, return the people to their work."

"Aye, Mr. Cameron." The steward was exact in his obeisance. "With your permission, Your Grace?"

Ewan was hesitant to let his people disperse. They were his people, and he felt the need of them. Just as he was loath to let Cat Sìth go, too. He wanted to be on his back again, in control again. "Enough havering. You haven't answered my question, Malcolm."

"Enough posturing." Malcolm turned for the door. "Let us go inside and discuss this like gentlemen."

Those had been his exact words that day—*let us discuss this like gentlemen.*

"You asked me for money."

"Entirely fanciful. Must have been quite a hit you took."

Ewan was sure now that he had not said anything about being hit. "It was, cousin. But you know that."

But Malcolm walked on, so Ewan had no choice but to follow. But he had learned the lessons of his childhood. "MacIntosh, stay with me."

"Wouldn't dream of letting ye out of my sight this day, Your Grace."

Ewan followed the sounds of Malcolm's progress through the house to the grand, mahogany paneled library with its shelves upon shelves, and balcony with more shelves upon shelves ringing the second story. Malcolm seated himself behind the massive desk in the center of the room. As if he owned the whole of the place. As if the keep of Castle Crieff were his.

Pride gripped Ewan's throat like a fist. That was his grandfather's desk.

His desk.

"Get up." He didn't give Malcolm time to settle into the seat before he was on him, catching him up by the lapels—and devil take him if the suit wasn't familiar—and bodily tossing him from the chair. "You're even wearing my clothes."

Malcolm scrambled for purchase, flinging his hand toward an open drawer, but Ewan had had more than enough. He had endured all he was going to take from his cousin and yanked him away.

Ewan kicked the chair out of the way, as well. "Let us stand face to face, like *gentlemen*, Malcolm. Isn't that what you said to me that day?"

His cousin's face, so very much like his own in form, went taut with understanding. "You said you didn't remember."

"I do now." The memory was stark. The two of them, face to face on the bridge, with Gow taking the reins and idling off to the side, just out of Ewan's vision. "I told you I couldn't finance you forever. Grandfather told you the same. He begged you to take up a profession—he paid for you to study the law and that came to nothing."

"I'm not a clerk," Malcolm spat.

"Those were your exact words that day, as well."

Malcolm dismounting his horse, and saying, "Can't we talk about this like gentlemen? Or must you loom over me like some bloody tyrant?"

"I am no tyrant," Ewan had answered. "But this morning I find myself out of charity with you and your constantly empty pockets."

"You must help me," Malcolm had pled.

"Must?" Ewan had answered. "I have already. Numerous times. Too numerous to count."

"Then what does one more time matter?"

Why had it mattered? Why would he not pay his cousin's debts out of family duty, if nothing else? Or had he been thinking of the future, and the family he wanted to have—the new life he was about to start with Greer—and known that Malcolm's claims would only grow larger and more outrageous with time?

He looked at his cousin now, tight-lipped and taut with some suppressed emotion. "You said, 'You can't mean to refuse me.'"

"But you did."

"Aye. I did. There was nothing more I could say to you. The time for kind words and good advice had already passed, as neither had been heeded."

"So bloody self-righteous."

"I am Crieff, Malcolm—it is my job to be righteous. Grandfather was as generous with you as he had been with me—we had the same allowances for years. You could have studied, could have taken up a profession, but you chose not to. You chose to spend rather than save and spend more than you had."

"Bloody prig."

Ewan didn't even bother to retort. He turned away, and gathered his reins to prepare to mount, and—

Nay, that was memory—pain, sharp and concussive echoing from his head down through his body and pitching him forward into the horse. He had groped for the saddle leather to keep his balance even as the edges of his vision closed in.

"You hit me." Another pain had erupted from his shoulder where a second blow landed. He had staggered sideways and went down hard on his left shoulder.

Ewan had to put out his hand to steady himself against the solid weight of the library desk.

"Again," he had heard over the screaming ache that ate him whole.

More pain, sharper, harder, more jagged, clawed at his temple.

A rock. Someone had hit him with a rock. From behind. Not Malcolm. Gow.

Ewan gripped the edge of the desk and tried to focus his gaze on Malcolm, who was moving away from him toward the doors. Getting away. Nay—closing and locking the doors. Locking them in.

"Is he dead?" That had been Malcolm's voice, high and tight with panic.

"Not yet." Gow, quiet and terse.

"Jesus look at the blood." Malcolm again, nearby.

They had stood over him, talking about him, while he bled. While he was so badly hurt.

"What if someone sees?" Malcolm's voice had hissed in desperation. "Get him off the road. There."

Hands had closed around his ankles like shackles to drag him away. He tried to struggle, to move. But he could not. Instead the pain had eaten him whole, chewing him up and spitting him out like a monster from a child's storybook—agony pierced his skull like teeth.

They were dragging him across the rutted rocky road, when Malcolm said, "Wait."

They had left him for a moment, and the agony subsided to a roaring ache. He had tried to breathe—to take in air, to push out the pain rattling through him like a runaway carriage. Tried to order his thoughts to push out the panic that crawled up his throat.

Hands had grabbed and turned him, pulling and tugging. They were going to help him now, he had thought. Surely his cousin would not let him die?

"Not much money." Gow's voice, measured and low. "But the gold's worth something."

"Do you mean his ring?" Malcolm had asked, his voice hushed and nearly aghast at what they were contemplating.

"Can't be the duke if he doesn't have the ring. And it'll make it hard to identify the body."

A gasping silence followed, and that was when Ewan knew they meant to kill him—they were killing him. They, his cousin and his servant, were the ones who had caused this pain, this endless agony.

There was a terrible pause—a hellish wait to find his fate.

"Take it." Malcolm's voice, cold with death.

Ewan had fought to open his eyes. Struggled to focus on the shapes of the men looming above, as they grappled to take the ring from his finger.

His hand had dropped to the ground, empty, and throbbing.

"Now what?"

The sharp snick of a dirk being unsheathed from Gow's boot was his answer. Ewan saw it, level with his half-opened eyes as he tried to think. "If he's not dead yet." Gow's voice was full of casual malice. "He will be soon."

Ewan tried to fight, tried to command his arms and legs to his bidding, but the pain ate him up again, filling his mouth with bile and his brain with agony.

No, he wanted to shout. No. I don't want to die. I can't—there's a lass I love—

But the words couldn't come out. They were swallowed whole by the gaping maw of pain as he pushed himself away from the blade. His back had come up hard against the stone wall at the edge of the bridge, stopping his flight.

There were only two choices—the blade or the bridge.

And he chose, shoving his legs under him, and tipping himself backward over the edge. And he was cartwheeling through the air until the sky hit him and turned dark. Liquid blackness sucked him down, down, down. There was nothing he could do but die.

Lady Greer Douglas
The Inn of the Three Sails
The Hague

1 August, 1792

Dearest, kindest, most beloved Greer,

I received your last from the Low Countries on Tuesday, and while very pleased to have your thorough and very useful reports of the canal systems, as well as the latest dairying practices of the Dutch, I profess myself most glad of the intelligence that you plan on returning home. The news from France has given me some anxiety for your safety, and I will be pleased to have you away from the Continent, and safe back upon these shores. Such sentiment may not surprise you, who know me so well, but I profess myself surprised at the strength of the feeling, which finds me in an almost agitated state of readiness to end my bachelorhood. We have done what we pledged to do—to give each other the time and freedom to grow up.

If you are in agreement, and find yourself in a similar state of readiness, I propose that we marry at Crieff this autumn, or as soon as you feel yourself ready for the burden of taking me on.

I will ask you to send your reply to Cameron House, Edinburgh, as business compels me there for meetings with lawyers, factors and agents regarding the final disposition of the estate which comes to me in full upon my four and twentieth birthday this month. I plan to return home to Crieff as soon as may be, where I shall await your coming with the greatest anticipation of happiness.

Your devoted, C

His Grace the Duke of Crieff
Cameron House
St. Andrew Square
Edinburgh, Scotland

16 August, 1792

Dearest Ewan,

I am in happiest receipt of your last, and my answer to your proposal is a most emphatic, Yes. Yes, let us marry ~ but at once! I, too, find myself anxious to return from the Continent to Scotland and begin our marriage as soon as may be. I confess that the fall seems too far away ~ I would be united with you as soon as travel and preparation allow. I will not write more, as the boy is waiting this instant to take my letter off to the packet boat but be assured that I am this moment on my way to you. I will send word the moment we have returned to Dalshee, and will set out directly to Crieff for our wedding, whereupon I will pledge myself,

Your most devoted, G

CHAPTER 31

*E*WAN'S HEART was thundering like hoof beats in his ears, blotting out all sound as his vision cleared to reveal the high-ceilinged library. He was not in the burn, choking on black water, but at home in Crieff, where the long lines of books stood sentry to the years in orderly rows. He was protected by his people, who were on the other side of the now-closed door. He was alive and with his murderous cousin, who had circled back to the desk.

"You're mad, dear cousin. Look at you, clutching the furniture like an invalid. Your brain is so disordered by your fall that I fear you're a danger to yourself and to Crieff. And we can't have that."

Ewan knew he would go mad if he stopped believing the evidence of his own heart and mind—he knew what he knew. "Nay."

"We'll make you comfortable at home while you convalesce, and find a physician better suited to your condition than that incompetent leech man from the village."

Ewan might have been confused enough to thank his cousin for his concern, but Malcolm was as Malcolm had always been—he could not keep the hint of gloating from his smile, the smirk that told Ewan his cousin had found find some bribable quack who would consign Ewan to the hell that was Bedlam for the price of some of Crieff's silver.

"Nay, *dear cousin.*" Ewan threw the bastard's own language back at Malcolm like a glove backhanded across his face. "Your days of lying and flattering and charming your way out of trouble are over. It really doesn't matter which one of you hit me—Gow may have done the foul deed, but you did nothing to stop him. *You* took my ring from my finger, Malcolm. Grandfather's ring. You knew what you were doing."

"And I know what I'm doing now." Malcolm dove for the open drawer, snatching up the pistol he must have concealed there, leveling it at Ewan's heart.

This time, Malcolm would make sure there was no coming back from the dead, no usurping his place as the Duke of Crieff. This time, Malcolm meant to do the deed himself. And he would not miss at such close range. "Move away from the desk."

Ewan decided he would do no such thing—he could not.

Because his gaze was caught by something left behind in the drawer. Something as bright and round as a penny. The face of a lass.

A lass he knew.

It was a portrait miniature, the glass cracked, and the gold frame dented from misuse. A portrait of a young woman who could only be a younger Greer—there was the familiar self-possession, along with the sweet mischief suspended in the depths of the warm brown eyes, and the wild fall of long, ginger hair, as bright and glorious as a penny in his palm.

This he remembered—this lass, this image of his beloved. This is what he had been looking at that day. That day by the river.

The sound of water and the wind through the trees filled his mind. He was seated on Cat Sìth, out of patience with Malcolm's droning complaint, wanting to be home. He had reached into his pocket for his timepiece but pulled this out instead. And there she was, smiling up at him, his bright lucky copper penny in his palm.

He took it now, holding the miniature fast in his hand, as if his grip might ease the hard, joyful hammer of his heart against his chest. "Greer."

"Yes, our lovely Lady Greer." Malcolm's frown dissolved into snide triumph. "Remarkably adaptable, isn't she, and pretty enough for the Highlands. She'll make a fine Duchess of Crieff for me, before she joins you."

For half a moment Ewan felt as if his heart might tear itself to pieces within his chest. But he would not allow it— he knew her thoughts, her heart, as well as he knew his own. Her affections were not changeable in the least.

"Nay. Though I were gone a hundred years, you'd not get her. She'd never have you. You're not worthy to so much as speak her name." The puzzle pieces locked into place, solidifying the past, with only a few remaining pieces. "Where are her letters? If I'm to be murdered again, I want them to hand."

Ewan rifled through the drawers, opening and slamming —they would be somewhere in this desk, close to hand. Close to his heart.

"Your sentimental little scraps of drivel?" Malcolm sneered. "How educational they were. How sentimental. But I learned all I needed to know to manipulate her before I burned them. Now stand away." Malcolm twitched the gun in his hands to bring Ewan's attention back where Malcolm wanted it.

It worked—time slowed and narrowed down to the small circumference of the barrel.

But Ewan would not do this to Greer a second time. He could not allow her to be so ill-used.

He scooped his hands under the edge of the desk, intending to upend the heavy oak piece onto Malcolm, and hopefully shield himself from the shot. But before he could so much as take the weight of the heavy mahogany in his hands, everything happened at once.

From above on the balcony came the sound of hammers being cocked back—Alasdair and Archie and Quince with guns trained on his cousin, who turned toward the threat, while from behind Malcolm, Greer rose up like God's revenge against murder and swung the butt of her fowling piece against the back of his cousin's skull with a crack that echoed off the wooden walls.

Malcolm wavered and started to go down, but still managed to swing his pistol wildly toward Greer.

Rage—blind, cold and deadly—erupted from him like a snake lashing out. Ewan was leaping for him, sliding across the desk to grapple the gun, and seize Malcolm by the throat, choking the lying, insinuating life out of him.

The charge went off, blowing an unholy loud hole in the high ceiling, raining smoke and plaster down upon them.

And then MacIntosh materialized out of seeming nowhere, with a brace of footmen, Geordie and Billy—Ewan was astonished to remember their names—who wrested Malcolm to the ground.

"Ye'll no' want tae do that, Mr. Cameron," MacIntosh instructed coolly, as he broke Malcolm's grasp on the spent weapon.

The footman pinioned his cousin's arms behind his back, while MacIntosh very correctly returned the weapon to Ewan. "Yer pistol, Yer Grace." And then, even more composedly, the steward stripped the cravat from his neck to bind Malcolm's wrists.

Ewan uncocked the hammer and emptied the burnt powder in the pan onto the top of the desk before he threw the weapon down. "By rights, I ought to thrash the life out of you," he told his cousin. He made himself step back, away from the villain, so he wasn't tempted to lay hands on him again. "But I'll save you for the hangman."

"You can't do that. You wouldn't—I'm your family," Malcolm gritted through the pain that was no doubt erupting in his head. "Think of the scandal."

"Scandal? Do you think I care for scandal?" Ewan had to grip his hands into the edge of the desk to keep from plowing them into his cousin's face. "You left me for dead. You and your man, with his boots and his knife, did your best to kill me. The fact that I'm alive owes nothing to you—your actions were the same whether I lived or died."

"It was an accident." Malcolm was grasping at straws to save himself.

"I don't think so." Ewan was not going to let him off so easily. "You don't bash a man's head in with a rock by accident. Or kick the air from his lungs and break his ribs by mistake. Nor pull a knife to finish what the rock and the boots had started without deadly intent."

"It was Gow with the rock and the knife," Malcolm swore. "I didn't do anything."

"You watched and did nothing." With each moment the memory of what had happened became clearer. "You stood and watched my life's blood being spilled onto the ground, and you did nothing. And no matter who did the deed, it is you who wear my ring, Malcolm. You who stood by and took what was mine by right."

"It shouldn't be yours," Malcolm spat. "It shouldn't be your right. I should have as much right as you to the fortune—"

"You did. Grandfather gave us everything the same—

allowances and opportunities. But you were never satisfied. You could have come to France with me, but you chose not to. You chose your fate just as assuredly as grandfather did."

"It wasn't fair."

Ewan stepped back from the desk. "Now you're the one who is taking like a madman, Malcolm."

"I should have had the right. I was older." Malcolm recited his complaints as if they were a litany learned long ago. "I should have been the heir."

So this was the essence of the constant friction—the murderous tension between them. "I am not going to debate the laws of primogeniture and succession with you. I don't make the laws, but by God, I follow them. What you suggest never could have happened. You're railing against fate, not against me."

"Grandfather could have made it so." Years of resentment poured out of Malcolm like poison. "He could have done what was right and given it to me. He could have done what was right."

"He did." Of this Ewan was sure. Their grandfather had done his best to form them both for Crieff. But only one of them had heeded the lessons. "You made your choice just as assuredly as Grandfather did."

"And so can you choose, cousin." Malcolm was not done with his recriminations. "All of this—this unpleasantness—"

"Murder is hardly unpleasantness, Malcolm."

His cousin ignored him. "All of this could have been avoided if you had simply given me the money as I asked."

Ewan held as firm as he had that day on the bridge. "All of this could have been avoided if you had simply not made alarming bets with dangerous people."

His cousin nearly growled, grinding his teeth in frustration. "Everyone does it. I'll warrant even you, my saintly prig of a cousin, do it. All gentlemen make bets. Why should not I?"

"I do *not*. I do not gamble. I do not make bets. I never have and never will. And neither will you from now on. Because you are dead to me. Take him away from me." He made himself speak in a more reasonable manner. "Lock him up in some cellar, or dungeon if we still have one."

"Indeed, Your Grace, the oubliette is still fully functional." MacIntosh managed to keep a straight face. "We'll toss him in there frae the nonce, while I send frae another magistrate."

"Another?"

"Your Grace will in time remember that he is the magistrate. But I should recommend in this instance, of consulting another." MacIntosh advised. "And there is the matter of Mr. Gow—similarly trussed by Dewar and ready for the oubliette."

"Aye." Ewan did remember. And he would, in time, remember all the lessons he needed to learn in order to do right by Crieff. "Keep them separated, if possible—let them stew in their own guilt."

"Just so, Your Grace." MacIntosh inclined his silver head. "As you wish."

"Thank you, MacIntosh. You are a wonder."

"One does one's best, Your Grace. Never less than one's best."

Never less than one's best. That was all he had to do—try. And with Greer by his side felt undiminished—together they could do anything.

He turned to her, and immediately she was in his arms, holding him so fiercely he knew she would never voluntarily let go.

"Papa is a magistrate—he will be in presently. He'll know what to do." She put her lips to the hollow of his throat.

"Why did you not wait for us? Why did you have to confront him in this dangerous way? He might have killed you."

"Because I had to." He could think of no other reason that made any sense. "And because, thankfully, he's not very good at murder."

"Your Grace." MacIntosh returned and bowed in apology. "If I may intrude to suggest one other thing, Your Grace?"

"Of course."

"The gravesite up the brae lies heavy on our conscience. Might I suggest sending the gardeners up to begin digging up the casket to see who lies within?"

"If indeed there is anyone." Ewan turned to his cousin. "Malcolm? Care to exchange that information for forgoing the indignity of the oubliette?"

"I had nothing to do with the coffin—that was Gow's doing."

"And where is your Mr. Gow?"

"Trussed like a grollached deer on the back of Dewar's pony." Greer supplied. "All your Dewar's doing."

"Dead?" he asked, wanting to be clear.

"Nay, lad." Dewar made himself known behind Alasdair. "Just laid out, like, after 'ee made the mistake of takin' a shot at me, same as 'ee did tae the earl. But wi' no better result, aye?"

"Aye." Ewan was glad the man was not dead. Let the gears of justice grind him down if they would. But he didn't want death on his hands, only life.

"I should have let him shoot the lot of you." Malcolm's sullen spite found a new outlet.

"You did, Malcolm—a fact we're not like to forget at your trial." Another thought occurred to him. "Did Gow serve with your father in North America? With the Seventy-Fourth Regiment of Foot Highlanders?" Ewan was no longer astonished at the arcane bits of information that his brain made available at odd times so long as they were useful.

Malcolm stared. "How did you know that?"

"Grandfather was intensely proud of your father, Malcolm—he kept your father's sword. It hangs in pride of place in the reception hall."

Malcolm was all sullen entitlement. "Why did he not give it to me?"

"No doubt he was afraid that you would pawn it." Ewan was done with his cousin's resentment. "But I think we have also narrowed down who it was that used my long Jäger rifle to shoot at the Earl of Shee—it was Gow with his infantry experience, wasn't it? Done at your command to blame me, and make Greer feel vulnerable, so she would marry you."

"It doesn't matter now, does it?" Malcolm spat. "He missed, and you're to marry the nosy bitch and get her money after all."

Ewan gave in to the spike of rage that spurred him to backhand his cousin across the mouth. "You will never speak of her in that manner, or even so much as utter her name again," he threatened. "Or I will wipe you from the face of this earth. Do you understand me?"

Malcolm just smiled.

The rage pulsed through him like poison. "Take my cousin up to the grave he had dug for me," he ordered. He turned his back on his cousin and addressed MacIntosh. "Open it up so that it may be ready for my cousin when the magistrate—whom he ordered shot at—comes to deliver his sentence."

Malcolm tried to pull himself out of the footmen's rough grip. "You wouldn't."

Ewan made himself as cold as the water of the river. "Better yet, take my cousin up the hill and make him dig it out himself. See how he likes standing in his own grave."

For the first time, Malcolm began to look afraid. "That was all Gow's doing—the body. I had nothing to do with it."

"And will he admit to that at your trial at the High Court at Lawnmarket? Will he stretch his neck to save yours? Paid him well, did you? Appreciated his underhanded work on your worthless behalf?"

"He's my blood—my mother's brother. He always encouraged me. Told me what was due to me. He'll do anything for me."

"Will he be loyal enough to take the noose for you?"

Malcolm was stunned into silence. "What do you want from me?"

"Justice." Of this Ewan was sure. "Justice for Crieff."

"While I'll get no justice." Malcolm was bitter to the last.

"What you might get instead is mercy." Ewan took a deep breath. "Tell me if there is an innocent person buried in my grave, and I will argue for leniency. For you to be put on a ship and transported, rather than be hanged. So long as you never step foot on this island again, your life will not be forfeit. You are my only family, Malcolm. And I will honor that bond even if you don't."

"Gow bought a pauper's body from St. Cuthbert's poorhouse."

"Ah." Alasdair's brow's lifted. "It seems our old friend the Reverend Talent is up to new tricks. I shall have to pay him a visit."

Ewan turned to his oldest friends, to the brothers of his heart, and to the woman he loved more than life itself. "Give me your honest opinion—am I doing the right thing? Greer?"

"Aye, my love," she agreed. "Mercy before vengeance. I've had my fill of coffins, without filling any more."

Ewan pulled her close and kissed her brow. "Then you shall have it. Send him away."

"I'll see you in hell, cousin."

"You may go to hell, Malcolm, but I am going to get married."

As soon as might be arranged. "Come." He took Greer by the hand and led her out, into the clean open air, where he could breathe and think. Where he could hear the wind whisper through the trees to calm the racing of his heart. Where he could propose the way he had always meant to. "It's not Glas Maol," he told her as they went through the gate to the walled garden. "But it will have to do."

"Do for what?"

"To show you. It was you." He opened his hand to revel her battered and shattered miniature, very much the worse for wear. "It was you all along—the penny in my palm." He held out the miniature in the flat of his palm. "It is you."

"Aye." She could not keep the tears from her eyes. "I gave that to you. Sent it from—"

"Italy," he confirmed. "You did. And *this* lass I know, I remember, this lass from the letters—the lass I wrote to."

"Oh, aye?" Her voice cracked with some bittersweet combination of disbelief and hope.

"Oh, aye. It all makes perfect sense now—the reason I couldn't remember you, this beautiful, gorgeously ginger creature, this fierce, kind woman, was that I had never met you. I know only my sprite, my lucky penny in my pocket who went with me everywhere. Though she was only a painting, not flesh and blood, she had been real to me."

"Am I real enough now?" Greer asked through the tears that rolled down her cheeks even as she smiled at him.

"You are more than real. You are mine, just as you always were. You were the last thing he tried to take from me—that day on the bridge, when he took grandfather's ring from my fingers, and rifled through my pockets, he pulled you from my hand."

She shivered in his arms. "I heard most, but not all of what happened."

"It doesn't matter anymore." But perhaps it did, because he went on. "It had been afternoon—the bright September sun had slanted thought the dark green trees. I was traveling along the tree-lined road, and the sun had been warm on my left shoulder—because I was going north. On my way home. To Crieff. To be married. To be with you."

He kissed the tears from her eyes. "I was so happy because I was going to be with you. And now I am."

"You've remembered it all."

"Not all, but most. But I know it doesn't matter anymore. I know that I will love you with every fiber of my being, and fiercely as you have loved and fought for me. I am at peace."

"And at Crieff."

"With you." He kissed her. "Will you have me, damaged as I am?"

"I like this man. I respect this man. And I pledge myself to this man forever more."

He kissed her again, slower this time, with all the joy and love and relief he no longer had to hide. "What say you to ending our betrothal, and at last getting married, my Lady Greer?"

"Oh, aye." His lass's smile was bright with her own brand of impish joy. "I beg that you would do so at your earliest convenience."

His Grace the Duke of Crieff
Cameron House,
Edinburgh
Scotland

1 September, 1792

Dearest Ewan,

I am arrived ashore in Britain, and as anxious as I can be to fly to you! But Mama says a certain decorum must be observed, therefore I write to ask your permission and blessing to meet you at Crieff three days hence. Please say yes! Oh, please. For I can wait no longer to be ~

Yours, G

Lady Greer Douglas
Dalshee House
Perthshire

Sept 6—

Dearest G,

Yes. Let us be wed in two days' time. With all my heart, yes. —E

EPILOGUE

$\mathcal{I}$T OUGHT TO have been a joyful thing to marry a man one had always loved, but despite her joy—or perhaps because of it—Greer cried. They were happy tears, but tears nonetheless.

But perhaps a couple who had suffered less, could smile more.

They were married just as they ought to have been, in the ancient kirk of St. Bride at Crieff, beneath the bright rainbow of the stained-glass window, and everything was exactly as it ought to be—her friends surrounded them, her Papa beamed, her Mama sighed, and her bridegroom was so handsome in a suit of embroidered silk velvet so fine that he outshone the sun.

She wore the silk dress Mrs. Malloch and Morna Beale had hand embroidered so patiently so very long ago, and which they had carefully revived without chiding Greer about the dirt and stains from that first, awful wedding day— the day her beloved had fallen, quite literally, at her feet.

But she would think of that awful day no more. Today was the first day of the future she had always wanted, always planned and hoped for. Today was a memory she would keep forever.

And so would her bridegroom, who at last, knew just what to say when her Papa bestowed her hand upon him. "Gie it laldy, now lass," he murmured as they faced the rector.

And she did, because at last the bright autumn sun shone high overhead, and everything was exactly as it should be.

FROM THE AUTHOR

Thank you for reading *Mad, Plaid and Dangerous to Marry*. I hope you'll take a few minutes out of your day to review this book – your honest opinion is much appreciated. Reviews help introduce readers to new authors they wouldn't otherwise meet.

THE HIGHLAND BRIDES

Mad, Plaid and Dangerous to Marry is the fourth book in The Highland Brides. While each book reads as a stand-alone, the series is best enjoyed in chronological order.

Mad for Love
Mad About the Marquess
A Fine Madness
Mad, Plaid and Dangerous to Marry
Mad Rogues and Englishwomen (coming soon)

To keep up to date on The Highland Brides, learn about other series (including The Dartmouth Brides and The Reckless Brides), sign up for Elizabeth's newsletter and get exclusive excerpts, contests, and more
http://www.elizabethessex.com

London, Early Spring 1790

MARIE CHANTAL AMÉLIE DU BLOIS never felt more French than when she was in London. Something about her seemed to mark her as different, as if the nightmare of their flight from Paris were painted across her face instead of the polite English smile she tried to give the world. As if her full French mouth were incapable of a sufficiently stiff upper lip.

But despite this deformity of character, she would continue to try to stiffen her lip, continue to wear English clothes and buy English bread while she shopped in English markets—she would become English through sheer dint of will.

Because she loved London.

She loved everything about the damp, down-at-her-heels city. Papa often said that London was dull in comparison to Paris, with all its fashion and art, but Mignon, as Papa called her, liked dull. She liked safe. And London's shabby pavements, leafy squares, and tidy shops felt entirely safe.

"Good morning, Miss Blois." Mrs. Parkhurst, from the house next door, nodded cordially as Mignon came along the uneven pavement.

Soho Square wasn't the most fashionable district of London, or the richest. But it would do very nicely. Because it was pretty, and green, and nothing bad could ever happen here, so far away, across the water from Paris, where bad things seemed to be happening daily.

"*Madame.*" Mignon curtsied and shifted her market basket to the other hip. "How do you fare this fine morning?"

"Tolerably well," Mrs. Parkhurst nodded her billowing English bonnet. "You are to be congratulated. I saw your father, earlier. He seemed very well pleased by the auction of his art at Mr. Christie's."

"Auction?" Mignon felt her stiffened upper lip fall slack. This was the first she had heard of an auction.

"Very pleased, he was." Mrs. Parkhurst was nodding in her genial way. "So nice to see him so pleased and well, after all your troubles."

Their 'troubles' had been broadcast about the square like poppy seeds by Papa. In his version of the truth, they had left France under the most horrific of circumstances. True, there was great turmoil and unrest in that country, especially for aristocrats, even disgraced youngest sons of disinherited younger sons—in Paris the slightest whiff of aristocratic forbearers had been enough to incite a mob.

But the plain truth was, she and Papa had managed to escape before the worst of the violence had found them. Because her papa, bless him, was a scoundrel, and scoundrels had a nose for such things.

Edinburgh, Scotland
June 1792

Lady Quince Winthrop had always known she was the unfortunate sort of lass who could resist everything but temptation. And the man across the ballroom was temptation in a red velvet coat. There was something about him—some aura of English arrogance, some presumption of privilege—that tempted her beyond reason, beyond caution, and beyond sense. Something that tempted her to steal from him. Right there in the Countess of Inverness's ballroom. In the middle of the ball.

Which was entirely out of character. Not the stealing—she stole as naturally as she breathed. But because the other thing that Lady Quince Winthrop had always known, was that the most important thing about stealing was not *where* one relieved a person of his valuable chattels. Nor *when*. Nor *how*. Nor even *what* particular wee trinket one slipped into one's hidden pockets. Nay.

The tricky bit was always *from whom* one stole.

When one robbed from the rich, one had to be careful. Pick the wrong man, or woman for that matter—too canny, too important, too powerful—and even the perfect plan could collapse as completely as a plum custard in a cupboard. Which made it all the more curious when she ignored her own advice, and picked the wrong man anyway. Whoever he was, he stood with his back to her, his white-powdered hair in perfect contrast to that red velvet coat so vivid and plush and enticing that Quince was drawn to it like a Spanish bull to a bright swirling cape. Unlike the gaudily embroidered suits worn by the other men, the crimson coat was entirely unadorned but for two gleaming silver buttons that winked at her in the candlelight, practically begging her to nip one of the expensive little embellishments right off his back.

A button like that could feed a family of six for a fortnight.

And while her itchy-fingered tendency toward theft was perhaps not the most sterling of characteristics in an otherwise well brought up young Scotswoman, no one was perfect. And it was so very hard to be *good* all the time.

She had much rather be bad, and be *right*.

So Quince took advantage of the terrific crush in Lady Inverness's ballroom, slipped her finger into the tiny ring knife she kept secreted in the muslin folds of her bodice for just such an occasion, and sidled up behind Crimson Velvet.

She did not pause, nor give herself a moment to think on what she was about to do. She ignored the chitter of warning racing across her skin, and set straight to it, diverting his attention by brushing her bodice quite purposefully against his back, while she nipped the button off as easily as if it were a snap pea in a garden.

The elation was like a rush of blood to the head—intoxicating and addictive.

And because that was what she did—regularly stole fine things from finer people in the finest of ballrooms—she wasn't satisfied with only the one button. Nay. Another six mouths could be fed, and Quince could live all week on the illicit thrill of having taken the second button as well, and gotten away clean.

Except that she didn't get away clean.

She didn't get away at all.

A very large hand clamped onto Quince's wrist like a shackle. A red velvet-clad hand.

Alarm jumped onto her chest like a sharp-clawed cat, but Quince kept her head, automatically tucking the buttons and knife down the front of her bodice, and winding her now-empty free hand around that crimson velvet waist. She pressed herself to his backside more firmly, and familiarly, and said the first unexpected thing that came to her mind. "Darling!"

Crimson Velvet went as stiff as a bottle of Scotch whisky. "Good Lord. What's this?"

Alarm faded as recognition, and something that really oughtn't be delight curled into her veins. She knew that deceptively easy tone. Strathcairn. Earl thereof.

Oh, holy clotted cream.

The Laughing Highlander, she had once called him. But the Highlander was not laughing now. He was looking down at her with a sort of astonished wonder. "Wee Quince Winthrop, is that you? Good Lord." He stepped away—though he did not let go of her wrist—to case her as thoroughly as she ought to have done him. "I would not have recognized you."

She had clearly not recognized him. But the man gripping her wrist was neither the powdered dandy she had imagined from across the ballroom, nor the amusing, carefree Earl of Strathcairn she remembered. This man was different, and as dazzling in his own way as the shining silver buttons she had secreted down her soft-pleated bodice.

Firstly, he was as irresistibly attractive as that red velvet suit—all precise, well-cut shoulders, and long lean torso that seemed a far cry from the rangy, not-yet-fully-formed man in his youth. But secondly—and more importantly—he was much more controlled, more…curated, as if he had carefully chosen this particularly splendid view of himself to show the world. As if he not only wanted, but demanded to be *seen*.

Quite the opposite of Quince, who minded her appearance only to make sure she blended into the crowd—if her sister told her this season everyone was wearing white chemise dresses, then a white chemise dress she wore, disappearing into a sea of similarly dressed swans.

By contrast, Strathcairn looked every bit an individual, and quite, quite splendid. His waistcoat was of the same saturated color as his coat, and his snow-bright linen with only the barest hint of lace was the perfect foil for his immaculately powdered hair.

On any other man such a look might have appeared plain and underdone, but on Strathcairn the blaze of unadorned velvet served to highlight the force of his personality.

And there was nothing she liked as much as personality, unless it was a challenge.

The earl appeared to be both.

"Why, Strathcairn." She made her voice everything breezy and cordial. As if her heart were not beating in her ears, and dangerous delight were not dancing down her veins. "It's been an age."

"Too long, from the looks of it." He stepped close—too close, not that she particularly minded—and looked down at her in a perilously attentive way, like a great, green-eyed tomcat eyeing up a wee mouse. The effect was most unsettling. It put her right off her stride. "Do you often embrace men you haven't seen in years?"

It had been exactly five years. He had briefly been one of her eldest sister Linnea's suitors then—newly elected a Member of Parliament, and headed to London, brilliant and ambitious. Quince remembered thinking the lanky Highlander was too tall, too clever, too canny, and far too insightful for tiny, fluttery Linnea, who adored nothing more than to be made a pet of.

Strathcairn hadn't seemed the type to keep pets.

Quince had been little more than a fourteen-year-old lass, but she had quite liked the young man's intelligence, nearly as much as his vibrant charm. Though what she liked best of all was his lovely, buttery smile that had made her feel like she was melting in the sun.

Strathcairn was certainly not pouring the butter boat over her now—his eyes might have been smiling, but from this angle, his chiseled jaw seemed to have been carved out of Grampian granite.

No matter. Quince was not Linnea—she was no one's pet. "I thought you were someone else," she lied without effort or qualm. "You've changed."

"So, my indiscreet young friend, have you." The barest hint of amusement in his glorious baritone was all that was necessary to bring back all the delicious torment of her youthful infatuation. "What in heaven's name did you think you were doing, calling me 'darling'?"

"Thought you were my Davie." Quince made up a convenient beau on the spot. "I must find where the darling lad's got to."

Strathcairn let out a low, disbelieving bark of laughter, but didn't let go of her wrist. "You can't be old enough to be making assignations with men, wee Quince."

He trespassed easily on the old acquaintance by calling her by her Christian name—if Papa's botanically inspired names for his daughters could even be called Christian. Strathcairn also crossed the lines of familiar behavior by turning her toward the door, and somehow settling her against his side in such a subtle, but insistent, way, that not a person in the place would have suspected she was being all but frog-marched from the ballroom.

Even though she was grown up now, and towered over tiny Linnea, Quince still had to leg it to keep up with Strathcairn's long strides, all the while craning her neck to get a proper close look at him.

He looked so different, with his hair powdered white, and this controlled look upon his face, as if his smile had been put away in a cupboard, like a cravat that no longer fit. This new Strathcairn was far more imposing, and much, much more intimidating looming beside her like one of the great statues at Holyrood Palace than he had ever seemed all those years ago when she had keeked out at him from behind the drawing room curtains.

But she was not four and ten now. Quince let him tow her only as far as a conveniently empty alcove at the end of the entrance hall, before she rounded her elbow out of his grip, and served him a sharp, instructive jab in the ribs— anger brought out the Scots in her. "I'd be much obliged if you'd take your great paws off of me, Strathcairn. You're creasing my gown."

He subdued his grunt of discomfort, but put a hand absently to his side. "My *paws*"—he gave the word a wry intonation—"are not great in the least. They're rather average. For a Scot." At last he let the gorgeously rough Scots burr rumble beneath the town polish of his Member-of-Parliament accent. "Your gown is barely creased, and not by me, but by that interminable crush. Or more likely by this Davie fellow. And who the devil is he?" Strathcairn's green gaze poured over her like chilly water. "He can't possibly be a worthy mon if he lets a lass like you caress him in public. You're too young for suitors."

By jimble, but he had grown into an even more attractive man himself over the years, despite this polished, urbane facade. Or perhaps because of it—his worldliness gave him an attractive look of experienced wisdom. Quite irresistible.

"I'm not young anymore, either. I'm nineteen."

This he acknowledged with a wry sideways slant of his head, as if she were so out of kilter that the acute angle somehow made it easier to see her. "A very bad age to be an accomplished liar. And flirt." Strathcairn finally released her arm.

Much to her chagrin—which was all the emotion she would allow to account for the strange warmth suffusing her face—she found she missed the contact. How disconcerting.

So she changed the subject. Without flirting. "What are you doing in Edinburgh?"

"I've come north to see to Castle Cairn now that my grandfather's passed on."

Something that must have been sincerity stabbed her hard in the chest. "I am sorry, Strathcairn. He was a grand auld gent."

It was the right thing to say—Strathcairn's whole demeanor softened enough to show her more of the young man she had admired beneath his curated veneer. Even those glittering eyes went soft at the edges. "Thank you. He was, wasn't he?"

"Aye." The Marquess of Cairn had been a cavalier of the old school, gentlemanly, generous and bold. He had raised Strathcairn when his son, Strathcairn's father and the prior earl, had passed away suddenly during Straithcairn's youth. "He'll be missed. Oh—that means you're Cairn now."

Strathcairn—for she could think of him no other way even if he were now Marquess of Cairn—lowered that chiseled chin, and nodded in rueful agreement. "Aye. And he's left large boots to fill. So I'm seeing to Cairn." He took a deep breath as if he were collecting himself before he raised his head, and added, "But before I head north to home, I've also been asked to see to a rather persistent problem plaguing Edinburgh."

A softer sense of alarm—or perhaps it was guilt—padded across her shoulders like a stealthy barn cat. She made light of it, as she always did. "The persistent plague of too many ladies and not enough gentlemen? I do hope you've come prepared to dance."

The first hint of a smile began at the far corner of his lips, as if he were not yet ready to commit to the strenuous exercise of a full-out grin. "No. I rarely dance." He shook his head in rueful apology. "No, the problem I speak of is a rash of thefts from some of the better households in the district. I've been asked to restore some sense of law and order within Edinburgh's society."

"On guard" was too simple and sensible a phrase to describe her reaction—Quince's skin went a little cold, and that sharp-clawed sense of alarm scratched its way down her spine. But she rose to the occasion—she knew better than most how to put up her weapons. To win any sort of fight, one had to attack, not just defend. And satire was the sharpest sword of them all.

"*Restore* law and order?" She made herself suitably wide-eyed and breathless. "I hadn't realized we were lacking it. Ought we to be on watch for gangs of housebreakers?"

"No, no. Nothing like that." He looked sage and worldly with all his unruffled calm, but she could see a tinge of riddy heat creeping over his collar. "Though it's too early to tell. But certainly too early for worry. Pray don't be alarmed, lass."

Quince's skin went all over prickly—nothing put her back up like being condescended to.

She sharpened up her sarcasm so he would not be able to so easily evade her point. "Holy sticky toffee pudding, Strathcairn"—she decided if he could trespass upon her Christian name, then she would trespass upon his old title—"imagine that. A gang of cutthroat housebreakers carting off priceless *Louis Quatorze* commodes to furnish their tatty tenement houses. How have the newspapers and broadsheets not been full of that?"

His smile confined itself to the outer corners of those intelligent green eyes. "No priceless commodes have been carted off."

"Auld occasional tables, then? Scaffy, mismatched chairs?"

"You needn't mock, lass. It's not ladylike." He put a hand up to rub the back of his neck, as if she really were succeeding in making him uncomfortable. Marvelous. And he had to subdue his growing smile—it started to hitch up one side of his mouth, as if he wanted to be amused, but was sure he oughtn't be. "If you must know, it's been very small items—smelling salt bottles, buttons, and the like."

And her with his two buttons down her bodice. She could feel them press into her skin as if they were biting her. Unsurprising since they were *his*.

Quince was too larky a lass to let a bit of her discomfort show. "Really? You've never abandoned Westminster, and come all the way north from London for some missing smelling salts?"

He had the good nature to look chagrined—that wary smile turned down sheepishly at the corners. "Not exactly. It's more complicated than that."

In fact, it was a great deal simpler than that. And she could not resist telling him so. "Well, it's a very good thing you told *me*." She lowered her voice in mock confidence. "Because I'm sure I know exactly what's happened to them."

He did not lean down to share her confidences. If anything, he became more upright, and even tilted away from her, as if he thought he could see her better from a distance. "You, lass?"

"Aye." She seized him by the upper arms, and man-handled him around—and by jimble if he hadn't the brawest, most firmly shaped musculature hidden under that soft, plush velvet—so he could follow the direction of her gaze. "There. Mr. Fergus McElmore has misplaced his snuffbox there, right under that vase of heather and broom. See? And there"—she pushed him in the other direction—"the Dowager Countess of Chester has abandoned her silver vinaigrette bottle in the cushion of her seat. Q.E.D. as you parliamentary types say." She made a dramatic flourish as if she were a theatrical barrister in court. "There is the *modus operandi* of your thefts, Strathcairn—silly stupidity at worst, simple thoughtlessness at best. Though in Fergus' case particularly, I think the thoughtlessness has come from an excess of Lady Inverness's fine Scotch whisky befuddling his poor wee numptie brain."

A fine coloring heat crept up Strathcairn's neck to his jawline. It lessened that impression of Grampian granite nicely.

He shook his head, but smiled nonetheless. "You think me foolish."

"I think whoever complained of their missing baubles is foolish, when they are likely only victims of their own excess —how *can* they be expected to keep track of so many possessions?"

He looked at her then—really looked, as if he finally saw more of her than the ghost of her pigtailed past. "You've a remarkably jaundiced view of society for a lass your age."

She was more than jaundiced. She was nearly lock-jawed with disdain. "I have a realistic understanding of human nature, Strathcairn. I think people are forgetful, and don't want to appear foolish, so they bluster and blame others for their own mistakes. And it is easy enough to blame the powerless"—she nodded toward the servants, who were most often the first to be accused when anything went amiss— "from the safe position of privilege."

"I take your meaning, lass." He acknowledged the right of her argument with a nod. "Nevertheless, it is my duty to look into the matter, to determine if it is indeed only a case—or cases—of forgetfulness."

"Then I should advise you to start with our hostess, and ask her what she does with all the flotsam and jetsam her guests leave behind after her balls." Because not even Quince, terrible magpie that she was, could take everything that was available—her bodice could only hold so much. "Perhaps she has the footmen cart it all up, and take it to the poor box at Canongate Kirk where they'll get better use of it."

The moment the words were out of her mouth she wished them back. She'd let her tongue run away from her mind, and run far too close to the truth for comfort.

And her suggestion brought Strathcairn's perilously attentive green gaze back to her. "What an agile mind you have, Lady Quince." And then for no reason she could fathom, he smiled at her—that gorgeous, gleaming grin she remembered of old. That mischievous, sideways curve of lip that made her feel as if she were being blessedly bludgeoned over the head with a five-penny slab of butter.

Quince nearly had to pinch herself to call her wits back under starter's orders. "Oh, pish tosh. Practical is what my mind is."

His smile settled back down to the corner of those sharp eyes. "Perhaps, but you've given me an idea—perhaps what I'm looking for is not a hardened criminal, but someone with the dowagers's vice."

Nay, nay, nay.

Clever, too clear-eyed man.

She had to divert him with something equally clever. "Carrying a vinaigrette is a vice? What do you imagine the ladies keep in there? Undiluted opium?"

Strathcairn shook his head, but he was amused enough to still smile. "The dowager's vice is the irresistible tendency toward theft. That is, the compulsive stealing of objects which are not rightfully theirs. It is commonly practiced by maiden aunties and elderly companions. And dowagers, of course. Hence the name."

Oh, by jimble. That sounded far too apt.

And the skeptical Scot in him had taken over—he was frowning at the row of seats at the far side of the ballroom where the older ladies, including some rather impecunious relations and companions, sat with their heads together in a comfortable coze. "They look perfectly harmless, but one never knows what might be hidden in their reticules, or tucked into their bodices."

Heat blossomed in that very place where Strathcairn's purloined buttons dug into her skin. Oh, he was clever.

But so was she. "Down their bodices?" She quite purposefully, and quite inexpertly, straightened her trim bodice, drawing his attention out the side of his eye to her small, but nevertheless eminently serviceable breasts. Mama always said a man couldn't think and look at breasts, no matter their size. No fool, Mama. And the clever padding Mama had insisted her maid sew into her stays made up for any natural deficit. "How do they find any room? Must be dreadful uncomfortable."

His brow rose as slowly as a guillotine over that acute eye. But his self-control was not equal to the task at hand, and his gaze strayed exactly where she had meant it to.

"Lady Quince." Strathcairn's lowered voice was absolutely irresistible when he forgot himself enough to let the Scots burr rumble. "Let me make right sure I understand you—are you *flirting* with me?"

"Am I?" Quince ignored the blaze of heat his voice and gaze kindled under her skin, and gave him her bright, knowing smile—all pleased lips and mischievous eyes. "What I am doing is trying to make you remember your duty, and accede to my wish to dance with me."

He regarded her with those too canny, too bright green eyes for another long moment before he answered. "Perhaps I will." He reached for her hand, and held her at arm's length for a lengthy perusal, as if he had not yet decided to grant her wish. "Yes, I definitely will. But before I do so, perhaps I ought to warn you, wee Quince, to be good. And be very, very careful what you wish for."

The heat that had blossomed under her bodice spread like wildflowers across her skin along the whole length of his gaze. And she liked it.

She raised her chin and gave him her slyest smile yet. "Oh, I am always careful, Strathcairn. But I had much rather be bad, and be *right*."

ABOUT THE AUTHOR

ELIZABETH ESSEX is *USA Today* Bestselling and award-winning author of critically acclaimed historical romance, including Reckless Brides and Highland Brides series. Her books have been nominated for numerous awards, including the Gayle Wilson Award of Excellence, the Romantic Times Reviewers' Choice Award and Seal of Excellence Award, and RWA's prestigious RITA Award. The Reckless Brides Series has also made Top-Ten lists from Romantic Times, The Romance Reviews and Affaire de Coeur Magazine, and Desert Isle Keeper status at All About Romance. Her fifth book, A BREATH OF SCANDAL, was awarded Best Historical in the Reader's Crown 2013. MAD, PLAID AND DANGEROUS TO MARRY is her eighteenth book.

When not rereading Jane Austen, mucking about in her garden, walking her beloved dogs, Ghillie & Brogue, or simply messing about with boats, Elizabeth can be always be found with her laptop, making up stories about heroes and heroines who live far more exciting lives than she. It wasn't always so. Long before she ever set pen to paper, Elizabeth graduated from Hollins College with a BA in Classics and Art History, and then earned her MA in Nautical Archaeology from Texas A&M University. While she loved the life of an underwater archaeologist, she has found her true calling writing lush, lyrical historical romance full of passion, daring and adventure.

Elizabeth lives in Texas with her husband, the indispensable Mr. Essex, and her active and exuberant family in an old house filled to the brim with books.

ALSO BY ELIZABETH ESSEX

The Reckless Brides

Almost a Scandal

A Breath of Scandal

After the Scandal

A Scandal to Remember

The Scandal Before Christmas (holiday novella)

A Lady's Gift for Scandal (holiday novella)

The Difference One Duke Makes (novella)

She Walks in Scandal (novella in *A Midsummer Night's Romance*
Anthology)

The Highland Brides

Mad About the Marquess

A Fine Madness (novella)

Mad, Plaid and Dangerous to Marry

Mad Dogs and Englishwomen (Coming soon!)

The Dartmouth Brides

The Pursuit of Pleasure

A Sense of Sin

The Danger of Desire

The Dartmouth Brides Boxed Set (with holiday novella *"Up on the
Rooftops"*)

The Kent Brothers Chronicles

<u>Between the Devil & the Deep Blue Sea ~ and ~ The Devil's
Own Luck</u>

*To keep up to date on releases and events, sign up for Elizabeth's newsletter
and get exclusive excerpts, contests and more, visit:*

http://www.elizabethessex.com

I also hope you'll take a few minutes out of your day to review this
book at your favorite book site– your honest opinion is much
appreciated. Reviews help introduce readers to new authors they
wouldn't otherwise meet.

www.ingramcontent.com/pod-product-compliance
Lightning Source LLC
Chambersburg PA
CBHW032112110726

47902CB00003B/557